Praise for

SALVAGED

"Elegant and inevitable, this is the prose equivalent of playing a survival horror game. Each piece feeds perfectly into the next. Beautifully written."

—Seanan McGuire, *New York Times* bestselling author of *Middlegame*

"*Salvaged* scared the hell out of me, and I write horror for a living! Madeleine Roux conjures real darkness with a brilliant novel that any fan of *Alien* will simply devour. Brava!"

—Jonathan Maberry, *New York Times* bestselling author of
V-Wars and *Rage*

"*Salvaged* is riveting and brutal, a study in scars. The masterful writing and bittersweet beauty of these characters will haunt you long after you finish reading."

—Ann Aguirre, *New York Times* bestselling author of
the Razorland trilogy

"Madeleine Roux's *Salvaged* is a breathless, claustrophobic twist on the SF thriller, full of deep space dread, conspiracies and malevolent alien spores, with a woman at the center whose courage was forged in all-too-human trauma. This is the *Alien* we need right now."

—Christopher Golden, *New York Times* bestselling author of
Ararat and *The Pandora Room*

"*Alien* meets *The Expanse* in this nonstop thrill ride. Rosalyn is a reluctant heroine on the run from her past; trapped on a ship with a terrifying alien presence, her resourcefulness and courage lend this unconventional space opera depth and heart." —Michelle Gagnon, author of *Unearthly Things*

"Roux's *Salvaged* is a tale of creeping horror and daring love, heavy with the weight of loss and trauma. Spooky fungus in space, devastatingly intimate hive minds, terrifying resource management and shockingly sweet romance combine in this love letter to redemption and recovery (and mushrooms)." —Caitlin Starling, author of *The Luminous Dead*

"Roux delivers a feminist sci-fi with plot twists, gut punches and a female lead with the strength of resilience."

—Mindy McGinnis, Edgar® Award–winning author of *Heroine*

"The rich description dumps you right into the world of *Salvaged* and won't let you go. Roux engages all senses; this is sometimes a good thing, sometimes bad, always brilliant. Needless to say, she had me at 'putrefaction.' In the coming years, writing courses will use *Salvaged* in the lessons covering 'how to immediately and completely hook a reader from chapter one.' You never thought you could care this much about cleaning. Rosalyn Devar may not be the space janitor we deserve, but she's the one we need. I loved it!" —Mur Lafferty, award-winning author of *Six Wakes*

"From the first searingly brutal line Madeleine Roux seizes the reader by their space helmet and drags them screaming and flailing up into the air ducts of this deeply engaging story of deep space horror. And she doesn't stop there; while a lesser writer might have been satisfied to just give you a tale of madness amongst alien horrors, Roux uses that as the skeleton around which she frames a deeper internal story about the ongoing legacy of trauma, assault and invasion. Truly remarkable and unsettling in the best of ways." —Jordan Shively, cohost of the podcast *Caring into the Void*

"Madeleine Roux's *Salvaged* is the fantastic sci-fi 'Beauty and the Beast' story you've always needed in your life." —Peter Clines, author of *The Fold*

SALVAGED

MADELEINE ROUX

ACE
New York

ACE
Published by Berkley
An imprint of Penguin Random House LLC
1745 Broadway, New York, NY 10019

Copyright © 2019 by Madeleine Roux
Penguin Random House supports copyright. Copyright fuels creativity, encourages
diverse voices, promotes free speech, and creates a vibrant culture. Thank you for buying
an authorized edition of this book and for complying with copyright laws by not reproducing,
scanning, or distributing any part of it in any form without permission. You are supporting
writers and allowing Penguin Random House to continue to publish books for every reader.

ACE is a registered trademark and the A colophon is a trademark of
Penguin Random House LLC.

The Edgar® name is a registered service mark of the Mystery Writers of America, Inc.

Library of Congress Cataloging-in-Publication Data

Names: Roux, Madeleine, 1985– author.
Title: Salvaged / Madeleine Roux.
Description: First Edition. | New York: Ace, 2019.
Identifiers: LCCN 2019014409 | ISBN 9780451491831 (pbk.) | ISBN 9780451491848 (ebook)
Subjects: | GSAFD: Fantasy fiction. | Science fiction.
Classification: LCC PS3618.O87235 S2313 2019 | DDC 813/.6—dc23
LC record available at https://lccn.loc.gov/2019014409

First Edition: October 2019

Printed in the United States of America
1   3   5   7   9   10   8   6   4   2

Cover art: Woman's profile by Lorado/Gettyimages; Solar system
by Dalmingo/Shutterstock
Cover design by Faceout Studio / Jeff Miller
Book design by Alison Cnockaert
Title page art: Abstract wave by Uniqdes/Shutterstock

For the survivors

Take hope from the heart of man, and you make him a beast of prey.

—Ouida

1

Rosalyn had endured disappointing birthdays before, but never one in ankle-deep corpse sludge.

She shifted her boots out of the reddish muck, swallowing hard as her feet suctioned to the floor. The job got more familiar but not easier. *Never* easier. And this was way beyond skin slippage, this was putrefaction on a level she had never seen before in person. Digital images just didn't capture it, really. The microscopic bacteria on the bodies were having a field day, turning once soft but decidedly *human* humans into a soup as dark and hideous as black gut blood, the kind of blood one never wanted to see squirt out of anything. But now she had to look at it.

Now it was her job.

Witnessing autopsies paled in comparison. Rosalyn closed her eyes tightly, feeling an unwelcome roiling in her stomach. The first time she saw a corpse cut open, she had excused herself from the cold, sterile lab to vomit. At private school, during dissection week, she had ducked out of the lab and away from the fetal pig on a tray and into the lavatory, swiping a bit of perfume under her nose; the smell of formaldehyde made her sick. She had to train herself to forget that sour taste in her mouth, to refocus away from the disgusting reality of decomposition, and turn instead toward one simple fact.

These had all been people once, people with families, and those families deserved answers and some small remnant of the deceased to bury. Dignity, somehow, would be fished out of this . . . this . . . Rosalyn opened her eyes but decided not to finish her thought.

The heavy vacuum canister on her back was already full, and she made her way along the edge of the ship's cargo hold toward the giant containment crate labeled HAZARDOUS, with its bright yellow plastic and two dozen warning stickers.

She turned down the environmental volume on her sealed suit, desperate not to hear the sound of her own boots sloshing through the remains of ten dead crew. Her coworkers. Distantly. She didn't know any of them, not really, but she recognized a few of the names on the manifest, people she had heard called over the intercom back at the Merchantia Solutions campus. *Tate Alonso, Adey Tyrol, Ji Gimble . . .*

"At least they caught the bastard."

"What?" Rosalyn shouted back. She adjusted the volume on her helmet with the LED panel attached to her suit's wrist, and spun to find her living coworker, Owen Cardew, staring back at her with wide eyes. Tapping the side of her head, she frowned. "Sorry, I went silent."

Owen nodded and joined her in the cargo hold, wading into the horror seeping across the corrugated floor. "They caught him. He's in custody. Sick fuck jacked the heat all the way up after he dumped the bodies in here."

"Yeah. That explains a lot," Rosalyn muttered. The raw truth of a body could be horrible. It could be beautiful, too, she thought, but lately she was just seeing the horrible parts. She had accepted the crew and ship salvaging job so abruptly that it took a while for the reality of the assignment to really sink in. Now it was sinking in, and hard. She closed her eyes again for a moment, then drew in a long, shaky breath and detached the vac from her suit, transferring the remains into the yellow containment bin. With hours of work ahead of them, she felt the creep of exhaustion start in her limbs. Irritating little lights twinkled in front of her eyes, a headache brewing, the cruel reminders that she was a ship ride and an hour-long shower away from a stiff drink.

It could be worse, she insisted, it could be like her second assignment, when a research vessel employee foolishly brought their cat aboard, and the thing had hidden in a vent until it died. After the ship returned, it had been Rosalyn's job to crawl into the narrow space and clean out the carcass. Her coworkers insisted it wasn't hazing, but they all had a good chuckle while she crammed her body into the vent.

"Happy birthday to me," she murmured, turning back to the job.

"You're not serious." Owen snorted and then sagged, pausing with the suction nozzle on his vacuum just above the pool of decomposed bodies. "Oh God, you are serious. It's your birthday? And you're here? What the hell is wrong with you?"

"I'm newish on campus, don't really have many friends yet. Didn't want to just sit around in the canteen being lonely, you know? Seemed sad."

"Sadder than this?" Owen turned away with a shake of his head. "If you don't win employee of the month, I'll bloody call for a strike."

"Thanks," Rosalyn said. It was mostly true, the no friends. The fear of being alone. Alone with her thoughts, or alone with a bottle of booze and then shortly thereafter passed out, deep asleep and far away from her waking thoughts.

"Any big plans after this?" he asked. "For the birthday, I mean."

"Oh. No. Just a hot shower, I think. A really, really long one. Never do much on my birthday, anyway. It's right next to Christmas, so usually it just got rolled over into the holidays."

"Bullshit. You should get double gifts. Your friends are cheap." Owen snorted.

Rosalyn managed a flimsy laugh but said nothing else. It wasn't her friends that insisted on the combination birthday and Christmas, but her family. The only person that ever paid much attention to her birthday was her best friend and best workmate, Angela Kerwin, who insisted on taking her out each year. They shared a birthday, though Angela was several years older. And they shared an addiction to work, though they relaxed their strict schedules on that one day a year, when they celebrated their birthday together. The Faubourg Sky Tower with its rooftop bar. They would sip lemon drops and watch the ships departing Earth, flashing toward the stars in tiny red blinks. Angela always stopped her before the night spiraled out into dancing or karaoke.

"Thanks, *Mom*," Rosalyn would tease, and then they would walk downtown to look at all the dazzling Christmas lights. Angela's last message had arrived a month ago. "I'm going to keep sending these until you ping me back," it said. "I know you're angry, but at me, too? Come on, Rozzy, I miss you. I want to tell you about everything I'm doing out here. It's wild. These samples . . . Your head would spin if you saw them. If we're right, we're going to change medicine forever. Okay, okay, I love you. Reach out."

"Well," Owen sighed. "Captain Murder Ship certainly isn't going to win employee of the month anytime soon." His vacuum whirred, then jammed, and he leaned down to pry a chunk of femur out of the hose. She couldn't help but watch him do it, so casual, like picking a booger, flicking it away. Not that she would do any differently, but still, it made her freeze. "Can you believe it? He just

snapped. Went completely mental and did in his entire crew . . .
They found him in a titty bar on Tokyo Bliss Station. Said he had
no idea who he was or what he had done. Yeah. I'll fucking bet.
Loser."

"Nobody just snaps," Rosalyn replied. She pretended to fuss
with her vacuum, no longer so keen on doing the work. No, nobody snapped. There were always signs. A short temper here. A
barked insult there. A strange, dark blankness in the eyes, colder
than the black void of space. Shark eyes. Inhuman eyes. Blame and
shame, but always soothed with an apology. Tearful *I love you*s after
the rage.

"Dunno, he had a squeaky-clean record," Owen continued.
That didn't matter either, Rosalyn knew. He lifted the barrel of the
vacuum hose up to his curved, clear visor and looked down it with
one eye closed. His was a face for smirking, and the smile lines
carved around his mouth and wrinkling at his eyes aged him. Certainly the work aged him, too. Rosalyn had spied more than one
gray hair in the mirror since starting with Merchantia.

"I looked into it. Couldn't help it, really. Morbidly fascinating,
that stuff, don't you think? Makes you wonder . . . could I do that?
Could I kill ten people and then go on holiday?"

"Let's hope not, Owen, we *are* alone on this ship."

"Right. Yes. Purely hypothetical, Devar. I'm one of the good
ones, nothing like this psycho . . ."

She listened absently to his assessment of the captain, and to his
wild conjecturing. There were worse people to do a job with. Owen
never went too far with the dark jokes, always stopping just short of
something truly disgusting, and he had no problem filling the silence with information about his hobbies, his family, his grievances
big and small. His wife and little boy lived on Tokyo Bliss Station,
but he had put in for a transfer back to Earth, he just needed the

5

money to get them there, and he had a little wrinkle-faced dog called Barry that farted itself awake every night and howled at him over long-distance video calls. The ringtone for his wife on his personal VIT monitor was some hideous new "Sexy Sadie" cover by the Late Nodes. Owen wore a newer model of the Vital Information Transmitter, silvery blue, one released specifically to celebrate Earth's space travel tercentenary. Tokyo Bliss Station marketing reps were pushing a huge retro culture package, rolling out 1960s kitsch by the freighter-load, hoping to drum up some nostalgia for the moon landing. Their new interactive video game deck was all about humanity going to the stars for the first time, a real tercentenary extravaganza. Rosalyn couldn't avoid the ads for it on her VIT, but she did avoid it on the station, even if it coincided with *her* first trip to the stars when she took the Merchantia job.

The Late Nodes blared through the hold now, interrupting Owen's close inspection of his equipment. He swore under his breath, stumbling back over to the containment bin while giving Rosalyn a sheepish glance.

"Take it," she said. "I won't tell."

The Late Nodes droned on about the world waiting for Sadie. Their take was darker, throatier, leaving behind the upbeat sway of the original.

"Darling, you know I'm at work . . ."

Rosalyn decided not to fire up her vacuum and interrupt the call, and she gave them privacy, shuffling carefully through the cargo hold toward the opposite end, away from the big bay doors. They had set up a low, temporary barrier to keep the remains from leaking out into the hall any more than they already had. She turned down the volume on her environmental suit again, determined not to hear their sweet, mundane exchange. It reminded her too painfully of things left far behind, on Earth, memories that she kept out of view but never seemed to outrun.

Her mother, Shireen, still called every day. *When are you coming home?*

On the rare occasions Rosalyn picked up, she'd just say, "Soon" and "I miss you" and "No, don't tell Dad I say hi." *Because I don't.*

Her ankle bumped something hard floating in the water. The extreme heat and time had all but liquefied the victims, but this thing bobbing in the muck was noticeably intact. Rosalyn squinted down at the small, blue tube in the pool of grayish red and crouched, fishing it out and wiping away the staining fluids.

There was a painful flash in her brain, a feeling like the sun searing across her eyes, and an even worse nagging sense that she knew what she was looking at. Sure, the small canister resembled any number of lab substances she had worked with in her previous life, but this bothered her. Her memory had gotten worse, alarmingly worse, since the drinking started. *Maybe that was the point*, she had thought in the midst of yet another hangover at Merchantia HQ.

Rosalyn stood and studied the tube, then reluctantly raked her eyes across the covered floor of the cargo hold. Together, she and Owen had put together an audio report of everything they found aboard the science vessel, a record that would later be used for company purposes and the inevitable charges against the rogue captain. The forensics team had already been through, though their stay was brief; this would all be settled out of court, the families hushed up with fuck-you money from Merchantia. Outer space lab work was, naturally, dangerous, and the NDAs they had signed were biblical in length. The murders wouldn't make a blip in the Tokyo Bliss Station or Earth headlines. A small article would be put out in the company newsletter. Just an outlying incident. Nothing to panic over.

During the walk-through, she and Owen had noted that the killer had emptied the cargo hold completely, dragging out the storage and supply crates and piling them in the hall, then sealing his poor murdered crewmates inside. The spare crates had been used to barricade the door, which was nonsense, since the magnetic seal was more than capable of keeping lifeless bodies inside.

She thought again of those heaped boxes. The captain had been alone on the ship with his deeds until the ship neared Tokyo Bliss Station and he could safely jettison in an emergency pod. What must he have felt, left in the cold, dark silence, with nothing but his dead crew and his crimes for company? Even the onboard AI Servitor, a kind of helper robot, had been deactivated and tossed into the hold, as if even lifeless, mechanical eyes were too cruelly accusing.

The boxes. Why push them up against the doors that way? The crew were all certainly dead, but maybe, Rosalyn thought, just maybe, the captain was still afraid and wanted to make sure whatever was in the cargo lock didn't get out. Perhaps he hadn't barricaded them in out of guilt, but *fear.*

The memory nagging at her before arrived, blistering in its clarity—she was back on Earth, in Montreal, at the lab with Angela while she introduced Rosalyn to all the newest xenosamples they were working with. Angela, direct and precise as usual, held up tube after tube, explaining to Rosalyn just what the substances inside might do for their project.

There was a little crayon smudge on Angela's white sleeve, the only hint of sloppiness on an otherwise immaculate person. She had kids, five, but she was always on time, always staying late. Once or twice, Rosalyn caught her on the VIT during lunch, giving her kids long-distance story time. *Busy the bee goes, "Buzz, buzz, buzz!" Dizzy the dog goes, "Woof, woof, woof!"* . . .

"This is from Callisto," she remembered Angela saying, a blue-tinted, clean tube pinched between gloved thumb and forefinger. "And frankly, I have no idea what it does. Not for long, though. We'll get on it tomorrow. Just . . . be so, so careful, Roz, like I said: We really don't know what any of this is yet."

Rosalyn heard Owen's vacuum start up again, and it startled her. She dropped the tube, watching it sink slowly into the human muck at her feet. It couldn't be the same kind of sample cylinder, and those were all so similar looking anyway. Montreal was at least five hundred *million* miles away. And then "Sexy Sadie" twanged through the hold again. It rang longer this time, and she heard more of the words. *Kind of an odd choice for a wife's ringtone*, she thought. Now Rosalyn saw a sheen of sweat on Owen's face as he raced to answer the call. He hurled her an apologetic look, but Rosalyn suddenly felt only sympathy.

Owen's ringtone was stuck in her head. She could recall the lyrics perfectly after so many hours on the job with him. She didn't remember the song being so condescending to the woman; maybe the Late Nodes' grittier take on the words brought out the darker vibe.

Rosalyn looked at where the tube had disappeared. A little cylinder of secrets. She glanced back at Owen then, wondering just what his strange secret might be. He seemed so happy, so bubbly, but weren't those smile lines carved awfully deep? Why did his face look taut now, as if he might at any moment break into tears? The raw truth of a human body could be hideous, and the mind? Uglier still.

2

Rosalyn peeled herself out of the environmental work suit, exhaling as she did, as if she could breathe out the last twisted eight hours of toil. A harsh, lemony vodka scent wafted out with that breath. It was a short ride back but it had felt like years and years, and she had indulged a little on the way. There were flasks that fit *perfectly* into an under suit. She half wondered if they had been invented by someone in the salvaging field.

The spare three-person crew of the *Salvager 5* had spent the ride back to HQ in almost perfect silence. Owen tried to start up with his theory of the crime a few more times, but he sputtered out fast when nobody joined in. She craved a hot shower and a drink (another one), and the cool, comforting darkness of her cramped room. It was only a hop back to the campus, a few hours after their initial light-speed jump, and climbing out of the suit felt like being born back into the world. The antiseptic white tunnels of the Merchantia headquarters weren't filled with fresh air per se, but it was a welcome relief after the musty, recycled air in her suit.

She, Owen and their pilot, Griz, were met at the air lock by an older man in a crisply pressed gray suit and narrow silver tie. Everything from his shellacked helmet of hair to his twinkling cuff links said HR. Owen bumped into her after a tech helped him out of his suit, and he swore softly against her shoulder. Her hackles were up and the others immediately paused.

"Suits don't come to the air lock," Owen muttered.

"Guess we're just lucky," she replied. "Maybe they'll throw a parade."

Griz, who rarely spoke but communicated plenty with his big, twitchy mustache, stepped up next to Rosalyn and grunted. She found a kind of comfort in their presence, though they didn't make much of a phalanx. In Rosalyn's experience, nothing good came of surprises like this. Why would someone this clean and presentable detach from their desk to mingle with the mere body janitors? They could've just sent a message if something needed doing. But then she considered where they had just been, and all of Owen's conspiratorial mutterings filled her head with noise. A rogue captain, crew reduced to mush, the boxes stacked against the doors, and that little floating tube hiding among it all . . .

"The crew of the *Salvager 5*," the man in gray said, opening his hands. "Welcome home."

Home? Rosalyn's eye twitched. The hall blinked with soft blue and green lights, a voice chiming over the intercom that they had successfully docked and disembarked. Those corridors and the surrounding launch bays always smelled like fresh bandages to Rosalyn, but now there was a new smell, a too-strong cologne that made her eyes water.

The man in gray closed the distance between them, casting a glance at the far-more-colorful suits the tech had collected. They had been rinsed off before ever being back on the salvaging vessel, but Mr. HR wrinkled his nose anyway. The smell of death was damned hard to get out, and hard to forget, even if Rosalyn was used to it now.

"I thought we might have a chat," he said. His head swiveled immediately to Rosalyn, inspecting her closely. She swallowed hard, keeping her lips sealed. Griz and Owen were good guys. They wouldn't tell on her; they wouldn't rat her out for having a quick drink on the ride back to headquarters. Hell, Owen had asked for a swig, too. Not that any amount of liquor existed that could flush out the memory of what they had seen in that cargo hold.

Rosalyn, admittedly, had taken more than a sip. She didn't like how close the suit was standing, but she kept eye contact, willing herself to breathe in short bursts through her nose, never letting the man get a whiff of her incriminating breath.

This is it, she thought with another twitch. *I'm canned.*

"A chat," Rosalyn repeated, monotone.

"A discussion. What you witnessed on this assignment . . . Well, we know it can't be easy. It's best we just touch base, make sure you receive the proper debrief. The proper counseling."

"Counseling?" Owen chuckled, walking past Rosalyn and down the freezing cold, tubelike tunnel of the air lock toward the outer launch bay. "Sure, mate. Sure. Let's get this over with, yeah? It's not something I'd like to dwell on."

"I'm good." Griz popped a breath mint in and went the same way, hands in his flight suit pockets, a whistled tune fluttering his mustache.

"It's mandatory, I'm afraid, for all of you," the suit said softly. Sternly. People listened to him, Rosalyn thought, and they did what he asked, even if he never raised his voice. But Griz wasn't people. Griz was Griz. She heard him snort before he turned and leaned against the circular portal that led to the bay.

"Mandatory," the suit said again, never bothering to turn and look at Griz. Then he stuck out his hand toward Rosalyn, his gaze fixed on her mouth. Rosalyn held back a shiver. She didn't like the way his face could remain so impassive, or his oozy corporate voice, or his overgroomed eyebrows.

"Josh Girdy," he told her, waiting until Rosalyn shook his hand. "I'll be with you in a moment, Ms. Devar. I'd very much like to know what you saw on that ship."

Rosalyn was the last to be called in.

The waiting room outside Josh Girdy's office teemed with the kind of comforts and style missing from the rest of the station. A few large fronds arched over the sofa where Rosalyn waited, and the coffee table near her feet was a long, low modern affair that gleamed like a polished tooth. A holographic display beamed down from the ceiling, a smiling white woman repeating the company's mission statement and policies with a hardwired smile.

Rosalyn tried not to sink down on the couch, but she was exhausted. She bounced her foot, impatient, feeling in her guts that these meetings were taking just a little too long. Griz had gone first, then Owen. Her fingernails would be bloody stubs by the time it was over. It wouldn't have bothered her so much if it didn't remind her of waiting outside her father's office to tell him she was quitting. The meeting had never happened. Rosalyn lost her nerve and left, deciding her sudden absence would send a louder message.

Her VIT monitor dinged with another message from her mother. Rosalyn checked the display, choosing the text version. It was hard still to hear her mother's voice, to detect the rising panic, and then the obvious despair.

I've gone back to Chennai with the relief team. Oh, Rosie, you wouldn't believe the flooding. You could join me. I know you would be good at this and we would be together. Your father . . .

Rosalyn tore her eyes away from the display and told herself the tears gathering behind her eyes were from the harsh lighting. Ever since leaving her previous job and Earth, she had existed in the razor-thin margin between screaming constantly and weeping constantly. She blamed the need for a drink. The impending stress of this HR meeting. She had never seen her mother's home, never gone back to India . . . Maybe it wasn't too late.

"Ms. Devar?"

The door had opened, Owen scuttling out. He wouldn't make eye contact with her. Rosalyn stared, willing him to look at her, but he refused. Owen never did anything very quickly, but now he all but sprinted for the door behind and to her left.

Standing, she mimicked the frozen smile on the holographic woman's face and stepped into the cool, silver space of Josh Girdy's office. It wasn't nearly as lively as the lobby. A single fake succulent plant sat on his otherwise empty desk. Rosalyn sat and bounced her leg again, smoothing down a company uniform hopelessly rumpled from her long day of work.

"Sorry for the wait," Josh Girdy said, rounding his desk and dropping into his chair, flinging out his tie to keep it from sticking into his trousers. "I know you're probably tired, so I'll try to keep this brief."

His lower lip stiffened, and he tented his fingers, bouncing them just like Rosalyn's leg. He was lying, and not with much skill. Just like Owen, he hesitated to meet her eye.

"So," he said, puffing out an exasperated breath. "Why don't you give me a reason to keep you on this team, Ms. Devar."

She froze. "Sorry? I thought this was a debriefing . . ."

"It is. Well, it was. But to be frank, there's no point in debriefing you if you're going to be let go."

Rosalyn flinched. *Let go.* Passive language. Cowardly language.

"Fired. Don't look so shocked, we both know you've been struggling."

Aggressive language. Somehow she didn't like that either, even if it was more to the point.

"None of my performance reviews have been poor," Rosalyn said slowly, feeling as if she had been dropped into a deep and icy pool. Her throat felt tight. Her leg bounced faster. "I know I have two absences but that's well within my allowed time off."

One, admittedly, was for a hangover. *Sick leave.* One lie hardly warranted all of this.

Girdy leaned forward, still tenting his fingers, and placed his wrists on the desk. Studying her, he blindly reached for a panel under the table, and a gently glowing holographic display like the one out in the lobby scrolled up from the smooth white surface of the desk. He flicked his eyes toward it and cleared his throat.

"Both of your cohorts on this assignment reported that you were drinking alcohol on the job. That you were . . ." He paused, squinting to find a direct quote. "Distracted, disoriented and unfocused. And this isn't the first time, Ms. Devar. I was hoping you would turn it around on your own but you haven't, so here we are. You've only been with us six months. That's a lot of screwups for six months. This job is hard on everyone, but if you're having trouble this early, then maybe it just isn't for you."

Rosalyn shook her head, then blinked down at her knees. Owen and Griz. She couldn't believe them. Had she really been so bad? Maybe it was worse—*she* was worse—than just what she could see. But she had tried to be discreet, maybe less so once she was off the clock, but that was her right. Still . . . that word, *discreet*, bothered her. If she had to be that way, then maybe it really was as bad as Owen and Griz said.

"I want to keep this job," she said quietly. There she was again, hovering between screaming and crying, knowing she had to strictly avoid both and look ahead, clearly, at Josh Girdy and his extremely unlikable face. "And you're right, I could be doing better. It's been . . . a very difficult year, you understand, but I'll clean it up. You have my word, Mr. Girdy. I won't disappoint you again."

He pinched his lips together and nodded once, then dismissed the display on his desk and waved a hand through where it had been. "That's fine, Ms. Devar, that's just a fine promise. But your breath smells like a distillery and you're on company time. This is sensitive work. Delicate work. We're dealing with the remains of valued employees. *People.* They deserve your full and *unaltered* attention."

That was some truly audacious shit, in her opinion, coming from the rep of a company that would gladly pay whatever it took to make the grieving families look the other way. They would sweep the murders under the rug, and quash any salacious reports before they could hit the mainstream outlets on Tokyo Bliss Station and then Earth.

Earth. She didn't want to go back. If she lost the job at Merchantia, she would be untethered again, and a failure at something else. She couldn't lose another thing, not *one more thing.* Leaving Earth had meant giving up everything, her family, her one friend, even her fish, Stanley. She genuinely missed that little guppy.

Rosalyn copied Girdy's posture, sitting up, putting her hands primly on the edge of his desk. "It's completely inappropriate to beg, I know, and I won't, but I will ask—*ask*—for another chance. Please give me one more assignment, and I can assure you the report will be very different." She saw his face soften, but not enough. A PhD from Berkeley and a nod from major alien biomedical publications and she was all but begging to keep a janitorial position. But she couldn't lose this, too, couldn't go back to Earth, to her father, to anywhere near *him*.

There was one last weapon in her arsenal, and she wasn't above using it. She needed the job. She wasn't losing something else.

"Please, Mr. Girdy," Rosalyn said with a sad half smile. "It's my birthday."

3

You'll be teaming up with Walters. Last chance, Devar. Happy birthday.

Dave Walters was a loudmouth and a loser, but Rosalyn shut up and took the assignment. She had to survive a quick turnaround, just one day of recovery before they left the station again, and Rosalyn spent it throwing out the bottles she had hidden around her company-issued apartment and gear. She meant to keep her promise to Josh Girdy, even if it meant feeling like a headachy piece of shit until the symptoms of withdrawal passed. With six self-help manuals downloaded to her VIT, she decided to eat something real before launch and the monotony of MREs.

The only place on the Merchantia campus that felt anything like Earth was the memorial garden, and there was usually silence there. Artificial sunlight streamed in through a silver web of skylights. Real grass and flowers grew, and a pleasant lightness of pollen floated in the air. It was always cool with mist. Occasionally the fake sun hit the real pollen at the right angle, and it felt like sitting in a room full of tiny fireflies. She dimmed the functions on her integrated augmented-reality display to make the atmosphere that much more peaceful. It was distracting to be bombarded with advertisements and stickers and whatever other bullshit streamed in through her implant.

Once, she had wandered into the garden to see that some jerk-off named Krant had left an animated crying emoji near one of the memorial stones. As a habit she turned off her AR's functionality in the garden after that. Vit Tech's slogan was *Life, vitally.* She hated that it was partially true—everyone needed their stupid implants now. Dating. Weather. Taxes. Shuttle times. Could the average person find their own ass without an AR sticker pointing it out to them?

Rosalyn chewed the sandwich she had gotten for lunch, and idly spun the silver canister of cola in her hand. It would be better if it had a shot of rum in it, but that was out of the question. More than twenty-four hours since her last drink. The jungle drums were starting, the throbbing in the back of her head that said it was time to find a beer or something. The ache, the sound, grew so loud it drowned out the rhythm of her own chewing. She closed her eyes, willing it away. *Stronger than that,* she told herself, *but not by much. Chew, chew, chew, just get through the rough bit. Just ride this out.*

That made her think of her friend Angela reading aloud to her kids, the simple little stories that lulled her children to sleep while she parented remotely from work. Chew, chew, chew . . . *Choo, choo, choo goes the train.* Rosalyn smirked, and for a moment the jungle drums faded and eased. Rosalyn had offered to cover for Angela numerous times, even just for an hour or two so she could run home to be with her kids more. But Angela was too focused on the work. On the data. "These samples," Angela would say, holding up a capped test tube, "are my children, too."

Rosalyn's AR display chimed softly, trying to coax her into a different kind of soda. The indicator blinked in the corner of her vision, a bright, vibrating cola can sprouting arms and legs as it danced to get her attention. She chewed loudly, to the point where she could only just hear the babbling of the artificial brook wending its way through the memorial markers and under the glass at her feet. If any other salvagers wandered through the garden during her lunch, she would quiet down the chewing, but only a little. With Owen and Griz stabbing her in the back, it was becoming clear that she didn't have many friends around. Rosalyn would chew as loud as she damn well wanted.

"Did you know trees can talk to each other?"

At the entrance to the garden, framed by a yawning arch, stood her onetime crewmate Alexia Courtney. Rosalyn's AR placed a blinking arrow over Alexia's head with a streamer showing her public profile. Petite and athletic, Alexia managed to look glamorous even in the shapeless sack of a jumpsuit they were all given to wear. Her dark eyes were wide now, and she smiled, dimples denting her cheeks.

"Hey, Alexia," Rosalyn said, rewinding the moment a few seconds and remembering the actual question. She dabbed at her mouth with a napkin. "Trees, mm? Is that a real thing, or is this some inside joke I'm not getting?"

Lunch was over. Shuffling boots and laughter filled the corridor behind Alexia. She came a few steps into the garden and lifted her fingers, wiggling them at Rosalyn. "Little roots talking to each other. Little wagging tongues."

"I . . . see," Rosalyn replied slowly. Well, Alexia's pupils weren't dilated unnaturally, so nobody had smuggled narcotics onto the campus. There were a few synthetic drugs coming up through the market, but Merchantia piss tested for those regularly. Maybe Alexia's AR was screwy. Sometimes the wireless patches failed to load properly and it gave Rosalyn a monster headache. So did the booze withdrawal, of course, a one-two punch that kept her lazing in bed long after she should've gotten up. But that was all over. New leaf, and all.

"Are you feeling okay?" Rosalyn asked. "We launch so soon, maybe you should get a quick med check before we load up . . ."

She consulted the clunky VIT monitor on her left wrist. Hard-coded information that was sensitive or classified went to the physical monitor. Vit Tech was too jumpy about body jacking to let companies send encrypted information that way, so old-school hardware it was. Four hours to launch. Alexia was one of the best pilots Roz had worked with at MSC, but she didn't exactly seem in fighting trim at the moment. Having her on the three-man crew would be the only thing making the presence of Dave Walters tolerable.

"See you, Roz," Alexia said, still smiling, and drifted out the door.

"Yeah." Rosalyn gave a short wave. "See you." And then when she was gone: "Jesus."

As if summoned by the ending of that strange interlude, a wiry, redheaded man bounced into the garden, hands in pockets, whistled tune on his lips. Dave Walters. Great. Rosalyn picked up her turkey and cheddar and began eating it, smacking her lips hard with every bite. Even subjecting herself to a painfully awkward launch with Griz and Owen again was preferable to working with Walters. Every woman on the station knew he was a pig, and Rosalyn had already strategically used one of her allotted absences to avoid an assignment with him.

But this was a test. Her second chance. Tests weren't meant to be easy.

Walters was of course the kind of person to advertise his relationship status in his AR profile. Single! What a surprise. And a Pisces not looking for anything serious. *Fascinating.*

"You see Courtney?" His song dropped and he let out a low whistle this time, rolling his eyes. "She's fuckin' blasted, man. Fruit loops. That last cleanup was a real shit show. Generator malfunctioned, raised the temps, practically cooked the bodies for weeks. Rotisserie research crew. Courtney said they were vacuuming up people paste for days."

"Fuck, that's awful." Rosalyn blinked hard. And weird. She had just seen almost exactly the same thing. What was going on? Apparently it wasn't the latest VIT patch messing with Alexia. Maybe Rosalyn was lucky to survive that horrendous cleanup without going mad and talking about whispering trees. Modern ships were equipped to drop temperatures the second no life readings were detected, keeping any dead bodies from decomposing too quickly, but things occasionally went wrong, sometimes the temps didn't drop and, well, people paste. She wondered at the likelihood of there being two similar cleanups back-to-back, though she hadn't heard anything about Alexia's being caused by an actual murderer.

"Poor thing," she added. "I finished something similar this week. It's hard to scrub those images out of your mind."

"She'll be out of rotation for at least a week. But who knows? Reconfig goes fast sometimes." Walters ambled over to her and swiped a potato chip out of her lunch. She grunted. Reconfig. That didn't sound so bad. Rosalyn could think of a few things she'd like to reconfigure in her head. "Happens to the best of us."

"We're scheduled to launch with her today," Rosalyn said, glaring. "The *Brigantine* salvage, they went blue two months ago. Who's replacing her?"

"Going blue" meant all souls aboard were deceased. The ship would beam red for a crisis, an SOS message, but blue if there was no hope of recovering living crew members. It was a little cold and tragic, she thought, but it allowed for proper allocation of resources. Triage. Living crew in danger had to take precedence.

Walters hovered. She groaned and pinched the bridge of her nose. "Please don't tell me . . ."

"Yup." So smug.

"That you're my pilot . . ."

"Mm-hmm." Even smugger.

"On the *Brigantine* job, and we're not getting a replacement for Alexia. Of course."

"You betcha," he smirked, and swiped another potato chip, munching with obvious relish. Not a second later, a message arrived on her VIT monitor catching her up on the new crew assignments. "You're in good hands, Devar, I can fly circles around Courtney. She's decent but she's got no style. And anyway, this sounds like a breeze. The two of us can handle it."

Rosalyn snatched up the remainder of her lunch before he could pilfer more of it. Then she pushed past her coworker, flinching away from actually shoulder-checking him out of the way. "I don't need you to have style, I just need you to do your job."

"Oh, I will," he assured her with a cocky chuckle. *Dick.* He breezed past her, as if ending the conversation was entirely his idea. Rosalyn froze and watched him swagger out of the garden and into the flow of salvagers leaving the cantina. "I'll do my job," he said over his shoulder. "With *style*. Four hours, Devar, don't be late! Hey, you should jazz up your AR profile, you know? An inspirational quote or something. Keeping it blank makes you look like a psycho."

Don't throw your bread crust at him. Only a child would do that.

Rosalyn crushed the last bit of her sandwich in her fist and imagined the bread sailing across the garden to land in his tangle of red hair. *Childish*, she thought with a weak smile, *but satisfying*. She crammed the crust and empty soda canister into the bag and drifted toward the exit, wondering if Alexia would be all right. *Hoping* she would be all right. The job got to everyone eventually. Two years was the max anyone stayed, then came a mandatory rest period. Outer space was terrifying. Salvaging was one prolonged exercise in confronting your own mortality. And it was dangerous. It was a job one only survived and never enjoyed.

Someone she didn't recognize cut off her approach to the door. A woman, short, old, with deep lines carved into her brown cheeks, drooped into the garden. Her arms were laden with a sleek tray, and on the tray was a pile of stones. Rosalyn silently made room for her to pass and then observed her going to the same bench and the stream where Roz ate her lunch every day. The woman knelt and carefully began to pile the rocks next to the bench. She stood and left without acknowledging Rosalyn, but her tread seemed lighter as she went.

Rosalyn couldn't help it—she waited until she was alone again to approach the piled stones. Just like the older woman, she knelt, squinting to find names and dates and messages carved into the rocks. It was like a little pagan outcropping, an ancient marker, so out of place there among the cold silver and glass fixtures of the base. She reached out and brushed her fingers over one of the stones—it was still warm from the other woman's touch.

She shivered, reading the inscriptions with her blood chilling by degrees, growing colder as she began to recognize the names.

MISATO IWASA, 2158–2269

PIERO ENDRIZZI, 2231–2269

TUVA SVERDAL, 2231–2269

RAYAN YASIN, 2241–2269

CAPTAIN EDISON ARIES, 2229–2269

"The *Brigantine*," she whispered, shutting her eyes tightly. In four hours she would be hurtling through space toward these people, not just their memorial markers, but their dead bodies. Flesh turning as hard as those stones. She could only hope they had gone peacefully, and that they would be found in a deep freeze, looking as quiet and whole as if they were only sleeping. This job had to be an easy one. Simple. She just needed to prove to HQ and Josh Girdy that she wasn't headed for a total meltdown.

It struck her as deeply morbid that Merchantia hadn't even waited for confirmation from a salvage crew before having the stones commissioned. Well, the *Brigantine* had gone blue months ago, so it was a safe bet, if a sad one. *Efficiency you can trust.* That was the Merchantia slogan. They tended to live up to that promise.

"See you soon," Rosalyn added, standing and leaving the garden at a near run. She had never bothered to read the other memorial stones, and this was why. Nobody wanted to know whom they were shoving into a body bag. Nobody wanted to know whom the people paste had really been.

Four hours. It would have to be enough time to get her head on straight.

4

As a child Rosalyn always climbed the same tree in the backyard.

There was only one tree to climb—an ancient, officially protected silver maple that anchored the house on Aberdeen more than
any concrete or stone foundation. Decades before, the boughs grew
heavy with snow in the wintertime, or so claimed her parents. Not
anymore. The leaves now soaked up the heat like tiny, brittle solar
panels.

It was a tall, tall tree, and she had learned to climb it early. Her
father would stand underneath and watch, and no matter how high
she climbed, no matter how little he became there on the ground,
she felt his nearness. He was there to catch her, close even when far.

He didn't feel near anymore. The *Salvager 6* hummed softly as the
atmosphere inside it grew warmer and the engines cycled, machine
and man preparing for the journey away from the campus and into
space. One last chance. Her head pounded. She wasn't just coping
with no booze anymore, but Dave Walters and no booze, as if this
assignment had been set up as the ultimate, brutal test of her will.

It didn't matter. Rosalyn was determined to prove herself, and
this time there wouldn't be any hidden flasks in her suit.

She stood in the small, empty bay that connected to the ship's air lock through a rounded, retractable corridor. Walters was already inside *Salvager 6*. New Classic 2210s rock drifted down the boarding walkway toward her. Alexia Courtney preferred classical, and so did Rosalyn. At least, she thought, it wasn't the awful synth-pop remakes Owens played. She had no idea if Griz even liked music; he never talked about much of anything.

Her pulse and temperature had started elevating since the moment she left the memorial garden. It felt safe there, but here, poised in front of the long metal tube and the ship at its end, she panicked. This was nothing new. Most salvagers got pre-mission jitters, even old pros. But this was different, her last shot, and it had to go off perfectly. Rosalyn didn't know if she was the only one who had gotten anxious tremors even during training, when they ran through scenarios in mock ships on base. Feet on solid ground, she was still shaken to the core like a complete chickenshit. The rooms were perfect re-creations of the innards of a salvage ship, and that was enough to make her heart race out of control.

So she did what she always did. She shut her eyes, took in several deep, deep breaths, pushed down the bad memories that resurfaced behind her closed eyes, and tried to immerse herself in the pleasure of breathing without a helmet.

"Any strong feelings about space travel?"

"Not really." Rosalyn had lied her way through her evals at the Merchantia Solutions headquarters back on Earth. Even hooked up to a lie detector apparatus, she had managed to get through the questions without raising any eyebrows.

"Paranoia? Claustrophobia?"

"Nope, nope . . ." More lies. Harmless, she decided; she was only mildly claustrophobic.

It came naturally, lying. She had gotten plenty of practice at her first job. It was a high-stress environment; drug tests and harsh evaluations were frequent. They were designing and engineering the future of memory medicine, of *longevity*, for God's sake, and you didn't get to perform a job like that if you couldn't handle a little stress.

Or a shitload of it.

Paranoia. Claustrophobia. She wasn't hooked up to an eval machine now, so she let the sweat bead on her forehead and her jaw grind back and forth. Rosalyn kept her eyes shut, forcing herself not to think about the tiny ship and its tiny confines and the tiny helmet that would lock over her head any second. Then her eyes snapped open, and she went rigid, the early, ugly rigor of an anxiety attack. A familiar tug in her guts, a familiar icy numbness in the tips of her fingers . . .

She was so engrossed in trying not to break down and dissolve into her panic that she didn't hear the footsteps approaching. An old AR advertisement had bugged out on her display and wouldn't refresh, blinking in the upper right corner above her eye. It was for Red Mars Mud Masques. *Wear it, remove it, reveal your inner goddess,* read the ad's text, scrolling by in a tiny window. *You're just five minutes away from the new you!* She stared at it, trying to pull herself back from a precipice that emptied onto a fall with no bottom. It was just the withdrawal, some nausea, nothing to be worried about.

"Jesus, eat something bad at lunch? You look terrible, Devar."

Walters. Her eyes snapped open and she let out a stale breath.

"Maybe the cheese was off," she said with a shrug. "Just a stomachache. It'll pass in a minute."

"Not that time of the month, is it? I'm sure they can find a replacement." Walters chuckled and leaned against the wall across from her. He had a lean, freckled, punchable face, a constellation of old acne scars and a narrow chin.

"Is this the kind of sparkling humor I can look forward to for the next week?" she asked. Her momentary panic vanished. Maybe she ought to be thanking Walters for sobering her up so fast. "You know, I'm senior on this trip, mm? And it would be my pleasure to pull rank." Rosalyn allowed herself a cool smile. "Because I'm sure they can find a replacement."

Walters put his hands up in surrender, cackling. "All right, all right. Fuck. If you're over your cheddar sweats, everything is green on board."

It was good that he was there. She couldn't panic now, not in front of him. Rosalyn nodded and pushed away from the wall. Serene. Calm. Totally in control. She didn't want Walters to find out this was her last chance at keeping her job, or he would just find a way to sabotage her. Hasty footsteps came from the other direction now, from outside the bay doors attached to the campus launch wing. The sliding doors hissed open and a young woman rushed up to them. She wore the crisp, simple blue uniform of the courier service that pinged between bases, delivering messages from as far away as Earth itself if signals were iffy.

"What's this? Nobody is allowed in here this close to launch," Walters said, crossing his arms.

The courier was out of breath. She nodded her head a few times, then shoved a small, silver package toward Rosalyn. "Just following orders. Control gave me the go-ahead to find Devar."

"It's fine," Rosalyn replied gently, taking the package. Her urge to stay friendly wilted when she read the sticker in the upper left corner. "Shit." And then under her breath, "Great timing, Dad."

"Oooh, Dad?" Walters popped up over her shoulder, catching a glimpse of the sticker before Rosalyn could jerk it out of his view. "Whoa. Maximillien Belrose? *He's* your dad? What the hell are you doing working this crappy gig?"

"It's a long story," she said softly. *And I wouldn't share it with you, anyway.*

The courier held out a digital pad to take Rosalyn's signature and confirm delivery. She waited until the courier had disappeared back out the bay doors before turning her head toward Walters. Her father had certainly gone to a lot of trouble tracking her down. Apparently, cutting him off from all social media and communications wasn't enough.

"It's complicated. Family stuff. Can I have a minute? I'll be right behind you."

To his credit, he nodded and backed off, then shook his head from side to side. "Damn. Devar's got a famous daddy. You just get more interesting by the second, don't you?"

I certainly hope not.

"I'll be *right* there," she reiterated with a thin smile.

Walters whistled his way back down the tube, and she could hear him chuckling to himself. There was a good reason she used her mother's maiden name on her application, and why nobody on base except for her boss knew about her family. It was the last name on that delivery sticker—Belrose—that had gotten it pushed through almost straight to the ship itself. That name opened all kinds of doors.

The return address made her hands go numb. The thought of that place, of her father and her old job, flooded her with so much rage that her system simply shut it out. It was too much to process, especially five minutes out from a mission. Better to go cold all over, to let the force of it bounce off her, as if she could harden herself into a little ball of steel.

Had she been warm once? She couldn't remember. Now she felt like ice all over.

She ripped open the silver packet and found a single ear chip inside. *Steel*, she told herself. And she would have to be, to listen to her father's voice again. It had been almost an entire year since they last had contact of any kind. Deep breaths. Closed eyes. She stuck the rubbery earpiece and its square, reloadable chip piece into her ear and tapped the little button on the chip.

Silence. Crackling. Rosalyn curled her fingers into fists and braced.

"Roz? Rosalyn . . . It's your father."

Obviously, Dad, thanks.

"I wanted you to know that I miss you."

On the message he cleared his throat, and Rosalyn ripped the earpiece out and shoved it in her pocket. Fuck him. She didn't need to hear him when she already had so much on her mind. Maybe it was an apology, she thought, or an explanation. Her father was never good at apologizing, something she had inherited.

"Everything okay here?"

She snapped her eyes up to find Josh Girdy watching her from down the corridor, hands in pockets, his outfit identical to his own from earlier in the week, except for the slightly darker tie. Nodding, Rosalyn cleared her throat, just as her father had done on the message, and gave a thumbs-up.

"Forget the thumbs-up," she said with an uneasy laugh. "Everything is okay. But it's all right to be nervous, mm? Always get a bit jittery before launch."

"Hate space travel myself," Girdy agreed. His shoulders eased back and he took a few languid steps toward her, peering over her shoulder to check for Walters. "I know our last interaction was, um, tense, but on behalf of the entire Merchantia staff, good luck. Have a safe voyage, Devar."

"Thank you," she said. "And I appreciate this chance. I won't let you down."

He took another step toward her, and another. Going rigid, she tried not to roll her eyes. He was trying to get a whiff of her breath.

"I can take a Breathalyzer," Rosalyn chirped, too chipper. "If you like?"

"Not necessary, not at all." Girdy waved her off, but she saw the little flicker of panic in his eyes. "Trust, am I right? That's what this is all about. The company, our mission here, all of it. Trust."

Rosalyn watched him internally meander around for a moment. Clearly, he wasn't finished, and he kept fishing in his pockets but never bringing anything out. His eyes darted up to hers, oddly blank and sharklike, almost black. She felt those drums in her head again, the pounding nerves, the sense that something bad was coming and she was powerless to stop it.

"Your reports really are good," he finally said, reaching to scratch nervously at his Adam's apple. "Thorough. Exacting. It's why, you know, we noticed, when things started to dip. But I listened to your report from this week. The Reevey case."

Captain Reevey. The killer. Not Captain Murder Ship, as Owen had so descriptively called him. Rosalyn nodded, still feeling as if she were somehow in trouble. Girdy kept rocking on his heels, never settling, never going still.

"It was solid work, Devar. That's partially why you're even here and not on a transport back to Tokyo Bliss Station. I'm interested to see how this goes. There's been, um, a string of this kind of thing lately, and to be completely honest, upper management is getting fidgety. First Reevey, then the *Quant-7* . . ."

The *Quant-7* had been Alexia's last gig, the one that had driven her to babbling about talking trees. Something was off. Two completely liquefied crews in one week? That was odd by any metric.

"This is a full code blue, and that doesn't look good for us, so please, if you see anything weird, anything that strikes you as unusual, make a note of it, all right? Maybe bring it to me first."

Rosalyn lifted a brow at that. What Girdy was suggesting wasn't procedure, and he knew it, blowing out a nervous breath and rocking faster on his feet.

"It was me, you know, that got you this last assignment," he reminded her, focusing those shark eyes directly into hers. "Favor for a favor?"

It was her turn to check that Walters wasn't around. She quashed the urge to squirm and shrugged. "You sound like you're expecting us to find something weird."

"It *is* weird," Girdy replied with a grunt. "People are dropping like flies around here, Devar. I think maybe one of us should try to find out why, and without all the, you know, stupid bullshit red tape upper management likes to toss up."

The drums in her head thundered louder. *Weird.* That was an upsettingly soft word to describe the total annihilation of three entire crews. It was strange enough that Girdy showed up personally to the launch, but his behavior made her even more suspicious. A slick guy like him would usually jump at the chance to impress upper management, but now he wanted to circumvent them? She smelled a rat, but whether that rat was Girdy or his bosses, she couldn't yet say.

He had her full attention. Rosalyn nodded, doing just like Girdy, putting her hands in her pockets to hide her suddenly sweating palms. She felt the message from her father there and squeezed it. Last chance. For this job, or for her to pull out. Maybe she ought to just tell Girdy to fuck off and she would find another way to run from her problems.

"Do this," he said, lowering his voice further and leaning in toward her. "Because it isn't just about second chances. It's the right thing to do. Three separate expeditions go dark, almost at the same time? That's a lot of dead people. That's a lot of questions that need answering."

Altruism or angling for a promotion? Rosalyn studied him but couldn't quite decide. Her coworkers deserved justice, that was true, but if this was all simply a series of unfortunate accidents, then there wouldn't be much justice at all, only funerals and filling vacancies at Merchantia.

"I get it," she said. "I'll see what I can do. What I can find."

"Good. That's good. Because, look, we've signed on to a lot of new tech partnerships lately—ISS, Belrose Industries, Beta Tech . . . It would be better if these deaths weren't ours, right? We do good work here; I would hate to think we were responsible in any way." His shark eyes glinted, and he said it with an oddly straight smile.

Definitely angling for a promotion. The more he talked, the more she became convinced Merchantia had done something wrong. Of course Girdy would want a slipup pinned on someone else. All of their jobs would evaporate if Merchantia had purposely caused multiple crew deaths. She had suspected negligence, but Girdy's black eyes suggested something worse. But there was more there, a name that made Rosalyn's ears burn. Belrose Industries. When she quit her job and left Earth, that partnership had just been a whisper among the board members. It hadn't mattered much to her then, only the science really interested her, but it certainly intrigued her now. Did her family business—her father's tech—have something to do with these catastrophes?

"So you're trying to pull a cover job," she said.

"No, no, no, just the truth, that's all I'm interested in. The truth! And if it's truth that exonerates MSC, then that's just great." Girdy chuckled and rolled his eyes. "Cover job. Ha. No, no, not necessary, just do your job," he said, and then added with another tight smile, "*thoughtfully.*"

Girdy laughed again and pointed a finger at her, still smiling, as if to verify they were old friends just joking around, as if he hadn't just all but told her to cover up for Merchantia's likely negligence. Pals! And he was just speaking candidly, like friends did. He stuck out his hand toward her, and Rosalyn reached out slowly to take it. The ready sequence had begun, blaring through the corridor, a red light flashing over them.

"What's going to happen to Reevey?" she asked, realizing he would feel how damp her palm had become. Reevey, of course, had quite clearly murdered his entire crew. No cover-up job possible there. "Will there be a trial?"

The handshake was quick, and in a flash Girdy was spinning away, striding down the hall, waving off her question just as he had waved off her desperation in his office.

"Dead. Hanged himself in his cell. Good riddance, right? One less mess for us to clean up."

His voice echoed down the corridor, and then he was gone. Rosalyn worried the message chip in her pocket and felt her head go suddenly quiet. No more drums, no more panic, just a strange emptiness.

A murderer. A mess. Just like his victims, no longer visibly human. An icy finger ran down her spine as she rubbed her thumb harder over the message. She no longer felt certain she wanted this last chance. But the thought of losing . . . of going back . . . that was as good as admitting defeat. And she couldn't shake the feeling that she needed to go, that the mention of her family business was no coincidence. She couldn't imagine *how* Belrose Industries could be involved, but if they were, it seemed right that she, a Belrose, should be the one to get to the bottom of it.

Walters was shouting at her from inside the ship. It was time to go. Rosalyn yanked the message out of her pocket, considered dropping it on the floor and smashing it with her boot. But she kept it, sliding it back into its safe little place.

5

"Feeling better?"

Rosalyn was hoping they could sustain an awkward yet steady silence. She was wrong, of course, because people like Dave Walters loved, loved, *loved* the sound of their own voices. He was staring at her intently. The *Salvager 6* buzzed with familiar energy, almost comforting, like the subtle back-and-forth rocking of a hammock in the breeze. But this was no beach trip, and Rosalyn's palms had not yet stopped sweating.

"Yes, definitely, I feel much better, just nerves," she said. It was oddly true. She didn't feel good, not at all, but she felt focused. As soon as they launched, she could put even more miles between her and her father, and Josh Girdy with his creepy shark eyes. "But it passed."

"I hope you mean that metaphorically."

Rosalyn managed a smile. "Wouldn't you like to know . . ."

"Was that an actual joke? Fuck. You *are* feeling better. Girdy doesn't usually have that effect on people. That guy makes me nervous. Something about his beady little eyes . . ."

Walters chuckled to himself. He sat to her left and a little behind, stationed at the front of the curved wall of monitors that fed them everything from cabin temperature, to speed, to distance to target and so on. Rosalyn understood how to read most of it, a requirement of training, one that had been a snap thanks to the complexity of her former job, but only a few core parts of information were really worth paying attention to at any given time. And as long as Walters stayed alive and vigilant, it wasn't her job to worry about the details of their flight.

She was cleanup and cleanup only.

You're leaving to be a fucking janitor?

It was a long leap from studying xenobiological samples against human biology to cleaning up corpses in space. When she left, her father's disdain for the job only made it that much more appealing.

"Yikes. This isn't much of a flight," Walters muttered. The engines purred more insistently, launch window approaching. She swiveled in her seat, watching Walters read over the mission summation. "These poor bastards almost made it back. They're on the edge of the system."

"No, they had just fueled up recently," Rosalyn replied. She had read the briefing the night before and once that morning. Leave it to her idiot pilot to do his homework six seconds before the test. "Whatever was left when they went dark the thrusters would automatically use to bring them back toward the campus. Speeds things up."

"You want to take bets on the state of things in that ship?" he asked, still looking over the briefing on his personal VIT monitor.

"Not really."

Walters sighed, leaning forward far enough to clack his helmet against the flickering green-and-black readout screens. "I thought a morbid sense of humor was required for this gig."

"Only if you're a dickhead." Rosalyn double-checked the harness securing her to the flight chair. "Have a little respect, Walters.

They had families, families that are waiting to hear about what happened to their loved ones. This is the third crew to go dark this quarter; we need to take this seriously."

"Whatever." He leaned back in the pilot's seat and checked his own harness, then signaled mission control for launch permissions. "Me? I die out here, I would hope somebody makes a joke over my dead body. Life's too short, can't be uptight all the time."

"Laugh at your dead body," she mused softly. "I'll keep that in mind."

"Ha. Ha. Now who needs to show some respect?"

Rosalyn tipped her head back and sighed hard enough to fog the glass of her helmet. The white mist of it bled slowly away as she stared impatiently up at the ceiling. "Get well soon, Alexia," she whispered.

The automated voice of the mission control Servitor filled the cockpit, effectively silencing their conversation. Most critical roles were being overtaken by Servitors now, biped artificial intelligence units that were completely obedient, error-free and—most importantly—cheaper in the long run than human employees. It was only a matter of time before their jobs were completely automated, too. But maybe it was the right decision to let AI Servitors do what they did—it wouldn't bother them to clean up the dead. There would be no more Alexias wandering the Merchantia campus mumbling about talking trees. Let the unliving handle the unliving, and see if doing it long enough drove even robots mad.

"All permissions in place," Walters chimed in when the Servitor's clear, slow voice cut out. "Monitors are green, engines green, and crew?"

"Ready on your signal," Rosalyn replied at once.

"Then we'll see you in a week, everyone," Walters said with a sigh, leaning forward to switch the flight controls to automated. The salvage ships were more or less shot clear of the campus base, and then, safely clear of all incoming vessels and the space station itself, the ship's controls would revert to manual. More than likely, Walters would just use the predetermined and charted course for the wreck and let the ship fly itself, but he would need to take over for small adjustments once they approached the *Brigantine*.

They both keyed in their personal, private number codes into the VIT units on their wrists. This was the final indication to launch control that they were both conscious and consenting to the mission beginning. Rosalyn punched out 1-1-1-8 on hers, struggling to hit the right numbers with the stubby fingertips of her gloves.

"Seven days," he added under his breath. "Then I'm taking a long holiday."

The internal countdown began. The engines roared. Rail mechanisms surrounding the ship began to squeal, spinning at incredible speed before engaging with the *Salvager 6* and flinging it straight into outer space and away from MSC.

"Time off is weird for me, but my birthday is always the worst." Rosalyn frowned as the narrow windshield opened, showing an unbroken and twinkling field of stars. Her father had insisted that it was ridiculous to celebrate her birthday *and* Christmas separately when they were so close together. Efficiency, that was his thing. Better to just fold it all into one. This last chance at keeping her job wasn't much of a gift either way.

"Not me. Got a calendar next to my bunk, been counting down the days to this trip for weeks. Second I get back, I rotate out and back to Earth. About time, too. Getting a little stir-crazy on base."

"That's good," Rosalyn said, distracted. She stared out at the vastness of space and the stars. They looked like a flat, unbroken wall, so numerous it was impossible to contemplate what might be going on around each and every one of those stars. They could hold civilizations yet to be discovered or, if the pattern of history held, just more emptiness, more planets unconducive to intelligent life.

"You've got a big family?" she asked.

Walters shrugged and wriggled down into his seat, getting comfortable while they hurtled toward their destination. "Not really. Just a sister, but she's got three kids and they like to hear my pilot stories. The oldest one? Alice? She eats up all the gory details. Shit, that kid is gonna turn out to be real weird one day."

Rosalyn smirked, glancing over at him. "Then maybe you should redact some of those details for her, don't you think?"

"You kidding me? That's the best part of being an uncle . . ." The spacecraft shook, hard, both of them jostling in their seats as the ship reached maximum velocity. Rosalyn felt her teeth rattle, the chattering almost loud enough to block out her pilot's voice. "'Sides, not my problem if she's a fuckup. Everyone will blame her parents, not me."

"Charming." She bit out the word and closed her eyes. It was always disconcerting to see the ship's instruments shaking around as they flew. It lasted another ten minutes or so, and both of them were silent, gripping their seats hard until the craft came to an abrupt stop and Rosalyn lurched forward, nearly propelled out of her harness.

"Hate that part," Walters muttered, sighing and glancing over the flight monitor. "Always makes my guts churn."

"Pilot, report." The mission control Servitor's voice filled the cockpit again.

"Green as you please," he chirped back. "FTL systems operable, ninety-nine percent functionality. Doesn't get much better than that."

It gets exactly one percent better, she thought with a grimace.

A quiet hiss chased through the underbelly of the ship. The FTL engines were locked until the pilot gave verbal confirmation that the jump could be made safely. Once they jumped systems, the *Salvager 6* would be far out of range of MSC mission control and they would need to function autonomously. Contact was possible, but beyond that, *Salvager 6* was at the mercy of Walters and Rosalyn.

Most pilots and crew members preferred the independence of deeper space, but not her. There was something comforting in knowing mission control could still pick them up if anything went unexpectedly wrong.

"You may engage FTL systems when ready, *Salvager 6*. Return in good health."

It was the usual line, and it never failed to sound a bit hollow coming from an AI unit.

"Next stop . . ." Walters said, selecting the FTL engines on his monitor, "three days out from Proxima Centauri b."

The ship shook again, this time more subtly. Rosalyn fancied she could feel the air charging with the energy it took to pull the craft through space with such unbelievable speed. *This* was the part she hated most. She might never conquer the feeling that humankind in outer space was unnatural, but outrunning light itself? If it was possible, then it obeyed the laws of nature, she conceded, but it still seemed like the result of terrible hubris.

She clamped down on the seat handles and held her breath—this was the truly gut-churning part, whatever Walters thought. A sensation of weightlessness came first, then full-body pressure, as if the atmosphere itself were trying to put a hand on your forehead and hold you back. When the FTL jump stopped, they would be rocked again, slammed back to normal speeds with an almost painful jarring.

The engines flared, and she could feel the sudden jolt as the FTL drive kicked in fully, rumbling power surging through the ship, making the soles of her feet buzz. Everything blurred, the stars, the outline of the windscreen; the instruments and everything surrounding her took on that same nauseating formlessness. The blur of her vision resolved into a single, huge spot of light in the distance. Rosalyn blinked through it, eyes nearly closed, her stomach and throat constricting as if they were in free fall.

It lasted longer than their quick shot away from the campus. She had been through this many times before, but never grew accustomed to it. It was more bearable on huge passenger ships, and the sheer size of those transports dispersed the shock of the phenomenon. The first time, in training, in a ship the same size as *Salvager 6*, she had vomited inside her helmet the instant they dropped out of FTL speeds.

Ever since, she forced herself to close in, to go numb and contained, squeezing every muscle in her body and gritting her teeth until impact came and the urge to vomit passed.

Her pulse pounded in her ears, and then a high ringing started, growing louder by the second, bringing with it the kind of migraine-inducing pressure that made her want to drop her jaw and pop her eardrums before they exploded. It was worse this time, much worse, with her head throbbing for a drink.

"Woo!" she heard Walters scream through his helmet. He whooped and laughed, banging his fist on the seat rest. "Nothing like it, right?"

The FTL cut out as scheduled, and the *Salvager 6* seemed to scream to a stop, though they drifted on and on, having been squeezed through that painful tube of light and sound and forced out the end, gliding into the neighboring star system, Proxima Centauri.

It was breathtakingly desolate. But there, not all that far away, hung a blob of silvery gray. The *Brigantine*. It was different from the field of stars around it. It drifted out there alone like a solitary mote of dust in a dusky sky.

I hate this shit.

Dead bodies. Five of them. She didn't want to think about what state they would be in, and could only hope for the mundanity of a malfunctioning air lock. A shiver traveled from the base of her neck to her toes.

You chose this life, she reminded herself, sitting taller in her chair. *Now do your job and bring them home.*

6

Rosalyn didn't fancy herself a music expert, but the Unpronounceable Sound barely qualified as music. So naturally, Dave Walters loved them and insisted that they be played on a loop.

"Do you have anything else loaded on your VIT? Please, this is fucking killing me, Walters." The oxygen and temperature levels on the *Salvager 6* had been stabilized, and while they finished their interception of the *Brigantine* and Rosalyn prepped for transfer, she liked to get some time out of the helmet. It also gave her the chance to lightly smack her forehead against the wall, a mean headache brewing at the base of her skull. Vodka would fix it, if she had any.

No. We're done with all that.

There were five bodies to recover and a company (potentially) to exonerate; vodka certainly would not help with that.

"If I have to hear one more hour of this noise, I'm going to fucking kill someone, and just a gentle reminder that there's only one other person on this ship."

From the cockpit, where Walters was attempting to sync their systems with the *Brigantine*'s, she heard him give a childish moan. "You have no taste, Devar. Or maybe you just can't appreciate TUS until you hear them live."

"That's possible?" she muttered. She couldn't see how anyone would willingly choose to listen, in public, to a wall of synthesizers screeching at random intervals. The "song" had opened with five minutes of nonsense poetry, followed by the lead singer making an odd groaning sound, which was allegedly the *real* name of the group. Insufferable stuff.

Rosalyn turned away from the stack of equipment crates she had been unpacking in the main bay of the ship. A red, curly head stuck out from the arched door leading to the cockpit, and Walters smiled at her. Or sneered. Then he winked.

"How do you feel about Station Bangers?" he said, and beamed, citing yet another improvisational techno-synth experiment.

"Fucking. Kill. Someone." She shook her head, then mouthed, "*You.*"

"Geez," Walters said, clucking his tongue and appearing fully in the doorway. He tapped the VIT monitor on his wrist with his forefinger. "Your heart rate is elevated, Devar. You should really relax. Not good to get riled up before a mission."

"Can we call a truce?" she asked, popping the lid off of a tester crate. She would need to use the individually wrapped testing nodes for taking samples of any biological material on the *Brigantine*. It was easier to load up with a few before boarding instead of making multiple trips back and forth between ships. "You must like the Late Nodes?"

"Yeah, yeah, yeah! Maybe I like your style after all."

"What a relief," she muttered. "Can that be our truce? Just please change it before I turn homicidal."

Walters picked their latest cover album and Rosalyn's teeth unclenched. Working in close quarters like this was difficult and often tense—a good partnership could make an otherwise deeply unpleasant job tolerable, and on lucky days, half-enjoyable. She and Alexia had gotten on like a house on fire right from the jump. Alexia was calm and professional, with just enough of a sarcastic streak to keep the missions amusing. As much as Rosalyn disliked Walters, he was right about one thing—it *did* take a kind of dark humor to survive salvaging. Alexia had that macabre side; it just didn't come with an unhealthy devotion to synth improv.

It will all be over soon.

Could be worse, of course; she could be stuck with Walters for a lot longer than their projected mission time of a week. Sometimes ships went dark in deep, deep space, and just getting to the wreck took weeks. Those missions required larger salvaging vessels, ones equipped with exercise facilities and more-comfortable sleeping quarters. Little hops like the one to the *Brigantine* were undertaken on smaller craft with less homey accommodations. A week of roughing it was deemed acceptable, but an already stressful task coupled with cramped quarters for weeks? Even more employees would lose their minds.

So that was a positive. Only a week. Rosalyn continued to sort out her kit, reminding herself that Walters was just about to rotate out for family time, and that maybe, just maybe, it wouldn't hurt to try to be amiable for this last trip.

Rosalyn packed her kit with extra testing nodes. Unlike Walters, she had done her homework. The *Brigantine* accommodated up to ten researchers. The only craft that ended up with messier salvage situations were exploration ships. Crews testing the edge of known space often ran into danger, and the missions had a tendency to end in bloodshed—even if Merchantia personality checked for resilience and stability in exploration crews, they couldn't always avoid space blindness.

It was a new thing, space blindness, the kind of sudden, previously rare condition that took over news hours and podcasts and medical roundtable discussions on Earth. You couldn't turn on the latest talk show without hearing things like, "Are we pushing crews too far?" or "The cost of the new horizon . . ."

Humans just weren't meant to be cooped up in little metal boxes in the middle of nowhere for years on end without relief. It did something to you. It chipped away at your humanity. MSC rotations were meant to counteract the side effects, but exploration was still important, and the human cost was, apparently, acceptable. Cryo-technology was still young and there were limits. Even her father's company, Belrose Industries, had been poking at the possibility of using drugs to alter brain chemistry and make humans more fit for long-term space travel.

Rosalyn cringed away from the thought. She had been on that project when *Glen* happened. God, but there was a time when she had loved that job. The research. The sense of urgency. The feeling that she was doing something important. If they could find a way to keep human bodies from negatively reacting to the length of space travel, then there was no telling how far people could go, or what companies like Merchantia would find with their probing missions. And of course there had been friends, like Angela, and like Lin, a new intern that collected vintage lunch boxes, and Saruti, who had walked Rosalyn through her first autopsy . . . She hadn't expected to miss them, or her fish, so much.

The work was easy to miss, too. Satisfying. Challenging. She had felt a breakthrough coming. Angela felt it, too, and had left to head up a new deep space research branch, keen to procure more samples, more data . . . The new position for Angela started just before everything imploded with Glen, and sometimes it was hard not to blame her for not being there. If Rosalyn had friends to tell, friends that would listen, maybe everything would've been different.

Maybe Glen would have lost his job. Gone to prison. *Paid.*

"You're gonna feel the bump any minute now."

She cleared her throat and nodded, finding that she had packed her kit from pure muscle memory. Testing nodes, atmospheric readers, blood and tissue containers, hover cuffs . . . Everything was exactly where it should be in the rectangular metal case engraved with DEVAR on the lid.

As promised, Rosalyn swayed on her heels a little as the *Salvager 6* made physical contact with the *Brigantine*. Walters had piloted them carefully, and it was so soft that she barely heard the impact of the two ships gently touching. It would take gradual, manual adjustments from Walters to position the crafts air lock to air lock. She listened to the soft hiss of the external jets as he used the piloting joysticks to find alignment.

"Just bring them home," she whispered, closing her kit and latching it. She stood and tucked it under her right arm, bringing it across the main chamber to the far wall and the long, waist-high metal shelf there. The main chamber of the *Salvager 6* was used for storage and general prep. All of the crates of salvaging equipment, food, and first aid and emergency supplies were strapped carefully to the walls. She tidied up the mess she had made preparing her field kit, returning the crates to their designated slots on the wall and securing them.

The chamber to the right was sealed, but it would serve as living quarters during their mission. Rosalyn looked at the closed door to that room for a moment, tightness gathering in her chest. She would be alone with Walters every night. The same panic had washed over her on the first missions with Owen and Griz. They hadn't seemed to even notice her, and gradually she stopped worrying that they were a threat. But Walters? If only Alexia were there with them, it would make it so much easier. Did she at all trust him? Did she *know* him? She had known Glen, or thought she did, and that hadn't meant anything in the end.

When he had slammed her against the wall, hurt her, it was like looking into a stranger's eyes.

Rosalyn shook her head and stumbled to the door, jamming it open. She could hardly breathe. Leaning against the wall, she forced air in through her nose and down, blowing it out slowly, repeating the exercise until her panic ebbed.

Pushing away from the wall, she walked into the kitchenette. Just beyond were two separate rooms, hardly bigger than shower stalls, which would serve as their bunks. Separate bunks. Her eye went at once to the heavy-duty locking mechanism on each and the attached keypads. She could lock herself inside and, no doubt, only a number code synced between her VIT monitor and the security panel would open the door.

It would have to do. It was enough.

She turned around to find Walters standing in the doorway to the cockpit, staring at her. That was a funny look. He lifted both brows, tilting his head to the side.

"I mean, it ain't the Ritz . . ."

"Just haven't been on a ship this small in a while," Rosalyn covered smoothly. She even gave a chummy little laugh. "Sardines come to mind."

"It's real peaceful," he said. "I get my deepest sleep in those things."

"Good to know," Rosalyn replied, closing the door to the living area and crossing back to the table. Her helmet rested there and she lifted it, lowering it over her head before giving a practiced twist to lock it into place on her flight suit.

"We're all cozied up," Walters told her with a thumbs-up. "You want to do the honors?"

"If you insist," she said, cringing at his choice of words. Soon she would be immersed in her work, totally lost to the dark ghosts that threatened from the back of her mind. On a salvage, she gave herself over to the details. She took refuge in the minutiae. Find, collect, record. Find, collect, record . . .

Rosalyn took up her kit again and walked with Walters to the air lock door. He had retrieved his helmet as well, since there was no telling what might go wrong during a sync up, or what the atmosphere would be like aboard the *Brigantine*. She tapped out the float sequence on her VIT monitor and waited.

She had always liked that term—*float*. It was like floating an idea, like giving the other ship a little wave to see if they were interested in saying hello. The float signal would hail every system on the *Brigantine* until something responded. It was as if they could coax one last word out of a lifeless body.

It only took about fifteen seconds before a green light flashed above the air lock door. Then came the familiar metal shift and *thunk* of the air locks recognizing each other and locking into place. Afterward, a quiet hiss beyond the door indicated the equalization of pressure and the presence of gravity stabilization. That was good. She didn't feel like bouncing around in zero g while she did her collection.

A series of quick, sharp beeps came from the pilot's VIT, and Rosalyn glanced over at Walters to see him frowning in confusion. He squinted at the tiny screen on his wrist and tapped it a few times.

"That's weird," he muttered.

"What is?" she asked. This was not a good time. She needed to keep a clear head.

"Have you ever seen this?" Walters asked. He held up his wrist, showing her a flashing alert. Red text began filtering across, and she hurried to read it aloud for both of them.

"'Crew redirect, stand by for instructions,'" Rosalyn read. "'*Brigantine* reclassified as non–mission critical.' Crew redirect? What the hell does that mean?"

"Give me a minute." Walters jogged back toward the cockpit, leaning over his display and sighing. She watched him key into the comm system, calling up MSC headquarters. The Servitor responded to their hail immediately.

"This is *Salvager 6*, yeah we're out here and we've made contact with the *Brigantine*. We just received some kind of alert about a crew redirect. Could we get confirmation and further orders?"

"Crew redirect," was the Servitor's response, as if it were the most obvious command in the world. She heard Walters snort. "Stand by. Stand by. Stand by . . ."

"This is ridiculous," Rosalyn hissed. "We're ready to go. Just tell them we can take another job after this one is finished, or have them send a probe. Can you confirm that the *Brigantine* is code blue?" she called out loudly enough for the comm to detect her voice.

"Affirmative," the Servitor responded. It then returned to repeating its standby message.

"And you can confirm that there are dead bodies aboard?"

"Affirmative. Stand by, stand by . . ."

Rosalyn turned back to the air lock. This was the third crew to go dark recently, and it needed to be handled. She didn't just need to prove herself, she needed to give the deceased and their families some closure. "I don't like wasting time. We're already here, Walters. Let's just wrap it up and get on to the next assignment."

"I don't know," Walters called out. He spun away from the console, taking a few slow steps toward her. Then he pivoted and pointed at the comm. "Maybe we should wait."

The Servitor suddenly came out of standby. "Redirect assignment confirmed—please proceed to the following coordinates for a refuel request. Repeat, redirect and refuel."

She could see Walters examining the coordinates and data streaming to his VIT. And she could also see the moment his face went white and slack. "You have got to be fucking kidding me." He glanced over at her. "It's some senator on a feel-good see-the-stars tour. His vessel overshot their window and now he's stuck. Idiot."

"A refuel?" Rosalyn wouldn't budge. "Talk about non–mission critical. His life support won't run out for days; they can send a fuel probe instead. There are *people* in there, Walters. I saw their little memorial stones. The senator can wait."

"No, Devar, come on. We'll get in deep shit for this." He closed the distance between them, joining her at the air lock. She fought the urge to shrink away from him. "You heard mission control."

"Yeah," she said. "I did. And Josh Girdy specifically asked me to look into the deaths on this ship, so this is me ignoring mission control. They can take it up with him if there's a problem. Who signed off on this redirect?"

Walters queried headquarters about just that, then stumbled over some name Rosalyn had never heard before. If it was Girdy's decision to send the redirect, she would take it seriously. This was his mission, he had chosen the crew, so any changes to the itinerary should be made by him and him alone. Rosalyn smelled a rat again, a rat that seemed determined to keep her away from the *Brigantine*.

Girdy needs to know about this, she thought. If this was all a mix-up, and Girdy really was fine with the redirect, then he ought to have been involved enough to sign off on the mission change himself. Her gut told her this wasn't his call. Her gut said, *Someone doesn't want you poking around.*

"Respond, tell them to send a fuel probe. Twelve more hours twiddling his thumbs won't kill the esteemed senator."

The Late Nodes still crooned through the ship, but their voices dimmed as the float signal was picked up by what was left of the *Brigantine*'s computer. It was like a soft, plaintive hello. Or maybe *help*.

"See?" she said. "It's a sign. Can you shut the music off?" Rosalyn whispered, glancing up at Walters. "I don't want any inter-ference."

"Oh," he muttered, scrambling to bring up his VIT. "My bad. Wouldn't want any interference while you fuck off and get us fired."

"Girdy will bail us out; he wanted me on this job. We won't get fired."

Before he could kill the music, the *Brigantine*'s systems responded. Instead of the expected, recorded rundown from the computer, the voice of an AI Servitor crackled over the speakers. It wasn't shocking that the *Brigantine* would have an AI helper on board, but it was strange that it wouldn't have shut down as soon as the dead hail went out. Efficiency. That was the Merchantia way.

"This is Servitor J-A-X Zero November, series type N . . ."

"What the fuck?" Walters murmured.

"Shhhh."

There was a pause, and then the AI completed its introduction, launching into a string of diagnostics regarding the state of the *Brig-antine*'s systems. It went on and on and on, a predictable list of prob-lems that she had already found in the dossier. Then, finally, Rosalyn sighed and pressed her finger to the VIT monitor, sending a return message.

"We're responding to a code blue," she interrupted. The AI fell abruptly silent. "We already have your ship diagnostics. We received a dead hail from your vessel. Can you confirm?"

"Confirmed," the AI replied succinctly.

She nodded, giving Walters a grin. A good sign. This talkative fellow had probably just failed to power down and had been putter-ing around the ship, waiting for them to come along. She almost felt sorry for it. Let that stalled senator stew for a while; this poor AI had been sitting there with a dead crew, alone and in the dark.

"That's good," she said into her wrist monitor. "Thank you.

We're expecting five code blues on board, crewmates Aries, Endrizzi, Sverdal, Iwasa and Yasin. Can you confirm?"

"You memorized all that?" Walters whispered.

She ignored him. There was another pause, this one longer. Rosalyn frowned and leaned in closer to her VIT, which was silly, considering the response would come from the speakers embedded in the ceiling above them. Walters breathed loudly next to her, practically panting. She couldn't blame him—there was no reason for a Servitor to take so long to respond. The dead crew ought to be obvious and his response similarly forthcoming. And logged.

"Confirmed," the Servitor finally said. The speakers crackled softly as the AI went on, and Rosalyn felt the blood slowly and painfully drain from her face. "Crewmates Aries, Endrizzi, Iwasa and Yasin present aboard MSC research vessel *705-B*, call sign MWC-70, all life readings green. Crew Member Sverdal deceased. Permission to board granted. Confirm?"

7

Walters gasp-choked so loudly it made her jump. "*Life* readings? Shit. Oh, shit. The crew are still alive in there? That's not good, Devar."

Rosalyn remained quiet, focused, staring directly at her VIT monitor and nothing else. Perspiration beaded on her forehead. Training had prepared her for this. She had run into all kinds of fuckups and glitches and misinformation on previous missions, not to mention liquefied cats and people, so there was no reason to over-react. Not yet, anyway. And if the crew were alive in there, then it would be huge news for Merchantia. Girdy would probably do a jig when they told him. Someone would get shitcanned for trying to redirect them to a bored senator. One dead woman was still awful, but four living was practically a miracle.

"Are you insane? Of course it's good. Still want to go off course and help that stranded senator? Just . . . just please be quiet and let me handle this," she hissed. "Servitor, give me the current location of the crew, please."

Walters fidgeted, then broke away from her side and began to pace. Clearly he had never run into a hiccup on a mission before, or the salvagers with him had kept the problems quiet. Rosalyn wasn't going to let this go pear-shaped because they couldn't keep it to-gether on their end. She reached out with her free hand and grabbed his arm, hard.

She didn't let go until the Servitor gave its response.

"Unknown. Confirm?"

"Yes, confirmed," Rosalyn said, squeezing her eyes shut for a moment. This was either a positive sign or a very bad one. "Can you give me *your* location?"

"Cockpit galley, confirm?"

"Great, yes, confirmed. And while you're there, give me a quick oxygen reading."

Rosalyn let go of his arm and locked eyes with Walters, shaking her head almost imperceptibly. Freezing, he kept eye contact, a light sheen of sweat glistening on his pale face.

"Oxygen levels holding at six percent, pronounced dangerous for humans."

She clucked her tongue softly, disappointed. No miracles here; it was just a glitch. Nobody would survive in oxygen levels like that, not for long, anyway. "Seal and secure your current location, Servi-tor. I'm coming aboard."

It was the pilot's turn to lash out and grab her by the forearm. Rosalyn shook herself free at once, glaring.

"Are you fucking crazy? You can't go in there, Devar, we don't know where the crew is! They could be alive."

She closed the communication link to the *Brigantine* and waited, leaning against the air lock portal while the AI followed her com-mands. She heard the whir and clank of the opposite air lock engag-ing, the doors aligning and then unlocking. As always, the sound made her adrenaline spike—it was time to do her job.

"Relax, salvagers run into stuff like this all the time."

"*I* don't."

"I'm serious, Walters, you need to calm down. That AI should have powered off ages ago; it's probably just low on cells. My guess? It doesn't have enough juice to sync all the new mission information and it's repeating back old data. I'll check the onboard databases when I get inside. Once we get that Servitor fully charged, it'll cycle in the new logs from the ship and match up with our dossier." She leaned against the exit briefly before glancing over the items in her case. The doors finished aligning and she punched the release lever next to theirs.

"Good to see you're so confident, but it sounds to me like you're writing fiction," Walters muttered, shaking his head. He was sweating, too. "Me? I'm staying put. You let me know if I need to rescue your ass. Or don't, you know, because I warned you, all right? You can't say I didn't warn you. Christ, we could be going to a cushy refuel job and probably, like, winning a medal of service or something, but instead you want to get messed up in this shit."

"Good to know where your priorities are at." Rosalyn shot him one last glance and then nodded toward the circular door as it gave, opening onto the tunnel passage like an aperture. "There are dead bodies on that ship, right? Our colleagues. One stupid glitch isn't going to keep me from getting them home."

He stared at her, unblinking, then rolled his eyes and took a step back, putting up his hands as he retreated to the cockpit. "You're sure this is all routine? I can get mission control on the horn again."

"Don't bother them," she said, scooting herself into the tunnel. She wouldn't prove much of anything if her last chance on the job ended before it really even began. And this had happened to her before or, at least, to Griz. One of the few times he ever spoke to her and Owen was when he explained away the glitches they ran into docking with dark vessels. Power and temperature fluxes

57

wreaked havoc on gear and crew alike. Servitors malfunctioned. Data was corrupted. Sometimes entire ships had to be completely refitted at HQ after an equipment problem. Or as Griz had so eloquently put it, "Surge and purge."

The gravity in the tunnel had stabilized and she moved about as smoothly as she could in the flight suit. "Let me get eyes inside and some power into that Servitor, then we can make the call."

Walters nodded slowly, and she watched him disappear into the cockpit before the circular door to their salvaging ship hissed shut. She was alone in the passage; her only communication with the pilot would come through the headset in her helmet. That was fine. She was eager to get this job over with—sure, she knew it was just some technical burnout causing the confusion, but that didn't mean she was sweating any less over it. Recovering code blues was tough enough on a flawless run, and there was no denying the jumpy nervousness fluttering in her chest.

Girdy had implied there was a remote possibility that more was going on than just bad luck.

I cannot believe I'm hoping for bad luck.

The other option was foul play, and she had seen where that led on her run. A cargo hold flooded with human soup. Until she saw for herself what was inside the *Brigantine*, she wasn't going to bother Merchantia HQ. After panicking and calling HQ too fast on her first assignment, she returned to her barracks room and found a baby bottle and a pacifier waiting on her pillow. She didn't hail mission control much after that. And besides, they would be alerted to the fact that she was ignoring the redirect if they called in the anomaly now. Did Girdy know about the redirect? Leaving too soon wouldn't get him or Rosalyn any closer to understanding why so many crews were going dark.

"This thing on?"

She flinched, Walters's voice blasting through her helmet. His voice crackled on the speaker, blown out.

"Please stop yelling." Rosalyn moved along the connective tunnel, pausing outside the door to the *Brigantine*. A tiny green-and-gold light flickered above the hatch, indicating it was unlocked and ready for boarding. She took a deep breath, feeling bruised on the inside from the force and speed of her heartbeat. *Just a glitch, Devar, keep it together.* "I'm at the door."

"Everything looks good, and the connection is fine. This patch of space is calm, shouldn't be in any danger of debris colliding with the tunnel," he responded, this time in a voice that didn't make her want to leap out of her suit. And then, in an even tinier voice: "You're still sure about this?"

"My first mission out I opened the target door and a dead botanist fell on me," she said flatly. "Things go wrong."

"Yikes. You didn't quit on the spot?"

"Our day can only get better from there, right?"

She heard Walters chuckle darkly on the other end. "That takes balls. I like it."

"No more chitchat, thank you very much, keep the talk to a minimum. I need to concentrate." Rosalyn hefted her work case, swinging toward the door. She pressed her palm slowly against the air lock release mechanism teamed to the *Brigantine*'s door and waited for it to respond.

"All right," she said shakily. "Going in."

Right on cue, the *Brigantine* opened to her, revealing a small, tidy room and another, smaller door. She sealed herself in, gravity in the antechamber stabilizing before she pressed through to the second door and into the ship itself. The temperature remained constant, regulated by her suit and the small oxygen canisters hidden in the flaps on her shoulder blades. The material was dense enough to keep her warm, dry and safe, a combination biosafety and space suit. There was no telling what smells or bacteria she would encounter on these missions, and the filtration system and heavy-duty gloves were meant to protect her from it all.

She let the security of that knowledge enfold her like a blanket as she switched comms to a general channel, allowing her to interface with both Walters and the *Brigantine*'s onboard AI.

The door led into a galley not unlike the one on *Salvager 6*, apparently used for minor storage and for traveling from one area of the ship to the next. Lights flickered overhead, nothing but emergency panels giving the ship a low, green glow. Her eyes adjusted slowly, tricked now and then by the strobing lights. To her left lay the sealed door to the cockpit, and to her right, another closed passage that would lead deeper into the *Brigantine*. It was a much, much larger vessel than theirs, equipped with more lodging for the crew, as well as several laboratories and sophisticated, atmosphere-controlled closets for storing research materials. She had memorized the schematic before launch, but seeing it in person was something quite different—for one, it was dark, and for another, it was bigger than she had visualized.

She paused just inside the galley, finding the floor damp and almost slick with something blackish. *Not again.* Only a few feet away sat a small folding table with the remnants of a card game and a few chairs, two knocked over and askew. She carefully padded to the table, making sure she didn't slip in whatever coated the floor. The lights strobed again, unevenly, and she gazed around at the walls, marveling at a strange blue flicker she hadn't noticed before.

Where was their Servitor? And what the hell was all over the walls . . .

"Devar? Hey. Talk to me."

Grimacing, she tore her gaze away from the strands of glowing blue on the walls and looked down at the card table. "Crazy eights," she said.

"Pardon?"

"They were playing cards," she added, noticing a distinct smear of blackish red on one of the spades. She waited a beat, spreading out one of the card hands and then walking away, slowly approaching the odd filaments of iridescent blue pulsing along the walls, as bright and spidery as human veins.

Rosalyn leaned in, squinting. "The floor is sticky. My VIT just keeps saying, 'Unknown Substance,' and there's something biological growing on the walls. God. It's everywhere. I'm actually getting a spore level alert *inside* a ship."

"That doesn't sound great."

"Here, grab the visuals," she said, using her VIT monitor to grant him access to the little camera affixed to her helmet. Anything in her AR display would stream directly to him. "See it?"

"Ugh. Yuck. Although . . . it's kinda . . . I mean, if you squint, it's sort of—"

"Beautiful," she finished for him, gazing around. "Definitely. Reminds me of those glowing caves, you know? With all the fluorescent mushrooms. Malaysia, I think."

"Nothing on the VIT?" he asked.

"No, nothing. Best I'm getting is 'Unidentified Fungal Growth.' Can you broaden the search from the *Salvager*? Maybe there's something in the MSC biological database."

Walters fell quiet while he performed the search. Through his mic, she could hear him tapping away at the console and breathing heavily. His VIT screeched again, trying to alert him to the refueling mission redirect. Rosalyn tuned it out. She moved farther along the wall, noting that the glowing blue growth became thicker as it neared the doors leading out of the galley, even disappearing into the creases along its edge, suggesting it had spread deeper into the ship.

"I'm going to take a wild guess and say this growth is our mystery killer," she said, sidestepping the door and following along the perimeter of the room. She needed to find that Servitor, and he was somewhere in the flickering darkness, powered down and waiting.

"You better decontam yourself for about a solid decade before you step foot on campus," Walters shot back. "Or on my ship."

"*Our* ship, thanks. And no arguments there. Anything in the bio database?"

"Nope, plenty of similar samples but nothing with that exact molecular structure. Closest thing I'm seeing here is *Mycena manipularis*, from Borneo, and something in the MSC database that I don't have the security clearance to view."

"Damn it," she muttered, turning and pausing, finding the Servitor huddled in the corner to the far right of where she had entered the ship. It was practically vintage. More modern models were skinned with simple, humanlike white latex to hide the metal skeleton. She preferred these older versions, with their charmingly mismatched eye sizes and three-fingered "hands." The ones made to look more humanoid were creepy, dead-eyed and unsettling. JAX's body was pure function, with a beak-like head and one "eye" for scanning and detecting crewmates' identities, as well as an "eye" for holographic projections and lighting in dark rooms. He was just over six feet, a sealed, tubelike chassis containing the hardware to keep him running.

"Found our Servitor friend," she told Walters. Rosalyn took the AI by its thin, metal shoulders and pulled herself closer, studying the front of the chassis until she located a small universal port on the left lower half. She fished a spare VIT power cell from her case and opened the small hatch next to the port on the AI. A smooth panel waited there for surface-to-surface wireless charging.

"I'm going to juice it back up with a spare battery. We need his data."

"Seems like you were right about the Servitor," Walters replied. His breathing had calmed. "If the crew were alive, you would have run into them by now. We haven't exactly been stealthy."

Rosalyn nodded to herself, lining up the battery with the charge surface before sitting down heavily on the stool near the AI. "The least hysterical interpretation of events is usually the right one."

"Yeah, yeah. You know, the cantina does a late-night tiki thing once a month—"

She squeezed her eyes shut. "Please stop."

"Oh, come on, ice princess, thaw out a little. Where are you from, anyway? Pakistan? Pakistani girls love me."

The Servitor thrummed softly, one eye flickering as the power began transferring and it booted into safe mode. "I'm Indian. Half. The furious half."

"I knew it. You're warming up to me." Walters coughed and then sighed. "Sorry. I . . . I babble and flirt when I'm nervous."

"Spare us both and try some deep breathing instead. *There.* We've got power," she told him, moving on swiftly. She would need to decontaminate for a decade for more reasons than one, she thought with a grimace. "You can come back online now, JAX, and hopefully, if my pilot is done making a fool of himself, we can sort out this mess." *And I can get back to my job, and then back to the station, and make sure HR knows I'm never partnering with Walters again.*

The Servitor blinked both "eyes" and found her, standing to its imposing height before nodding its head once. "Power levels at six percent and climbing." His larger orb eye had already scanned and identified her. "Greetings, Merchantia Junior Salvager Devar. Welcome aboard the *Brigantine*, a Class A—"

"No time for that, friend, sorry," she interjected, holding up a gloved hand. "JAX, access the *Brigantine*'s itinerary, try a month out from failure."

Walters had begun breathing heavily on the other end again. Hopefully he would keep the nervous flirtations to himself.

JAX's crisp, automated voice filled the galley, echoing slightly. "Mission day sixty, refueling contact with unidentified civilian craft. Mission day sixty-three, scheduled resupply stop with MSC vessel *809-T*, freighter class; mission day seventy, scheduled stop with moon base Terralon, Proxima Centauri system; mission day seventy-five, unscheduled contact, Coeur d'Alene Station, Proxima Centauri system. Unavailable, unavailable . . ."

"Unavailable?" Rosalyn sat back on the stool, crossing her arms and studying the Servitor with a puzzled frown. There was more than one red flag waving wildly in front of her face. Civilian contact. Unscheduled stops. Maybe Girdy's instincts were right. Something strange was going on.

"Define 'unavailable' for me, JAX. That's a new one."

"You've never gotten that from a Servitor before?" Walters asked. He sounded winded. Spooked.

"It's probably just an error, like the life-forms reading. He's a second-run model, practically a relic now. No offense, JAX."

The Servitor tilted its head to the side. She imagined it grinning wryly at her. "None taken, Junior Salvager."

"Define, please," she prompted it.

"Unavailable: designated classified or otherwise corrupted."

"Fantastic," she muttered. What a headache. She was going to get herself and Walters fired over a faulty robot. Sighing, she pulled a cable out of her bag and ran it from one of many small data link ports in the Servitor's chassis to the lifeless monitor near the door covered with flowering blue growth. "All right, JAX, access the ship's data directly. Search for anything relevant in itinerary, manifest and navigation. I want to know about these 'unavailable' stops, specifically the unscheduled and civilian contact."

"Might I remind you that our job is to just clean this shit up and leave? Let the lawyers deal with this Sherlock shit."

"There's unidentifiable blue matter all over the walls, and something is suspicious with both the life-reading scanner and now their Servitor. I'm not going another step farther inside this wreck without knowing what I'm getting myself into."

Walters swore incoherently on the other end.

"Unavailable."

"What?" She turned back to the Servitor, which appeared to be staring somewhere over her shoulder. "Say again."

"The data you requested is unavailable, Junior Salvager, my apologies."

Her helmet was going to fog from so much sighing and mumbling. "JAX, run a self-diagnostic. Has anyone tampered with you recently?"

The lights in the Servitor's eyes went very dim and then brightened. "Permissions accessed and altered, mission day eighty-three."

Rosalyn blinked. *Shit.* "Eighty-three?" She consulted her VIT briefly and shook her head. "No, that isn't possible. The salvage signal started beaming on mission day seventy-nine. Who changed your permissions?"

"Unavailable."

"Agh!" She smacked the domed Plexiglas of her helmet with her fist. "I'm getting seriously tired of that word." Standing up fast, she kicked the stool back with her heel. Her foot connected harder than she intended, and the chair tumbled across the room, knocking loudly into the card table. One of the abandoned hands of cards skittered softly to the floor.

She was about to turn back to the Servitor when she heard an answering noise through the sealed door. It was like a groan, a deep, metal scrape, the sound of something huge and hard and inhuman waking up.

"Did you hear that?" she whispered, freezing.

"Get out of there," Walters said, just as softly. "Devar? Get out."

The noise came again, louder, and when her gaze drifted to the sealed, growth-covered door, she noticed it had begun to shiver. She heard scrabbling through the mic, as if Walters had fallen off his chair or ripped off his headset.

"The crew," she breathed, feeling insane. How could they be alive? The oxygen levels were dangerously low. The ship had beamed a code blue.

"Life signs green," the Servitor chirped back, almost cheerful. It swiveled, facing the door with her as if expectant.

"That's not possible." She knew the AI would contradict her, but she wasn't saying it for the bot. The door hissed, and she felt the galley lurch under her feet. She stumbled, half tumbling to the card table and using it to hold herself upright. Her hands buzzed with fear, tingling, and she shook them out, trying to regain feeling. Trying to regain control. The jungle drums sounded in her head again. If only she could have a drink, sit down, just close her eyes and *think* for a moment.

It's just the ship settling, or one of the engines trying to cycle.

"Look at the live schematics!" she demanded, shouting into her mic. More shifting and scratching on the other end. What the fuck was Walters up to? She actually needed him now and of course he was completely useless. "The door . . . the, um, the east door of the air lock galley, is it locked?"

"Uh, yes! Both locks are functioning," Walters finally stammered back. "Shit, sorry, I'm getting my suit on, you can't be alone in there. Something is going on . . ."

"Idiot. Stay on the *Salvager*!"

"I'm not leaving you alone!" he thundered back, voice breaking.

Rosalyn shook her head hard, clutching the table again. *No, no, no, stupid idea . . .* "Servitor," she said, breathless, "lock down this area. Do you understand? Nobody in or out."

The AI swiveled away from the door and regarded her, one eye flashing as it attempted to do what she said. The light dimmed a little and its head drooped. "Command failed, override in place. Portal Two unsealed. Portal Two unsealed . . ."

Rosalyn's eyes bugged. Portal Two? The doors were numbered clockwise from the air lock, which meant . . .

She gasped and spun, the ship creaking around and under her, all the air, all the focus rushing out of her as she turned and stared directly into the big, bright glowing blue eyes of a human. Blue. Glowing. Her mind raced as she went suddenly deaf to the Servitor and Walters's hyperventilating panic on the headset. She knew this face, but not with those eyes.

The dossier. The crew.

Rosalyn searched helplessly for words but nothing came out. Her eyes roamed over him desperately, from his face—tinged a deathly, unhealthy robin's-egg color—to his hair, black and ruffled, part of it missing, his skull gleaming and exposed, and over that, a pulsing web of the glowing blue growth. Oh God, where was his helmet? How could he *breathe*?

"Hello," Rayan Yasin said with a curious half smile and a squint. "Have you come to join us?"

8

"Join . . . you?" Rosalyn's gaze slid back and forth between Rayan's huge doe eyes and the open wound on his head. She hadn't trained for this, but had anybody?

"Devar? Devar! Hey, tell me what's going on over there!" Walters shrieked at her over the comms, but in between the words she could hear frantic scrambling. "Tell me what the fuck is going on!"

There was a solution here if she just kept calm and prevented the situation from spinning further out of control. Her heart wanted to fly out through her mouth, but fainting in fright wouldn't save anybody, least of all her.

So the crew was alive, or maybe that was too big of an assumption. Join *us*. So there was more than one person left alive on the ship, and that would have to be dealt with. Rayan Yasin looked at her steadily, his smile hopeful, like a kid on his first day of school hoping to make best friends.

She thought of the training emergency vids they had showed her on the station, and one in particular sprang to mind. A salvaging vessel had been boarded, and the quick-thinking woman piloting the ship managed to record a hail right in front of the pirates. She kept it vague. She didn't give her attackers any reason to retaliate. Communicate the situation. Remain concise.

Avoid escalation *at all costs*.

"Your name is Rayan?" Rosalyn asked slowly, sweeping her eyes behind him, keen to know if the rest of the crew was hiding in the cockpit with him. Her pulse hammered, but she could control this if she just played it safe. Strange as he appeared, the researcher did not seem hostile, and she might still negotiate her way back onto the ship with Walters.

"That's me," he said, laughing, almost goofy. *What the fuck*. He ducked his head shyly and nodded toward the cockpit. "I had JAX keep an eye on your ship; we scanned you when you docked. You're the salvager, so that makes you Rosalyn Devar."

"And my pilot is Dave Walters," she replied. Clear and slow. The internal systems on the *Salvager 6* would record all of this, and if this went south, the recovery people back on the station needed a perfect file. Otherwise they would be walking straight into a trap, just like she had. "He's listening in right now, and he wants to come aboard and see what's going on in here. He's worried that I might be in danger. I'm not in any danger, am I?"

"Devar! Shut up! It's not much of an ambush if you tell them what's coming . . . Shit, shit, shit!"

Rayan's eyes blew wide. "Oh. No, that's not good. Please, tell him not to do that." He flinched, his eyes flaring even brighter, so bright they were nearly two beaming white lights. Muttering in another language, he smacked the side of his head. She took the opportunity to sidle closer to the air lock bay. Walters wouldn't be much help in the ship, but if he successfully opened the doors, they might have a chance of fleeing back to the *Salvager*. "Please . . ." Rayan's head flew up. "You have to tell him to stay where he is."

"Did you hear that, Walters?" she asked, licking her lips nervously. "Rayan wants you to stay put. He's injured, major damage to the top of the skull."

"How major?" Walters was out of breath and still fumbling. Any minute now he would be finished suiting up, and then Rosalyn needed to be at the air lock door, ready to make an escape.

She looked again at the splintered skull, the bits of flesh and black hair tufted up around the edges, and the pulsating blue net of *something* covering it like a strange bandage.

"Catastrophic," she breathed.

"Is he staying away?" Rayan asked, insistent now and advancing on her. The walls around them glowed brighter, dazzling and sapphire. The Servitor followed obediently behind Rayan, clearly no help to her at all.

"Yes," she lied. "He's not going to board, he promises. I promise, too."

"That's . . . that's good." The intense brightness in Rayan's eyes dimmed a little and he glanced sheepishly at his boots. "I don't want to do this at all, but you need to follow directions. If you don't follow directions, then I'll have to restrain you. Mother just wants what's best for us."

Mother?

He was reaching for something in his off-duty crew suit. The jumpsuit had multiple deep pockets, a few sewn across the chest, others positioned under his hips. She braced, expecting him to pull out a knife, or some kind of makeshift weapon, but instead he produced a clean, new syringe device.

Rosalyn fixated on the glistening needle, taking another tiny step toward the air lock doors. "There's no need to make threats, Rayan, we're on the same side here. We both work for Merchantia,

right? You wouldn't hurt a coworker. We only came because of
the code blue signal; we thought you and the others were hurt or
dead."

"Threats!? Shit, I'm equalizing the tunnel, Devar, I'll be there
soon, okay? Just . . . fuck, I don't know, just keep him distracted!"
Through his mic, she heard the distinct hiss of the *Salvager*'s door
decompressing.

Suddenly, JAX shifted closer to Rayan, standing at his side, its
automated voice overlapping with her pilot's. "Air lock doors engaged, *Salvager 6* safely linked to *Brigantine* main galley."

"No!" Rayan slapped the side of his head again and lunged for
Rosalyn. She wasn't prepared to fight him off, but she tried to
dodge, yanking her arm out of his grasp and backing up toward the
exit. "Hold her, JAX, we need to . . ." He flinched, head jerking to
the side as if pulled by a leash. "Hold her!"

Fighting a metallic, inhumanly strong AI was not the same as
fending off a lanky lab researcher, and JAX's hand closed around her
wrist tight as a cuff. She screamed, sure now that she had lost complete control. The Servitor would not unclamp no matter how hard
she pulled and twisted. Sweat gathered in her helmet, pouring into
her eyes, condensation filming her view now that her breathing
grew too fast and panicked for the suit to automatically dehumidify
the polycarbonate visor. Still, even through that fog, she could make
out Rayan's glowing, crazed eyes.

He lunged for her again as she heard the air lock on their side
whir to life. Dave was coming. Dave would be there any second,
she thought, but still too late.

The syringe in Rayan's grasp plunged toward her, and she
shrieked, writhing and punching at him with her free hand until the
syringe flew out of his hand, clinking softly against the wall.

"He . . . he tried to stab me! Fuck!" *Calm, calm, calm.* But she couldn't pull herself back from the fear now, from the rage.

"I'm hurrying!" Walters reassured, his mic crackling as he passed into the equalized tunnel. So close. She just needed to get in range and hope that Walters was smart enough to come armed.

"Do not let those doors open!" Rayan screamed. He was not a large man, but his voice boomed through the galley.

JAX's grip did not slacken as he attempted to block Walters's access to the ship. She could see the flicker in his "eye" as the Servitor connected, and he answered a moment later. "Error. The *Salvager 6* maintains priority access to our vessel."

Gasping, Rayan scrambled away, toward the cockpit, his voice trailing behind him as he threw himself through the arch. "No! That's not right!"

"Researcher Yasin," the Servitor prompted stoically, "the *Salvager 6* will retain priority access until the code blue is lifted. The *Brigantine*'s autonomy cannot be restored until—"

"Then lift it, lift the code!" Rayan screamed back.

Rosalyn clamped her hand over her bruised forearm, commanding herself to regain control of the situation. That started with her doing whatever she could to help Walters when—if—he got through the doors.

"Don't lift the code," she said, winded. "Please, JAX, I'm begging you. We came here in good faith, and right now we have command of the *Brigantine*. Obey your programming. Listen to me . . . Leave the code intact."

"Just be quiet," Rayan whispered, almost panting. Rosalyn leaned back, his breath fogging her visor. "Lift the code, JAX, do it. *I'm* your superior, she isn't part of the crew. Lift it!"

The Servitor did not release her, but he seemed to regard them equally, weighing the options while Rosalyn wondered if it was possible to die from sheer panic. She slumped back against the wall, fighting the AI's strength, inching toward the air lock doors.

At last the bot managed to make a decision or run through its programming or whatever it took, and it looked in Rayan's direction. "Lifting the code requires a full reset of onboard ship functions."

"I don't care." Rayan was sweating now, too, seething, his eyes flaring white again. Then he seemed to recall something and froze, blinking. *"All* functions?"

"Yes, sir, all functions. The lockdown on bays two and three will lift, sir."

"Shit. Piero and the captain . . ." He wiped at his face, but time was running out. Behind her, Rosalyn heard Walters fumbling through the tunnel toward them. He would reach the doors in a matter of seconds.

Her heart lifted, one last gust of energy—of hope—breaking through the fear. Maybe these two would debate and hesitate just long enough for her to get the fuck off that ship. The portal to the *Brigantine* hissed, the galley pressurizing, one step closer to letting her unlikely savior in.

9

The burn behind his eyes was incredible. Rayan could hardly see through the pain and the fine web of blue lines that splintered across his vision.

But he could still make out the woman in front of him, huddled back against the doors, her face screwed up in a mask of fear. He hated that. Hated that anybody could look at him that way . . . But of course she did. Of course he deserved that look. He was only trying to help, but sometimes helping looked like something else entirely. Like violence. No. He was not violent, could never be violent.

And then there was JAX. This was impossible. More impossible was time, and the decision bearing down on him like a ship at speed. They needed her VIT credentials. Above all, they needed her VIT, and that was at all bloody costs. They needed to get back to Mother. Mother came first. So he closed his eyes, just for a tiny respite, just to see if he could escape the throbbing in his skull and heart for a second, and then he spoke, trembling.

"Do it, lift the code. Reset."

It was a quiet order, and he didn't give it lightly. The thought of Piero on the loose again . . . He shuddered, listening to the *Brigantine* snap to life, engines cycling, lights attempting to turn on but only managing a flicker, and of course, the most important part, the air lock functions resetting.

"No!"

He hadn't heard a wail like that since Iwasa found Sverdal's body. It stilled the blood in his veins and he clenched his fists, watching as the woman slipped her fingers between the Servitor's hand on her arm and the slick material of her suit, prying his metal fingers off and spinning, sending JAX skidding toward the cockpit. She hurled her body against the air lock doors. He could see over her shoulder through the small, circular window in the door—the tunnel uncoupled, whipping free and then floating in the nothingness of space.

And with it, the pilot. All of his anger with her for lying vanished. It was only natural to try to escape, it was only natural for her crewmate to lend assistance—

No, child, you were foolish. Reckless. Once this new one relinquishes her VIT data she will join them, but she is not like Mother's original children. You must control yourself, darling. No more silly schemes. No more syringes. Think of your family. Think of your mother.

He felt for her. But he stayed at a distance, numb with guilt as the interloper in his head went quiet again and he was left to his own thoughts. That was almost worse. Rayan could feel remorse, but the *thing* in his head? He didn't know *what* it felt beyond determination. Endless hunger. Constant *need.*

Mother needs you. Mother needs this. Mother needs that.

The salvager pounded her fists on the door, shrieking. Her body faced away from him, but even so, Rayan knew she was weeping. Over her shoulder, he saw the pilot spinning away into the stars, his mouth wide open. The biggest and worst surprise of his life.

I killed him.

Yes—the other voice in him rose—*for us. You killed him for your family. For Mother.*

"I'm sorry . . ." Rayan managed. He would burn up in his brain
for this, and suffer, and he would pray later for true forgiveness, even
if he felt certain it would never come. "Walters was his name? I'm
sorry, but you don't understand, I have to—"

Her grief changed then, spiraling out, snarling into rage, and she
turned on him, slamming into his chest and sending him flying back
against the card table. The little white rectangles fell around them,
floating onto her back and his head as she tackled him to the floor.
His back exploded in pain from the sudden impact, and at once
Foxfire—Mother—consumed him, rushing over him, dulling the
sting and summoning his own anger.

"*No!*" he shouted. JAX had already lumbered over and yanked
her off of him by the elbows. His control returned and he sighed,
covering his face with both hands before sitting up with a groan. "I
did what I could . . . and then I did what I had to. You should've let
me inject you. You should've let me! It will help! I'm sure it will
help, the experiments, the allium . . ."

"What the hell are you talking about?" she shrieked back, struggling against the AI, kicking out both legs in frustration. "You
killed my pilot! You killed him. What the hell is wrong with
you? What did you try to stab me with, huh? You want to kill
me, too?"

"No!" There were too many questions. His brain throbbed and
throbbed, Foxfire grappling with him, but Rayan subdued it for the
moment, rubbing at his face. "No, I . . . I wanted to help you. I
didn't mean to hurt you, okay? I tried to save you. Joining hurts. It
shouldn't be forced on anybody."

"*Save* me? Save *me!?* I thought I was here to save *you*, or what the
hell was all that about?" She was gasping for breath and reeling, her
eyes unfocused.

Rayan climbed slowly to his feet. He wanted to tell JAX to let her go, but that didn't seem wise just yet. "I didn't try to hurt you. It's protection," he said, and pointed to his own head. "Against this."

She went still, her dark hazel eyes sliding to the bent syringe on the floor. "I need to sit down," she said. "And you"—she pointed a shaky finger at him—"you need to start from the beginning. After that, you can sync up with the *Salvager* for a tow, then I'm taking you and whatever this sick shit is back to MSC."

Clearing his throat, he gave a tiny nod. "Okay."

It was kind of an affirmation, just enough to calm her down and just enough to be a lie.

"JAX? Release her."

"Sir, I detect elevated levels of both—"

"Let her go, just do it."

The Servitor took a step back, its clamp-like "hands" loosening. The woman tumbled forward, sneering, and snatched up one of the tipped folding chairs. She righted it and sat down hard, dropping her face into her hands for a long moment. Soon, she stood again and collected the syringe, studying it briefly before snapping off the needle and sliding the tube into her pocket. *Smart*, the voice inside him sneered. *Smart and prepared. Troublesome.* Rayan didn't disturb her, but he felt something stirring in the ship, a dark echo, a familiar hum in his head that was both of him and not of him. Someone else was waking up.

Oh no.

"So?" she groaned, finally staring up at him. Her cheeks were pale, streaked with tears. "Start from the beginning."

Outside the galley doors, down the corridor, he heard the distinct lurch of the heavy storage-bay doors unlocking. The mechanism stuck a little as it gave, they could all hear it, and their heads turned simultaneously toward the portal leading deeper into the

Brigantine. The sound resonated like a low howl through the hull, sending a tremor through his legs.

Rosalyn Devar's eyes widened as she sat up straight. "What was that?"

"I'm sorry," he told her earnestly, trembling at the footsteps that came toward them. "The others are waking up."

10

Rosalyn had been there before, in that breathless, deep panic that seemed to flatten out time and sharpen the senses. It wasn't calm, exactly, but a falling away of every noncritical thought and impulse. She had been there before, curled up on the floor, in pain and shock, faced with what felt like the impossibility of the next moment coming, and the next, and the next after that. Rosalyn looked down at the bulge in her pocket where she kept the syringe. She had been there before, but this time there was no running away.

"JAX," Rosalyn heard herself say. Her own voice sounded distant, as if emerging from underwater. "Reseal this door, please. Lock it tight."

Walters was gone. Dead. She was alone on a ship full of strangers and some kind of biological threat. There was nothing left to do but focus and survive.

The engines had cycled, but only ship-critical systems remained functioning. She could hear the diminished hum of a ship running with locked thrusters. Likely plenty of fuel remained, but the code blue had sent them drifting toward headquarters, and now that the system had logged the linkup between the *Salvager* and the *Brigantine*, the ship would cease its trip. They were stranded. If she could somehow unlock the thrusters, she could pilot the *Brigantine* back to the *Salvager 6* and leave the forsaken hulk far behind.

It was a fantasy, of course, but she needed a fantasy just then.

"Door sealing." JAX snapped to action quickly, as if eager to be of use. The lights in the galley flickered, dim, less bright than the blue mass glittering along the walls and ceiling. It wasn't much, but she heard the locks engage on the door and called it a victory. One step at a time. Even in a panicked state, it was critical to plan. Rosalyn glanced at Rayan, who fiddled sheepishly with the ends of his shirtsleeves.

"How much time before the rest of your crew gets through that door?" she asked. Rayan stared at her and shrugged.

"Depends on how motivated they're feeling," he said softly. "And, well, considering I locked them all up for their own good, they're probably pretty motivated."

"And dangerous?"

"*They're* not dangerous," Rayan insisted. He paced to the locked door, putting his ear to it. "At least, I don't think so."

Rosalyn smoothed her gloved hands down her thighs, a self-soothing gesture she hoped would stop her from wringing the guy's neck. "The way you said it—'*they're* not dangerous'—what do you mean?"

"Misato and Edison are my friends, they wouldn't want to hurt you, or anyone really. Piero is, uh, Piero. He's got a bad temper, but he's a good person. They're all good people. They were, anyway, before . . ." He gestured helplessly to the blue glowing all around them. *In* him.

"That blue stuff is keeping you alive," Rosalyn observed. In her many years of studying medicine and biotechnology, it was like nothing she had ever encountered. "You shouldn't be able to breathe in this atmosphere, and your head wound—" His lips tightened at that, maybe a sore subject, so Rosalyn pivoted. She wanted to keep him from lashing out again. "But somehow that blue substance is controlling you or . . . or what, Rayan? Help me out here. You said you wanted to protect me with that injection, so give me something to work with."

"I want to," he said, darting forward. She went rigid and he backed away, looking crestfallen. "Yes, the Foxfire controls us; it tries to, anyway. It was just a few spores at first, a fungal infection, probably started just in the lungs, but now it's everywhere, growing and spreading, and it's doing the same inside us. Bit by bit we're losing ourselves to it. It *talks* to us."

His eyes flared almost white hot again and he swore, clutching his head.

"I take it this 'Foxfire' doesn't want you helping me?"

"Yeah," Rayan sighed, shaking out the pain. "I've been fighting it, but I didn't know if the others were, so I tried to keep them locked away. I coded the ship and sent the hail. Oxygen levels are fine, I hacked JAX to report whatever I wanted. The Foxfire would've just spread to a rescue crew, but salvagers have those suits, right? Those are equipped with powerful filters, decontamination protocols . . . so I thought you'd have a fighting chance at least."

Rosalyn went quiet, studying him for a long time. The door to her right groaned, a sudden weight slamming against it. *Bang, bang, bang.* She jumped, and so did Rayan. Her mind began spinning—she still had no plan, but Rayan could be an ally if she played it right. If he was telling the truth, of course. But how could she trust him? If that blue Foxfire stuff was trying to control him, then maybe it would make him lie, too.

She needed to know more. So much more. She wouldn't know enough before whatever or whoever was behind that door broke through the manual locks. Rosalyn hurried toward the cockpit. This wasn't her usual ship, but they all used similar technology, issued by the same company. An unlocked plastic case sat next to the cockpit bay, a standard-issue emergency kit. The blue mass had formed over it, making it just a blue lump, as if purposefully trying to conceal what was inside. Rosalyn shoved that thought aside and knelt, swiping away the growth. To her surprise it was thin and vine-like, the glowing blue spores breaking up and into the air as she touched them. Behind her, she heard Rayan give a moan of pain. The flowers . . . the glow . . . Were even their pain receptors linked?

It sounded like he murmured, "Oh, please hurry."

The banging started up again, harder this time. Rosalyn groped blindly for what was inside the crate, fighting the low light in the galley. She powered on her overhead light, finding what she was looking for.

"What do you think he has?" Rosalyn called over her shoulder. "A door jammer? A wrench?"

Rayan was quiet for a second and then said, "It's big and metal." Another pause. "Like a crowbar."

Great.

"You can sense that, huh?" she asked. It would be fascinating if it weren't so terrifying. That racket didn't sound friendly. Rayan had to be an anomaly. The rest of the crew would probably murder her on sight if this Foxfire stuff had totally taken control of them. "Or just an educated guess?"

"Bit of both. What are you looking for?"

"This." Rosalyn stood and turned to face him, brandishing a collapsible fire extinguisher. It wasn't all that big, but the blast packed a punch, and if she aimed it right, the powder had a chance of blinding an attacker. She sighed and pulled the pieces apart, reassembling them into a functioning extinguisher. Out of the corner of her eye, she noticed Rayan shaking his head.

"It's no good," he whispered fiercely. "If I can see you, so can he. He'll know what's coming. When we're this close to each other, it's almost like my mind, my eyes, are his."

She refused to put down the extinguisher, choosing instead to take a few steps toward Rayan. Maybe he could see the wild panic in her eyes, and maybe he could see her chest pumping hard under the suit, but she tried her best to give him a straight look.

"No bullshit," Rosalyn said, hazarding a hand on his shoulder. "You can help me. We can help each other. Please, you could be my eyes right now. You could help me get out of this. If he can see through you, then the reverse is true, right?"

JAX whirred softly, feet clacking as he took a few steps toward the door and spun to face them. "Manual lock integrity at twenty percent."

"Rayan . . ." Rosalyn spoke slowly, wincing each time the door was slammed into. "I know a thing or two about xenobiological samples, we used them all the time at my job," she told him. "I studied it for a long, long time. It was my whole life before I went into salvaging. Maybe we can, I don't know, figure something out together. If you get me back to the *Salvager 6*, we could work on this, just you and me. Maybe there's a way to reverse things, a cure, if you figured out a vaccine—"

"It's not a vaccine," Rayan stated flatly. He closed his eyes. "Basically just garlic."

"What?"

"Manual lock integrity at five percent and failing," JAX interjected.

Bang, bang, bang.

They both glanced at the shivering door.

"Sulfur compounds," he went on. "I was trying things on samples, and something about the allicin must be toxic to the spores. An organosulfur compound from *Allium sativum*. Garlic. It wouldn't protect someone for forever; they would probably need ongoing injections."

Rosalyn nodded, but she could hear the hinges on the manual locks screaming with each hit of the crowbar. They were running out of time. Sulfur compounds and whatever else could wait until she wasn't facing down a homicidal crewmate.

"That's a start," she breathed. "It's a start, and with your knowledge and mine, we can do something. You can help me. You can help me get back to the *Salvager*. We can . . . we can incapacitate him together, unlock the thrusters and get to the *Salvager* to regroup or, hell, just get on it and *leave*. What's keeping you here?"

"N-Nothing," he stammered. "And everything. My head. *My head*. Mother is . . . I . . . can't. I can't do that." Rayan flinched, gripping his skull again with both hands. "I want to. I really want to, maybe I can—"

Rosalyn heard the manual lock give on the other side. The lockdown sequence would lose priority on emergency settings, the ship relying on good old-fashioned bracketed stops to keep the doors in place. It would do a decent enough job sealing them in if there was nobody tampering with them.

The Servitor hobbled toward them. "Manual lock—"

"Has failed, yes, thank you, we know!" Rosalyn shouted.

She ran to the door and flung herself to the side of it, putting her back flush to the wall and raising the fire extinguisher. This time the crowbar was aimed at the door itself, not the locks, and it only took a few hits and a kick of a solid boot to send it crashing open. Rayan collapsed into a heap, holding his head and rocking back and forth. She could just barely hear him sobbing as a huge man rushed inside.

He was just a blur, but big. Too big. Rosalyn took a deep breath. She had been there before, inside that fear, inside that helplessness.

Never again, she said silently. Before the man could spin toward her, she smashed down the trigger on the extinguisher, a huge cloud of white enveloping him. He shouted in confusion and staggered back. Rosalyn pounced, raising the metal canister high before bringing it crashing down.

Through the mist of white and the glowing blue, black blood squirted out to meet her, splattering with a sickening gush across her visor.

11

Piero howled with pain. His ears rang, wet, warm blood running into his mouth as he clawed at his eyes. *The bitch.* The bitch had blinded him. She would pay for that—she would *die* for that. There was nothing but fury inside him, fury and anguish. His hands stung from where the crowbar had bit into his palms, and now it felt like she had split his face in two. He wiped and wiped, covered in whatever she had shot him with and his own blood. Clever little thing.

And Rayan had helped her. With every *crash bang crash* of the crowbar, he had been seeking his clustermate. Why was Rayan trying to keep him out? What was he hiding? The cluster spores in the galley were no use, their senses not nearly as keen or as helpful as Rayan's actual eyes. It was like screaming at someone across a canyon. His own voice rang back, but there was no answer from Rayan. He banged on the door and tried to see through Rayan's eyes, but something stopped him. It was infuriating.

Which made him laugh. Of course. Piero threw back his head, lying flat on the floor, laughing and laughing, letting the horrible blood run freely into his mouth. He swallowed. Who cared? It was no use trying to fight the two of them, and besides, they needed her alive. Just for a little while the clever little shit had to live. He wiped at his eyes again and finally realized he could see. Blinking through the stinging, he gazed up through a lingering white fog at Rayan and the woman. There had been only glimpses of her through the cluster network as he made his way from the crew deck, Rayan keeping him from getting the full picture.

Mother—Foxfire—would be furious with him.

A sense of urgency had swept over him once the ship reset and the doors cycled. Mother told him to go and go fast. Things were happening. Something lucky had fallen into their laps. Something very interesting. Something that Mother wanted desperately to know more about. Piero's laughter died out until it was just a soft, mirthful hoot. Of course Rayan had bungled this. Or maybe . . .

He's winning her trust, the dark voice inside of him suggested. *He's lowering her defenses. Perhaps he is the clever little shit. Trust your brother. Trust your cluster.*

Piero let that possibility wash over him. It felt good. And anyway, he didn't really like violence, preferred to avoid it. It was so *volgare*. His father smacked him around only as a necessity. That was a good policy. Who knows? He might have swung that crowbar too hard and killed the girl before Mother got what she needed out of her.

"That wasn't very polite," he said up to their astonished faces. It came out garbled. One of his teeth was chipped, he now realized. They had been murmuring to each other but he didn't bother to listen. He had to play this Rayan's way. Make friends. He could do that. Friends relaxed. Friends let you pour them a drink. Let you in. Let you *help*. And then? Well, his father always said, *If you can pat a man on the back, then you can put a knife there, too.*

Rayan dropped down next to him, his teeth clenched in horror. "Piero . . . I'm so sorry. I should have stopped her. I didn't know what to do."

He waved the young man off. Such a worrier. They had the advantage now. She was outnumbered, this salvager. Piero reached through their shared network, through Mother, trying to calm Rayan, reassure him, let him know they could work together to outsmart the woman. His thoughts were more open now, but jumbled. It was impossible to tell what he was thinking.

"You . . . you were pounding so loud on the door. It sounded angry."

Piero nodded, then reached up and slapped the boy gently on the side of the head. "You locked me in the dorms, you motherfucker, of course I was angry. What was I supposed to do? Even jerking off gets old."

His eyes slid to their visitor. *Prisoner.* She hadn't struck him again, so she was either cautious or naive. Possibly both. He tried to smile, and wondered just how gruesome it looked. Very, he hoped.

"Ah. Pardon my language," he said to her, winking.

The woman recoiled, but did not lower the fire extinguisher clutched in both hands. That explained the white vapor all over the place and the godforsaken stinging in his eyes.

"Help me up, Rayan, my head is killing me."

Rayan clapped a hand over his arm to help lever him up, but the woman took a big step forward.

"No," she said, kicking the crowbar away from his side and across the galley. Clever. "You can stay right there."

"And I thought *I* had a temper," he murmured to Rayan. Inside, he felt his chest growing hotter with irritation. But he remembered that they had need. Mother had need. He glanced briefly at the glowing VIT on her arm and swallowed to keep from spitting at her. They needed that thing; the one on his own arm had gone dead. Useless.

Why hadn't Rayan tricked her into removing her helmet? The

oxygen levels were stable, and just one gulp of spore-filled air would put her on the path to Mother's embrace. His eyes slid warily between the two now, his faith in Rayan dimming. Something was wrong.

"What is this, Rayan? I thought we were friends. She's been here five minutes and you trust her more, eh? Do you even know her fucking name?"

"It's Rosalyn," the other man said, exasperated. "And . . . I don't trust her. But I don't trust you either, Piero. I . . . don't think I trust anything anymore. Listen." He swiveled on his knees and looked up at the woman, Rosalyn, his eyes glittering and huge. "He's bleeding so much, can I just get him to the med bay, please?"

The woman stepped back, still brandishing her makeshift weapon, and squinted at them.

"Does it matter? I mean . . . doesn't that stuff keep you alive no matter what?"

"It doesn't mean he can't feel the pain," Rayan shot back. "I can do something for that, at least."

Piero let his head dip back, playing it up. He was in pain, *tremendous* pain, but already he could feel the Foxfire inside him going to work, its soft, warm tendrils making their way through his body to the wound. Already there was a scar forming, a light web of blue knitting his split skin back together. And the pounding in his skull . . . well, that was nothing new, really, although his headaches were less severe now. They began to vanish when he stopped fighting the war inside and just sounded the retreat. Mother became gentler when he played into her hands. He wondered if that was where the sudden rage came from, the Foxfire, or if that was always inside him, and if there was really any difference at all now between him and the thing unfurling inside to heal him.

"Fine," Rosalyn finally said. "I'm not a monster."

"That's one opinion," Piero muttered, inhaling between his teeth as Rayan helped him slowly to stand. "*Che palle*, that hurts like hellfire. Damn your aim, woman."

"I'm watching you," she told him.

The nozzle of the extinguisher remained firmly between them. Piero slung his arm over Rayan's shoulder, leaning heavily on the smaller man. He took the salvager's measure with what sight he had, but decided she really was pretty, Indian maybe, a bit tall for his taste, with even brown skin, huge hazel eyes and a clean-shaven head. That was a pity. He pictured her with a head of long, flowing black hair and almost started salivating.

Not that she would be interested in him, but Piero liked to look. She wasn't his type, not with that bald head, but hair could grow. Misato was old as dirt, and Rayan didn't want anything to do with him sexually after the Foxfire took them. He had been bored nearly to death waiting for Rayan to let him out of the dorms, but maybe now things would get exciting. He looked again at her VIT. Yes, very exciting indeed. With her credentials they could get back to civilization and then there would be a world of possibilities, for him and for the hungry seeker inside.

Piero tried to scratch his chin casually, giving the woman a lazy smile, one that had worked plenty of times before on much prettier women.

"What do we do with her? I wouldn't leave her alone with JAX or the cockpit," Piero said. The sharp, summery scent of lemons drifted around him. That was happening more and more as the Foxfire deepened its hold.

Something about the salvager was achingly familiar. He couldn't explain it, couldn't explain it at all, but somehow he had seen her eyes before, hazel, big, filled with tears, filled with laughter . . . A memory, like a building fever, burned across his brain. *How could I possibly know her?* If he knew her, then maybe he ought to trust her . . . But no, no, that wasn't right either. She wasn't part of the cluster; she wasn't one of them.

Rayan gave her a furtive glance, then nodded toward the mangled door to their left.

"He's right, Rosalyn. I'm sorry," he sighed. "But you have to come with us. You can bring the fire extinguisher if that makes you feel better."

Something sparkled to Piero's left, down the corridor, past the destroyed door and in the shadows of the halls covered in the thickness of Foxfire nodules that glowed like blue flame. Their leader. *Mother's favorite*, he thought sneeringly. His presence was so strong it made the fringes of Piero's vision stutter, his bones almost vibrate.

"That won't be necessary," their captain said. In the cavernous dark of the hall, Piero could only see two glowing blue eyes. "She'll be coming with me."

12

Outnumbered. Trapped. Friendless.

Her one gambit had not paid off—Rayan had caved, and now she was being escorted down the narrow, tubular corridor toward more of the unknown . . . Rosalyn hugged the fire extinguisher to her chest. She felt almost dizzy with fear and the drums in her head, the withdrawal symptoms. Never before had she craved a drink that way. Almost like oxygen. It would just take the edges of this sharp terror away, sand it down to something manageable. Or something she could forget.

At her side, JAX clipped along, energized by the fresh battery she had put in his chassis. Piero and Rayan followed behind her. They didn't need to say a word; the threat simply existed. Hemmed in on all sides. *Bloody trapped.*

Maybe the woman aboard, Misato, would be more amenable to helping her. She couldn't understand it—if this Foxfire thing was trying to control them and they had some shred of self-determination left, why wouldn't they try to work with her? And what had happened to the other woman, Tuva? They didn't even speak about her, and JAX had described her as deceased. Maybe she had passed before the Foxfire had a chance to spread.

Rosalyn swallowed hard. There was clearly something human left in these people, but she couldn't let them get near other humans or they would simply spread the Foxfire farther and farther. No doubt that was the goal. Of the Foxfire, of course, but now of its hosts as well. Her heart clenched with pity, but there was something else, too . . . Revulsion. Dread. She had seen the fury in Rayan's and then Piero's eyes when the creature inside them took over. Mother, or so they called her. Bizarre. The flash of white eyes . . . the total lack of humanity . . .

Shuddering, she watched the man ahead of her move deeper into the research vessel. She hadn't yet caught a glimpse of his face, but there was a tired stoop to his shoulders. The others had fallen in behind him immediately, and so she could only deduce that he was the last male crewmate, the captain. Where was Misato, she wondered, and what would happen when they reached wherever he wanted to take her?

A fire extinguisher wasn't going to do much damage against three grown men. She needed a new weapon and she definitely needed a better plan.

Reason first, she cautioned herself. *You're outnumbered, remember?*

"Where are you taking me?" she asked, trying to keep her voice as neutral as possible. But even she could hear how small, how terrified she sounded.

"We're going to talk in private while Piero gets his face figured out," the man ahead of her said. He hadn't introduced himself, and didn't seem interested in speaking until they found that privacy. His voice was pleasant, confident, low and almost musical.

"I won't hesitate to defend myself," she warned him.

"Clearly." The captain managed a short laugh, shaking his head. "Piero never had a pretty face, but now?"

"Eh, I can hear you," Piero groused from behind her.

She had to agree with the captain. The tall Italian had a face as friendly as a hatchet, deeply lined, with a too-big nose and a razor-sharp chin. He was probably someone's taste, someone who courted trouble. In the dossier picture he had ice-blue eyes, not so very different from the glowing orbs shooting daggers at the back of her head. His crude swagger reminded her of . . .

No, she couldn't think about Glen just then. It all felt too close, too similar. She hadn't been outnumbered in Conference Room B, but he had sixty pounds on her and the red-hot dangerous fire of a man enraged burning away inside him. It almost made her laugh, thinking how she had been afraid of Walters and their close quarters aboard the *Salvager 6*; now that seemed a million miles away, and quaint by comparison. God, Walters. They had *killed* him. He was out there spinning and spinning, shattering into smaller frozen pieces until he was nothing but dust.

They had come to a stop and Rosalyn didn't notice, lost in thought, and she nearly walked directly into a storage locker at a fork in the corridor. She gasped softly in surprise, then watched Piero and Rayan hobble away and down the left fork, disappearing. As they went, Piero looked at her over his shoulder, face streaked with blood, his right eye split to the bone, where miniscule blue webs were already forming, a spidery net gleaming in the wound. He air-kissed at her and she turned away.

"Vile," she whispered.

"This way."

The captain had already started down the right fork. Strangely, he turned up on her AR nav bar. Other users in the system would appear as icons that grew brighter the closer they got, but of all the crew he was the only one registering on her display. That was important, she thought, doubting that the rest of the crew would have forgone the implant for integrated AR. Occasionally she ran into someone way older that had never gotten around to having the procedure or mistrusted the tech, but those folks were few and far between. Integrated AR technology was so convenient and widespread, it was almost a no-brainer to opt in for the implant.

JAX waited until she began to follow. It felt almost like a betrayal, knowing the Servitor was there to keep her in line. This tech was meant to be harmless. Maybe that was an avenue to explore if she ever got a minute alone . . . Rayan had hacked the permissions on JAX once, but that meant it could be done again. She wasn't necessarily familiar with Servitor tech, but it couldn't hurt to try.

"I'll talk to Piero," the man ahead of her said. "Tell him to watch his mouth."

Rosalyn didn't respond. Instead she stared at the back of his head, running silently through the dossier she had read not twenty-four hours earlier. That could work to her advantage, too, she thought, knowing these people. Or at least, knowing who they *had* been. So far what she had seen made sense—Rayan was a crack biology and xenobiology graduate, top in his class and young for the position and money he was making at Merchantia. Piero was just muscle, and probably the most dangerous—ex-military turned mercenary turned glorified security guard. The samples on these vessels were sensitive and expensive, and piracy was uncommon this close to headquarters but not unheard of.

She called up the ship schematic on her AR display. The captain was leading them closer to the extensive storage needed for crew supplies, specimens and experiments. The area on the map marked MAINTENANCE ACCESS was getting closer, as well as a labeled hatch leading down to the bay for rovers and collection vessels. *Storage, storage, maintenance*, she thought, counting off the circular doors as they went by. It wouldn't hurt to keep her bearings, even if those bearings were covered in that same glittering blue web of growth and spores. Her display continued trying to identify the growth, but the progress bar remained empty. Did that mean they could see her wherever she went in the ship? Was each of those glowing nodules another vigilant and watchful eye?

They stopped outside a regular storage hatch. JAX remained close, in easy striking distance. Still, he was an old model, and could possibly be knocked over with enough shoulder force. And then what? Rosalyn waited, watching the hatch door hiss open.

She held the extinguisher at the ready.

"Aren't you nervous?" she asked. "To be alone with me, I mean. I attacked your friend."

"He's not my friend," he replied flatly. Then he stepped into the doorway, gesturing for her to go through. When she hesitated, the Servitor lightly clamped her forearm and tugged. "And no, you're . . ." He trailed off, but he sounded almost sad. "I want to trust you. I don't know why, but something tells me I can."

I wouldn't bet on that, buddy.

Rosalyn stumbled through into the storage bay. It was roomy, most of the crew-supply crates pushed to the edges of the space. Someone, the captain, probably, had dragged a mattress onto a few crates and stacked more around it, making a kind of sleeping cubby. The growth had infiltrated it, pulsing lightly along the cubby ceiling. It reminded her of the dumb little glow-in-the-dark stars she had stuck to her bedroom ceiling as a kid. She had tried to bring them to boarding school, too, but they were confiscated. Back then she had wondered when she would go see the stars herself, and if she would get to, and now here she was, wishing she could go back.

A folding table was set up to the left and it was littered with notes, monitors and the captain's VIT, which had either been powered off or run out of juice.

She wandered to the middle of the bay, still clutching her one and only weapon.

"And besides, what exactly would make me nervous?" he asked, walking with that same tired gait to the table and putting both hands on it. She wondered why he wouldn't face her. The Servitor stood between her and the door, which closed, sealing them inside.

"You're going to, what, knock me upside the head with that canister, then go finish off the rest of my crew, but also somehow deactivate JAX, pilot the ship alone and get to safety? That the plan?" He finally turned around, resting his lower back against the table and crossing his arms over his Merchantia crew jumpsuit. "You would also have to decontaminate yourself and your entire ship or risk bringing Foxfire with you. Oh, and good luck explaining this mess to HQ. They'd probably quarantine you for life just in case. Did I miss anything?"

Rosalyn worked her jaw back and forth, feeling stupid. "I'm not sharing my plans with you."

The captain gave her a slow, wry smile and then spread his hands wide. "Go ahead. Bash my brains in. It won't do a damn thing. The Foxfire will just fix it all up. You've seen Rayan, right?"

"What if I cut you into little pieces?"

One dark, thick brow raised above the rim of his glasses. "Hadn't thought of that. Worth a shot maybe."

Rosalyn frowned, finding his laughter a little annoying.

"You're not like the others," she said softly.

"Better looking, you mean."

"Ha. Ha." She rolled her eyes, taking a careful step toward him. The lighting in the storage bay was as dim and infuriating as it was in the rest of the ship, but he had set up a few emergency lights near the table, giving her a better view of his face. Bookish, she thought.

Kind. *Tired.* Tired and handsome. The kind of man she would give a second look in a bar under extremely different circumstances.

"I've managed to keep my situation in check," he added, taking off his glasses and scrubbing at his face with an open palm. He stroked his short beard for a second and then put his spectacles back in place, sighing. "Meditation helps. Music, too, one song in particular. If I can keep a familiar tune in my head then I can . . . feel more like myself."

"That's good," Rosalyn said. She hadn't meant to sound so excited. "Right? That's good. That means you might actually listen to me."

"I wouldn't go that far." He laughed again, but it was humorless. "I'm Edison—Captain—Edison Aries. But I'm guessing you know that. Salvagers don't go in blind, right?"

"I know who you are," she replied, nodding. "I'm Rosalyn Devar. MSC fell for Rayan's fake code blue, so here I am. My pilot . . . he's dead. Rayan cycled the engines while my pilot was trying to get in."

Edison crossed his arms over his chest again and grunted. "Foxfire cycled the engines. Rayan would never do that, he's a good kid."

"Fine, well, I don't want to argue semantics. Someone on your ship killed my pilot. Fair?"

"No, not fair. It wouldn't have happened if we weren't . . . all fucked up like this."

Rosalyn scrunched her eyes shut and turned around.

"You're angry," he said softly. "It's understandable."

"Yes, obviously I'm angry. I just . . . I want to shoot this thing at your head so badly but I can't. I . . . I'm trying to keep this civil. Believe me, I'm trying, even if I don't seem very good at it." Rosalyn spun to face him, half tempted to chuck the extinguisher across the room in frustration. "I'm not an idiot. I know I can't take on all four of you and an AI, and I'm not going to try. What should I feel if not angry?"

Edison nodded, sucking in his lower lip and leaning hard back against the table. "Scared. Confused. I get it. Tell me, what did Rayan spill about us?"

Spill. That was an interesting word choice. She couldn't help but mimic his strained posture. When the adrenaline lagged, there was nothing left behind but exhaustion. "He said he sent out the hail to get someone dispatched. When I first came aboard, he asked if I was here to join all of you. So he must have wanted me to come; maybe he thinks Merchantia can find a cure or something."

"He lied to you. Not that he can help it. Rayan didn't send that hail."

Rosalyn narrowed her eyes, taking another tiny step toward him. "What?"

She could tell he was fighting the urge to laugh again. "Are you surprised? There's an alien mushroom in his brain telling him what to do."

"But the code, the hail . . ."

Edison nodded, waving her off. "Oh, some of his intentions might have leaked through, but it wasn't his doing. I should know— Foxfire is in me. It's in him. So we're all in it together. If Rayan managed to get you here, then Foxfire wants you here, it's that simple. If this weren't part of the plan, I'd know, I would feel the panic in the system." He closed his eyes and swayed on his feet a little. His mouth went slack before he straightened up and added, "She's not calm, exactly, but in control. And you . . . You're not getting the reaction I would expect."

"What do you mean?" Rosalyn's skin crawled. She didn't like the thought of that thing in him having opinions about her.

"I mean it's confused. When I look at you the voice goes silent, then so loud I can hardly think, but it's mostly nonsense. Noise. Like when you turn a speaker up too loud and everything crackles around the edges. And when the Foxfire is quiet, I want to trust you, but I know that's not me feeling that . . . Maybe it's because you're the only one outside the cluster, but none of it makes any sense. It's like I *know* you."

"All you need to know about me is that I'll do whatever it takes to survive," she shot back. Then, softer: "And you don't know me."

"No," the captain said, blank. "No, I suppose I don't know you, so why do I feel like *she* does?"

She let that sink in for a moment, all of what he had said about the voices and the noise, and especially the strange reaction to her in particular. God, if only she could sit down and take some notes, try to piece together the nature of this thing's biology. All living creatures had an imperative to live and flourish; this was simply Foxfire's way of doing it, she knew, even if it felt invasive and sinister. Mother Nature was not exactly concerned with warm fuzzies.

"She?" Rosalyn asked.

"It thinks it's our mother," the captain said. "We're her children. I don't even know if it's really that sentient or if it just knows humans tend to listen to their mothers. A back door. A way to win our trust."

She shuddered. "God, this Foxfire stuff, it thinks it can control me just like it's trying to control you, right? It's a symbiotic relationship until it has total dominance over a host, so can't you tell exactly what it wants?" she asked. "We could use that, you know. If you wanted to work with me. If you wanted help. Maybe we could outsmart it somehow."

"It's not a two-way street all the time, Rosalyn," Edison replied. He gestured back and forth, trying to clarify. "It's like whispers down a hallway. Voices in another room. My guess? She—*we*—needs your credentials for something. We've been locked out of the MSC comm systems and databases. The hail system works but that's about it. This low on juice, we're dead in the water out here, especially after we linked up with the *Salvager*. We're not even on autopilot toward campus anymore."

"That doesn't make any sense," Rosalyn replied, shaking her head. "Your credentials shouldn't get locked out, even if HQ thought you were all dead. There's a grace period before your access goes dark."

Edison shrugged. "Maybe they figured us out, maybe they knew something was wrong."

"And sent me and Walters straight into a trap?" She scoffed and then laughed, and then went dead quiet. Girdy. Did he know more than he let on? He had been so nervous about this particular crew . . . Maybe Girdy discovered something concrete after launch and sent that divert order. He might have been trying to protect her and Walters from the *Brigantine*. Or maybe it was just a normal divert order, one she had stupidly chosen to ignore. Girdy hadn't signed off on the redirect, so her instincts told her it wasn't him. Someone above him wanted to keep them away from the *Brigantine*, and it was obvious now why. If they knew about the Foxfire infestation, then Girdy was right, someone was deliberately sabotaging crews who wound up dead.

Or taken over.

Edison was watching her, so she met his eye steadily.

"I'm not giving you my VIT credentials, and only I know the password."

"Obviously." Edison winced, eyes flashing, fighting something back. "Piero will try to threaten it out of you. Rayan and Misato will sit there for the rest of their lives trying all ten thousand possible combinations."

"And you?" she asked, a little nervous to hear the answer.

"Me?" Edison gave a short laugh. "I don't want your VIT credentials, Devar. I have something else in mind altogether."

"Like what? I'm no idiot. You're not going to trick me."

Rosalyn watched him turn away. She wished he hadn't, she wished she could see his eyes and make sure they weren't glowing white. How could she trust a single thing he said? Shifting a step to the side, she carefully watched the table he loomed over, and studied his eyes in the glossy surface. They didn't change as he put both hands on the table and lowered his head, taking a deep breath.

"Ha. No," Edison said. "Like revenge."

13

Deception, Mother was beginning to realize, was a human's greatest asset. They told half-truths or complete falsities without hesitation. Revenge. Her favorite child wanted revenge. This more than anything else frightened her. She had watched the other children fight in their myriad ways, watched the young biologist crack his head open in despair, not knowing such a mistake only made integration easier. A wound must be tended to by the body itself, resources allocated and diverted, leaving the nervous system less guarded.

No such opportunities presented themselves with her favorite, the captain; in fact, he seemed to be growing stronger in his defenses. She was losing him. *Losing him.* It was impossible. They should have been fully integrated by now, thoughts, desires and actions utterly linked.

His mother. His mother was always the tunnel that led deepest. Edison seemed to pity and even like the woman that had come aboard their ship. The salvager. His mother had always told him to be kind. *You never know what someone else is dealing with.* That would make this difficult. His instincts led him to be gentle with the salvager, and that was not what Mother wanted. But. *But.*

Being Mother was not enough. She had to become *his* mother.

Tunneling. Tunneling deep. Edison protected his memories well, but the salvager had thrown him off balance. His mind was preoccupied with her, with what to do with her, how to help, how to gain her trust . . .

Mother needed that trust. Mother, mother, mother . . . It was a concept that worked so well to bore into the humans, but she hadn't been specific enough, she saw that now. And so she burrowed deep, and used his distraction to her advantage. The memories surfaced, slowly, seeping up like water through mud. An image emerged. His mother. Diana. Tall and dark-skinned, with short fingernails and rough hands, perfectly straight posture, black hair braided in neat rows back from her forehead. Little ribbons and medals glistened on her chest. It didn't appear as if she smiled often, but when she did? Oh, when she did . . . it lit up his entire life for days on end.

Mother. Diana. But what did all those rows of ribbons and medals mean? Foxfire tunneled deeper and new concepts broke free, there to be examined and integrated. Military. This woman had been a warrior of a sort, an aggressor. But then she was kind, always kind, to Edison. More ideas seeped up through the mud of time and distance. Her life as a warrior meant she was often away from home. He missed her. He lived to impress her. Straight As. Valedictorian. Tidy room, *clean* room, always spotless.

He was a child suddenly, kneeling on the blue carpet in his small attic room. Everything, from the carpet under his knees to the air blowing in through the window, smelled strongly of lemons. Lemons but wrong, too sharp, like a cleaning solution, something unnatural . . . His mother knocked on the door, then entered holding a large faded box, one of her rare smiles brightening her face. Crossing the floor, she carefully lowered the box until they sat on either side of it. Her ribbons and medals were gone. Edison liked her better out of her uniform; that was when she was more *Mom*.

"It's fragile," she told him, gently lifting the lid on the box. "Come and look at this, baby."

"What does it do?" he asked.

"Music," she said. "It plays music in the old way, with big circles like this. This one is new, but you still need to be careful. See, baby? You lift this little neck and then put it down when the record is spinning."

They sat like that for a long time, just sitting and listening. Diana let him keep the record player and gave him a box of albums. Another day. More music. His mother was somewhere else in the house, the smell of spaghetti sauce filling the whole place. Just before dinner, Edison put on his favorite record and started to dance. Even Foxfire felt the joy of it, the freedom, a boy alone in his room kicking and flailing without rhythm or care. Then he kicked the record player, hard, the music scratched and spun out, and the fragile plastic neck snapped.

That was when another Diana came out. No smiles. Stern.

"What did I say, Edison? I told you to be careful. I can't believe you'd be this careless!"

Grounded. Grounded for a week. Edison didn't know what that meant. He barely left the house anyway, just school and homework and the record player, but he didn't even have that anymore.

A third Diana appeared, sick and sleeping, tubes and tubes and tubes everywhere. A machine controlled everything about her. The place they kept her smelled like medicine and sorrow. Edison was older, and he didn't say much, just kept his vigil and played music for her on his VIT, the same music from the record player, but never the album he was listening to the day he kicked the neck and snapped it. So many people came and went. Corporals. Generals. Edison let them put solemn hands on his shoulders, let them murmur, and apologize and pray.

Edison just kept looking at the machine breathing for Diana. One day he would have to tell that machine to stop.

Memories offered themselves up to Foxfire constantly now, a steady, overwhelming stream. "Mother" had always been the key, but this was something more. She couldn't just be the idea of mother, no, she had to be *Diana*. Rarely smiling, firm-voiced, little-medals-on-her-shoulder Diana. Control, ever fleeting, was close now. Mother Foxfire sensed his defenses lowering, the shock of those painful memories providing the necessary smoke screen. Look here, it seemed to say, look at this loss, this grief, let those emotions bombard your reasoning. *Sink into this sadness and then Mother will make it all go away.*

What had felt like scrabbling against a steep uphill climb flattened out into a smooth and focused road. A path to integration.

And at last, for a moment, Mother truly had him.

14

It was a short lapse on his part, but that was all it took.

One minute, he was seeing his own hands right there on the table, and the next his mind was somewhere else. *Something* else. A ghost from his past shimmered to the fore, knocking him off balance. He hadn't been drunk in a long time but he remembered the sensation, and God was it similar. His vision blurred and his limbs moved on their own. A spinning, nauseating pit formed in his stomach, a well of helplessness that deepened by the second. And worst of all, he could see it on the woman's face the instant he changed.

"Revenge, *yes*," he heard himself say, but his voice was huskier, labored. Words came out of him, words he wanted to say, but now they were all in the wrong order. He felt his feet shifting and he lumbered toward Rosalyn, gait uneven, stuttering, as if he were a toddler learning to walk, all momentum and no grace.

"You will help us. The credentials . . ." His hand turned into a claw and he pawed at the air in the direction of her wrist. "With your credentials we can use the network again, and the navigation systems can return us to the station. Mother . . . Mother wants to go home."

Rosalyn was backing away from him, her face pale with fright. That pit in his stomach filled with acid, and he drowned in it, so disoriented that he forgot momentarily how to fight it back. How to swim. Her back hit the wall near the door, and Edison watched her pound at the console to try to open it while still keeping her eyes on him.

He had closed the distance, staring down at her from his height, the alien in his body distorting her image until she warped into something small and fragile. *No.* He had to swim. He had to find air. There was a way back to control but his thoughts jammed. A word, an idea, danced on the tip of his tongue, maddeningly close . . .

"The credentials. If you were one of her children, you would want to help Mother. It would be easier"—Edison heard his voice and shuddered at the raw edges of it—"if you surrendered. The process is painless. Let Mother embrace you and find bliss. With us you can be loved, with us you can be *believed*."

His skin felt on fire. Those weren't his words at all now. But the Foxfire had made a mistake. Bliss. Tokyo Bliss Station. His favorite artist was on the stage, the horn soaring, the drumming vibrating in his shoes. He knew this song and he forced himself to hum it. A good memory could drown out the monster in his head. The monster that had begun to sound just like his real mother.

And so he hummed, and hoped it would be enough to drag him to the surface.

That didn't do him any favors with Rosalyn, who shook, raising the fire extinguisher to defend herself. Edison felt the Foxfire clench and react well before he could, and he backhanded the canister out of her hands. It flew across the room, landing with a loud *clank* in the corner.

He heard Rosalyn give a panicked cry as her hand punched the door console again, mashing enough buttons to send the door hissing open. She tumbled away from him and down the hall. Even through her suit he could hear her ragged breathing. The Foxfire made him give chase, but he kept humming, the notes going higher, wilder . . .

His tread was heavy as he ran after Rosalyn, following close on her heels as she scrambled to get away, clumsily finding her way down the corridor and back to the fork, then around that bend and toward the crew deck.

Edison was coming back to himself, he could feel it, but he had to hurry, had to break the surface and gasp air before he did something to hurt her. He would never forgive himself . . . never . . . Rosalyn found her feet; faster, faster she pounded through the halls until she hurled herself through an open door and slammed her palm on the wall. The door didn't close and she swore, backing away from him, cornering herself in one of the labs.

"Get away from me!" she screamed, turning in circles, hands running over the lab countertops, looking for anything that could be used as a weapon.

Tokyo Bliss Station. The music. He just had to keep humming that song, tear his mind away from her and the moment and get lost in the music. But his feet just kept going and soon he would be in striking distance. Mother wanted her. Bad. The noise filled his head. Mother's noise. She was furious. Something about Rosalyn set her off in particular. *There is something different about this girl . . .* She was going to rip the suit away from her, her last line of defense, and expose her to the spores and the network and the bliss *no matter what it fucking took.*

Edison saw his own hand rise as if through a heavy fog, but the music! The music! He had it now, the beat and the scales and the notes. His fist flew, but he corrected it just in time, sending his knuckles crashing into the wall next to Rosalyn's head. She collapsed to the floor, scuttling away and breathing hard.

He let his hand go limp. The pain came as soon as the control did.

"Shit," he whispered, sweating. "It just . . . It caught me unawares that time. It sounded just like my mother, I couldn't, I couldn't . . ."

"Stay away from me," Rosalyn hissed. "Just stay away!"

"I know, I know." Edison put up his hands and turned around, walking slowly and deliberately to the door. He breached the hall and gave her time to watch him swivel back around. The cold storage rooms were one of the few areas with clear plastic shields that could be lowered for lab observation. Edison put the shield in place, and it dropped between them with a soft *plink*.

He knocked gently on the barrier. "Get up. You can lock the shield from your side."

Rosalyn hesitated, then climbed to her feet and approached, eyes so fixed on him it made him go rigid with embarrassment. He deserved that look.

"Six-five-seven-five is the code," Edison told her. "It's my administrator's key."

"Which you could input from that side, too," Rosalyn shot back, breathless.

Edison shook his head, lowering his hand. "No, the lab side has priority to protect samples and keep things locked down during decontam. No one can get into that room unless you let them."

"Or you cycle the engines," she pointed out.

"Sure," Edison told her. "But I won't do that."

"Right. And I'm just supposed to trust you after . . . after *that*?"

Sighing, he leaned his forehead against the shield, his breath fogging it a little. "What do you want me to do?"

Rosalyn studied him through the shield for a long time, and he didn't dare raise his eyes. The last thing he wanted was to see in her gaze what she thought of him. *Monster.* That acid pit in his stomach sizzled again, but this time out of shame.

"Let me go. I'll take one of the evac pods and pilot it back to the *Salvager*, then I'll leave. I won't tell anyone about you or what I saw here. Please. Please let me go."

Even if he wanted to, even if he could . . .

"I can't let you do that," Edison murmured, squeezing his eyes shut. "I jettisoned all the evac pods a week ago. As soon as I realized what was happening to us . . . I couldn't let any of us get out of here and risk spreading the spores."

She made a tiny, hopeless sound. "You can still let me go. I'll find a way to get to the *Salvager*."

"Mother, I mean, the *Foxfire* won't let me," Edison told her. It was true, but he did wonder. He wondered if he could fight it back long enough, keep his own mind and desires long enough to unravel whatever plan the monster inside had. It was too risky. If he failed, if he hurt her . . . "I'm sorry," he said. "It won't let me."

Even through the shield he felt her go cold.

"You're pathetic," Rosalyn whispered.

"Believe me"—Edison pushed away from the barrier and showed her his back—"I know."

15

Vodka. She needed vodka. The worst of the withdrawal symptoms had passed, she thought, but no, here they were again, louder and more insistent than ever. It was like a drum in her head, an itch in her throat, a burn that went from her tongue to her hands and made her fidget constantly. Just one sip of something would make this all feel far away, like a nightmare she could laugh at in the morning.

Morning. *Sleep.* How was she supposed to sleep? Rosalyn paced, flexing her hands and then stretching out her fingers, over and over again, hoping the pattern would somehow become soothing. It didn't. The little room she had locked herself in was bathed in the harsh orange cast of emergency lighting. With her mind jumping from thought to thought to thought she almost didn't notice the one thing that was conspicuously absent from the room.

No Foxfire.

Rosalyn scrubbed at the bloodstain on her visor with both hands until the dried muck flecked away. She searched along the walls, floor and ceiling but found there wasn't a trace of the blue glowing stuff. Outside the safety of the plastic shielding, the flowering spores ran right up to the doorway and then stopped, as if shying away. She turned around, staring for a moment at the decontamination chamber next to the cold storage lockers.

It was just fungal matter, sophisticated, surely, but could it actually know not to come near the decontamination area? Was it possible even the growth itself was afraid of the room?

It wasn't a triumph, but at least she felt relieved that she might have blundered her way into the safest part of the ship. Her suit came standard equipped with environmental filters, but this much contaminant in the air would wear them out quickly. At least in a more or less clean zone the filters wouldn't be bombarded with spores. Eventually the suit's filters would need to be replaced, and she didn't imagine they had an infinite supply aboard.

But that was about where her luck ran out, she thought, going to the cubby and bench near the lab equipment and sitting down hard. She leaned back and called up her AR display. Without a recognized network connection, she would have access to only limited functions, but she could at least start a running list of what she knew and understood about her circumstances. And she still had the crew dossiers. Maybe she could mine those for more information . . . They were all clearly dangerous, the crew, but it seemed like Edison was using his own memories and past to somehow fight back the Foxfire's control. If she knew the crew, then if they turned on her again, she might be able to call up some tidbit from their profile to bring their humanity back.

Rosalyn snorted. God, that was idealistic. She let the text app idle on her AR display, staring through the blinking cursor to the door and the glowing corridor beyond. It was true, what she had told Walters; in the darkened ship the pulsing blue covering the halls was almost *beautiful*. Either the exhaustion was really taking hold now or the millions of scattered turquoise spores were flashing slowly in time to something, and if she concentrated, the rhythm of it seemed like a heartbeat.

Madness. The crew was mad and now it was gripping her, too. She knew their environmental suits were meant to withstand a vast array of contaminants, but she couldn't imagine any salvager had run into something like Foxfire before. Rosalyn called up the factory warranty for her suit on the AR display, skimming the fine print for exactly what the suit protected against.

Contaminants deriving from molds, fungi . . .

That made her feel marginally better. The suit would keep her protected as long as it maintained integrity, and there was a chance that Rayan's experimental injection might be developed into something truly useful. But how long would that work? The crew was not the least bit stable, and it would only take another outburst to compromise her suit and expose her to their horrible fate.

She laughed again, hoarse and fatigued, letting her body go limp against the wall as she drew her knees up to her chest and hugged them. Self-preservation was a stupid idea. Triage was probably the best bet. Solutions, solutions . . . She couldn't let this stuff spread any further, she decided, it had to stop here, with them. With her. It was the shock or the fear, she also knew, that made hot tears gather behind her eyes and spill down her cheeks. She would have to die. They would all have to die. No Merchantia ships were equipped with self-destruct functions, but there were plenty of ways to destroy a vessel, and destroy it she would.

The finality of it, the simplicity of it, felt like comfort and resolution. When she woke up she would know what to do, but she would need strength and rest to do it. God, she didn't want to die. *She didn't want to die.* But what else could she do? She had seen the wild inhumanity in Edison's eyes as he chased her through the ship.

He would have killed her. Piero would have killed her. These weren't men and women anymore, they were aliens, trapped and doomed, imprisoned in their own bodies.

Rosalyn let her eyes droop and then close, knowing what had to be done, tears still streaming out of her eyes as she fell fast asleep.

16

Misato Iwasa did not have time for this shit. She had been deep in conversation with the monster in her mind, the one that cruelly called itself "Mother," and they had just been starting to get somewhere. Time. Time was in short supply, and she needed every single second available to her before . . .

Before it was too late.

There was nothing for it. Edison prowled outside the door, not knocking but lingering, and she could sense him easily through the cluster network binding them together; even without it, his noisy pacing would've given him away. And through that same network she repulsed him, letting him know firmly that she was not in the mood for visitors. She would never again be in the mood for visitors, not until she found a way to beat back the enemy and win the war raging in her head.

Mother. Ha. This thing was nothing like her mother.

She sighed and opened the door to him.

"The eternal optimist," he said by way of greeting.

"And what should I do? Give up?" Edison towered over her, but he always seemed to shrink a little in her presence, as if faced with a disapproving teacher.

"No, no, that's not like you. How's that working out? The optimism."

Misato had barricaded herself in the women's crew quarters. At first she hadn't noticed the forced lockdown Rayan had put them under, because she so rarely left the familiar comfort of their sleeping area. It had been the natural place to stay, a place she knew well while everything inside and outside of her unraveled and became unrecognizable.

She padded to the kitchenette to her left and ran the tap, then started up the 3-D extruder, choosing one of the preprogrammed modes that would print her a cup and a spoon. They were running low on coffee, probably because she did almost nothing but drink it and drink it and let the caffeine speed her thoughts. It helped, she knew, one small advantage in this mind war of attrition.

If Tuva were still alive, she would scold Misato for hogging it all for herself. She missed Tuva so much, even with the scolding. Such a serious girl, but sometimes Misato managed to make her laugh.

"Coffee?" she offered him. "No, never mind. You didn't come here for that. Something is wrong. The salvager."

Edison crossed to her, leaning against the wall and watching as she filled the newly printed mug with water and waited for the coffee to brew. She didn't have long to wait, and soon the room filled with the earthy perfume of the grounds soaking.

"How can you drink so much of that stuff? Everything puts my stomach off," he said.

"You have your humming," Misato replied gently. "I have this to keep me human. Stop stalling, Edison, it's bothersome. I was making progress before you barged in here."

"I didn't barge—"

She put up a weathered hand, silencing him. "What's the problem? Sit down. You're so jumpy it's making me nervous."

"Ha. Yeah. I'm the jittery one." He chuckled darkly to himself and followed her and her steaming cup of coffee to the round table positioned in the middle of the kitchenette. "How many cups is that? You're gonna take off like a rocket if you don't cool it with the caffeine, Iwasa."

Misato ignored him and sat down, realizing with a worrisome jolt that it didn't hurt her back as much as it used to. Her brow furrowed as she blew idly on the steaming mug.

"What?" Edison asked, watching her closely, just like he always did. It made him a good captain, that ability to observe his crew with constant intensity.

"My back," Misato replied with a grimace. "It should hurt more than it does."

Edison nodded gravely. "It's the Foxfire. You should see Piero. The salvager smashed his eye damn near in half and he's waltzing around like nothing happened. And Rayan . . ."

She closed her eyes and sighed. That had been a terrible day. All the days were terrible now, facing the slow, inexorable conversion of her own mind and body, but there was something viscerally awful about seeing the young biologist in so much shock and pain. There was a fight, screaming, the churning, masculine adrenaline flooding the room before Piero lashed out, mocking Rayan for the voices he kept saying he heard in his head. It had been a friendly game of cards, normal, and then Rayan lost it, smashing his head into the wall over and over again, picking up a ration container to continue the job. The blood had sprayed over her hands and the cards, and then there was an odd flicker in his eyes and he slumped over, shattered.

That was just after Tuva's death, when the Foxfire was still new in them, before anyone's eyes were blue, before she had to put consistent effort into untangling *her* thoughts from those proposed by the enemy. But then Rayan hadn't died. He should have, and very quickly, and so they had only given him something to dull the pain and send him off in comfort. But he never passed, and slowly, to their growing horror and fascination, the blue webs appeared, spidering over his white naked skull, protecting his fatal wound until the exposed bone nearly disappeared.

She shivered and held the mug close to her chest for warmth.

"I don't like it," she said finally.

"Piero can deal with it. He had it coming, trust me."

Misato snorted. "That's not what I meant. I don't care what happens to that brute. He got us into this mess in the first place."

Edison's dark brown eyes snapped open wider. "Not this again. There's no proof, Iwasa. Just because you hate his guts doesn't make him guilty of anything but being an asshole."

She lowered her head and eyed him through the steam rising between them. It made sense, of course, that Edison didn't believe her, but it was quite sad, she thought, that he wouldn't open himself up to possibilities. Even upsetting ones. Maybe a good captain had to look for the good in his crew no matter what.

"Edison, don't be naive. What else explains it? He was so insistent that we take an extra day on Coeur d'Alene Station, that we take that shipment . . . It stinks, reeks, really, and you know it. Tuva knew it, too; that's why he killed her."

"*Also* just guesswork," he said. "Tuva's headaches were getting so bad she was practically blind. It was a seizure, you said it yourself. There were no marks on her body. Nothing."

Muttering to himself, Edison rubbed at the whiskers on his chin and pushed his chair back, balancing on the two back legs and bouncing a little with nerves. It didn't bother her. Eventually he would come around to believe her. That, or she would find a way to toss Piero out the air lock and call it done. Unlikely, of course, given their relative sizes. But nobody ever accused Misato of being uncreative.

"I'm not here to get into that with you. Again." Edison adjusted his spectacles, one hinge taped up for a fix. She had offered to print him a new pair but he wanted to keep them, sentimental reasons, he said. "It's the salvager, like you said."

"You can complain about her if you like, but I already admire her. If she smashed up Piero's face, then she's my kind of gal. There's something about her, something different. Maybe I met her on campus before. I must have, her face is so familiar."

His lips quirked to the side. "No, I feel the same thing. It's like I know her. I get this unbelievable headache when I look at her, like it's painful. The Foxfire reacts to her, I mean I almost . . . The Foxfire took over and I frightened her."

Misato stared at him. The mug almost slipped out of her hands. She made her right hand into a fist, testing it, finding there was less and less sensation. To her horror, the mug's surface barely felt hot to the touch.

"What did you do?"

"I lost control." Edison closed his eyes, letting the chair crash back down to the floor. He squeezed the bridge of his nose just above his glasses. "Mother wants us to join her to the cluster. She's going to try and make you do it, too."

Misato's brows raised in surprise. "Stop calling that thing 'Mother.'" A pause. "So, she's not infected yet?"

Edison shook his head and sighed. "Not yet. Rayan concocted some temporary vaccine that he wants her to take, but he missed her with the syringe. And she has her hazard suit. Salvager tech is made expressly to keep this kind of junk at bay. She's well protected . . ."

She heard the implied *for now* in his statement and withered.

Slowly, she put out a hand to Edison and covered his knuckles with her palm. As she leaned toward him across the table, he couldn't help but keep her gaze.

"We have to protect her, too," Misato said softly. Seriously. She wouldn't wish this private torment on anyone, especially some poor innocent woman that blundered into their nightmare. Something flared at the back of her mind, pain suffusing the crown of her skull. The Foxfire was furious with her. *The network was a gift. Joining the cluster was an honor. The girl should be so lucky to fuse with us and . . .*

"Agh!" she cried out, then quickly gulped the coffee. The hateful thoughts receded. For the moment. It was Edison's turn to squeeze her hand.

"Breathe," he said. "You can fight it."

"It's . . . I'm all right." Misato took another quick sip from her mug. "Where is she now?"

"Cold storage lab. She's safe from us. I gave her my code to keep the contamination shield in place. The Foxfire won't go near that room for some reason. Rayan thinks it's afraid of the decontam pod."

Misato nodded, feeling more like herself. "Fools. We should have jumped in that thing the second the shipment was compromised."

"There's no point in dwelling on it," Edison replied shortly. "We're here now. We're here, but she doesn't have to be. I don't care how bad Foxfire wants her, we need to fight it."

She stood and returned to the kitchenette counter, refilling her mug and dawdling there with her back to him. "Frankly, Edison, I'm afraid to ask."

"Coeur d'Alene Station," she heard him say hoarsely. "With her VIT credentials we could access the coordinate log and thrusters and go back, get to CDAS and make sure whatever got us doesn't get anyone else. The whole place might be contaminated . . . All those people. We have to be sure."

Misato spun to face him, splashing hot coffee on her hands. She didn't feel the burn of it, just the wetness dripping over her thumb.

"If you want to protect that woman, you won't take her anywhere near CDAS," Misato hissed. "What makes you so sure that's even your idea? 'Mother' could be telling you to do it. Anyway, if there's Foxfire somewhere on that station, then it's a death trap. It's bad enough she's mixed up with us, now you want to steal her identity and put her in more danger? You're heartless, Edison. Just get her back to that ship of hers and be done with it. You know it's the right thing to do."

He was quiet for a long moment, running his fingertip along a flaw in the table. His head drooped lower. She had always thought him a handsome man, but the Foxfire was taking its toll. There was gray in his beard, and the smile lines at his eyes were deepening. His left hand seemed to shake constantly with some kind of tremor.

"I don't know what's right," he told her. "I don't think I can let her get away. The Foxfire wants her here; it's going to make us keep her here."

"So you're playing right into it?" Misato marched over to the table and slammed her mug down. She took him by the shoulders and shook. The glowing blue of his eyes twinkled, threatening white, but he seemed to beat it back. Thank God. He could overpower her without trying, and she needed to be heard. "I get it, Edison, you want to be the big bloody hero. You want to save the whole galaxy. Sometimes you don't get to do that, sometimes all you can do is just keep things from getting worse. We don't know what's on CDAS. It could be—"

The warm emergency lights in the quarters blinked, twice, the ship suddenly juddering, the floor beneath them shaking before the lights went out altogether. They froze, bathed in the glowing turquoise Foxfire clinging to the walls and ceiling.

"What was that?" she whispered.

She saw Edison close his eyes and snap them open again. "It's not one of us," he murmured. The engines whined, the ship drifting through space still while the floor again shook.

"It's her, then," Misato said, following him to the open door and into the corridor. "What do you think she's doing?"

"I don't know," Edison grunted, navigating easily through the pitch black. "But I doubt it's friendly."

17

Messing around with highly dangerous, highly volatile tech fueled by an hour or two of restless sleep was not an ideal plan by any stretch of the imagination, but desperation did funny things to the body. And the mind.

Rosalyn blinked three times in rapid succession, twisted into a pretzel in the engine compartment. On a whim she had used Edison's captain's code to access this part of the ship and gained a much-needed second wind when it actually worked. Onboard ship engineering wasn't exactly her area of expertise, but a few generalized undergrad courses and the ship's schematic would have to be enough. All MSC vessels ran on the same tech, and that backstabber Griz had broken his usual silence once to drone on about the refinements and upgrades the entire fleet had received recently. That kind of thing was exciting to him, apparently.

Solar panels did the bulk of the work, Griz explained, giddy by his standards, and now Rosalyn was glad she had half listened. Even far from any suns, the panels could soak up traces of light particles. But once those stores were depleted or the ship voyaged too far from any light source, the engines defaulted to the radioisotope thermoelectric generators. Both methods were incredibly safe, but the newer RTGs had to be handled "like babies" according to Griz.

She could hear the pilot's monotone voice as she unsealed the maintenance panel in engineering: *Those puppies kick in too fast and you've got more than a fire, you've got one inferno of a shit storm.*

Scrubbing at the grime on her visor, Rosalyn leaned in closer to the panel, coming face-to-face with the lighted screen reporting on the technical health of the ship. All of it could have been more comfortably accessed from the cockpit, but Rosalyn wasn't chancing the trip. JAX and the others would be lurking in the halls, and she had been lucky to make it to engineering in secret. There was no telling how long she had, but sooner or later one of the crew would check on her in cold storage and find that it was empty.

It felt wrong, her fingers hovering over the life support and fuel readouts. The *Brigantine* was in decent shape, and would easily survive the trip to headquarters. Once the thrusters had cycled, they had begun gently carrying them back toward HQ, reinstating the code blue. The solar coating and RTGs had plenty of juice, but without a way to actually direct the thrusters, she would never make it back to the *Salvager 6*. It was floating out there somewhere, abandoned, but the code blue kept her from redirecting their trajectory. Maybe she could risk trying to override the code, but if she failed or was incapacitated, that would give the crew the ability to fly *anywhere*. That was a different plan for a different reality, she thought. It was too risky. If even one spore escaped decontamination on her suit, she could spread the nightmare to an entire corporate campus.

But what if. What if she could escape this hell without dying? What if she could get back to her ship and find her way to HQ, warn them about the state of the *Brigantine* and go through a few rounds of decontam and a rigorous scan, a physical, quarantine, whatever it took to scour every trace of Foxfire from her and the suit . . .

Even that very unlikely scenario required murder. The crew would never let her escape, and the technical readout and schematics confirmed that all emergency pods had been jettisoned. Destroying the *Brigantine* was the only way to make sure Foxfire went no farther. It was the most responsible, if hardest, thing to do.

Her forefinger hovered over the touch screen, the words LIFE SUPPORT glowing just below. She could cut that and see if it made a difference, since her environmental suit had plenty of oxygen left in the canisters. Sighing, she tilted her visor against the edge of the panel. No, she had seen Rayan's wound. He should be dead. The Foxfire might not even need oxygen to keep going. Plenty of fungi were anaerobic. She sincerely doubted the growth could survive the frozen vacuum of space.

She had climbed up into the engineering ducts so confidently. Sure, her hands had been shaky from lack of sleep and her eyes and brain throbbed with exhaustion, but there had been a certain fire under her feet that shoved all of that discomfort aside. Now, faced with actually ending the lives of four strangers and her own, Rosalyn hesitated.

A wave of nausea rippled through her stomach, and she clenched her abdomen to keep from vomiting. What if they could be cured? What if all this mess could be used for something good? The fungus could knit wounds back together, perhaps even elongate human life . . . No. *No, no, no.* There was no silver lining to this disaster, only suffering. It was pure arrogance to think she could somehow spin this around and make it out okay. *You can't turn shit into sunshine*, Angela liked to say, usually when Rosalyn came by her office to vent.

"I'd say this qualifies as shit all right," Rosalyn whispered, pulling her head back and scrolling down the readout panel. Cutting off the core functions to solar power might bring up the RTGs quick and hot, bypassing gradual transference of power and forcing the ship to call too fast on the RTGs to keep life support and other key systems online. It was a long shot, Rosalyn decided, but a long shot she had to take, and take immediately.

There was activity down the corridor, just a door opening and closing, and she only heard it softly but still . . . She checked the onboard monitoring systems. The security cameras were still turned off. That was good. Her first step in the duct was cutting the cameras. It had caused an unexpected power surge, but just a short one, and Rosalyn hoped the crew had mistaken it for routine during the ship's emergency state. She had sealed the hatch back up behind her to make it look like nothing was out of the ordinary in engineering; if the monitoring systems were on, it would be easy to spot her in the ducts.

It was time to make the call. She scrolled and scrolled through the systems menu and stopped. Solar panels. She could do it, cut them manually and without warning, and hope the abrupt loss of power would trigger a deadly chain reaction. Rosalyn took a deep breath and nodded, her finger trembling as she pushed it toward the display.

A single footstep sounded on the cold metal floors of engineering. Then another. The steps were definitive and echoed. She froze, listening as the person came closer with a heavy tread. *Thunk, thunk, thunk.* Had she left any sign of her whereabouts outside the hatch? She had been so careful to seal everything up so it would look completely normal. The monitoring functions were off.

They must have swept the whole ship looking for her and finally gotten around to engineering. Well, that was fine. She had pulled up the solar panel readouts and she had her plan.

"Rosalyn?"

It was Edison. God, she was an idiot. She had turned off her AR display to concentrate, and if she hadn't, she might have seen the little indicator telling her he was approaching her location. She didn't creep back down the duct to peer out of the screw slots to check if he had white or blue eyes. It didn't matter. The second he realized what she was up to, the Foxfire would take over and she would be assimilated. Forcefully. Sweat beaded on her forehead, dripping down over her brow and into the valley along her nose.

"I know you're there," he said calmly. *Just a trick, he's trying to get you to drop your guard and engage.* "I know you're there, I just don't know what you're trying to do."

There was no point in staying silent. His AR was probably flashing with the indicator, telling him she was right above his head.

"Go away," Rosalyn said flatly. "I just want to be alone."

"What did you do to the ship? JAX says someone is screwing with the monitoring systems manually and he can't override it." A pause. He shifted closer, and she could hear him breathing heavily outside the duct hatch. Her leg was cramping up and she twisted a little, wishing she could wipe at the sweat dripping down her face. She was trapped now, with her one way out blocked by Edison. *No, not by him, by the stuff taking over his body.*

That didn't help. She didn't need to sympathize with a person she was about to kill.

"Don't try to open the hatch," Rosalyn warned. She heard whispering. Someone else was out there with him. It was easy enough to guess that Piero wasn't there, otherwise she'd already be fighting him off. "I'm holding a loaded gun," she added. "Don't make me use it."

More whispering.

"You have a gun?" Edison finally asked, incredulous.

She sighed. "No . . . not literally. Just go away, please. It's harder to do this with you here."

Rosalyn regretted the words as soon as they tumbled out. Why did it matter? This asshole had chased her through the ship. He would've killed her if he had the chance, or at the very least forced her to be exposed to the fungus.

He's not human. None of them are human anymore, right? This is mercy.

It had to be mercy.

"What's harder to do?" He sounded nervous now, afraid. His voice was suddenly hoarse and shaky.

She knew the feeling. Her finger moved closer to the panel.

"I'm killing us. All of us. It's the right thing to do."

Silence. No more whispers. Rosalyn expected the hatch to be ripped away, to be faced with wild, bright white eyes and clawing hands. But none of it came. Her hand began to tremble in earnest, perspiration stinging her eyes. Then tears formed there, not just from the stinging but from terror. She didn't want to die. Closing her eyes, she tried to stop the shaking in her whole body. *They killed Walters, Rosalyn, and they'll kill you, too. This is just the death you choose.*

"I see."

Two words. Why did they stall her? Maybe it was the resignation in his voice. Or the sadness.

"D-Don't try to stop me," Rosalyn stammered. "I've made up my mind."

"Okay," Edison said. "You do what you have to do."

A shaky hand had stopped her before, ruined her career, ruined everything. She wouldn't let it happen again.

"I will," Rosalyn said, pressing her fingertip to the touch screen, disabling the solar panels, closing her eyes as the ship's RTGs kicked in hard, a terrible force sending her crashing back against the wall. Her head slammed into the base of her helmet, and she saw a brilliant kaleidoscope of stars, and then *nothing*.

18

The minor fire that broke out on solar panels S8 through S10 was contained by the ship within seconds. Bright, crisp light flooded engineering, blinding Edison until Misato, hands covering her eyes, shouted, "Lights to half!" It was dim again, mercifully, and he shook the spangles out of his vision.

He hadn't realized how long they had lived in almost complete darkness.

The woman in the hatch had gone silent, but he had heard the bang of her body against the duct wall. Edison glanced at Misato, who had gone rigid as they both listened to the ship cycling systems, bringing itself back online to full. Full. No more emergency status. No more code blue.

"What did she do?" Edison asked, taking a gingerly step toward the maintenance hatch. There was no movement within.

The much shorter woman marched past him, going on tiptoes to loosen the hatch. Her iron-gray bob was streaked with lighter silver and swung back and forth as she worked. "Ballsy move. She cut solar panels hoping the RTGs would overload from the increased stress. Didn't work so good."

"Why didn't you think of that?" Edison groused, taking a step back and letting her pry at the hatch. "You're a goddamned engineer, Iwasa."

"The *best* damned engineer," she corrected. "And the best damned engineer doesn't try something that could fry the ship for good. Or, you know, fry all of us. What she did was practically suicidal—even most pirates won't try it when they find a dead ship. She was trying to blow us all to hell. Instead she just brought us out of being stalled."

"Not sure how to feel about that." He helped her pull down the heavy cover on the duct hatch and leaned it against the wall. Being far taller, he could easily peer inside. The woman was slumped over, utterly still, one foot kicked out toward him.

He watched her for a moment and saw the slow rise and fall of her chest through the suit. Alive, at least, but that would probably wind up being a disappointment for her.

"Why didn't you try to stop her?" he heard Iwasa ask.

"Why didn't *you*?"

Edison glanced down and to the left, and saw the old woman cross her arms and shrug, a twinkle in her eye even through the blue glow of the Foxfire.

"I'm not afraid to die. I'm only afraid to lose myself." Iwasa looked away from him, but he could tell she wasn't finished. "And besides, I was sort of curious what she would try. I know this ship like the back of my hand, and I was pretty sure she couldn't kill us from there. Now, if she found a way to get at the plutonium in the RTGs, we'd be having a different conversation."

"Yes," Edison said, venting a dark chuckle. "We would."

"Anyway," Misato mused, scratching at her chin, "I have no idea if the fungus can survive extreme temperatures. Even space might not kill it off."

"Something to think about," he agreed. "Something to test."

"What the hell was that? Do you see this? We're back online, baby!" Piero had slid into engineering with a spin and a whoop, Rayan not far behind him. The Italian danced over to them, his right eye split through the middle, the bone and sinew beneath protected by a thin web of blue. The flesh all up and down the right side of his face was black and purple with bruising. It was gruesome to look at, but seemed to bother Piero not at all.

And he noticed the open duct hatch. And he noticed Edison turn and shield it from his view.

Yes, protect the salvager. Her bumbling has come to nothing. No, not nothing; she has helped.

He was not, he insisted silently, protecting her because she had accidentally cut the code blue. In fact, he didn't know why he was standing guard like that, only that he didn't want Piero anywhere near Rosalyn. The short stints when he slid into Piero's mind through the alien network were enough to convince Edison that he never wanted to go near the man's thoughts again. He could never control how much he saw, or how long it happened. The glimpses into Piero's mind were brief, shattered fragments, never enough to make out anything more than flashes of dark memories. Foxfire wanted Rosalyn's information and mind, so Piero would probably protect her, too, but Edison didn't trust him.

It was confusing and his head hurt, and he didn't want to deal with the Italian just then. Or ever.

"Don't get too excited," Rayan said, lingering near the door. He fidgeted nervously with something in his pockets, having changed into a lab coat. The collar was splashed with dried blood, his or Piero's, it was impossible to tell. "The nav systems still want active credentials. We're not going anywhere unless Rosalyn gives up her password."

"You're missing the point," Piero replied. Laughing boisterously, he shuffled back over to Rayan and clapped the young man with rattling force on the back. Rayan jerked forward. "The code lifted. HQ will notice that and send more ships. We don't need her, eh? We'll be better prepared when the next morons show up—we take their credentials instead and we can go wherever we please. Rayan can send another hail, and we can dump this bitch out the air lock."

Edison scrubbed at his chin, stowing the urge to toss Piero out into space instead.

"Captain . . ." Inching forward, Rayan stared up at him with his huge eyes, lower lip trembling. "We could give her the injection while she's out cold"—and here he glanced nervously at Piero—"if you want to keep the Foxfire away from her."

"Bullshit. Don't waste the syringe," Piero said hotly. His momentum was all in his shoulders as he stalked toward the engineering hatch. It was familiar body language, the seething masculine coil of anger tightening his shoulder blades together as he came face-to-face with Edison. God, that blow to the face really had made Piero terrifying to look at.

His lip curled up and he craned his neck to see around Edison's head. "We can use the cells in her suit for something, yeah? Let me have a go at her VIT, I bet I can crack it."

"That's not happening," Edison told him sternly. He could see into the man's face where the muscle and skull had caved in. A jagged piece of cheekbone stabbed out from the split in his skin. He was strangely odorless, as if the Foxfire had drained him of all human markers.

Piero leaned back on his heels, sweeping his eyes up and down Edison's face before his sneer deepened. Maybe he recognized the matching posture, the planted feet, the puffed chest. "Ha. Fine. Put it to a vote, then. You Americans love your democracy. We want her VIT credentials, don't we? So we can actually fucking get somewhere."

"I'm no thief," Misato said, joining Edison and extending the wall between Piero and the duct.

"Rayan?" Piero spun, his swagger returning as he jutted his hip out toward the younger man and pointed double finger guns at him. "You're with me, I know you are. This is all a waste of time. Let's get you back to the lab where you belong. A *real* lab, not this satellite bullshit. Back to campus, to life, to wine and food and pussy. You're just too tense, we all are, nobody thinks right trapped on a little ship with three other people for this long."

But Rayan was shaking his head midway through the speech, his eyes fixed on the tops of his shoes. "I don't know. The campus . . . We would just make things worse."

"Ignore him, Rayan." Edison took one step backward, putting himself closer to Rosalyn.

"Motherfucker, don't touch her, we haven't voted yet." Piero slapped a hand in Edison's direction before closing the distance between him and Rayan. His lip curled up toward his split cheek, Piero leaned amiably on Rayan's shoulder, dipping his head down, one roguish curl falling over his forehead. Then his eyes seemed to go unfocused, a white, glittering curtain dropping over them.

"We had a plan, Rayan. Mother has a plan. The woman is not important, only her cooperation is important. Violence is unnecessary, she can simply join the cluster and contribute her credentials and knowledge voluntarily."

Edison lurched away from the hatch, watching Piero's hand clamp hard over Rayan's shoulder. They were still learning about the strange connection between them, but there was no doubting that proximity strengthened that bond. All in one place like that, they had made themselves vulnerable. Piero and Rayan, he knew, were the most lost to the Foxfire, and now he looked on in horror as Rayan gritted his teeth, fighting but helpless, as it took control of him, too.

"You're sick," Edison snapped at Piero. "You let that shit rule you? You're a coward."

"We rule over you, too," Piero—the Foxfire—told him.

Pain seared through Edison's head, and he heard Misato cry out in alarm before dropping to her knees. She put both hands over her face, shivering.

"I never *let* you do it," Edison shouted through the hot knife slicing through his brain. "I never want you to do it."

Rayan's head snapped up suddenly, frosty white blazing out from his eyes. "Violence is unnecessary. We can gift her bliss. Connection. This is the compromise."

"No."

"What is she to you? A little crush? Aw." This was new. This was Piero's shithead attitude mixed seamlessly with the alien's intentions. His eyes were pure white. His voice was his own. "What is she to you? We're your crew. Your cluster. *Listen to your mother.*"

Crew. Cluster. None of it meant anything anymore. Rosalyn was the most human thing on the ship, and that was worth saving. Not one more person was going to experience this; Edison was going to fight through it no matter what, he decided, even if he was the only anchor keeping the ship from blowing away in the storm. On the floor next to him Misato wasn't giving up, though her shoulders trembled harder and harder.

Warm, tempting tendrils licked at the edge of his pain. If he just gave in, the suffering would be over and he could sink into the Foxfire's influence like a waiting bath.

"No," he repeated. *"No."*

Edison charged at them. Moving made it easier to resist. Running with all of his weight behind one shoulder, he forgot about arguments and reasoning. It was not an elegant solution but a solution nonetheless. Misato stumbled to her feet, grunting in agony as Edison rushed by her, catching Piero off guard. He was already off balance, leaning so hard on Rayan, and now it was easy to aim right at his armpit and send him reeling back toward the door.

There was a loud *crack* as they collided, and Rayan spun away, managing to land against the wall and huddle there, his eyes still wild and silver.

Piero was back on his feet in an instant, growling, hurling himself toward the door as it shut with a hiss. His fingers curled into talons as he reached for the control panel on the other side, but Edison was just a little faster, inputting his captain's code and locking him out.

He hadn't noticed how hard he was breathing, but he leaned against the door, listening to Piero swear and kick. Fixing his crooked glasses, Edison turned around, sliding down a few inches while Piero huffed and paced on the other side.

Then he knew, or sensed, that Piero had put his palm gently on the door. "We are your cluster, your family," he heard Piero murmur. It didn't sound anything like him at all. "We are not the enemy, Edison."

He closed his eyes, made a fist and pressed it against the portal. "You're sure as shit not my friend."

"Let him in." Rayan rushed toward the door, slamming his fist against the panel uselessly. Without Edison's code there was no opening the portal. Outside, Piero laughed and laughed, adding his own fists to the racket. "Let us in! *LET US IN!*"

The biologist was screaming now, louder and louder, frantic, and Edison didn't know if his aching head could take one more shout like that.

"LET US IN! LET US IN!"

"You have to stop that." Edison's voice shook. Whatever Rayan was doing called to the monster inside him. It snarled and snapped, desperate to get out, determined to open the door and let Piero and the chaos back in. "Rayan, listen to me, you have to control yourself."

He didn't like manhandling the kid, but there were precious few options. Misato joined him, taking Rayan by the shoulders as he bucked and shrieked, both fists banging on the door panel. Clamping a hand over the biologist's mouth, he made a soothing sound over and over again, as if trying to settle a spooked animal. *Shhhh. It's okay. Think of a memory. Something that's just you, anything that's just you. Shhhh, calm down now.*

It was as much for Edison as it was for the kid.

Misato met his eye over Rayan's shoulder, her mouth a thin line, but he looked quickly away from her, afraid. Proximity was dangerous. Easier now, he thought, without the screaming, to keep hold of his humanity. But still.

At last Rayan stilled, no longer squirming and kicking at them. He blinked rapidly, the bright terror in his eyes dulling until it was the usual dimly glowing turquoise. His hands closed gently over Edison's wrists. On the other side of the door, it had gone quiet, Piero's giggling vanishing down the corridor. Even without the silence, Edison sensed he was gone.

"Are you going to be quiet?" he asked Rayan, stern as a parent.

The kid nodded yes.

"All right, don't make me regret this." Edison let him go, watching the biologist stumble away, his clothes rumpled and still bloody, his thick black hair sticking up in every direction, revealing the grisly wound below. He wondered if they all appeared that haggard and dirty. Human needs, human instincts, had become distant desires, an occasional itch that he was too distracted to scratch. Showers. Food.

Contact. It was like the alien thing inside him was slowly setting aside everything that made him a man and discarding it.

"I'm sorry," Rayan whispered, huddling in the middle of the engineering room with both arms wrapped around his middle. He shivered as if freezing cold, avoiding eye contact.

"Forget it," Misato said as she hurried to the door panel. "You can apologize later. We locked ourselves inside here, and Piero has access to the cockpit. To JAX. With the Foxfire controlling him like that . . ."

"I know." Edison pinched the bridge of his nose, wishing fruitlessly for his headache to subside. At least the beast in his head had calmed for the moment. "Not my finest idea."

Rayan perked up, but his face was streaked with tears. With a few faltering steps toward the door, he raised his hand and closed his eyes. As he did, a crisp, mechanical female voice spoke across the intercom system.

"Emergency broadcast parameters met. Fire damage detected. Foreign matter present in crew-critical quadrants . . ."

"He's going to send an emergency hail," Rayan whispered, shaking his head. "He wants to lure more ships here. He wants to expand the cluster."

19

She woke to a deep slicing sensation in her stomach.

Hunger. When was the last time she had eaten something? Rosalyn blinked in the cool semidarkness. She didn't recognize where she was at first, and sat up, fast, too fast, her vision spinning from the sudden rush of blood. Whatever she was lying prone on was quite soft and accommodating, padded and slick with some kind of plastic coating. Her eyes adjusted gradually, and she instinctively reached for her face, breathing a sigh of relief when she felt the protective bubble shielding her from the ship's compromised atmosphere.

"You're safe, chickadee."

Rosalyn started, twisting sharply to the right. She hadn't noticed the small old woman sitting next to her, hands folded around a full white mug. The last crew member, Misato Iwasa. Her AR display fragmented into a few pale squares, forming boundaries around the various parts of her face and body to identify her. One square highlighted her delicate mouth and the mole next to it, another what would have been brightly inquisitive brown eyes. At least, that was what was shown in the dossier picture that popped up in the upper right-hand corner of her display.

A fish tank lined the wall behind her, bathing the room in

SALVAGED

watery blue light. The spores had spread into the tank, and there didn't seem to be a single fish inside swimming around, just floating turquoise threads along the surface.

"Hi." Rosalyn didn't know what else to say. There was a dull ringing in the back of her head, and her skull felt soft, like a bruised apple. She groaned and stretched, glancing around the room, her AR helpfully providing the schematic overlay and informing her that this was the medical bay and attached wet labs.

"Are you hungry?" Misato Iwasa asked conversationally.

"Wait . . ." Rosalyn's memory was returning along with her vision. They were obviously still on the ship and obviously not dead. She squeezed her eyes shut and sighed. "It didn't work, did it?"

"Your quaint little plan to blow us to hell? No, afraid not. Not a bad idea, but you ended up doing us a favor. Well, not us. *Them.*" She pointed to her eyeball and shrugged. Just like Edison, she seemed to wear the weight of their plight on her shoulders, sinking down toward the floor as she took a long sip from her mug.

"You're . . . not angry." Rosalyn squinted at her, her stomach twisting again with hungry anguish. Sitting up, she dangled her legs off the padded examination chair. "You're not angry. Why are you not angry? I tried to kill you."

Misato's thin brows went up and she snorted above her cup. "Did you try to kill me, chickadee, or them?"

"Them," Rosalyn admitted. "But them also means you."

"And you." Misato stood and crossed to the laboratory counters opposite where they were sitting. There were two small, refrigerated lockers, one with a taped label reading SPECIMENS, DO NOT EAT and the other labeled FOOD, DEFINITELY DO EAT.

She opened the latter and rummaged. Half watching her, Rosalyn reached for her VIT, inputting her personal code and checking the life on her oxygen canisters. If she wanted to stay alive and healthy, which

141

she hadn't decided on yet, then she would need to maintain enough juice in her suit and a reasonable oxygen level. Even if the oxygen had stabilized on the *Brigantine*, she didn't trust the filtration system in her suit to deal with the Foxfire spores indefinitely. For the moment she retained plenty of oxygen, but the filters were another story. To keep her safe, they were dealing with a spore-choked environment. Eventually those filters would need to be replaced, especially after constantly processing such heavily contaminated air.

"Hungry?" Misato called. She returned from the lockers with a few ration pouches.

"How did you know?"

"Your stomach is growling something fierce. No way you thought to stop for a snack while sabotaging the ship." It was a gentle accusation, given with a smile.

Rosalyn took the pouches from her and felt her face grow hot. "I thought it was the right thing to do."

"It still is, probably." Misato took a seat again, brooding over her mug, and Rosalyn's gut growled just at the sight of the steaming liquid heaven in the cup.

"God, that looks so good," Rosalyn muttered. "I'm starving."

"It's coffee, probably not the best for an empty stomach." The older woman nodded to the pouches in Rosalyn's lap and smirked. "How do you plan on eating those?"

She hadn't even thought that far ahead. Studying the pouches (sweet potato puree, freeze-dried turkey cutlet, reconstituted apple crumble), she chewed for a moment on the inside of her cheek. Soon she would have to use the bathroom, or make the uncomfortable decision of letting the suit cycle and expel her waste for her.

"Cold storage has the decontam chamber and a bathroom. I might be able to finagle something."

"Or I can," Misato suggested. She rolled away on her chair for a moment, then flicked herself back with her heels, returning with a small touch tablet she had taken from a messy examination table. "Hold this."

Rosalyn took the mug from her while Misato brought up a simple drawing app on the tablet, sketching rapidly with her fingers, making an improbably precise schematic, as good as any Rosalyn might find loaded up on her AR.

"You worked on the Io Station Project for the Global Alliance," Rosalyn said softly. "You're practically a legend on Earth. Your dossier . . . I mean, it's incredible. Why are you on the *Brigantine*?"

"Vacation?" Misato glanced up at her and winked, still working diligently. "I had my fill of irrigation rigs and sulfur dispersion systems, thought I would give bioengineering a look. Or maybe I just have an addiction to school. Here . . ."

Turning the tablet around, she held it up for Rosalyn to see.

"We can run the nonlethal decontam hoses to the atmospheric regulator in cold storage. You can take my oil atomizer and run it, too. With some oregano oil and melaleuca, you can create a hostile environment for the Foxfire." The schematic was way beyond Rosalyn's understanding, but she nodded and took a photo of it with her AR display.

"Oregano and mela . . . mela what now?"

Misato laughed, a belly laugh that shook her whole body. "Melaleuca. In combination they're lethal to most fungi."

"I see. So why didn't you try it on yourself?" Rosalyn asked gently.

"Oh, we did. Just made us sick. By the time we tried ridding our bodies of the Foxfire, it was too late." She took her coffee mug back and chugged from it. Afterward, her smile had faded away and Rosalyn felt like a jerk for prying. Still, she was part of this mess now, too, and any weapons were good weapons in her estimation.

"Right. Forget I said anything. I'm sure you tried everything you could."

The old woman stroked her thumbs down the sides of the mug. She looked so tired, and the smiles and laughter seemed thinner and more fragile in hindsight.

"Is this what you were out here to study?" Rosalyn asked. "The Foxfire?"

Misato shook her head and took in a deep breath, turquoise eyes flickering a little as she sat back in her chair and crossed one leg over the other. "Oh no. Other xenobio samples? Definitely. Foxfire was never part of the mission. CDAS had intercepted some pirates with alien contraband, and Merchantia Solutions wanted us to take them and study them in various environments, zero g being one of them. It was exciting stuff, top-level stuff, so they brought me on."

Rosalyn frowned. "Top-level stuff? That doesn't make any sense. The dossier said you're running a routine research vessel . . ."

With another big belly laugh, Misato finished her coffee and twirled the cup between both hands. "Yes, yes, I'm sure that's what the dossier said. No offense, chickadee, but I don't think a salvager has clearance to know about what we were doing out here. Not that it matters now, poke around all you like. Take pictures. Spread the word . . . if you can."

Rosalyn made to stand up, moving slowly, cradling the food pouches in one arm as she lowered herself to the floor with her left. She flinched and made a face.

"You got quite a jostling in that engineering vent," Misato said.

"I can feel that." Her shoulders felt like they had been run through a blender. On the counter behind Misato someone had lined up a row of insulated drink cups, each labeled with the crew's names. One was missing. "Speaking of poking around," Rosalyn said slowly. "One cup missing. Can I ask what happened to Tuva?"

144

The old woman closed her eyes tightly, then opened them to stare into her empty mug. "She died just days before the first sign of Foxfire. A brain tumor, maybe, a seizure . . . Rayan found her asleep in her bunk, not a mark on her, just . . . gone."

"I'm so sorry," Rosalyn murmured. "On top of everything else that's happened, what a nightmare."

"She knew something," Misato said. Her jaw hardened, and she looked up suddenly. "I don't believe for a second it was a tumor or whatever else Piero keeps saying. He put her mug away somewhere, he can't stand to look at anything that reminds him of her."

"Why not?"

Rosalyn had forgotten all about the food packets in her arms, remembering what Girdy had warned her about on the launch platform. Her stomach hurt again, throbbing with intuition. This was the second time blocked clearance had come up. A mysterious death. The Foxfire itself . . . not to mention the other doomed expeditions and Reevey's inexplicable, murderous madness.

Either it was a trick of the light or the blue glow in Misato's eyes dimmed a little, as if the humanity there ached to win out. "Because he killed her. I've been in his mind. We've all been in each other's minds. He's hiding it well, there are fragments, suggestions, but when I try to think of it through him, I just keep seeing this room. The aquarium. But I *know* he did it."

"How?" Rosalyn asked, breathless. "Why?"

Misato vented a low chuckle. "She had this thing. She couldn't stand a lie. At first I found it irritating but after a while it grew on me. Toward the end she had these violent headaches, and we all told her to rest, but she kept trying to corner Piero. She knew something. She must have known something. I know Piero did it, I just don't know how."

A heavy stillness fell between them. Misato seemed to drift away,

her thoughts somewhere else entirely, or maybe the Foxfire was trying to reach her again and tear her away from Rosalyn. More than
anything she felt sorry for Misato. She had tried her best to kill the
entire crew, and this woman was still helping her. It made her wonder if there wasn't just a sliver of humanity in there, but more. *More.*
Trusting anyone was a mistake, she knew, but asking for help didn't
necessarily require trust. And maybe trust would come, maybe she
could sway Misato to her side for good.

"I could help you look," Rosalyn said softly. At once she saw the
flicker of interest, of hope, in the old woman's eyes. "If you can keep
the others away from me, if you help me, then maybe I can find out
what happened to Tuva. To be honest, I want to know, too. It might
tell us how this whole Foxfire thing got on the ship in the first place."

Misato didn't hesitate at all. "I will do what I can to help you.
You have my word. Thinking of Tuva helps. She was such a brilliant
woman. And she's . . . right there. Right on the other side of the
Foxfire, something recent and clear and good."

One person on her side. Maybe she could convince Edison next.
One by one she could convince the crew to fight hard, and fight on
the side of humanity. If it took solving Tuva's murder, then that's
what Rosalyn would do.

"Did she leave behind anything?" Rosalyn asked. "If she had
suspicions that Piero was up to something, she might have taken
notes on her VIT."

Misato shook her head, turning to put her mug back on the
counter, next to the named canisters. The light from the aquarium
shifted over the back of her jumpsuit, pale and spangled. "There was
nothing."

"That's pretty suspicious," Rosalyn pointed out. "Aren't you
worried Piero will realize you suspect him of something? You two
do sort of share a mind."

"Let him find out," Misato replied. "Finding the truth for Tuva matters more. Honesty, truth, justice . . . that was everything to her. Do you understand?"

Rosalyn dared to walk closer, knowing it was risky. She couldn't trust anything the crew said, and she knew it was possible that Misato could lash out just like Edison had. But somehow she felt safe, or at least, in that moment, Misato seemed like the closest thing to human she had found since boarding the ship.

"It means you're still human," Rosalyn said softly. She looked at the row of cups, and at the end where Tuva's should have been. Girdy had told her to be on the lookout for something strange. The Foxfire was strange, obviously, but this mystery was something else. Something human. Maybe it would lead her away from the infestation itself and closer to what had caused it in the first place.

Her hunger, then, seemed very, very small.

"Did you keep the body?" she asked, hoarse.

Slowly, Misato nodded.

"Show me."

20

Something remarkable was happening. They stood in the cockpit together, a wall of flickering light dyeing them a vivid grass green. *Like the foothills in spring outside the* città. It felt like the whole of the universe was open to them now, an endless horizon of opportunity, and all thanks to Mother.

No, thanks to the girl.

Ah yes, the girl, the salvager who had split Piero's face down the right side and with it, forged an opening for Mother. Ingress. Progress. The wound had weakened the body and opened the way, defenses lowered and useless against Mother's assault. The gash was a wide-open door that led to the heart of him, and when the wound began to heal, it healed with the strong blue filaments of the cluster.

Mother was there, standing next to him, or so it seemed. A figure hovered in the corner of his eye, the suggestion of a luminous blue being.

Piero was hers. He moved now with Mother guiding his hands, with deft and determined fingers, not a hint of hesitation or fight left in him. He was freed and they were one and it felt almost painfully good to be *whole* that way. Mother understood now, understood what others of their kind had experienced—the undeniable rightness, the *bliss*, of union.

This was bliss. This was the human man improved and connected completely to the cluster. The ship may as well have been part of him, living and breathing as his skin, just one more organ but one that they now occupied. The corridors and rooms spread out all around him at all times, a map with a trillion spying eyes. And Mother felt that it was better for the man, that this human Piero had achieved a kind of grateful resolution.

Like going home. Like running to Mamma's arms. *She was always so warm and soft, and smelled like Bottega Veneta Eau de Velours, vintage, a precious bottle passed down and down, rationed like wartime essentials, just a dab behind her ear but* oh *how it delighted the senses! Oak and jasmine, but rosemary, too, from her hands and the bread she made on Sundays. Mamma hugged him tight and lifted him from the floor and swung him around. They would have to go soon, to the new colonies. The tides were rising, swallowing their town like they swallowed Venice whole. The water was coming for them, terrible, inexorable, with a hunger that could not be negotiated or stopped.*

And there, as he hugged her and buried his face in her neck, he smelled a heavy men's cologne, overpowering and foreign, and there was the lipstick smudge on her collar, transferred from that same strange man's fingers. From her lips to his skin to her blouse and now to his cheek, an indirect kiss that soured his stomach in an instant. Stay, Mamma, he had pleaded, stay and make bread again, don't go give your lipstick away to strangers.

That was how Mother got in. The hate was there, just waiting, a box redolent with mold, hiding in the very back corner of the cupboard. The wound had ripped off the lid and let the hate spill out, hate Mother found and swam up like a poisonous river running swiftly to the core of him. *Piero.*

Stay, Mamma. Stay!

She hadn't, of course, which Mother reminded him in a bombardment that came not by the second but by the nanosecond, then constantly.

When she finally did stay, it was only to take him away from everything he knew. Mamma swept him up into her arms once more and said it was time to go to their new home, far away, across the stars to a place called Io.

But all my friends are here, he screamed as she carried him into their simple house.

You will make friends on Io, too, my heart, you'll see.

No! he had screamed and screamed, beating his fists against her breast. He was already large for a child and he felt her wince, but she kept on carrying him anyway.

What about my friends? What about the old men playing dice? Who will take them? Or the stray dogs? Will the water swallow them all up?

I don't know, his mother had said, gripping him tightly. *Someone will look after them. You're hurting me, Piero.*

Of all her many betrayals, this one cut the deepest.

The hate, the hate, the hate. It was so powerful. This new mother of his, born from the Foxfire, knew the power of his hate. But she would never hurt him the way Mamma had hurt him.

"I will never make you do anything you don't want to do," Mother said. She was still hovering there, just out of sight. Perhaps he was imagining it, but it felt like she touched his shoulder. The smell of jasmine came to him suddenly, and he felt the urge to cry. The touch on his shoulder grew stronger, and he let Mother embrace him, wrapping her arms around him completely.

"I don't want to hurt anybody," he heard himself whisper. "I didn't mean to hurt anyone."

Mother hushed him. The perfume was all around him, painful and familiar, the scent of his true mother's blouse, of her room. He had loved her little room on Earth, so small and cozy, with plush carpet faded by sunlight. Their new home on Io, cold and square and hard, never seemed to retain the smell of her, even when she was still alive.

"You're a good boy," Mother said, stroking his hair. It was matted with dried blood. "My heart, my heart, you must be strong, and you must listen. You may have to hurt again, but only for me. Only for our family."

Her hands felt just like his real mother's, and the scent of that perfume made him cry harder. She held him there for a long time. When he opened his eyes, just a bit, there was no one really there, just his own arms wrapped around him as he rocked back and forth. But when he went back into the darkness, Mother returned and soothed him.

"I should have stayed there," Piero said softly. "I should have stayed and drowned with the old men and the dogs."

"No, hush now, there is no time for sadness. Would you like to hear a song, my heart?" Mother rocked him harder and Piero nodded against her. Her voice was that of his mamma's, but somehow sweeter and more melodic. "Busy the bee goes, 'Buzz, buzz, buzz!' Ollie the owl goes, 'Hoot, hoot, hoot!' and Mother goes: 'I love you.'"

The song repeated until Piero no longer wanted to cry. He stood up straight, feeling stronger, Mother's hand still cupping his shoulder.

"What should I do?" he asked.

"You know what to do," Mother replied. "You're such a brilliant boy. A mind for numbers, for codes. For secrets. The salvager is just a small problem. No challenge for such a brilliant boy."

Just a small problem. He had taken care of Tuva when she discovered his secret, and he could clean up this mess, too. The cluster needed to grow, and now, thanks to the girl, the answer presented itself. Mother had asked him to be clever, and so he had snatched the code blue idea from the biologist, a sneaky scheme, but this was more direct. Even if it brought human engines of war to them, it was worth it. Any opportunity to expand the network, to add more children, was worth the risk.

And Piero agreed. He scrolled quickly through the available emergency commands at the piloting console. HQ, Piero considered, would see that their ship had gone green again but that might only make them suspicious. A cry for help would be better. Wiser to look the wounded lamb than the hidden wolf.

"You're so clever, my heart," Mother told him. "I knew you would find the answer."

"Emergency broadcast parameters met. Fire damage detected. Foreign matter present in crew-critical quadrants . . ."

Shit. That was the best they could do. No follow-up to assure HQ that they were docile, just trapped. The nav systems went haywire. Anything. Anything. Lies. But Piero's damned credentials were blocked. There was no way to get a specific message out, and the screen flashing **ENTER VALID EMPLOYEE IDENTIFICATION** blinked and blinked, taunting them.

They still needed the bitch's credentials. A minor problem. Piero was free now, part of Mother, inconvenient human reactions to force and violence no longer a prohibiting factor. Being human had never felt the way he did now—utterly submerged in the acceptance of another being. And there was the promise of more acceptance from more beings. As their family grew, that love and warmth would only increase, multiplying with every mind Mother added to their cluster.

But it itched, this human skin that locked him and Mother inside. Piero lifted his right hand and scratched at his cheek, at the gash healed over and through with connective webbing. Picking and picking, the raw edges of human skin around the opening caught on the fingernail and Piero dug in. Mesmerizing, the repetitive motion of the nail and the finger, the human skin resistant and then pliable, peeling away like the rind of a soft cheese, revealing the scintillating web of turquoise blue below. Better, that. Better the fine blue lightning over the muscle tissue. Better and better the more the skin came away. The body shivered but the mind delighted.

"You look so beautiful," Mother said. "My beautiful heart."

Soothed, he almost forgot the blinking irritation of the screen.

ENTER VALID EMPLOYEE IDENTIFICATION

They reached out together, he and Mother, not with hands but with the mind, traversing the intricate network that connected them together. It was stronger now, that bond, and they sensed each spore, each flowering shock of blue along the ship's walls and ceilings. The crew had left the engineering bay, their locations pulsing noticeably, like three proximate hearts.

Misato and the salvager were traveling together down the corridors. Reaching out through their cluster, Piero prodded at Misato's mind, searching for her intention. She resisted him, as always, but he was stronger now, stronger through Mother. Images flashed before him—a hand, a fish, a lock of white-blond hair.

Tuva. She was taking the salvager, the *interloper*, to Tuva. Piero snarled. It would be a short but infinitely satisfying hunt.

21

"We put her in the body drawer," Misato was explaining, pulling on the long silver handle at about waist height. "She should be well preserved."

Rosalyn took a deep breath, preparing herself, as she always did, for the sight of a corpse. The air felt stranger when a dead body was nearby. This one, however, was just as Misato expected. Preserved. Tuva Sverdal might have been taking a nap, her eyes closed, her lips slightly parted as if she had just exhaled. Her skin was ghostly, ghostly pale, almost like chalk, thin, blue veins visible along her jaw and forehead. Blond hair fell to her shoulders, parted in the middle, and her eyelashes were that same snowy color.

"You removed her suit?" Rosalyn asked.

"I wanted to check for marks." Misato deflated a little, sagging against the deep drawer. "After that, I couldn't get her back into the suit myself. Too heavy. It didn't seem right to ask the men to help."

Rosalyn nodded, gesturing for her to pull the drawer out farther. Already gloved, she leaned forward toward Tuva and carefully pulled back her eyelid. Normal. From what Rosalyn could see, there were no outward signs that the Foxfire had tried to take over her body.

"Did you consider an autopsy?" she asked.

"Of course," Misato said. "But the others disagreed. They wanted to leave it to HQ when our assignment was done. Then the Foxfire happened and, I hate to say it, but I think we all forgot about her in here." She sighed and let go of the drawer, taking a tiny step back.

Something down by Tuva's waist caught Rosalyn's attention. She picked up the woman's wrist, holding it up closer to the light on her visor. There was a small tattoo, black ink, in a language Rosalyn didn't speak. Right away her AR display highlighted the words with a shimmery box, translating.

"Fight back," Rosalyn whispered, then looked at Tuva's closed eyes. "Is that what you were trying to do? Fight back. Maybe I'll get one of these if I ever make it out of here alive."

"You would've liked her," Misato said. "She was a survivor, just like you, always spoke her mind. A bit uptight, maybe, but I prefer the word 'precise.'" Chuckling, she did an impression of a stilted Norwegian accent. "Whenever the drinks came out, she would say, 'This is a science vessel, Iwasa, not a party barge.' She had a strong gut, listened to her intuition. *Hated* Piero. They didn't get along from the jump, and now I realize she had some . . . some suspicions, deep ones, and we were fools to dismiss her."

Flinching, Rosalyn put the woman's arm back down and leaned in to get closer to Tuva's face again. It was partially to keep Misato from seeing her expression, or her reddening cheeks. She had always shied away from that word. *Survivor.* Running away from her entire life didn't feel like surviving, it felt like hiding.

"I'm no survivor," Rosalyn murmured.

Misato dropped it. "Did I miss anything?"

Rosalyn was about to pull her head away from the corpse when she glanced downward from that angle, noticing a slight distension in Tuva's midsection. As if lightly pushing on a balloon, Rosalyn palpated the stomach, a thin stream of air releasing from the mouth. A small indicator in the bottom-right corner of her AR display flashed, then became brighter, then enlarged itself so that it could not possibly be missed.

A warning.

"Cyanide gas." Rosalyn said it almost as a question.

"All bodies produce that," Misato began saying, but Rosalyn shook her head hard, running her eyes over the AR warning again and again.

"Not in this quantity, no way," Rosalyn told her. "That wouldn't make sense. Look at the body. I mean, I know she's Scandinavian and all that, but she shouldn't be this pale. Even in death, that color is unnatural."

"You think she was poisoned." Misato drew back from the body, putting both hands on her head before turning in a circle. "Where would Piero find a form of cyanide on the *Brigantine*?" She began arguing with herself, rapidly, pacing. "Tuva was bright. She would have smelled it, she would have . . ."

Rosalyn let her talk through the possibilities, only catching snippets of her rapid theorizing. Rosalyn retreated to what they absolutely knew, which wasn't much, but evidence always trumped conjecture. She interrupted Misato, who spun to face her, eyes glowing only faintly blue, as if the Foxfire had somewhat retreated.

"Brain tumor," Rosalyn blurted out. "You said everyone thought it was a brain tumor. Why?"

"Tuva suffered from debilitating headaches, shakes . . ." Misato explained, giving the dead woman a forlorn frown. "They worsened just before she died."

"Which would mean she probably took a lot of headache medicine. A lot of pills, a lot of capsules . . ." Rosalyn rolled along, feeling she was close to something, feeling as if the answer were lurking somewhere on the edge of her tongue. She shut her eyes tight and sighed. "The aquarium. When you tried to look in Piero's thoughts, you saw the aquarium. Why would you see that?"

Before Misato could answer, Rosalyn shoved the drawer shut, locking Tuva back inside. She reached for the older woman's wrist and hauled her toward the ladder and hatch that led out of what most MSC employees just called the dead drop. Every ship came equipped with a space to store anyone that happened to pass away on a mission. The temperature-controlled slots would preserve a corpse until the ship reached HQ and an investigation could be conducted. The hatch led up into the suit storage room, one that shared a wall with Edison's makeshift hideaway.

"The aquarium," Rosalyn said again, pulling Misato along once they were out of the hatch and plunging into the blue-tinged corridor.

"What about it?"

The story spinning into sense in her head had made her careless. Rosalyn pulled up short, but still ran headlong into Captain Aries. Edison blinked down at her, curious and oddly calm. *Probably doesn't want to spook me*, Rosalyn thought.

"You should get back to the decontamination lab," he said, his brows pulled down in concern. "Piero is up to no good."

"I know," Rosalyn replied, then gestured to Misato. "We know. Come on, you may as well come along."

"What?"

She didn't answer, pushing ahead to the corridor split, then taking a right. Her display helpfully brought up the ship schematic again, but she was learning her way around. They passed her lab space, then another fork, which she took a soft left on and brought them into the crew lounge area where Misato had woken her up not long ago. Everything was exactly as it had been, including the cups lined up on the counter. Rosalyn paused, taking in the room and then marching over to the aquarium.

There were often blanks in her memory, things that had washed themselves away out of desperation or protection. Her memories of the past had once been a solid, colorful painting, but now it was far more like a watercolor, parts faded or gone altogether. There were gaps, redactions, all over recent events. The drinking didn't help, she knew, but more than that, she could tell her mind was doing it to shield her. But now and then, small memories returned with crisp clarity.

She had cleaned Stanley's tank one last time, saying goodbye, hoping Saruti would do a good job with him. He would go live on her desk at work, occupying a space there while Rosalyn forfeited hers. That last time and every time she cleaned his tank, a familiar warning would pop up as she emptied the cleaning pellets into the water.

"Stanley," she breathed, staring up at the watery light of the aquarium.

"Who?" Misato asked. She and Edison joined Rosalyn, standing just a few inches behind.

"My pet," she said, confidence building. Striding over to the counter, she followed its edge until she reached the end, and the logical place for a trash bin. Kneeling, she reached in and plucked out a pill bottle. Shaking it, a few capsules rattled around inside.

"Tuva didn't have an AR implant," she continued, popping open the bottle and dumping out the remaining capsules. "If she had, it would have flashed up on mine when I examined her. Those things emit a weak signal for months, usually for memorial stuff. Which means . . ."

"She wouldn't have had any warning," Misato finished.

As soon as the capsule was in spitting distance of Rosalyn's visor, her display flashed another warning, this time detecting concentrated levels of cyanide.

"Stanley," she said, standing. "My pet fish. There's a form of cyanide in aquarium cleaner. It comes in powder or capsules."

Misato and Edison regarded each other for a long moment, silent.

"Son of a bitch," he finally muttered. "Misato, I should have listened to you."

"I knew it. I knew he did it." Misato turned away from them both, going to stand in front of the aquarium, her hands spreading across the ripples of light on the surface. "What did you find, Tuva? What did you know?"

"She must have had a bunk," Rosalyn said. "Personal items. Maybe there's something there that you missed. Just knowing that Piero poisoned her doesn't mean anything unless we know why. The Foxfire already has him; it's not like he's going to get a trial, right? We should take another look."

Edison's head jerked to the side suddenly and he put up his hand. "Yes, yes we should." Then, more softly to Misato, "He's coming."

"I sense him, too. He's angry."

Rosalyn tensed, dropping the pills back into the bin as Edison advanced toward her fast, grabbing her by the arm and dragging her toward the rear of the crew lounge before she could protest. There was a hatch past the freezer and food storage, one similar to the ladder that led down to the dead drop in the cold room. Edison pushed her toward it when she wouldn't move, and Rosalyn stumbled into the ladder's rungs, then took hold.

"Just climb, the rear bunks are up there. Tuva's things. Just climb, damn it."

Scrambling up the ladder, she heard the first signs of footsteps from outside in the corridor.

"Faster," Edison hissed. "She's coming."

22

"She?"

Edison stomped the hatch closed behind him, swiveling the manual lock into place with the toe of his boot. As he did so, a light flashed in front of his eyes. *Mother.* She—it—was learning him. Now whenever he felt her ghostly touch on his shoulder, he would turn to find his own mom staring back at him. She always wore the thin smile of a disappointed parent, her lips pursed, one hand on her hip, ready to ground him for not cleaning his room or taking out the trash.

"Mother," he said, lowering his voice. Piero and Misato would be just below them; they would have to keep quiet. Even if Piero sensed Edison there, and he would, he might not be able to make out their entire conversation. "The Foxfire appears to us as our mothers. It's a trick. A really, really fucked-up trick. But it . . . can work. That's how this thing gets to us."

"Sure," Rosalyn murmured, drifting farther into the bunk galley. To Edison, she appeared lost in her thoughts, moving down the line of bunks in her bulky suit on almost tiptoes. "You're all out in the middle of space, suddenly you start hearing things, things that sound like your own mother . . . It's the stuff of nightmares. Were you close with your mother?" Gazing around the room, she reached out to touch the surface of each bunk.

"Yeah, we were close," he said. "I was afraid of her, too. Military woman, and boy did she expect the best. When you made her happy she was sweet as pie, but let her down?" He whistled.

"I know it. My father was—is—the same way. Perfection or nothing. It's exhausting." She stopped suddenly, about halfway down the row, and spun to face him. Her dark eyes squinted at him, and she frowned. With her hair shaved off, it was impossible not to notice her immense, startling eyes. "Are you . . . all right? Are you going to attack me again?"

He saw her eyes dart around, probably for a weapon.

"You're safer with me than you are with Piero, and besides, I'd like to help you if I can." Edison stayed near the hatch, preparing to defend the way in if Piero decided to smash his way through again.

"Why?" she asked. "I imagine it would be easier to give in. Misato is fighting it hard. She wants to help me, too, but why you?"

"Because I'd like to stay human," he said with a chuckle. "I'd like to get rid of this. Be myself again. I don't know if it's possible, but we have to try."

"God. And that thing inside you is probably doing everything it can to sabotage that attempt." She sighed and pointed to the bunks. "I suppose this one is Tuva's? Why are the others empty?"

"There are a few bunk areas on the ship, but a small crew. Tuva liked the solitude."

"Good girl," he heard her mutter. "Misato was right. I would like her."

Edison watched her crouch in front of the one made-up bunk. The blankets and sheets were cleanly in place, pulled taut and precise. A military habit. Edison recognized it right away. Her trunk of personal items was pushed against the foot of the bunk, which seemed to levitate, though it was fixed at the head area to the wall, a neat little illusion of engineering. It provided more space underneath, but Tuva hadn't used it, apparently.

"It's unlocked," Rosalyn noticed, pulling open the trunk. "Isn't that unusual?"

"Tuva had this thing about lying and secrets. She thought being an open book was the most important thing in the world. I . . . didn't really get it."

"Enjoy lying, do you?" She glanced up, and her half smile told him she was teasing.

Muffled voices came through the floor below them, and he put a finger to his lips.

"Keep it down," he said.

The room was almost completely dark except for the blue glow of the Foxfire along the walls and the automatic light on Rosalyn's suit visor. She swayed a little, grabbing the trunk for support.

"Are you all right?" he asked softly.

"Just tired," she said. "And hungry. Is there another way out of here? We'll be trapped if . . ." And there she trailed off, busying herself with the trunk.

"He won't hurt Misato. At least . . . I don't think he will. Shit, I don't know, he does seem to be changing." Edison took a few steps deeper into the bunking area, but didn't want to get too close. He could only imagine what she thought of him after he had chased her through the ship. It felt like another person altogether had done that, but the flicker of fear in her eyes told him otherwise.

He didn't want to frighten her again, and he hardly trusted himself.

What are you waiting for, baby? You can help us all. Help your mother and rip open that silly suit. Rip it open. She can join us. You can give her bliss.

It never learned. Edison hummed to himself, as quietly as he could, pushing back the voice in his head. He imagined it like a boulder, halfway up a hill, his whole body braced against it, each note he sang forcing it back up bit by bit. The concerts he had gone to on the station always seemed to turn the tide. He wondered if that would change, if the thing inside him would get smarter and more dangerous. It seemed almost a guarantee that it would.

"I know that one," Rosalyn said idly, picking through Tuva's things. A small ball of string, a necklace, an old and cracked VIT chip. "The Late Nodes, right? My old salvaging partner was obsessed with them. The covers especially."

"Didn't mean to bother you. It just helps."

"I don't mind," she laughed, wry. "Just as long as it isn't the Unpronounceable Sound."

"Never. I would never, never do that to you," Edison said solemnly. That made her smirk and glance his way. Again, he was caught for an instant by her consuming eyes. "You're a music person?"

"Sometimes."

"Like what?" he asked, watching her study the broken VIT chip.

"Oh, mostly women screaming into the microphone. And Beethoven. I like Beethoven."

The voices below them grew louder and they both fell silent, listening. The floor was too thick to make out any distinct words, but Edison's head pounded, full of terrible noise. His face grew hot, and he shivered, feeling, seeing and hearing only flashes of the argument.

He wouldn't do that. You're lying. No, no, no! Listen to me, listen to me . . .

Then, just as quickly as it had come, the noise lessened and his head felt unusually empty. Stillness. Footsteps. The lounge below resonated with nothingness, and for a moment it was quiet except for the buzz of the engines and the FTL core. He yearned to hear a bird chirping or a siren, something, anything that would remind him of personal stillness on Earth. Now it was only that dull hum, a sound that he imagined might come from the center of the world.

"It wasn't Piero," he said finally. "It was Rayan. They're gone now. They were arguing; he doesn't want to believe what Piero did to Tuva."

"Why did you believe me?"

The question came quickly, but it cut through to him somehow. Edison stared at her, confused. "Why wouldn't I?"

"I don't know. You barely know me. You didn't believe Misato about Piero, about her suspicions that he was up to something and attacked Tuva," she pointed out. Reasonably, in his eyes.

"I should have believed her," Edison said. "That was a mistake."

"So why did you believe me, then?"

Edison sat on one of the bunks a few down from Tuva's. Leaning forward, he rested his wrists on his knees, still watching her. "Misato is fighting this, like you said. Staying connected to her seems to help me keep Mother at bay. The music helps. And . . . you help. Your humanity. Your youness. Foxfire still doesn't know what to do with you. I can't get this feeling out of my head that I know you somehow."

She laughed a little, then snorted. It was endearing, but Edison tried not to notice.

"What if I'm the last human you ever meet? God, that's a depressing thought," she muttered.

"I don't think so," he said. "I think you're—"

She coughed.

"Just fine," he finished.

Rosalyn's hands went still, and he couldn't help but wonder what she would be like out of the bulky suit. Tall, of course, that was obvious, and slender. But it was impossible to get the real make of a person when they were three inches deep in coated plastic. She cleared her throat, shifting, no longer keen to glance his way after that last comment. From where he sat, he could swear her cheeks had turned pink.

"Wait." Her entire body went rigid, her hands stopping along the bottom of the trunk. She picked at something there, then gasped. "A false bottom. I suppose Tuva wasn't totally against secrets, mm?"

"What is it?" Edison couldn't help but jump to his feet.

"Just . . . a worker's badge. It's been printed, extruded, like a copy." Rosalyn held it up for him to see. It was flat, about eight inches by five, with a photo, reflective scanning tag and company branding. The badge had been tucked into a clear plastic sleeve and attached to a black lanyard. "Danny Russo? His Merchantia file says Piero Endrizzi. Christ. Which one do you think is real?"

Edison joined her near the trunk, waiting until she offered the badge to take it.

"ISS?" He turned the thing over, but the badge didn't seem like anything special. "Incorporated Shipping Solutions. They're partnered with Merchantia now; they handle all of our biohazard and dangerous materials. Maybe it's just his old job."

"Then why the different name?" Rosalyn asked. "Look at the issuing date. That thing is current. ISS . . . Why does that sound so bloody familiar?" Standing, she snatched the badge back, pulling it up close to her visor for a look. Rosalyn pulled the badge out of its transparent sleeve, and a tiny slip of paper, no larger than her pinky nail, fell out. Crouching, she picked up the folded paper and carefully opened it up. It had been squashed into an accordion, but once she flattened it, she could see tiny, handwritten print.

"Anything interesting?" Edison asked, squinting over her shoulder.

"Numbers," she said. "Coordinates, maybe?"

She used her VIT monitor to scan the numbers. "I can't do a networked search, but I can at least run these against the downloaded MSC data on my VIT."

It didn't take long for a match to appear. They weren't coordinates at all, but dates.

"These are launches," Rosalyn breathed. "They're all in the MSC database, which means they're all our launches. Science vessel launches. For the *Quant*-7, and . . . that was Alexia Courtney's gig, and Reevey's command . . . These are the recent code blues. Entire ships that went dark under suspicious circumstances, and every single one of them left campus before Piero joined the *Brigantine*."

Edison whistled. "That doesn't sound good."

"And ISS handles biohazard deliveries? That can't be a coincidence. This must be what Tuva found, and why he had to kill her. It's the Foxfire, Edison, it has to be. He must have been handling it for ISS and brought it aboard for some reason."

Josh Girdy, the son of a bitch, was right. Someone had gone to considerable trouble to get Piero's tainted biohazard deliveries onto science vessels. But why?

"Shit," he muttered. "We need . . . we need to know more. This is heavy."

You know all you need to, baby. Why does it matter? You're with us now. You're with your cluster, your siblings, your mother . . .

"*Stop using her voice!*" He hadn't meant to shout, but it gnawed at him each and every time, hearing the horrid monster in his head use Diana's voice like that. Rosalyn's eyes could have swallowed him up for their size.

"She sounds just like my real mother," he whispered, pinching his forehead. "It's . . . not easy."

"Think about that song," Rosalyn said, humming a few off-key bars. "Or Misato. Or me."

He did. He did think about Rosalyn, breathing hard, seeing in those huge eyes the kind of sympathy he hadn't expected to find. Sliding the badge copy into her suit pocket, she swayed again, and, carefully, he put out a hand to steady her.

"Tired," she said. "Sorry."

"Don't be sorry, that's—" A series of red lights flashed above her visor, three tiny dots that lit up in sequence. "Bad. That's bad."

"Yes, it is," Rosalyn almost shrieked, putting both gloved hands over the bottom of her helmet, as if reaching for her mouth to gasp. "It's my filters. My clean oxygen. All these spores . . . They must be wreaking havoc on the filtration system. Oh God. *Oh God.* What do I do?"

Edison took hold of her more firmly, guiding her by the shoulders, turning her toward the ladder. His mind raced. One lone human on their ship and her only guarantee against the Foxfire was about to fail. He should've seen it coming. Damn it, he was the captain, after all; of course this level of air corruption would jam up a suit after this much exposure.

Captain, captain, captain, be the fucking captain.

"We . . . Shit. We find you new filters and hope like hell they're not already contaminated. We can get you back to the lab," he said, kicking open the hatch. "You'll be safe there, right? You can breathe there until I find new filters."

Rosalyn closed her eyes and reached for the ladder, her face turning pale behind the visor. "If you find new filters," she whispered, trembling. *"If."*

23

He expected suit storage, just next to where Edison made his home on the ship, to be empty, but he was not alone.

In the corridor, surrounded by the pulse-throbbing glow of the Foxfire nodules, Edison felt his own pulse jackhammer. In his heart he knew—knew—that what he was seeing was not real, but it made him stutter to a stop nonetheless. The door to his makeshift home was open, too, though it had been jammed closed for a long time. Rayan had tried to keep them all sequestered, and while Edison slept, and waited and stewed in his quarters alone to fight the Foxfire in his head, he came to the conclusion that the young scientist had bought them valuable time. Being apart like that seemed to make it easier to control the fight. Not win, of course, but maintain a shred of humanity while the Foxfire bled into his every thought.

And now it was bleeding over again, and badly.

Edison stopped just inside the suit storage door, watching, listening to his mother hum an old Earth tune. They were lucky to still have a house on Earth, given the state of things. GATE, the Global Alliance Technology Effort, had convinced the United States government to start evacuations. Resources were drying up. Floods. Quakes. Hurricanes. Only government and environment critical would be allowed to stay. Diana Aries had finagled a pass for them, her long service in the army granting them reprieve.

Their neighborhood gradually emptied out, but Diana stayed. Even when Edison took his own posting and left Earth, she stayed. Whenever he got back it was the same damn thing—homemade spaghetti and his mother singing to herself at the stove. Garlic and oregano filled the kitchen, filled the house, and he was a little kid again at heart, hiding in his room, knowing his mother would be furious when she found out he had broken his record player.

The vision in front of him in the suit storage room, of Diana at the stove, flickered. Oregano and garlic. Something about that smell, all over him now, seemed to disrupt the illusion. But then it strengthened again, and oddly, the room filled with the smell of citrus. When he took one more step inside, she turned.

Oh. This day. *That* memory.

Diana dropped the stirring spoon at the sight of him.

"Surprise," he said with a chuckle, but the spoon, messy with tomato sauce, hit the floor. Edison rushed to pick it up, burning himself. He swore and looked for a rag to wipe up the stain on the floor.

"That's all right, baby," she said. "These hands aren't so sure these days."

"Let me help. I've got you."

Edison rinsed the spoon, stood with her at the stove. He noticed the tremor in his hand was in hers, too. His had started with the Foxfire, but hers?

"You got any good news for me? What about that promotion you were sniffing out . . ."

"No, ma'am," Edison said, shrinking.

"Next time, then. Next time." Her fingers went stiff, and she fumbled for the spoon.

"You all right?" he asked. His demeanor always changed around her. Edison could relax, take off the military man, just slide into home. The vanishing accent of her roots crept into his voice, a tiny flicker of Atlanta.

"I'm just fine, baby. Just fine."

Edison saw her hand flex before the spoon dropped again, but this time he caught it.

"What's going on?" he asked. "Why no hug?"

"Of course I would hug you," Diana whispered. "I just don't want you to feel how brittle these bones have become."

Edison felt the memory flicker around him. At his side, his mother stirred nothing, just a wooden spoon going around and around on top of a stack of dirty environmental suits. She was blue, all blue, made of glowing turquoise starlight.

"It's in my bones, in the marrow," she told him, gruff. "The cancer. I'm gonna feed you and then we're gonna sit for a long time."

"There are options." The words came out too fast, like a reflex.

"No options but one," she said. Diana put down the spoon and shook her head. "I know you aren't going to take clean filters out of here. I know you won't do that to me."

Edison froze. The spoon was gone. The scent of garlic and oregano vanished, leaving him in the rubber and antiseptic stink of the storage room. He backed away from her, from his faintly glowing mother.

"Baby, listen to me. You can still win her over. She's pretty, right? You like her? That's just fine. You win her over. Just pick up the filter, air it out a little, then give it to her. She won't know the difference and then she can be with us. Be with *you*."

"I can't do that, Mom. I can't." Edison backed away until he rammed into the closed closet behind him. Wincing, he stumbled to his left, his head exploding in pain. He wondered if that was how Tuva had suffered before the end, when her brain felt like it was being lanced with fiery needles.

The captain. Be the captain.

Edison scrambled across the room, to the low bank of plastic shelves bolted into the wall. Several labeled bins held the accessories needed for suit maintenance, including emergency patches, extra gloves, shoe covers and visors, as well as a bin specifically for the new, sealed oxygen filters. He smacked the bin open, reaching in to find their stock was low. Dangerously low. He thought immediately of Piero. Had he tried to sabotage the filters? If so, he had missed two. *Two.* He had no idea how long those would last Rosalyn, but it would just have to suffice.

Listen to me.

The voice was right next to his ear, shrieking, still his mother's voice but twisted and rising, higher and higher, as she closed in on him. Before it had been a tender hand and a whispered song, but now it was madness.

Baby? Baby? Listen to me. Listen to me!

He ran, scattering the other bins to the floor as he fled the room. The sealed filters were jammed under his arm, removing the temptation to scratch at them while his mother's furious voice chased him down the corridor and to the barrier, where Rosalyn waited.

The moment he saw her, the voice cut out.

Silence. Nothing. Just the normal hum of the ship and the muffled sounds of Rosalyn puttering around in the lab. She hadn't noticed him there, and he commanded his pulse to slow, his breath to ease . . . Their alliance was already on thin ice; the last thing he needed was for her to see him gasping and wheezing with terror.

The whole place was a mess, the ceiling panel ripped open, some kind of schematic of hers drawn on the wall in black marker, tubes, wires and hoses hanging down like so many loose guts. No, not a schematic of hers, but one belonging to the genius mind of Misato Iwasa. *Just a simple airflow bypass system using a reversing valve.* It was a bleed from Misato, their connection through the cluster giving him flashes of the engineer's knowledge.

A freestanding atomizer near the kitchenette puffed out a constant stream so thick Rosalyn looked like a mad scientist in some alchemy dungeon. She had pulled one of the safety respirators from Rayan's research lab, the straps dangling down her back, and they swung freely as she stood on a chair, trying and failing to screw together two hoses with a connector.

Glancing past her legs at the schematic, he cleared his throat and tapped lightly on the clear shield separating them.

"That would go a lot faster with a multi-tool. There should be one there," he said, pointing to the kitchenette. He had startled her, and she wobbled on the chair, spinning too fast and nearly toppling to the floor. Rosalyn caught herself, holding tight to one of the hoses dangling out of the ceiling, then nimbly leapt down to the floor.

"Bottom drawer," he added. "Sorry for surprising you. I've got the filters."

"You knocked, thank you." Rosalyn smiled, as if that small courtesy meant everything. "How many did you find?" Then she pointed vaguely upward as she went to the drawer he had indicated, kneeling. "Did you notice? The hail Piero sent stopped."

"Two," he said with a sigh, and waited until she lowered the barrier and he could shove them through quickly. Rosalyn took them immediately to the decontamination pod. "The damage is done. Even a round or two of that hail will draw attention. I don't need to tell you what that means."

"I don't know what you think I can do about it," she said, her voice muffled and mechanical in the respirator. She had found the multi-tool and snapped it open, climbing back up on her chair to work on the connector again. "Can't unpluck a chicken."

"You can't turn shit into sunshine, but we can hope they don't notice the signal," he said.

Rosalyn froze, her huge eyes turning on him. "Where did you learn that saying?"

"I don't know, just . . . somewhere. Why?" Now that he thought about it, he couldn't remember saying it until very recently. Maybe it had bled over from one of the other crew members.

Her gaze drifted away from him and she shrugged, but something was clearly wrong. "It's nothing. Never mind."

Nodding, he leaned against the door frame, stroking his chin thoughtfully again. She had a stronger build than he expected, the tight thermal tee under the environmental suit showing an athlete's body, muscled shoulders tapering down to a narrow waist. A swimmer's frame, maybe. The bubbled visor of the helmet had distorted her face, and while the respirator covered her mouth and chin, he was surprised by how delicately defined her nose and brow were. Her voice and posture screamed prep school, maybe even one with a GATE endowment. She had the lightly accented, almost British voice of someone educated abroad and at incredible expense. It contrasted hilariously, nicely, with her now-unkempt, half-jumpsuited appearance, like a trustee turned junker.

"Maybe we could just beam out some Unpronounceable Sound. That would keep everyone away," Edison teased.

"Don't be cute," she muttered.

"Okay, no cute. How about curious?" Edison asked. "What's this project of yours?"

"I need a place to eat and bathe, so Misato gave me some ideas for rigging up a kind of decontamination chamber. The diffuser spits out oregano and melaleuca oil to kill off any rogue spores. I'll have to put my suit on before I leave, of course, but it's something." Rosalyn trailed off and looked at him again, one hand landing on her cocked hip. "Thank you again, by the way, for the filters."

"You're welcome," Edison replied. "I'll, um, I'll try to find more. Just . . . thought I oughtta hurry. Listen, I know you probably want me to get lost so you can sleep, but I think we should talk."

"That sounds ominous," she said, jumping down from the chair. Closing up the multi-tool, she slipped it into her cargo pants and grabbed a food pouch from the kitchenette counter. The room only became mistier as the hose system she had finagled kicked in, one of the open tubes hissing softly as it released some kind of gas.

Rosalyn pulled the respirator down and ripped open the food pouch, squirting it efficiently into her mouth. Sweet potato. He hated the stuff but it got the job done.

"You sure it's safe?" he asked, nodding toward the mask.

"AR display says the only foreign traces are on those filter packs you gave me, but with the respirator on I should be safe. I'm already decontaminating them. Afterward, I can crack the seal," Rosalyn said. She ripped open another food pouch and dispatched it just as readily. "I added Foxfire's composition to my atmospheric app; it tracks the air quality for me."

"Smart."

"Just practical," she deflected, mouth still full of mush. "So what are we talking about?"

Edison inhaled deeply, forgetting that he hadn't quite formulated his question yet. The corridor around him was dark, the crew having adjusted to the low emergency lighting to the point where it was more comfortable to exist in semidarkness. He wondered if the Foxfire was making them sensitive to the light.

I can help you see so much more, baby. Trust your mother, trust me . . .

No. He swore once under his breath and then began to hum, quickly, almost frantically, closing his eyes and filling his head with the song. Not now, not now . . . He didn't care how nuts it looked; he needed his bulwark against the encroaching corruption.

"Don't go haywire on me," Rosalyn pleaded. "Should I sing, too?"

"No. I won't," he promised, snapping his eyes open to see her there, lovely but afraid in the fog. She had moved closer to the barrier, her knuckles white around the empty food packet in her hand. "I won't do that ever again."

"Ha. And don't make promises you can't keep." Rosalyn tossed the packet over her shoulder. "I scrounged up a hell of a lot of food packets. Maybe I'll just wait this out. Even mushrooms need to eat."

"Yes," Edison replied flatly. Coldly. "Us."

She glanced away.

"Is that really what you want? Because that hail is going to bring more ships, which means more victims or it means we all die. I don't think they'll discriminate, do you?" Edison hadn't meant for it to sound so cruel. "And besides, I thought we were starting to get along."

Rosalyn bit her lower lip, avoiding his eyes. "Maybe. Look, about before—in engineering—I thought it was the best way to end this. Quick. Painless."

"You don't have to apologize. We all get it."

That drew her head up, both of her brows rising. "I wasn't going to apologize for being cornered, but I am sorry for what's happening to you."

Edison wasn't surprised by her frankness or wounded by it; he could hardly expect her to be unfailingly sympathetic when he had nearly hurt her. And it was nice, if awkward, to *talk* to someone. Someone with human eyes.

"You can't imagine what it's like," he told her in a hushed voice.

"To have something take control of you like this. To feel this powerless."

"Yes," Rosalyn said, just as softly. "I can."

He frowned and tried to think of the right thing to say but she cut him off, tossing her nonexistent hair back and sucking in her cheeks. "I know what it feels like, and I'm sorry. You didn't ask for any of this to happen, and it's certainly not your fault."

"I'm sorry, too," Edison said. "Yeah . . ." He still felt unbalanced by her response. She knew. Right. Of course. He scrambled to come up with that goddamned question. Any way he phrased it she would be put off, so he decided to just be direct and hope for the best. They were running out of options. And time. They had a day at the most, he figured, before the Merchantia ships turned up to investigate, maybe far less if someone in the area was redirected to their coordinates. At the risk of sounding insensitive, he blundered on.

"So, all right. Well. There's no polite way to say this, I guess, but I think you and I need to make a deal. Or a promise. No, a deal."

Her face relaxed a little, full lips quirking to the side. "A deal?"

"We can't be here when those ships arrive, it's too unpredictable, and I think we both would like to avoid more people getting contaminated with this bullshit. But without access to the thruster controls, we're just sitting ducks. We need our scanners back on, the piloting mode fully engaged, and then we need to get the hell out of here." *At least it came out coherent*, he thought, watching her mood darken by the word.

"We've been over this," Rosalyn spat. "I'm not giving you my credentials."

"And instead?" He gestured broadly. "Look around! *We're running out of options.* If we just sit here, we're as good as a baited trap. More ships will come, and there's no guarantee I can control the crew long enough for you to warn them and escape. Things are getting worse. You can't see inside our heads, but trust me, it's worse."

"That's not a deal," she said.

"What?"

She rolled her eyes and marched up to the clear barrier, poking it as if to poke his chest. "Let's say I play along, mm? You get my credentials and we avoid the Merchantia ships. Then what? That's only benefiting me so far, and a deal by definition cuts both ways."

Damn. Edison ground his teeth together, wishing she hadn't caught on. It would be simpler to explain later. Simpler, but meaner.

"Fine. Fine. I want to go back to CDAS and make sure they didn't accidentally run into Foxfire like we did. If we took all of it and nobody else is infected? Then *fantastic*. Great. We can part ways. You get dropped off at the station and you can report the contamination, get us quarantined and shipped off to be studied or whatever else. I just cannot—*cannot*—live with myself knowing I had the chance to do something and didn't." Edison turned away from the glass, pacing, removing his spectacles to find that when he rubbed his eyes, tears had formed there. Why wouldn't she listen? She had to listen. This went so far beyond them only a selfish idiot would refuse to take action.

"It's my job," he added quietly. "I'm the captain. It's my duty to protect people. I failed to do it with my crew, but I won't fail you and I won't fail the rest of goddamned humanity."

He waited and waited, convinced she would refuse him again. She appeared to be listening, really listening, and maybe even softening up. Then he felt a tender hand on the back of his neck. He shivered.

We can fix that, baby. Give her bliss. Give her our gift. She can refuse nothing if she's one of us. Let her join the cluster. Be kind to her. Be generous.

"Agh."

Edison grabbed his head, squeezing his temples, falling back against the shield from the sudden blast of pain in his skull. Vaguely, he heard Rosalyn tapping on the other side of the barrier.

"Edison? Edison?!"

That helped. Her voice seemed to call him back, though the sizzling in his brain lingered as he righted himself, wincing.

"I'm all right . . . I'm fine."

"Oh, thank God." She sighed and took a step back from the barrier. It was her turn to pace. "If we're going to do this, then you need to promise me you'll do whatever you can to keep the Foxfire from taking control. Understand?"

"Yeah, obviously, I'm not a fan of it, either."

"This is serious," Rosalyn chided. She was pacing faster, working up to something, her hands rubbing together as if they were numb with cold. "I need to trust you, even though you're all *brainwashed*. And you need to trust me, even though I tried to blow us all to hell."

He had to give a wry snort at that. "What a pair."

"Well?"

"An alliance of convenience," Edison agreed. "I'm in. Misato will help. She likes you, and she hardly likes anyone."

She gave one sharp nod. "All right. Jesus, okay . . . How do we know which shipments or whatever have the Foxfire? If those launch dates we found with Piero's badge are correct, then he could have delivered Foxfire to other ships. Whatever he gave to Captain Reevey made him go mad and murder his crew, but I didn't see any bodies on that ship that reminded me of Foxfire symptoms."

Down to business. Edison appreciated that, and it was something to keep his focus. If his mind was too unoccupied, too free, then the Foxfire had a way of creeping in and exploiting that idleness.

"Rayan never incinerated the sample crates we picked up on CDAS, so we still have the serial numbers, the labels, everything. Maybe we can run a full search of any shipments coming or going to see if there are more samples on the station," Edison explained, his eyes tracing her path back and forth across the room. "We have the badge Tuva found and those dates, too. ISS will have their own docking bay. If we find those same delivery dates in their system, then we have proof it wasn't just Piero working on his own."

"And if we can lock down the cockpit, I can send a message to HQ, tell them the situation and make sure they don't intercept us without a full quarantine crew ready." Rosalyn picked up his idea as fluidly as if it were her own. "And . . . and . . . we can get a call to CDAS, have them run a scan of their inventory before we even get close. Hell, I mean, we could even link up with the *Salvager*, get us all aboard and just tell MSC to annihilate the *Brigantine*."

Edison snagged on that, making a face. "No . . . too risky. If any part of the Foxfire survived the blast, it could just be picked up by a junker."

"Damn, all right, fair point." At last she quit pacing, standing near the chair under the exposed wiring and hoses of the ceiling. He almost didn't notice. Something was wrong. There was an abrupt absence in his thoughts, a space where none had been before, like a bulb going out in the night.

He tilted his head to the side, trying to chase that feeling. What was missing?

"Edison? Hey. Hey? Everything okay?"

"No," he breathed. He risked it, letting the line between his thoughts and Mother's blur until the whole connective tissue of the Foxfire network spread out around him, the growth becoming thick veins, redolent with life and sight. The veins were not as obvious as his fellow crewmates, Misato back in her quarters, Rayan moving about the lab, both bodies vivid and blue, limned in light. An image flashed across his brain, incomplete and hazy. A starched white collar, a smudge of something dark pink. Lipstick.

You can't see your sibling, can you, baby? Where did he go? Find him.

Edison shuddered, his mother's voice shimmering through his head, her touch feathering across his shoulder again. She was right. Piero was nowhere to be found, no longer a weak signal on the periphery but a void altogether.

"Where is he?" he whispered aloud. "Piero . . . It's like he's vanished."

"What?" Rosalyn joined him at the barrier again, both of her palms pressed against it. "What's wrong?"

"I can't sense Piero. The others are right there but . . . I can't . . . I can't feel him anywhere. I saw something from him, a fragment of a memory maybe, just a smudge of lipstick on someone's collar. *Shit.* It doesn't make any sense. I can always feel them, just distantly. Always."

She sounded incredulous. "How is that possible? Can't you feel each other through the network?"

"Yes." Edison scrunched his eyes shut and then opened them. "I don't know. In engineering he completely lost it. I think he's stopped trying to fight the Foxfire. You didn't see it but . . . God, it was insane. M-Maybe she's shielding him, shielding him and punishing us."

Her eyes were huge and liquid, reflecting his own terrified turquoise stare. He didn't know what to say to reassure her. He didn't know what to say to reassure himself.

"Punishing you? Punishing you for what?" she wondered.

Edison didn't look away from her, even if he wanted to shrivel up and hide from what he had to say. "For this," he told her. "For you."

24

Rayan was saying goodbye.

There were many things he still ached to do, but a goodbye seemed the best. The fire in the solar panel array had shocked him out of something, out of a deep and deceptive well of optimism that had kept his cruelest, darkest fears at bay. The salvaging crew arriving had been like a shaft of light piercing a leaden sky, but now he saw that beam of light for what it really was—a scouring flame. The lick of flames on startled skin before the real burning began.

All of his hard work lay before him. Not all of his work, but all of his work relevant to Foxfire. He had been the one to name it that, and it took. Oddly, he felt a pang of pride knowing even the alien consciousness inside him had also adopted the name.

Foxfire, then Mother.

It was from a phenomenon well known on Earth, bioluminescent fungus that grew on decaying wood. Sometimes the more whimsical called it fairy fire, but that didn't seem right. No, *Foxfire* sounded appropriately volatile. Aggressive. This was no fantastical forest of dancing lights, but a slow descent into a separation of self, the ripping of the identity from the mind. His research had led him to find that this bioluminescence was the closest known thing to the molecular structure of what now infested the *Brigantine* and her crew.

Earth. The thought of it made him want to grieve. He had only experienced it at the state-of-the-art virtual reality Dome on Tokyo Bliss Station, spending hours and hours wandering through re-created stages of Earth's history. He liked the 1980s best, a far, far distant time of new tech and synthesizers and cocaine. Parts of Tokyo Bliss Station reflected those neon sensibilities, the arcade district in particular, so maybe that was what made it all feel like home.

Sometimes he got nauseated from being in the VR for too long. It often gave him vertigo, but it was worth it. He visited his parents' hometown, but only when it was still thriving and lively. If he closed his eyes and concentrated, he could still see the sunset making a riot of the mosaic tiles on the Wazir Khan Mosque. Once, he invited his mother to come along and experience it with him, but she wouldn't or couldn't.

"It was hard enough to leave," she told him. "It would kill me to go back."

For a while the virtual insides of that place had been his talisman against the Foxfire. He would fetch his mother's prayer rug from his locker, kneel and go there, really go there, sit and listen to the chanting and find temporary reprieve.

He kept the rug close by while he studied the Foxfire samples he had collected from himself and the others and the interior of the ship. Of course, there were pure samples from the contaminated crate they picked up from CDAS, but he wanted variety. A broad sampling might let him see tiny changes, and track if the cellular structure changed once the fungus interacted with human tissue.

Like many of the experiments he had done in his life, the results thrilled and terrified him. Never had he come across a compound that spread this rapidly. Fungus could not self-replicate, but somehow this substance grew out of control, colonizing at a rate that was dizzying to observe. A part of him admired its elegance, its efficiency, an almost self-sustaining system that, when viewed under a high-powered microscope, appeared beautifully symmetrical. Even engineered. No, that was a ridiculous idea. Nature and evolution were profoundly startling, and it was egotism to think humans were responsible for this. He had made himself the most unique test subject in a moment of panic, the voices in his head, ones he couldn't explain or stop, driving him to self-harm. During vanishing moments of sleep, he could still feel the cold bite of the ship's plating as he slammed his head into it again and again.

So verily, with the hardship, there is relief, verily with the hardship there is relief.

His mother had given him a small handkerchief with that phrase from the Quran. It was just threads in his pocket now, loved to near nothingness. This, he thought, was also an act of love, taking every scrap of information he had collected, compiling every gleaned observation and laying it all out for someone healthier to understand.

"Your curiosity makes you a good scientist," his dissertation advisor, Dr. Marcel Kio, had told him at a department party. "Your innocence makes you an outstanding one."

Innocence, Kio had gone on to say, was hard to find and even harder to preserve. An innocent mind allowed for all possibilities, especially the ones a more cynical person might discard.

"I've never heard you say the words 'that's impossible' and that's . . . well, usually impossible," Kio added. Probably a little drunk.

Rayan didn't drink, but now he half wished he did. This whole process might be easier if he could take the edge off. But this had to be done. He wasn't giving up; he was assessing all available data and coming to the most accurate conclusion: He was losing this fight, faster than he had hoped, faster than predicted, and all the innocence and optimism in the world couldn't change that.

One had to go where the data led, and the data led him here, to this drafting table with the sum total of his work. It would be impenetrable for most people, but if the *Brigantine* was found and quarantined and studied, then someone at HQ would find it useful. It was, at least, a record of what had happened and proof that they hadn't gone down without a fight.

He winced. He didn't want to fight with his crewmates. Whatever had happened between him and Piero in the past felt like ancient history. Space was lonely, Piero was so . . . odd. And confident. Maybe he ought to regret it, but that seemed silly now. At the very least, the other man never made him feel discarded; all the parameters had been decided up front.

You're such a beautiful boy, Piero had told him. Nobody had ever called Rayan beautiful before. Cute? Sure. Sweet? Definitely. Beautiful was different. When he closed his eyes and breathed in *beautiful*, it felt like walking through the peaceful, reverberating halls of Wazir Khan.

A rare, sweet memory that had been all but obliterated by Piero's swift and mean descent, Rayan mused. His official task was done. The record was straightened and set. There was a blank space on the right side of the drafting table, and he ran his palm over it and thought. He retreated to his locker across the room in the lab. They weren't allowed many personal effects, just enough to keep homesickness at bay, so Rayan pulled out anything of his that held sentimental value, and returned to his monument.

Gently, he folded his mother's prayer rug and laid it on the blank space. On top he placed the printed photo of him and his brothers. Before his AR chip was fried, a holographic display would leap out of it, and his oldest brother Ehsan's hand would appear behind his head with rabbit ears. They had gone on vacation to Xi'an Station, just the four of them, learning to surf at the wave pools and watching artificial sunsets beamed live from the remnants of Navagio Beach.

Ehsan had gotten fall-down drunk and proposed to a waitress at one of the floating bars, but neither of his brothers snitched. Smirking, Rayan would put his forefinger on Ehsan's face. That waitress still sent the occasional poke over VIT Chat.

He pulled the shreds of handkerchief from his cargo pocket and laid them reverently next to the photo.

So verily, with the hardship, there is relief, verily with the hardship there is relief.

Last, he put down a handwritten Valentine's Day card from his first and only girlfriend, Maya. They had met in undergrad, then dated on and off until Rayan got serious about his dissertation and things evaporated. Even Rayan's mother begrudgingly liked Maya. She was short and plump and always wore dresses that would be hip six months in the future.

"Everything but her eyeballs is pierced," his mother had complained. But nobody could resist Maya's crooked smile.

To my perfect cinnamon roll: You're going to crush this shit. See you on the other side.

Maya had gone into chemical engineering. Both of them were born and raised on Tokyo Bliss, and when they were still furtively bringing up marriage, they both wanted to have the ceremony on Earth. Something so serious, so important, should be done on solid ground, they both agreed, even if it would cost a small fortune and take months to get clearance.

He heard a footstep behind him at the entrance to the lab. That was strange. He usually sensed anyone coming before they arrived. That narrowed down his visitor nicely.

"Rosalyn?" he asked, turning and finding himself face to chest with Piero. "*Oh.* What did you . . . what did you *do* to yourself?"

Rayan wasn't foolish enough to think his own grievous flesh wound, covered in a protective layer of Foxfire growth, was anything pretty to look at, but this was something different. Something ghastly.

Piero's skin hung off his face and neck in chunks, pulsing blue light spearing out from between the tears. There was almost no flesh left around his eyes, making them protrude, bulbous and unnatural.

But his old friend—his old *lover*—smiled. His teeth looked whiter and more threatening with no lips to define the grin. "It's only flesh. Flesh is not really part of us. The cluster, the connection, we're her children and we should reflect her."

Rayan swallowed with difficulty, choking back the urge to vomit.

"Am I speaking to Piero?" he whispered.

"Yes."

Rayan sighed. "Am I speaking t-to Mother?"

"Yes."

He was cornered against the drafting table and all of his hard work. Piero inched closer, already crowding him uncomfortably but now actively pressing Rayan's lower back into the lip of the table. The academic side of him had wondered what full integration with the Foxfire would look like, though perhaps his innocent curiosity meant he lacked the capacity to imagine this outcome. It was more terrible than he expected, and now he wished he didn't know the answer to his silent question.

"So this is what will happen to me," Rayan mused, trembling. His eyes bubbled with tears, every new rent discovered on Piero's face making him feel more powerless with grief. "This is what the end looks like."

Piero, or the Foxfire taking his form, tilted his head to the side. His expression grew blank and then puzzled. The connection he had lost to Piero now blazed, and he felt overwhelmed by the hurt and confusion radiating through their shared network.

His eyes were the same turquoise blue, but a dazzling white core stared out from each, a dollop of liquid mercury shimmer.

"I called you beautiful," Piero said in a voice unnervingly mingled with a woman's. "Am I not beautiful, too?"

"Don't do that," Rayan said, pushing against his chest with both hands. It was pointless. Piero was bigger and stronger, and they both knew the corruption dulled pain. Fully integrated, he probably felt invincible. "Don't. Don't use something good between us against me now. It isn't fair. You didn't call me beautiful, Mother, Piero the man did."

"Fair." Piero tried out the word as if tasting a new and perplexing flavor. "I see."

"No, you don't see." Rayan sighed and beat his fists on Piero's chest again. The other man took hold of his wrists, squeezing until Rayan saw stars. "You don't get it because you're not one of us. A human. Those memories are special. They're not weapons. Do you hear me? They're not weapons."

He stopped fighting, feeling light-headed and disoriented. The familiar pulsing headache began at the base of his skull and he moaned. *No, not like this. I wanted to be in control of when it happened.*

We are in control together, dear one.

It was the voice of his mother, soft, sweet, flowing seamlessly in and out of Punjabi.

Why not join us? Why not be a true child and a true sibling? Struggling, struggling, struggling, and for what?

"Stop that," Rayan whispered weakly. "I don't want to talk with our minds. I hate that."

"Everything in your mind is a weapon," Piero said aloud, humoring him. "Every thought, every memory, every delight, every sorrow is a weapon she will use until she gains control. It's painful, Ray, I know, but it can end."

The table bit deeper into his spine and he winced, falling back against it, his elbow landing on the prayer rug he had folded there. One touch of softness, like a pleasant memory, the remembrance of a tiny joy long past and almost forgotten. The rug. The mosque. His talisman. Rayan reached for those hours upon hours in the VR Dome as a reflex, guessing it was fruitless but thinking that it mattered to fight all the same. Exhausted, run-down, he felt the temptation to surrender as it rose and crashed over him. But it was important to fight.

Fight back. That was the little tattoo on Tuva's wrist; she had told him so, reluctantly. Fight back. He missed her, even if she never seemed to like him very much and her weird food stank up the lounge.

"What is this?" Piero had at last noticed what was fixed to the drafting table. He leaned down, his head looming over Rayan's shoulder. Confusion. Amusement. Rayan now felt the other man's emotions as if they were his own, and the whiplash of it was nauseating. Tiring. He was so tired of fighting, but the fighting mattered. His memories of the mosque were fading, disintegrating in front of his eyes as if burned away, one tile an ember that floated away, one window a bit of ash there and then charred beyond recognition.

She's learning, Rayan thought. *Not just learning but adapting.* The biologist in him couldn't resist asking Piero, "How did she get you in the end?"

Their eyes met, and for a brief instant the blue grew more

powerful, bleeding over the white pupil. But it was just a flicker, and Piero's lipless mouth drew down into a ragged grimace, more drooping hole than human mouth.

"You'll soon know. Can't you feel it? She's so close. She's felt even closer since the salvager came. There's something about her . . . Mother will be stronger when the cluster has her, and we'll have her soon."

"Shut up about that crap for one minute," Rayan said, irritated and angry. "We've all been resisting somehow. Yeah, it's been getting harder but still . . . It felt like something I could maybe win over or, I don't know, delay. What did it?"

The Foxfire considered him through Piero's glittering eyes for a long moment. It was hard not to flinch away from his horrible face, but Rayan steadied himself. He wanted to know this one thing, because maybe if he knew, there was still a way to hold on. Yes, he had been ready to say goodbye, preparing for it, but if there was a chance . . . if there was a chance, however miniscule . . .

"What do you hate?"

Rayan blinked. "Hate? I d–don't know, not much. It's not healthy to hold grudges."

Again Piero fell silent and again he considered Rayan, studying him, and he sensed an odd force tugging at his brain. An invasion. The Foxfire was searching for answers and it hurt, more than a headache, a needling, precise pain that blossomed over his right eye and spread.

"*Shit!* What are you doing?" Rayan tried to reach for his head but he was pinned to the table, able only to flail and groan with pain.

"There. Obvious but poetic. I can't believe she didn't find it sooner."

His vision frayed at the edges, spots and spangles blotting out his sight, more and more, like raindrops collecting on a windowpane until everything was blurred. The sensation in his head was incredible, white-hot, lancing agony that made him finally go boneless. He would have collapsed to the floor if Piero weren't keeping him upright against the table.

"Ignorance. You hate ignorance." Piero was nodding, but he could only see it vaguely. He hadn't expected the transition to hurt this much. Stupidly, he had assumed it would be gentle, just a gradual sinking into darkness. A fade to black. Rayan couldn't see at all then, but he felt Piero's breath on his face, warm and loamy.

"This is the key that fits any lock . . ." His voice sounded far away, trapped behind the wall of pain and muffled by it. "She's found it, what you hate, and what you hate makes you vulnerable. Now unlock for her and the pain will stop. The pain will end and you'll join the family."

25

"Then we just need Piero to leave the cockpit, and—hey. *Hey.* Are you falling asleep on me?"

"Son of a bitch, sorry." Rosalyn shook herself awake, sitting cross-legged with her back to a chair. There was no missing the deep blue smudges under her eyes, or the way her limbs sagged toward the floor.

"I haven't really slept," she added, glancing at her VIT. "In forty-eight hours. No wonder I'm agreeing to this insane plan."

Edison shook his head, crouching down on the other side of the barrier. The diffuser cycle had switched, and now only a light vapor hung in the cold storage chamber. He wondered what would happen if the shield dropped and all that fog rolled out to him. Nothing good. Every treatment Rayan and Misato came up with only made them sick as hell and weak, which probably only made Mother Foxfire happier. A compromised immune system was a party for viruses; he could only imagine what it meant for the Foxfire.

"I know you're exhausted," he said, tilting his head to the side. She pulled her knees up to her chest and stuffed a yawn behind her fist. "But that doesn't mean my plan can't work."

"Mm. Yes," she mumbled absently. "Very achievable."

"I'm gonna remember that you get real agreeable when you're exhausted."

Rosalyn narrowed her eyes, hugging her knees. "Agreeable can turn into horrifically grumpy, just you wait. And anyway I'm not much of a partner in this endeavor if I'm asleep on my feet." Her eyes closed slowly, as if completely beyond her control. "I can't sleep now. Not with Piero going completely AWOL like that. It creeps me out. You I sort of trust. Him? Nope."

Edison didn't know if he ought to tell her, but if this partnership was going to work, then honesty would be key. Frowning, he slid to the floor completely, sitting across from her with his hands resting on his ankles. "Rayan is missing, too."

"What?"

"I know. Well, shit, no, I *don't* know. I don't know what it means, Rosalyn." The hairs on his arms stood up and he patted them down nervously. "It just happened. He was in the lab, I could sense him there, now he's . . . just gone. It's like Foxfire disappeared him. Swallowed him."

Her eyes were wide open now. "This is going to sound really cruel, but do you think . . . do you think it means they died or something? What if this stuff doesn't want to control you but kill you?"

"That should scare me but it doesn't." Edison leaned his head against the barrier and sighed. He felt weary, too, though his body tended to resist sleep. The dreams he had lately were terrifying, nothing like the nightmares he experienced in the past. The worst part was that he knew why the dreams frightened him so much— they weren't his dreams at all, but the thing inside him going into fitful rest, showing him a glimpse of its unconscious thoughts.

He shuddered just remembering it. "This thing is too virulent. It wants to spread. Killing my whole crew wouldn't accomplish that."

"I suppose," Rosalyn granted him. She looked more alert,

slightly panicked, her hazel eyes scanning the hall behind him. "But the spores are in the air. It just takes exposure, right? If those Merchantia ships turn up, the situation kind of takes care of itself."

"No. They'll be suited up like you are. You're lucky Rayan met you at the cockpit. If it was Piero, he would've gone straight for your visor."

Now it was her turn to shiver. "What an image."

"Sorry."

"No, it's fine, you're right." Rosalyn shrugged, trying to conceal another long, long yawn. She stretched like a cat, and it was kind of cute, he thought. *No. Not helpful.* It was bad enough that she was prettyish, not his type, but maybe his type was changing. *Or maybe the Foxfire is changing you.*

"What?" he heard her say, and he coughed.

"What what?"

She rolled her eyes at him, which was becoming routine. "Your eyes went all soft focus. Don't tell me we're both falling asleep. Kiss your sweet plan goodbye."

"It's not that," Edison said, flailing for a distraction. He found one, but it didn't exactly put him off that dangerous path. "I was just wondering . . . your AR bio is blank."

"So is yours," she shot back ruefully. "Are you chatting me up to keep me awake?"

"Maybe. Is it working?" Edison smirked, then pulled his head back from the barrier. It had knocked his glasses askew so he fixed them. "Besides, what should my AR profile say? 'Infected with alien fungus. Lost in space. Probably gonna die soon. Dogs, jazz, single malt.'"

"You're a dog person?" she asked, laughing softly.

"Yeah. Is there any other kind?"

"Uh-huh, cat people, and they are completely terrible."

"Amen to that." Edison high-fived the glass and had to chuckle as she air-fived him back.

She rocked back and forth a little as if in thought, then pulled the chair behind her around and made a pillow out of her arms, laying her head on it. "I'm more of a double-malt girl myself, but nobody's perfect."

"Look at us building bridges. Next we might actually think our way out of this bullshit pit."

"Don't get ahead of yourself," she murmured, scrunching up her nose and closing her eyes. "You're the only one with a functional AR chip. How does that work?"

Edison made himself more comfortable, turning and leaning against the door frame, kicking his legs straight out to the front. His back didn't ache, nothing ever did except his head, but it was still nice to feel casual. It was too soon to say if she really trusted him, but this seemed like progress.

"My guess is the Foxfire corrupted the others' but managed not to fuck mine up. That's just a stab in the dark, though. It's been helpful to have it. The music, the photos, the memories . . . I can't say for sure, but I think it's keeping me closer to human." *And so is this.* He watched her half nod, but he could tell he was losing her. She was drifting away and, selfishly, he wanted her to stay.

"Helpful for you," Rosalyn remarked. "But also helpful for the Foxfire, don't you think? It just has more information, more access, more ways to understand you and control you if you have a working AR chip."

Edison paused. "I hadn't considered that. Damn, and I thought I was the lucky one."

Yawning, she replied, "You still might be. Maybe it's still a net win if it helps you stay in touch with your human side."

"How long do you need to rest?" he asked softly.

Her words were so slurred he almost couldn't make them out. "Not long. Just an hour."

"Sure," he said. "I can give you an hour. I'll post up here and make sure nobody bothers you, all right?"

"S'mmkay."

She dropped like a stone. Edison hadn't seen anyone fall asleep that quickly in, well, ever. It was like a spell had been cast, awake one second and gone the next. It wasn't that he missed her, exactly, but that the silence afforded unique opportunities for the Foxfire to emerge. The quiet, lonely hours were always the hardest.

Because this is just a distraction, baby. "Buzz, buzz, buzz," goes the bee, keeping busy, be as busy as you like, it's only a matter of time. You'll join us.

Edison sighed and rubbed his temples. Preventive measures needed to be taken. He summoned his AR display and brought up the music app, choosing his usual calming playlist. It could've been a salt circle, his spiritual protection against the coming Foxfire incursion. On a lark, he opened his AR public profile and changed it. Charming or desperate? He couldn't decide. Either way it was something. Something for her. The monster inside him had been gaining ground steadily, it seemed, until the salvager arrived. It made him wish she had arrived sooner, the tossed pebble that rippled hard across the pond.

The steady mechanical thrum of the *Brigantine* normally put him at ease, but in that moment it was different. Time generally had less meaning in outer space, but for routine and health, MSC kept their workers on an established day/night cycle, synced to Earth. Most space stations did something similar, the prevailing national territory determining which time zone they chose to follow. Merchantia Solutions, based out of Vancouver, timed their workdays accordingly. He liked it. Even if the connection to Earth was artificial, it was still a connection, however tentative.

Several facts dawned on him at once as he sat in the semidarkness watching Rosalyn Devar sleep. One was that he would never see Earth again. In fact, this ship and the innards of Coeur d'Alene Station were likely the last places he would ever know. Fucking miserable. The second fact was that the ship was unusually quiet. Too quiet. Most hours Rayan could be heard tinkering away in the lab, dropping things with his clumsy enthusiasm or crying excitedly over a particular discovery. Even during the lockdown Rayan imposed, Piero made plenty of noise just to remind everyone he was still there and still pissed. Occasionally he could be heard punching or kicking the walls and door. Misato never made a racket, but Edison sensed her burning brightly in his mind.

It deeply unsettled him, this remarkable silence and the as-yet-unknown implications. He knew he couldn't move from that spot as long as Rosalyn slept. Piero was up to something, and even if the questions and curiosity were eating Edison up, he couldn't leave her. A captain didn't abandon his crew, and Rosalyn had become part of the *Brigantine* whether she appreciated it or not. He had failed Piero miserably, and probably Rayan, too, but it didn't have to be that way for Misato or Rosalyn. There had to be hope, or there was no point in keeping this vigil or resisting the voices in his head.

There was a third fact making itself known: Rosalyn drooled quite a lot while she slept.

The music twined softly through his head, the only noise beyond the hum of the ship. Free-form jazz worked the best against the Foxfire, he found; the unpredictable notes defied patterns, skipping and stopping at random, too wild for the monster to anticipate. Anything repetitive put him in the most danger. In the early days, those first ugly, awful days, they had all compared notes, trying to find ways to quiet the sudden voices in their heads. In the end, they each found a different solution. Rayan had his memories of Lahore.

Misato had her coffee. Edison had his music. But Piero . . . Piero never told them what helped him. Maybe the horrible truth was that nothing helped and that was why he seemed to sink the fastest, with nothing there to hold on to.

Or maybe, just maybe, he was a traitor, and the guilt had gotten to him as quickly as the infestation.

Rosalyn's head slid off her arms and onto the chair. No way that was comfortable. If he could, if it was possible or even appropriate, he would've liked to slide a pillow under her cheek and drape a blanket over her. After what she had seen, after what she now faced, she deserved to get some good, solid rest.

The salvager tried to kill you, kill your family. She will try to do it again.

Enemy at the gates. Edison dropped his glasses in his lap and scrubbed at his eyes. He had to stay awake and alert, lest the Foxfire catch him in a moment of weakness. It would be far too dangerous to lose control now when Piero and Rayan had vanished and Rosalyn was all but catatonic. Vulnerable.

Yes, baby. Vulnerable. Break the shield. Destroy the barrier. Let her join the family.

"I'm not doing a single fucking thing you tell me to do," Edison muttered aloud. "I don't care who you sound like."

And how do you know that? How do you know this wasn't intended? We want you to remain close to her. We want the temptation to become too much.

"Bullshit."

Is that you saying that? Are you even you anymore? No idea original to your mind but to ours. You know this; you know our desires are intertwined.

"Not always." Edison sighed and cleaned his glasses on his thermal crew shirt, then set them back in place. "Not now."

I know you're plotting against us, baby, I know you like her; we like her, too. Mother knows what you're up to.

"Yeah?" He felt crazy speaking to himself this way, but if he didn't, if he only talked back to the voices in his head, it made it easier for them to swirl together. A thought could be his and then seamlessly become something else, tainted and ripped from his control. "If I'm plotting against you, then try and stop me."

Oh, we will. We are.

A hand like a vise clamped down on his shoulder. Edison leapt to his feet, throwing his right arm out for balance and slamming it against the clear barrier. He kept his balance, but his attacker had the upper hand. Of course he didn't have to look. Piero peeled away from the darkness as if he were part of the shadows. He wasted no time, shoving Edison back against the shield and then reaching for his head, Piero's huge hand closing over Edison's face before cracking his head back against the barrier again and again. Something snapped. There was a crackle like the breaking of thick ice.

No. The shield will hold. It can't break, it can't . . .

Edison lashed out with both hands, landing one blow, but it was a weak one. There was no coming back from this ambush. He couldn't see, couldn't think, not with Piero's giant hand smothering him and blocking his eyes. Their connection returned with a vengeance, pure, obliterating emotion rolling off Piero. Edison gasped, hearing his glasses click softly as they landed on the floor.

Rage. Frustration. *Elation.*

His chest felt giddy, as if that excitement in Piero had nested itself effortlessly in his body. Then he was flying or tumbling, jerked away from the barrier, his thoughts a jumble as he fought off the other man's emotions. More than the disorienting blows to the head, those unfiltered feelings left him reeling and confused.

There was a soft sound behind him and then laughter, but there was no telling if it was his voice or another's.

26

Shattered. Shattering. She opened her eyes, the world black and blue, glowing, glowing so brightly as if fused to a dream. A fluorescent smiling skull glittered in the dark outside the chamber, hovering there before she recognized the springy mane of hair and the powerful frame attached to it. Piero. She opened her mouth to scream out a warning but nothing happened.

Nothing happened and everything happened.

Piero fell on Edison with unnatural speed, grabbing him by the head and lifting him to his feet before using his skull like a rock to break the flimsy shield. *Slam, slam, slam.* Rosalyn watched in mute horror as a hairline fissure splintered out from the contact point, and half expected the barrier to crash inward and expose her to the corrupted ship's atmosphere. But then Piero ripped Edison away, his spectacles dropping to the floor with a tiny bounce.

The violence ended as abruptly as it began, Piero flinging Edison into the darkness. Rosalyn scrambled to her feet, floundering in a frenzy of dread and confusion. Her environmental suit lay in a heap near the decontamination chamber and she hurled herself toward it, cursing the number of toggles and seals that had to be meticulously done and redone to ensure total security. And the filters. The filters.

By a stroke of luck they had finished their cycle in the decontam pod. She ripped them out, punching the old filters out and into a hazard bin, breathing hard enough through her respirator to faint.

"Fucking shit, fuck," she mumbled, hands shaking as she switched in the new filters and raced toward the door. But she stopped herself. No. This was panic speaking. This was haste. She had to be smarter than the thumping war drums in her head that said, *Go, go, why are you fucking dawdling, GO!*

Edison couldn't sense either Piero or Rayan. Against Piero she stood little chance. Against them both? She needed more than adrenaline to save Edison, if he could be saved at all. Of course she had to try, because three grown men against her spelled quick and total doom. Misato might be helpful, but could she really rely on another person when the infected crew were dropping like flies?

Fight back, she thought. *Fight back.*

She paced, and then raced to the 3-D extruder, wondering if she could at least print some sort of weapon. Most printers were prohibited by law from doing so, and only a sophisticated hacker could change that. The machines were calibrated to automatically scan schematics for known weapon parts to avoid the rampant proliferation of 3-D printed guns, knives and bomb parts. She didn't have time to mess around with sorting through the six million available printing formats either. Rosalyn shook out her trembling hands, then smoothed them repeatedly down her legs. Her leg. Her right leg. She gasped, releasing the sealing valve on the right leg of her suit, allowing her to access the plain jumpsuit beneath. Panting, she thrust a hand down into the pocket of her cargo pants.

The multi-tool. It wasn't much, but it had a decent enough utility knife and corkscrew, and both of those could sink handily into an eye or throat. Clearly those infected with Foxfire were dulled to pain, but a good enough slash would likely be incapacitating. She didn't need to kill anyone, just get them out of the way long enough for Edison to fight back or run.

Or run. To where? She had Edison's captain's code, but that could only do so much. There were no evac pods, no truly safe places on the ship. Her little hideaway chamber was the most secure place, she thought, but if Edison got inside, it would make him immensely sick and expose her one safe zone to corruption.

Think. Think. Think.

Starved of options, Rosalyn brought up her AR display. There he was, the indicator blinking softly at the very top of her vision. That was a good sign, at least; it meant his display was still functioning, and if his chip hadn't been completely corrupted by the Foxfire, then maybe he was still fighting it off. Piero and Rayan seemed to fall to it in a flash, so there was no telling how long she had to act. Her heart twisted as she stared at the display—Edison had changed his public profile.

Dogs, jazz, single malt

She wanted to cry. No sleep, hardly any food, and now her one solid ally, the one person who seemed at least partially reliable, had been attacked. It was bad enough before, but now the enemies were turning on one another, and somehow that was so, so much worse.

"Hey."

Oh God, Oh God . . .

But it was only Misato. She put one palm on the shield, lightly, pressing her other forefinger to her lips. Luckily her eyes were blue and not the stark, terrible white of Foxfire's control.

"He took Edison," Rosalyn whispered hoarsely. "Piero is . . . he's like a demon. His face is all shredded, skin hanging off of him, his mouth . . . Jesus, it's a nightmare, and all I have is this stupid fucking multi-tool with like a two-inch blade and . . . that's it. That's all I have. *He took Edison.*"

Misato nodded, her silver hair and eyes glowing brightly in the darkness. "I need you to stay calm, Rosalyn, you're shaking."

"I know. I know. I just . . . What the hell are we going to do? Can you, I don't know, sense him? Is he all right?"

"Yes, but the others . . . I can't see them. As hard as I try, they're just not there." Misato slowly reached into her cargo pocket, pulling out what looked like a homemade machete, a weapon cobbled together from a plastic chair leg and a jagged shard of the ship's interior.

"Jesus Christ! Where did you get that thing?" Rosalyn rushed to the glass, her helmet bumping gently against it.

"It was a precaution, in case I wanted to take my life peacefully."

"Yeah. There is *nothing* peaceful about that thing."

"No," Misato agreed, inspecting it. "Hm. Perhaps not. Perhaps that works to our advantage. Come on, we need to fix this. For Tuva?"

Rosalyn nodded, panting, then transferred the multi-tool to her left hand, gripping it tightly. *Tap, tap, tap.* There went the code. No turning back. The shield went up with a quiet hiss, and she joined Misato in the quivering darkness. She felt suddenly aware of every sound, every breath, every reverberating buzz of the ship's body. There was a metallic *click-clack* behind Misato, and Rosalyn reached to pull the older woman back. JAX teetered into view, not a single light shining on his chassis or head.

"It's okay," Misato said, twisting out of her grasp. "He's with us."

"But how?" Rosalyn whispered. "I thought Rayan hacked his functions."

"The kid? Sure. But I'm an engineer. I could make JAX perform *Swan Lake* if I wanted to," she replied, inching carefully down the corridor.

"Isn't that programming?"

"Yeah, obviously." Misato snorted, JAX sticking close to her side. "I had to even the odds for us. Piero has to be stopped."

Rosalyn caught up to her, brandishing her multi-tool knife at the darkness. "He was already a murderer, now . . . I don't know. I don't know what he did to himself. This is getting out of control. I mean, it was already impossible, but it seems like the Foxfire is accelerating or something. I'm not . . . can I tell you things? Is it safe to say anything to you, or will you just feed it back to them and betray me?"

"You don't have to tell me," Misato replied, coming to a stop. "Edison shared it all. Your plan, that is."

"What? That . . . but he . . . he didn't tell me that . . ."

"No, because you don't trust anyone here, but he does. Maybe you should consider it, too. Just a friendly suggestion."

Rosalyn considered that, standing there frozen and afraid in the darkness. What was she going to do? Take on a woman with a homemade machete and her faithful Servitor? Alliances had to be made, as much as she hated it. As much as she still didn't fully trust any of it. This was as close as she was going to get, she thought, not real, deep friendship or trust but a convenient partnership, one that would hopefully last long enough to survive this sudden mutiny. There was a plan to enact as long as they could wrest control of the ship back from Piero.

"No, I do. I like you. I would like you a lot if we weren't here. And I trust you; you wanted to do the right thing for Tuva. I . . . trust *or something* you. For now. Anyway, how are we going to find them? We can both see Edison, I've got my AR, but we have no idea where the other two are."

"You're not the only one who can fit into an engineering bay duct," Misato murmured. "JAX is monitoring the security feeds."

"Crewmates Endrizzi, Aries and Yasin are currently located in starboard observation."

"Christ, you're good. You did all that just now?" Rosalyn was feeling increasingly confident in this temporary alliance. She was grateful, at least, that the one person available to her as an ally was intensely, scarily smart.

"You're terrifying," Rosalyn added with a shiver.

"Ha. Just resourceful. I went to work on the cameras and JAX as soon as Piero went dark. Rayan came to see me and he was scattered . . . worsening. Something was different, and I prefer to be prepared," Misato explained. She began moving down the corridor again, keeping her makeshift weapon at the ready, and Rosalyn copied her.

"Why starboard observation?" she asked in a whisper. "What's there?"

In the glow of Misato's turquoise eyes, Rosalyn saw the old woman's mouth harden into a grim line.

"The brig."

"Crew member Iwasa?" JAX interjected. "Pardon the interruption, but it seems pertinent: Crewmate Endrizzi is attempting to access the communications hub directly."

"Directly?" The engineer drew up short and Rosalyn stumbled past her. "Define 'directly,' JAX."

"With his fists," the Servitor intoned matter-of-factly.

"Oh no. Oh, that's not good," Misato breathed. "Show me the feed."

JAX lit up, his chassis becoming a milky white that then filled with a camera stream from starboard observation. The two women crowded around him, leaning in for a better look. The image was murky and difficult to make out, and there was no sound, but toward the back left corner of the gently curved room, next to a large observation window, was Edison, locked behind what looked like the same tough, clear shielding from cold storage. He shouted something unintelligible, and Rosalyn heard the echo of it in real time, muted by the doors and corridors between them.

Piero had ripped a smooth, silver panel from a waist-high bank of storage bins near the brig. His fists came away with spools and spools of green cording.

"God, what are they doing to him? And what are they doing to the *ship*?" Rosalyn whispered.

Misato squinted and then shook her head. "JAX, where is Rayan? I don't see him there. Find him on the cameras."

The faintly glowing image stream on the Servitor's curved body went dead and then cycled at impossible speed through all the available cameras on the ship. Darkened room after darkened room flew by. When the cycle ended, JAX tilted his narrow head to the side.

"Unavailable."

Misato blew out a frustrated breath and then glanced at Rosalyn. "He's somewhere. Keep monitoring the feeds, JAX. We need to know if Rayan turns up. The *second* he turns up."

"He's probably hunting us," Rosalyn offered. "They know you, right? They know how capable you are."

"How capable *we* are. I told you, Rosalyn, you're a survivor, which is why we need to change course. Piero will kill our chance of getting a warning signal out. He's already sent his SOS; he doesn't need to do anything more but sit and wait for more ships to arrive at these coordinates," Misato said, taking off briskly down the corridor.

Rosalyn leapt to keep up, forcing down the exhaustion, a bone-deep brittleness that felt as threatening as the man tearing open the ship to rip at its guts.

"No, no," she quickly said, putting a light hand on the shorter woman's shoulder. "What about Edison? You can still sense him, right? That means he isn't a lost cause yet."

Dogs, jazz, single malt

Rosalyn blinked. Was this just sentiment talking? The lack of sleep could be compromising her ability to think straight, but it seemed wrong to just leave Edison there and potentially lose another friend. Ally. She meant *ally*.

"We'll be totally outnumbered if Edison goes," she hurried to say, watching Misato's eyes flick back and forth as she no doubt made her own calculations. "We have to protect the comms, that's priority one, right? I need to get a message out to HQ and stop them from coming here. If we go to the cockpit now, that means I have to put in my credentials, and if we go down, then the Foxfire has free rein of the ship. We're not outnumbered, not yet, but that could change. And fast."

"Our chances of success greatly decrease against three opponents," JAX chirped. "Crewmate Yasin is approximately one hundred and sixty pounds, suffers from asthma, and possesses no military or martial arts training. Crewmate Endrizzi is approximately two hundred pounds, with extensive experience in Krav Maga, judo—"

"Yes, we get it." Misato waved him off impatiently. "Then we stick together and go straight for Piero. He probably sent Rayan to ambush us if we tried for the cockpit." The engineer set off back down the passage, and Rosalyn tried to keep pace. "I don't like the idea of fighting Rayan, anyway. I'd rather put it off. He's a good kid . . . What a waste."

Rosalyn watched her take a hip flask out of her left cargo pant pocket and chug it. She wouldn't have minded a spot of liquid courage herself, but that would have to wait. Her AR display kicked in, highlighting the flask before Misato tucked it back into her pocket. $C_8H_{10}N_4O_2$. Coffee.

"This is *all* a waste," Rosalyn told her quietly. She didn't know why they were whispering; it was doubtful that their whereabouts were a secret to Piero and Rayan. "I could be in Mile End having a Pisco sour right now."

"So why aren't you?"

Rosalyn breathed hard out of her nose, shaking off the nostalgia. It wasn't helpful. She could have stayed at Belrose Industries. She could've pushed harder to get Glen sacked. She could've filed the police report. Or just quit and stayed on Earth. Or taken a million other paths that didn't lead to a knife in her hand and panic in her heart.

She had been so sure that the blaming voice in her head had been excised like a malignant tumor, but no, a few dangerous cells remained. *This is your fault. Why didn't you just divert to refuel that senator? Walters would still be alive. You might never have even ended up on the* Brigantine. *You didn't have to sabotage the ship; look where that got you.*

It had been like that after Glen, too, a never-ending series of twisting passages she walked in her head, each of them leading to a different outcome, each of them placing blame firmly at her feet. There were so many warnings. Angela had told her to dump him and get out. And when he snapped, when he proved everyone right . . .

It came to her like a flash. Edison standing there on the other side of the barrier with hooded, sad eyes, and her own words looping back toward her, and the way he had relaxed once she said it to him, like a huge weight had been torn from his body.

You didn't ask for any of this to happen, and it's certainly not your fault.

She breathed in, she breathed out. The words felt like something she could believe in, so she did. Blame was a labyrinth that never ended, and she wouldn't get lost in that maze again. Couldn't. She had survived Glen and she would survive this. Rosalyn glanced over at Misato, a woman she would have liked to meet under any other circumstances.

"I had to run away from something," Rosalyn finally answered. "I needed some distance. Or perspective. I don't know."

"How's this for perspective?" Misato asked with a snort. "Bet you're wishing you hadn't run away. I can't imagine it was anywhere near as bad as this."

"No, just different," she murmured. "A different kind of hell."

"You've been through hell? Good. Then you might just be tough enough to help me untangle this mess."

Rosalyn held back a weary sigh. "And what does that look like?"

"For now? Getting rid of Piero. Disabling Rayan. Keeping Edison halfway human. Sound okay?" Misato had led them through the snaking tunnels of the ship, down a steeply curved ramp and to another closed, circular door on the lowest level of the ship. The collection rovers were in a bay nearby, with the only other entrance hatch besides the one she had initially entered through with Walters. Rosalyn brought up the schematics of the *Brigantine* on her AR and nodded. Starboard observation was just through the door and around a quick right-hand corner.

"Sounds like something, and that's way better than nothing," she agreed. "Which is what I got."

"That's the spirit," Misato teased, but Rosalyn could hear the edge in her voice, the tremor of nervous energy. "You got anything new for me, JAX?"

The Servitor remained quiet, and no lights flickered in his head or body.

Misato shouldered up to the rounded door, hefting her makeshift weapon and nodding once. "Then we go for Piero, hit him hard. We have to stop him before he disables our comms."

JAX sidled up to the door panel and disengaged the seal, allowing them into the corridor beyond. It was still and mostly dark, the only light emanating from the strands of turquoise Foxfire glittering along the ceiling, thousands of little eyes watching them, measuring them, twinkling with what felt like anticipation.

27

Piero still remembered exactly what Io looked like as the transport descended. Like a moldy golf ball. Like a burnt pizza with all the cheese scraped off. It didn't look friendly or like home, and his skin itched with nervousness as they breached the atmosphere and the transport rattled hard enough to make his teeth clack.

His nose had been pressed against the cool observation window for an hour. Mamma sat next to him, legs primly crossed, her high heels on the bench next to them. Traveling was a luxury, she told him, so it was important to dress your best. Her long, tanned legs were drawing glances from other passengers. Some were there for short trips; others were destined to stay. A small blond girl Piero's age had tried to show him a game with AR creatures you could chase and keep as pets, but Piero didn't have the expensive tech headset it required. He wanted to cry, but shoved her instead.

"Don't look so cross," Mamma said as he glowered out the window.

The naked pizza moon was getting closer and closer, and he could see the faint outline of the colony boundaries, the great pulsating dome that protected the new cities from the hostile atmosphere of the sulfurous moon. They had learned all about Io in school. Chinese was the most common language spoken and Piero's Chinese was very bad, almost as bad as his English. Signorina De Luca had called the colony *un miracolo*. A miracle.

The great silvery grids of the colony grew sharper, ripples cascading along the protective dome, a swirling mist buffeting against the city limits, as if an army of ghosts tried constantly to storm the gates. What was visible of the ground through the mist was teal and orange, deeply pitted and hilly, but the colony sat on a carved-out rectangular depression, as if some giant had come along to scoop out a flat place for his sandcastle.

No trees. No sandboxes. No stray dogs or old men playing dice. He would miss those old men, their red noses spotted with age, their hats always tilted against the roaring sun. And he already missed the dogs, with their wet, curious noses always pushing into his pockets, looking for sweets.

"*Nǐ hǎo, wǒ de míngzì shì Piero,*" he mouthed to the window, fogging it. He practiced again and again. It was the only phrase he had ever spelled perfectly on a test.

"Mamma," he said softly, not wanting the blond girl and her family to overhear.

"Yes, darling?"

"When do I get a better headset? The VIT Fives have been out for *ages*." In the window reflection he saw his mother sigh and bend down to rub her swollen ankles. He wished she wouldn't; the other passengers kept staring at her when she did that.

"You will waste your time with it. You will just play games all day and never study," she said.

"I won't. It isn't fair, I need it for English, for Chinese. The Fives do all the translating for you, you don't have to try at all!" he cried, forgetting that he didn't want to draw attention to their fighting. To their poverty.

Mamma gave one of her sweet, indulgent laughs and leaned back on the padded bench, reaching up to comb his messy curls with her fingers. "We will ask Domenico for one when we are all settled, mm?"

Domenico. Her lanky, gray-eyed lover. Piero hated the man and his ugly gold watch, his paisley shirts. They were old-fashioned and gaudy, just like the man himself. He always smelled of too much garlic and played football terribly, stumbling over his flat feet and blaming it on his shoes.

"Never mind," Piero whispered to the rapidly approaching ground. "I don't want one."

His forearms had been resting on the back of the bench, but he pulled them away, running his nails nervously back and forth over the pleather cushion, scratching and scratching until his mother tsked him and slapped his hands.

What was he doing? Where was he? Where was Mamma?

Piero looked at his hands. Were they even his anymore? He could barely feel the bunches of cord in his hands, green and warm, fresh from the insides of the ship. Starboard observation sketched itself in around him, dark, lit with soft yellow filaments above the panoramic windows and the familiar blue growth that pulsed in harmony with his heartbeat. He felt it there and all around him and in the man trapped in a clear prison to his right.

The ship. The *Brigantine*. Somehow, Mother had lost control of him for an instant, but instead of reality he had slipped far, far into the past. Parts of him still existed then, but those parts and his whole belonged to the cluster. They had work to do. They had problems to solve. The salvager had inadvertently helped them, but now she and the as-yet-unclaimed Edison and Misato plotted against the collective. Wayward, naughty children. Of course, they would be subdued in time, but the cords in their hands, the comm network, took priority.

"I know you can hear me. Listen to me, you little shit, let me out of here right now. *Let me out.*"

It was a stroke of genius, the brig, the only compartment on the ship that a captain's code could override from the outside. Two threats neutralized, two to go. He—they—felt almost giddy, on the verge of a breakthrough. The beautiful bright fungus covering the ceiling seemed to trill, flashing faster and faster, signaling their shared excitement. It was a sensation but also a verse that filled them, spurring, exciting, a fragment of something greater that kept Piero's hands busy with the cords, twisting, snapping, breaking, breaking. Faster and faster . . .

Mother liked to make up rhymes for him, so he made up some of his own. *The knife in the hand goes stab, stab, stab. The blood in the veins goes spill, spill, spill . . .*

Piero had given Tuva the pills to save himself, and giving a pill or two wasn't so hard. He wasn't a killer, but Mother was changing him. Everything was different. Killing Tuva didn't sit right with him, but choices had to be made. He wasn't going back to Io. He wasn't taking another shit job with shit money. Merc work hardly paid the bills with military-grade Servitors coming online. His contact at ISS had been clear—the package would be at CDAS, and it needed to be transferred to a vessel, any vessel, and studied. If Piero could just do that, just put the package into a controlled space and record the results, he would be set for life.

But not if that Norwegian bitch intervened. Not if she ratted him out before he opened the first canister.

On CDAS a mask and vaccine tab had been left with the package. The mask seemed redundant, so he skipped it, and took the vaccine. Bad choice. Big mistake.

Mistake? But now you have me. Now you have your family, your mother. My heart, they're coming. They're coming. The women. The betrayer machine. They're coming.

Faster, faster. The Foxfire marked their steps, an alarm ringing from the corridor around the corner to the very core of his body. There was a delay, but only a slight one, so he stood, hands full of warm, wrapping cords, and waited, verse and song louder than the shouts, just as much words as drums pounding in the deep dark of him.

The knife in the hand goes stab, stab, stab. The blood in the veins goes spill, spill, spill, and Mother says it's time to kill.

More verses. More drums. His head and hands pounded. He was ready.

28

Before they pushed into the starboard observation room, she took one last nip from her flask of coffee. Synthetic arabica was all she had left, and even that was running low, but it was better than nothing. Besides, she just needed the taste memory, not the real deal.

Your supplies won't last forever. We're coming. Mother is close now, but you know that.

"Shut. Up."

"Sorry?" Rosalyn stared at her blankly, her little multi-tool held up like she was going in for a heist. Comical, but at least she looked ready.

Misato held up her own weapon, larger but no less ridiculous. "Nothing. JAX, you go in first. Get up some speed, charge him. You've got fresh batteries from Rosalyn, so you should be able to give him a good wallop. I just need him distracted."

You just seem distracted, that's all.

That voice. Misato blinked hard. This time it wasn't her mother. Maybe the Foxfire had sensed that wasn't working, that Misato had never been close to her parents. It was like being inside herself twice, a nested doll, experiencing the present but also the past. Something about that phrase had dredged up a memory that fell around her close, a tight curtain of vaporous thought. She was back in Musk Hall, prepping for a bioengineering exam she hadn't studied for enough. That was okay, she'd wing it like she did most times. This shit just clicked for her. Systems. Patterns. The logic of the body and the machine had a symmetry that she liked.

Jenny was different. Jennifer, her Jennifer, younger by almost a decade and bright as hell. She was like Rayan, too smart for her age, and too naive. It was never going to last between them. Misato was hungry for deeper space and deeper mysteries, and Jennifer was gorgeous, smart but shallow. Not *shallow* shallow, just shallow when compared to what lay beyond the ever-expanding human boundaries. Misato hadn't lived well past one hundred to hole up in a condo on Tokyo Bliss Station and watch younger, hungrier people get what she wanted. Setting up the Io colonists had been the adventure of a lifetime, but she had more than one lifetime in her, she was sure of that.

Coffee. Jenny drank her coffee black, strong and acid, nasty enough to strip the varnish off a rocket. Fake sunlight poured in through the channel of overhead "windows" in the massive library, a loving re-creation of the now-lost Osaka Station. It was half of a low glass pyramid attached to a more traditional ten-story data library. The air in the main study area was always cool and swirling, kicking around the warmed dust smell of hundreds of busy computers. All around them, students typed away, hunched over their tablets and keyboards, eyes red with weariness.

But there was no tablet in front of Misato, just Jenny's hands wrapped around a steaming silver canister. Her hands were heavily tattooed, Jupiter on one, Mars on the other, exquisitely rendered and as colorful as the actual planets. Two formulas were inked across her knuckles, coffee on the right, ethanol on the left.

Misato watched the letters and numbers deform as Jenny

drummed her fingers on the canister impatiently. She needed answers, Misato just needed to look at her. So pretty. A star girl, born in a man-made paradise, never seeing Earth or the Philippines of her mother or the Netherlands of her father. *Maybe one day*, Jenny would say, *maybe one day we can go to Amsterdam together and get high as fuck, wander the canals, eat a stroopwafel or some shit, you know, be romantic.* Her black hair was pulled back in a dizzying twist of tight braids, a little dusting of stars tattooed under her left eye.

So pretty.

"It's not about . . ." And here Jenny squinted, eyes sliding to the side as she read what was open on Misato's AR display. They had linked displays months ago. "Cortical Dynamics Underlying Implant-Related Seizures, is it? It's me. It's us. It's this bullshit again."

"I love you, Jenny."

"That's a cop-out." Jenny was thirty-eight, but she may as well have been a decade younger than that. Age didn't seem to touch her face, as if even her own cells sensed changing that perfect dark skin would be a crime. "Love. Blugh. Okay, genius, get back to work. I'll stop distracting you."

She pushed back her chair and leaned over the table, then crawled up onto it, bridging the distance to plant a sloppy kiss on Misato's cheek.

"There's a poetry thing the JAXA kids are doing. I'm already late," Jenny said, giving a fluttery wave. Of course she would want to see Japanese astronauts reciting poetry. "I'll ping you later."

"Okay, I love you! Bye."

The smell of coffee, rich and homey, lingered. Jenny never pinged. Maybe she knew Misato was going to leave anyway; maybe she just found someone else. A poet. Someone who had all the time in the world to eat stroopwafels. That wasn't Misato, but now she wished it was.

"Misato? Hey! Am I losing you? Please stay with me."

Vaguely, she felt someone digging in her pockets. The curtain lifted and there was Rosalyn with her huge hazel eyes that always looked so worried and her bald head. Rosalyn waved the coffee flask in front of Misato's face but she pushed it back.

"I'm fine . . . I'm . . . We should go. We're wasting time."

"What was that?" Rosalyn pressed. "Did the Foxfire say something?"

"No," she said. "It was just . . . I thought I saw a ghost. I'm fine now, let's go. JAX? Breach the room."

They ought to take their time, or at least form a better plan. The time for pep talks had passed, and Misato was spooked. What the hell was that? She had vivid dreams occasionally, and strange visions when she dozed and the Foxfire directed her unconscious imagination, but that was like a total split from reality. The coffee had smelled so close, the steam from the canister warm, Jenny's sharp perfume twining around her again for one lovely moment . . .

JAX moved with unnatural speed, uninhibited by the limitations of human mobility. He dropped into an odd crouch and then onto all fours, dashing forward with quick, jerky movements. He wasn't designed for military purposes, but his chassis and head were hard enough to drop anyone to the ground at full speed. Misato urged Rosalyn forward with a nod, and together they turned the corner, five meters or so behind JAX's opening salvo.

Starboard observation was as dark as the rest of the ship, not helpful for Rosalyn but no disadvantage for Misato. Her eyes now seemed well suited to the darkness, immediately homing in on Piero, standing just as he had been on the security camera footage. JAX shot toward him, flying across the floor like a four-legged bullet. In the brig, Edison let out a shriek of surprise, both palms flattening against the clear shielding. JAX met his mark, but Piero was ready, hunching down at the last second, bracing for impact and then throwing his shoulder into the Servitor as it hit.

Misato had been right about one thing; JAX really was made of strong stuff.

The Servitor ricocheted off Piero's shoulder with a sickening *crack*, then continued on, barreling with total momentum into the clear, tall rectangle of the brig. Then came another *crack*, a louder one, and a high metallic sound, likes two knives scraping together. The clear sheeting couldn't take the impact, splintering and caving in at three distinct points, then falling, collapsing inward. Edison threw himself backward against the wall, flattening himself to avoid the sharp edges.

Piero's shoulder hung loose in its socket, but that seemed to bother him not at all. He righted himself at once, smiling with his ragged wound of a mouth. JAX's blow had knocked his arm out of alignment and torn away most of the muscle, revealing the shards of slick white bone beneath. It seemed even starker and more naked, bathed in the glowing blue threads that also hung in shreds around his arm.

But he didn't come for them as Misato expected. Instead, he turned, surprisingly adroit in his mangled state. He had stripped to the waist at some point, his jumpsuit in tatters, the broad planes of his chest torn clean of human flesh, and the bright blue strands pulsed quickly, mimicking whatever adrenaline flooded his body.

JAX had lodged himself in the brig next to Edison, his head somewhere inside the wall panel. The rest of him jerked and spasmed as if in death throes.

To her credit, Rosalyn ran in without hesitation, holding her little multi-tool up and diagonal to her right shoulder, preparing to slash. But Piero was faster, and more reckless, diving toward Edison in the brig, using the chaos to grab the captain by his forearm and swing him around. With his other hand he pressed on Edison's upper back, forcing him to his knees and bringing his neck perilously close to the jagged edge of the broken sheeting.

"Wait!" Misato cried out, a hot flicker passing across her forehead. Piero—the Foxfire—wanted in, badly, wanted to control the whole chessboard and not just half the pieces. Part of her almost gave in, not out of weakness but desperation. If she were strong enough, stalwart enough, she could connect to him and try to appeal to whatever was left of his better nature.

Rosalyn heard her, stopping mere feet from the two men, her weapon still raised and trembling.

"He'll do it," Misato breathed, staring into Piero's silvery-white eyes. There was nothing left of his humanity, she thought, nothing there but savage allegiance to the Foxfire within. This was something new, an evolution. Before, the Foxfire had felt invasive, surely, but the takeover had been gradual and almost friendly, as if the monster could cajole them into buying its propaganda. This was not negotiation but bare hostility.

She could see Rosalyn's nerves now as she bounced from foot to foot. The salvager glanced back toward Misato, her eyes huge and glossy, mouth dropping open and freezing there as if to ask, *What do we do now?*

Worst of all, Rayan was still lurking somewhere on the ship. Misato looked behind her, but the corridor was empty. Inch by terrible inch, Piero was forcing Edison's head toward the sharp edge. The captain fought him, lashing out with his fists, punching into a body that was long past recognizing pain. The man had torn most of his own flesh off; a few hard blows to the stomach landed like a child swatting his father.

Edison was trying to mouth something at them, one word over and over again.

Stall.

Rosalyn must have seen it, too. She took a few faltering, careful steps toward the two men but stopped when Piero gave a more determined push on Edison's neck.

"Slow down," Rosalyn said. Her voice was muffled through the environmental suit, but Misato heard it clear enough. "Just . . . just wait one minute, okay? There's something I want to know. Something . . ." She glanced at Misato for reassurance and received a tiny nod. *Yes, chickadee, keep going, keep him talking, whatever time we can gain back is critical.* For what, Misato didn't know, but it was better than watching her crewmates decapitate each other. The comm hub to their left was a disaster, which meant he had probably been successful in cutting off their voice to the outside world. The best outcome they could hope for now was keeping Edison alive.

"Questions are pointless," Piero hissed.

Sweat dripped down Edison's beard, landing on the shattered remains of the brig and splashing.

"F-Fair enough," Rosalyn stammered. "But what about a trade? Is that pointless?"

Piero's white eyes flashed. A trade. The Foxfire was clearly intrigued. The shiny blue spores above them on the ceiling seemed to dance as if electrified.

"A trade," Piero echoed. "What could you offer us? You're weak. We have the advantage."

"I have something you want," Rosalyn continued. "Something you've been trying very hard to get. I think it will benefit us all, really, and nobody will have to die."

He stared at her for a long moment. Misato tried to take a step forward but he saw her, head tilting to the side as he squinted in her direction. She froze, holding up her weapon as if in surrender. *Shit.* This stalling thing wasn't doing much of anything.

"What is it you think we want?" Piero asked, eyes sliding rapidly between her and Rosalyn.

Even through the bubbled visor, Misato heard the troubled gulp Rosalyn gave. Of course, it made perfect sense. Rosalyn's arrival had seemed to stir something in the Foxfire, provoking an extraordinary reaction. It was only logical. *Logical*, Misato thought with a quick shake of her head, *but stupid*.

Rosalyn didn't look back. She seemed to be staring directly into Piero's eyes, into the core of the monster holding them all hostage. Her voice was small but firm and sent a shiver down Misato's spine.

"Me."

29

The bastard alien inside Piero was thinking it over.

One simple word had brought the whole screaming panic of the moment to a standstill. She could hear Edison's shattered breathing, and Misato's, too, and her skull ached from the deafening pound of the blood in her ears.

She had stared the devil in the eyes before. *I've been here*, she thought. *I've seen the snake coil before the strike. I've seen the humanity fall away from a man until there's nothing left but madness and rage.*

It was going to work. Or at least, this part of her hastily patched-up plan was going forward. The rest? Well, one step at a time. It had been her mantra after Glen; it would have to serve again now. One step at a time. Shave your head. Throw out your makeup. Wipe the lip gloss off your mouth and smear it on your jeans. Go to space. Lose yourself. Remake yourself. Forge something new.

A snarling beast had tried to control her before and won. *Not this time, motherfucker.*

"Admit it," Rosalyn pushed. "You want all of us. You're hungry for more bodies. More knowledge, right? You want more knowledge for the . . . for the cluster. You want to be mother to us all. It'd be stupid to throw Edison away. Look at him. He's strong. He's smart. He's got . . . he really likes dogs. I don't know if you know this because you're not from Earth, but that's a big deal to us humans, so don't toss him away when you can have us both. It's simple math. You . . . you *can* do math, right?"

She couldn't tell if he was grinning or hissing. Most of his face was a sloppy, disfigured mess. His grip seemed to relax a little on Edison's neck, and the captain half smiled at her, his face shiny with sweat. It was working. Or something was happening. It was an improvement over the pandemonium.

"Mother sees the wisdom in your suggestion," Piero said slowly, as if debating each word. "She knows you. She . . . knows your face. I know your face. But she does not trust your intentions."

"Why not? You said it yourself, you've got the upper hand."

"You think Mother is foolish. You think she's blind." The canopy of blue above them twinkled, a grim reminder of just how much she was up against. She wondered if maybe in addition to a master engineer, bioengineer and programmer, Misato was a champion javelin thrower. That would simplify things considerably.

"I know you're not blind," Rosalyn replied, fighting impatience. "Just be realistic, you want me to calm down. We'll just go in circles unless we . . . unless we find some kind of truce."

"Truce," the Foxfire—Piero—tested the word, hesitating.

And he wasn't moving. Rosalyn knew what they were waiting for. All she had to do to end this was remove her environmental suit. She had assumed they would get to this point and that another part of the plan would occur to her, but now she was drawing a blank. Either Edison or Misato performed a miracle or they were going to be stuck in a standoff for eternity. Then again, Piero could simply call her bluff and slit Edison's throat.

She wondered if that would matter. Well, of course it mattered, but in the abstract . . . Piero looked to be held together with a prayer, yet his strength was overwhelming Edison's. Even Foxfire couldn't survive a severed head, she thought with a shudder.

Rosalyn slid the multi-tool into her suit pocket and sighed. Then she reached with both hands for the seal clasps on her visor. Edison and Misato made a sound in unison, one a gasp, the other a groan.

"Don't," Edison whispered. "Rosalyn? Don't."

She met Edison's eyes, blinking once, calmly, hoping he got the message. Not much of a message, but she did at least have a brain cell or two to rub together. She fidgeted with the seals, letting the thickened pads of her gloves rub uselessly over them. Grunting, she yanked and yanked, throwing in a theatrical twist of her hips for good measure.

"Shit," she muttered. "It's stuck."

"It is not," Piero growled. "You're stalling."

"It is! *Ugh.*" This was rolling the dice, she thought, knowing she could easily slip and actually release the seal and blow it all in spectacular fashion. Misato took a few shuffling steps toward her.

"*No.* Do not assist her. *Stay where you are.*" Piero leapt to his feet, one hand still gripping Edison by the nape, but his stance was considerably less menacing.

"Christ, I should've had a maintenance check on this thing months ago. Procrastination is a real bitch," Rosalyn chattered to herself, still pulling at the seal knobs, letting her fingertips slide off at the last second each time. Putting some real muscle into it, she screwed up her face, the actual, very not-pretend sweat on her face adding to the performance.

"It's not coming free," she whined. "*Shit.*"

"Enough. Mother is impatient." Piero lunged toward her, annihilated arm swinging grotesquely as he barreled in her direction. His better arm lifted, long fingers stretched out toward her as he slammed into her, sending them both crashing to the ground. She felt the floor hit her tailbone with a *crunch* and she winced, crying out, pushing against the dead weight of Piero's body as he crushed her into the tiles.

His huge hand landed on her visor with a *smack*, slick white teeth gnashing as he leered down at her.

This was the moment she had feared, the loss of control, the panic, the same stomach-churning sensation of knowing a bigger, stronger, *angrier* body was on top of her. Hot tears poured down her cheeks, into her ears, itchy and slimy. Why couldn't she move? Why couldn't she see? It was getting hard to breathe, hard to think. Every time she tried to draw air, it choked her.

Not again, not again, not again . . .

She blinked rapidly. Someone was screaming. A blur rushed above her head and she heard Misato, but it was so far away. There was a sound like rushing water, quick, sloshing bursts. Everything was fading. When the tears finally cleared, she was staring up into Glen's face. Square chin. Icy gray eyes. Perfectly stubbled jaw.

"You don't speak to me that way. You do not ever speak to me that way, Roz. It is so fucking condescending, okay? I don't know why you have to be so smug all the time. It brings out the worst in me."

Not this time. Fight back.

"No!" she heard herself scream. "No, no! Never again. *Never again!*"

When it was Glen on top of her she had fought back, too, but this was different, all new but somehow also all terribly familiar. She *knew* that she could fight this, knew that she was more than strong enough. Her left hand slid into her pocket, the only motion she could manage, and her fingers closed around the multi-tool. It was like someone else was guiding her, her own ghost aiming the two-inch knife, finding with luck or experience the base of the skull, the approximate location of most AR implants. Her own ghost plunged the knife in deep, breaking off, hitting something harder than bone.

The hand covering her visor shook, peeling away and leaving a long smear of blood.

Sound, vision, feeling all rushed in too fast and she drew breath as if resurfacing from deep, dark water.

The weight on her chest lifted and she watched Piero roll to the side, the multi-tool still stuck in the base of his skull, the AR chip shorting, sending him into a seizure. She had spent countless hours studying methods of integration with AR, always careful to make sure their tech didn't interfere with the implant and cause irreparable damage. And she had been good at it. Careful. Precise. But someone had pushed her to the ground, invaded her, and the only thing that numbed the panic was vodka. Then gin. Losing time. Skipping work. Glen was such a nice guy, who would ever believe her? Running. Running. Running until she was there, watching Piero shake and seize.

It was only a temporary solution, and Rosalyn watched Piero scuttle back against the wall, tangling himself in the cords he had pulled from the *Brigantine*. His legs shot out in front of him as he reached with his better arm for the knife in his back.

It wasn't enough. She had to finish him off. *Fight back.* Maybe Tuva was watching somehow, lending her strength. Rosalyn crawled weakly onto all fours, blearily finding she was not the only one fighting for her life. The blur above her head. The sounds of rushing water. Rayan. Foxfire would have their ambush after all, taking a page from her slapdash handbook, their second piece on the board arriving with a fire extinguisher, filling up the observation room with blinding white foam.

30

They were both moving to help Rosalyn when Rayan appeared, announcing his arrival with a blast from a fire extinguisher. His timing couldn't have been worse. A wall of white mist separated him from Rosalyn, but he saw Misato fight through it, screaming, her shiv raised high and ready to strike.

He lost track of her in the foam gouts that came one after another. Judging from their direction, Rayan was trying to protect Piero, who was struggling somewhere against the wall. Panting, Edison wiped at his face, shielding his eyes, peering into the disorienting fog long enough to see Misato slide toward Piero, jabbing her makeshift sword into his chest, pinning him to the wall. They both made horrible sounds—she an anguished cry and he a wet gurgle. Froth bubbled and spilled from his mouth like a secret. Rayan laid on the fire extinguisher again, leaping over Rosalyn to smash the heavy butt end of the extinguisher against the back of Misato's head. She went down hard, landing in a heap at Piero's feet.

It was then that Rayan turned his attention to Edison, charging him, brandishing the extinguisher canister like a battering ram. Edison planted his feet loosely, dodging, pivoting to use the man's momentum against him, just as Piero had done to JAX. It worked, but only for a moment. Rayan spun to meet him, slipping a little on the extinguisher residue covering the floor but not enough to lose his footing. There was no telling if Rosalyn was in a state to help him; Edison was on his own.

He lifted his arm just in time to block a close-range blast, his arm aching with the sudden freezing cold of the powder. Coughing, he gasped, the spray leaving him breathless. Rayan swung the canister, missed, then brought it back on the rebound, managing to clip Edison's shoulder. The kid's eyes were white, furious, his expression alarmingly blank, as if he had no idea that he was in the middle of bludgeoning his own captain.

"Rayan! Stop! You don't have to do this!" Edison shouted, batting half-blindly at the fire extinguisher, hoping to knock it out of Rayan's grasp.

There was no answer, only rage and another flurry of blows from the biologist. Edison let them come, waiting for an opening and finding one when Rayan swung too forcefully and overbalanced. Jamming his shoulder into Rayan's, Edison reached for the extinguisher, and they wrestled against each other. Under ordinary circumstances Edison felt confident he could outbox the kid, but this wasn't Rayan's strength against his—Rayan's body knew no fatigue, no pain, and his sole purpose now was to do as the Foxfire directed.

"Let . . . go," Edison growled. "It's over. Just let go."

They danced back and forth, one gaining ground until the other found a reserve of strength and pulled and pulled, dragging the other man down until the canister was at their knees. Edison's fingers were slippery with sweat, numb with cold, and he could feel his grip failing. A sudden female scream made them both freeze, hands clasped over each other's as they looked up in unison. Motes of foamy white powder settled slowly to the floor, as soft as a snowfall, and beyond that stood Rosalyn, trembling, backing away from them and into the adjoining corridor. But Edison didn't watch her for long.

She had screamed at Piero, at the slow, horrible push of his hands against the pinning knife that drew it through his body. His face was as blank and inscrutable as Rayan's, which made it all the more horrifying, seeing the knife disappear into his chest cavity, the thin pole of the handle jutting through before that too was gone, in him, then out the back of him as he came free. He had torn a massive hole in the center of his body, the bottom of one rib visible as he staggered to his feet, seemingly unaware of the catastrophic wound that oozed fresh blood down his abdomen, soaking into his jumpsuit trousers.

All at once the canister flew out of Edison's hands, ripped away, his stunned disgust the only distraction Rayan needed.

No, he thought with a grunt, *no*.

The hit to his chin seemed almost like an afterthought. It was hard enough to knock him dizzy and send him spiraling to the floor, but not enough to disable him entirely. Rayan was no longer interested in him, it seemed. Instead, he strode purposefully away, joining Piero as they followed Rosalyn out of starboard observation and into the corridor.

His body shook with panic. Misato hadn't moved. On elbows and knees, Edison pulled himself across the floor, giving sluggish chase, head spinning.

We'll come back for you. When the salvager is ours we will return for you.

"Fuck that," Edison spat, fighting for breath in a room that felt like all the oxygen had disappeared. The extinguisher powder felt like ice in his lungs, but he slithered through it, ignoring the spreading numbness in his forearms and knees. He tasted blood in his mouth and swallowed with a wince. It was no use. He was too slow.

Give up, baby, give up. Just lie down. Mother will take care of you. Go to sleep. Can I sing you a song?

It was agony, and the Foxfire did little to numb the pain. He climbed up onto his knees and then to his feet, ignoring the surge of needle pricks through his joints. All this carnage, all this chaos couldn't be for nothing. This was his ship. He was the captain. In the hall, just before watching Rosalyn go to sleep, he had promised her he would do whatever he could to fight the Foxfire. Her AR marker blinked at the top of his vision and he followed, dragging his feet with every impossible step. Voices bled in from the corridor. He passed the broken Servitor, and Misato on the floor, and the blood-spattered cables hanging loose from the wall.

The corridor yawned before him, glittering blue, the voices getting louder and louder, Rosalyn's AR indicator becoming a more solid triangle as he stumbled along.

Edison fell against the rounded wall, shoving along it, eyes trained forward, determination the only thing putting one foot in front of the other. Now the voices were audible, clear even, and he slid around the corner, sagging with exhaustion, both hands on his knees as he caught sight of Rosalyn, hands up in surrender, her back to the rover bay doors.

Two of them. One of him. But he couldn't leave her like that, couldn't give up now. Piero closed in on her, his shredded arm swinging loose, a macabre pendulum marking out the last seconds of her freedom. Rayan was at his side. They seemed to be waiting for some signal, or else Foxfire, in its growing hostility, was enjoying this sick chase.

Rosalyn flattened herself against the door. Edison saw her hand run up along the wall, her knuckles brushing the little LED touch panel at shoulder height. Her head turned and she saw him, eyes fuzzy behind the dirty visor of her suit. One knuckle tapped against the panel, then another, and Edison caught the faintest, saddest smile on her lips. He shook his head, but braced anyway, throwing himself across the hall and grabbing the handrail there.

He saw that strange smile one last time before the bay doors opened behind her with a force that shook the entire ship, the outer seal disengaging, sucking all three of them into the cold vacuum of space.

31

Whiplash. Tumbling. Tumbling, burning, turning . . . *agony*. It felt like Rayan's spine had cracked in half from the force of the sudden gust that pulled him out the doors and into the rover bay. What was once an orderly garage with rows of well-kept vehicles and drones was now caught up in a funnel, as if the entire ship were being drained out and into space.

Space. He had one fast glimpse of it and then he was somersaulting, reaching out for anything and everything. His hands found purchase on a rubbery stump, no, a leg. Rosalyn's leg. He was holding her by the ankles, feet kicked out behind him as the doors beyond her closed. No more of the glowing blue matter was sucked out the vortex behind them, but the rovers and drones banged hard against the sealed locks keeping them in place. A few stray crates that hadn't been secured disappeared so quickly it was like they simply ceased to exist. It wasn't wind pulling on them but the terrible inward breath of a hundred gods, sucking them away, ripping at them as a burning iciness crept over his body.

His body. Rayan felt the insurrection inside as he held on with all his strength, the Foxfire not quiet, not at all. It rioted. He closed his eyes against the howling windy gusts and cried out, dry, frozen and feeling his fingers slip. He imagined a million little seeds inside him scattering, or a thousand spiders scuttling for shadowy holes. A place to hide. Respite. But there was no respite. The outer ship doors were open, and space would vacuum them up unless someone pulled the lock.

A shape tumbled by, big and unwieldy, and then he felt a painful jerk on his left calf and glanced down in a panic, his hair whipping, his vision growing duller as everything in the rover bay was swept away. He was being pulled apart. Loose, grainy crumbles came free from the wound on his head, one boot going with them.

Piero. Piero had fallen out of the *Brigantine* in the tumult, latching onto his leg but only just, his mangled arm and its hand the only connection to Rayan, to life. To salvation.

Why did he have to come back into his body now? *Coward*, he thought, wishing he could summon the Foxfire back to shame it. Cowards. *Cowards*. Abandoned at the moment of greatest peril, of death.

No, he heard a soft, drowning voice say, *I saved you once, dear one. Mother resurrected you from certain death. Here is a human's ungrateful heart laid bare.*

"Go!" he screamed. Tears dried and froze and crackled instantly on his cheeks.

Rosalyn glanced down at him. She felt him struggling and must have thought his one screamed word was for her. In a way it was. Time slowed. He looked up at her, beautiful but afraid, clinging to the safety rail just inside the rover bay. She had looped one arm around it and then the other, finding a strong grip, but not strong enough. Space would pull them out, destroy them, turn them to icy dust.

Time slowed.

He was in the galley just outside the cockpit. Piero was kicking all of their asses at crazy eights. *I hate this game*, he had said, throwing down his terrible hand. *Why can't we play tarneeb?*

Misato had offered to switch games but Piero wanted to keep fleecing them. It was just a big show, a way to one-up them all. Piero was like that. He was being confrontational because Rayan had found something shady on his tablet. The Italian had been drinking grappa, and it smelled so foul coming out of his mouth that Rayan thought it must be paint thinner. Piero left his tablet open, and Rayan saw one of the banking tabs. How could he have that much money and still work exploratory jobs for Merchantia? Who would bother? Well, besides Misato, but she was weird that way. Piero was a mercenary; mercenaries didn't do charity.

What's this? Rayan had thought it funny. *Piero, you're loaded. When we get back you're taking me somewhere nice on Tokyo Bliss Station.*

Don't look at that. Why would you look at that? What are you, a spook? Mind your own business.

It was such a harsh response. So defensive.

I didn't mean anything by it. Relax.

Shut up, you relax. Hand me the bottle, cazzo.

The voices got bad during crazy eights. Not just bad, intolerable. Every time he tried to play a card, a small voice inside him suggested something else. It was like he was going mad, like he could suddenly read minds. The voice would tell him what card Edison was about to play, and then it would happen. Again and again he was right. *This isn't real. This isn't possible.*

The round ended and Piero won, then stood, doing a ridiculous dance, pretending to hump Edison's head out of his sight.

He's going to go get his bottle of wine. He wants to celebrate.

Who's up for a drink, eh? Piero had done just as the voice predicted. It didn't make sense. It was maddening, as maddening as the headaches and the strange dreams. Every night he dreamed of a lady all in blue, tentacles reaching out for him, strangling him until he shrieked and flew awake.

He slammed his own forehead on the table once, then did it again. At first it felt sort of good, or at least, it was a distraction from the voices and the headaches. Then he stood and did it more, harder, leaning back and throwing himself against a low support beam. The rest of the crew tried to stop him, but it was too late; he was going to get the voices out by any means necessary . . .

On the contrary, it only made things worse. The voices grew louder, more persuasive, until he couldn't sort out his thoughts from the stranger's. He thought maybe it was the blue lady's voice inside him, but no, nothing so beautiful could hurt this much.

He had let it in, sped it all up, given himself that wound, and when he woke up, numb with drugs, he saw it on all their faces: *You were not supposed to wake up.*

In Wazir Khan Mosque there was a pale red archway, tapered, with stones worn by time and cruel winds. Leafy plants grew in the corridor beyond, leaning into the pathway to find the sun. A gate lay at the end of the passage, an open walkway above with three embellished arches. The walls there were yellow swirled with crimson, like a droplet of blood dropped into tea. He pictured his brothers in those arches, waving to him, beckoning him. They weren't smiling, they didn't look happy to see him, but even their sober greeting felt like going home. He wondered where they were just then. Io, probably, or Tokyo Bliss Station. Ehsan had taken a job on an orbital cruise off Mars. Hamid wanted to go back to school for colonial horticulture. Behram just drifted. Typical youngest. Free and unconcerned, always certain to land safely after a fall.

He moved toward the gate, toward his brothers. There was

pressure on his leg, but he barely felt it. His skin and sinew felt stiff, as if he were becoming stone.

So verily, with the hardship, there is relief, verily with the hardship there is relief.

When he tried to open his eyes they were crusted and cold, as if held in front of an open refrigerator. He tried to blink but nothing happened. A kind of jagged cork wedged in his throat. Rosalyn held on still above him, safe in her suit.

But Piero. Piero pulled and pulled, trying to swing himself up even as space performed its horrible transformations. Crystals grew all along his half-naked body, frosting the silver-white eyes, the torn chest, the threadbare muscles in his destroyed arm. While he still could, Rayan looked down, then kicked weakly at the other man's hand. Again. Again. The toe of his boot nudged at the hand curved around his ankle, and to his horror he realized Piero could not let go; his fingers had frozen into place, hard and brittle as rock salt.

Go, Rayan thought. *Let go. Let go now. I'll go, too, but not with you. Not with you.*

Piero didn't give up, trying to force his way up Rayan's leg. But space moved against him. There was no fighting its inexorable pull. No sound, no sound, but in his mind he heard the crack, the shivery snap as the exposed bone and strained sinews of his elbow gave, and Piero flew away, spinning and spinning as the stars claimed another soul.

It was time to be charitable. To forgive.

Whatever you were, whoever you became, for a little while you were beautiful. We were beautiful together. Forget Mother. Forget her. Remember yourself.

Rayan couldn't see. He didn't know what Rosalyn looked like as he nudged his fingers free of her boot. He didn't know if she looked relieved or sad, or if she reached for him. He had already said goodbye, made preparations. His work was in the lab, his memories and his mementos, too. Somehow it didn't scare him so much, because at least he had chosen to let go.

It didn't feel at all like he expected. It didn't feel like anything at all.

32

"No! Hang on! Shit, shit. *HEAR ME!*"

Her ears rang in her helmet. She had been screaming at Rayan for what felt like an eternity. In reality, it had been thirty, maybe forty-five seconds. Her arms were about to give out, but even so, if she reached—if she just reached—maybe she could save him. She had to try to save him, because in those last seconds, when Piero's arm snapped and he was ripped out of the *Brigantine*, Rayan had glanced her way and his eyes were his own.

Rayan had spun free of the bay doors when she saw them slowly start to close. She gasped, losing strength in one arm, reduced to clinging to the railing with one precarious hand. The force was too much, and the doors were closing too slowly. By the time they met and the bay pressurized, she would be long gone.

Oh God, oh God, not like this.

Only one more minute. Thirty seconds. *Anything.* But it had been hard enough holding on for that long, especially with the weight of two men dragging behind her, pulling as inescapably as space. Pain shot through her elbow, a sprain maybe, or just her muscles failing on her at the last possible second. She screamed, yanked, going boots over helmet as she careened toward the sliver of stars between the doors. Worse than floating forever in a void, she was going to be extruded into paste.

Rosalyn put her hands out in front of her, desperate, wishing there was something feasible to grab, but the rovers locked to the walls were just out of reach, and the little opening in the doors was coming fast. She spun once, twice, watching in mute horror as her death approached. Just an inch of space light, half an inch, then . . . nothing.

Floating, she bumped gently into the closed doors. Listened with sobs of hysterical relief as the seal engaged, the lock pressurized, and the gravity stabilizers kicked in. She fell with a thump to the ground, laughing and crying so hard she could barely breathe. On all fours she hiccupped and gasped, hiccupped and gasped, trying to chase down the lump of certain doom in her throat.

"Rosalyn! Holy shit, it worked. Rosalyn!"

Edison limped toward her, then managed to pick up the pace and reach her, falling to his knees and taking her shoulders as the magnitude of what she had just survived hit full force and she vomited into her helmet, slumping into an unconscious bundle at his knees.

She didn't know how long she had slept or how she had gotten to cold storage, but she woke slowly in the fetal position, the right side of her face soaked, lying an inch deep in cold, sour vomit.

"We tossed a fresh suit in with you. Can you hear me? How's your oxygen? You should check the filters."

Rosalyn sloshed herself upright. She was almost sick again from the smell, but managed to swallow it down instead. The shield held, a tiny fissure down the middle, but it was otherwise intact. Edison stood on the other side. He had changed into a fresh crew uniform, a tight, collared thermal tee and baggy cargo pants.

Her eyes filled with tears at the sight of him.

"What? No! No, don't cry. Hey . . ."

"It's going to happen," she wheezed. "The crying. A lot. Hasn't . . . hasn't happened in so long. Just let it be. Christ, are we really alive?"

Edison gave a dark laugh, nodding. "Apparently." Then he pointed to the clean, white hazmat suit next to her. "You can run it through the decontam chamber. Misato is pumping the vents extra hard in here so you might feel a little light-headed. She just wanted to make sure all the junk on your suit was killed off."

The diffuser was on, too, the herbal, sharp scent of melaleuca oil and oregano flooding the room, tingeing the oxygen coming in through her helmet.

"Can you give me a minute?" Rosalyn asked. He throat was hoarse from being sick and screaming so much. "I should . . . I'd like to clean up."

"Take all the time you need," Edison said softly. He tapped his temple. "You know where to find me."

She would. Her AR indicator for him was full and blinking, showing him right there on the other side of the shield.

"Wait!" she cried, lurching unsteadily to her feet. *Oof.* She was intensely dizzy, stumbling to the door and catching herself on the frame. "The comms. The signal. Can you—"

His face fell, and Edison shook his head slowly, glancing away. "They're fried. Piero did a number on the long-range hub."

"*No,*" she whispered, leaning her helmet against the wall. All that chaos, and for what? "Then we need to get moving. He didn't find a way to sabotage the thrusters, did he?"

"Nope."

Rosalyn puffed out a breath. That was something, at least. "I'll sync with your display. You can have my credentials, all right? Just get us moving out of here. The last thing I want is more casualties."

"You sure? We hold out long enough, maybe we could explain it all, right? Once they dock with us, once they—"

"No." She hadn't intended to sound so vicious, but she was exhausted and her stomach was already turning again from the stench in her visor. "Listen, I appreciate what you're trying to do here, but we can't risk it. We're a baited trap. Look at what happened to Piero and Rayan. It could happen to you, too."

Edison didn't respond, but she saw his brows knit together over his glasses with hurt as she turned away. It was simple, sending the linkup request to his display. Once he accepted it, Rosalyn could freely send information and vice versa. She composed the message and attached her credentials, then shuffled toward the decontam chamber and the shower. When she looked over her shoulder to make sure she was alone, Edison was gone.

It was a relief to peel herself out of the suit. She was never going to get the smell out of that helmet, she thought with a sigh. Her chest felt like someone had cracked it with a power hammer. Every muscle in her body protested as she carefully stripped and hauled herself into the decontam chamber. A shower would feel nicer, but that would have to wait. Keeping herself free of Foxfire was priority one, even if she was desperate to soak in scalding hot water for a few hours or days.

That reminded her . . . She glanced up at her AR task bar. Eight hours had passed while she slept. As much as she needed that sleep, she worried about what might have transpired in the interim. She couldn't imagine what Misato and Edison were thinking. They had lost two of their crew and probably JAX, too. Rosalyn had no idea what to feel. In the moment it had all felt right, necessary, but she would never forgive herself for not trying harder to boost Rayan up. Piero was a lost cause, a killer, but something in the younger man's face told her there was still something in there to salvage. In the end, it looked to her like he had let go on purpose. She ached to think of him turning endless circles in space. Nobody deserved that. Maybe if she somehow survived this disaster, MSC could send out recovery probes. But no. Her heart sank. They couldn't send out recovery probes, couldn't risk bringing his remains back to the campus and contaminating the whole place. If his body was found, they would need to incinerate it.

Rosalyn leaned against the well of the chamber and pulled the protective mask over her mouth and nose, closing her eyes. The cool puffs of air drifted over her shoulders, and she shivered, clenching her gut to keep from crying. More and more, she knew survival was nothing to expect. Nothing to even hope for. They were on a suicide mission now, with a one-way trip to CDAS and nothing beyond. She hardly cared what they found there. What did it matter? Foxfire had to be eliminated. Merchantia and GATE had to be warned. Her only realistic goal was making sure nobody else went through this hell.

An image of Piero pulling himself along Misato's knife floated across her mind and she retched, a thin stream of bile leaking out of her mouth and down the seam of the protective mask. She wasn't sad to see him go. But was he really gone? Wasn't his consciousness shared with Edison, with Misato? They had done so much to shield themselves from Foxfire and the others, maybe they could hold on a little longer.

The chamber beeped quietly, indicating the cycle was complete. Rosalyn dropped the mask and tiptoed out and around, into the shower, turning on the hot water with a giddy sound. One small pleasure. One small relief. She smoothed her hands over her shaved head and leaned into the water stream, letting it scour the mess from her face and neck.

She dreaded leaving cold storage, her little haven, but eventually she would need to confirm their course. As much as she wanted to trust Edison and Misato, as much as they had proved themselves her allies, she knew there was still an unknown element inside them. They could pilot the *Brigantine* straight to Tokyo Bliss Station and assimilate millions of innocent people. And anyway, she owed Edison an apology for snapping at him over the coordinates. She couldn't say for sure, of course, but it seemed wiser to keep the remaining crew on her side. They would never really be friends, couldn't be, but it would be far worse to see them become enemies.

Edison accepted her linkup, and a tiny green circle appeared next to her pending message. Soon the thrusters would unlock, and they would be on their way to Coeur d'Alene Station. His icon on her display blinked and she pulled her face out of the water, reading his changed public profile. It was blank. No more dogs, jazz or whiskey.

Ouch.

Rosalyn shook her head and plunged her face back into the spray. *Wise up, you moron, it's better this way.* Yes, better. Better to keep the crew at a distance. Better to harden herself now knowing what the inevitable was likely to be. Still, it stung, way more than she expected or appreciated. On a whim, as a starter apology, she opened her own public profile and added to it.

Vomiting profusely into helmets since 2269

Maybe it would help smooth things over. Maybe it would make him crack even a small smile after the horrors they had just survived. She stumbled out of the shower, kicking over her old jumpsuit as she did. The fabric pooled and toppled, and out came the syringe body and the badge Tuva had found.

And something else.

Rosalyn crouched, picking up the little hard-coded message her father had sent the day she left. She hadn't listened to the whole thing, but now it seemed right. His indifference—his failures—couldn't hurt her anymore. She had forgiven herself for everything that had happened with Glen. Staring down Piero's madness, fighting him off, had felt like the best apology she could give to her old self.

Sliding down to the floor, she adjusted the respirator and pulled on a towel, then sat in the dissipating steam, listening as her father's voice pierced the whir and hum of the little sterile room.

"Roz? Rosalyn . . . It's your father." She tensed, but let the message play through. "I wanted you to know that I miss you. And happy birthday, of course. Damn. I'm a day late, aren't I? Bugger it." The message cut out, then started up again. "Happy belated birthday, darling. I know we haven't spoken in a long time, and I know you won't come home, so I won't ask. That makes your mother want to strangle me, but I won't ask. There are just . . . things I needed to say."

Rosalyn braced, pulling her knees up to her chest and hugging them. The tears, the ones that never seemed to come when she was stuck in the space between screaming and sobbing, came freely.

"Glen is out. I should have believed you, I did believe you, it's just . . . his position at the company, what he did, what he knows about our books, if he turned on us, there would be an alphabet soup of agencies up my ass over it. I had to give him money, Roz, a lot of money, to keep quiet. When you went away I was happy, at first. I know how that sounds. But there are things we've done here, places we've gone, that were wrong. There's tech we messed about with, samples we found, that we should have turned over to GATE right away. Maybe it's better that you're gone. Not because I don't want you here, because I do, and not because I don't miss you, because I do, but because it might be safer. But then, your mother tells me you're with Merchantia now, so maybe not."

He let out a long sigh, and so did she. Then she covered her mouth with both hands, the sounds inside too big to let out all at once.

"Didn't you and Angela have the same birthday? I remember you two giggling together in the lab over it, over a cupcake. Red velvet. God, she's gone, too. I don't think we'll see her again, she loved that project too much, but I shouldn't have let her leave. This is what I mean, Rosalyn, there are things I can't tell you, things I wish I could tell you, but then you would be in more danger. Just tell me you're safe, all right? Give me a gift on your birthday. Late birthday. Typical me, I know. I love you, Rosie girl."

For a long time the message kept going, and she heard him breathing on the other end, loudly enough that he might have been right there next to her. Something had opened, a door she hadn't expected to ever find unlocked. She opened her AR archive of messages, adding that one to the collection of notes from her mother, from Angela, from Saruti . . . Angela had reached out for months, even after her big move to the outer space campus, and then one day it just . . . stopped. Angela's messages stopped just a month before their shared birthday, not that they could celebrate together this year. There wouldn't be cocktails and cupcakes, but even a call would have been nice. Wiping at her mouth, Rosalyn sighed into her palm; she didn't know if she regretted leaving Earth, but she mourned the bridges she had burned so recklessly in the depths of her pain.

Rosalyn sat in the damp towel, staring into that open door in her mind, letting the light pour out and wash over her. Her father was still in the wrong, but it was more complicated than she believed. Or maybe not. She didn't know what to think, or what she would've done in his position. The urge to talk to him, to understand, almost soothed away the brief surge of relief. She felt shaky with the acidic burn of fear in her stomach. Coincidences were piling up, too many to ignore, and she had to wonder if the timing of her father's company merging with Merchantia was key. Josh Girdy suspected a cover-up. Someone had tried hard to divert Rosalyn away from the infected

Brigantine. Other ships coding. Piero, or Danny, whoever he was, murdering a crewmate, lying about his identity, holding on to a dated note that lined up with the launches of doomed expeditions . . . Was it just resentment bleeding in that now she knew, or felt, that her father and Belrose Industries were mixed up in it all? It didn't seem possible, but then, none of it did. She had seen things nobody could expect to see, survived things nobody would expect to survive, and the pieces twining together in her head made an awful kind of sense.

Angela had left Earth with her own project, a dangerous one, one her father made sound like a suicide mission, but in every one of Angela's unanswered messages, she made it sound like they were going to cure all the world's ills. If only she could talk to Angela over lemon drop cocktails, she would know what to do, and that she was okay, alive, just working hard and video calling her kids, the same old Angela, mother as much to her test tubes as she was to her human children.

She almost sent off a message to Edison, and then to Misato, but she stopped. They were in pain, too. A part of them was still human, and that part had to be grieving. Rosalyn stood and returned to the shower, standing under the hot water for a long time, wondering if she would ever speak to her parents again, or to Angela, or to anyone totally human.

But maybe that was all wrong. Maybe it was more important than ever to stick by Edison and Misato, to find in them the humanity that was left and nurture it like a fragile seedling growing in a storm. It would be hard, knowing that it might be over for them soon, but a voice inside her said simply: *Fight back.*

I can be your friend, she thought. *Just don't make me be your executioner.*

33

Jenny had loved cults.

Aum Shinrikyo, Order of the Solar Temple, Heaven's Gate, Dohring-Waugh, the Lighted Path, Scientology. The psychology of it fascinated her. Utter devotion in the face of overwhelming scientific evidence. Religion they both understood, if shakily, but cults were something different. Jenny sent Misato article after article, and snippets of video she found in the Musk Hall archives. Some of it was back in the days of film, and the grainy quality of the images added to the mystical allure.

"All these people thinking they're going to, like, hop on a comet and sail to enlightenment. It's bonkers, right? But you have to respect it." Somehow, they always landed back on this topic. Jenny had been particularly animated that night, gesticulating wildly as she alternately guzzled wine and cola and wolfed down sushi. "But didn't we kind of do the same thing? Earth is an afterthought now. We hopped on starships and flew to a totally new reality. Shit, I wasn't even born on a planet. If I could go back in time and meet one of these people, they would think I was, like, Xenu or some shit."

When the Dohring-Waugh fanatics hijacked a passenger ship and crashed it into the surface of Mars, Jenny was there to give Misato

the play-by-play, even though every news stream covered it in pains-
taking detail. It hurt that Jenny couldn't see how uncomfortable the
coverage made her; the cultists had been convinced the Io colonies
were going to become prisons, the colonists used as lab rats. The
crash was their act of protest, or maybe they really thought they
could somehow land on the surface of Mars with few supplies, no
expertise and only sheer blind hope to save them.

Misato humored her, and when the hurt passed, she even preferred Jenny this way. This was far preferable to her more morose
moods. Banks of ceiling-high fish tanks surrounded them, suffusing
their table in cool light, wobbly yellow and green lines undulating
over their plates and cups. The waiter had disappeared long ago, not
bothering to return since they had already paid the bill and were
now just finishing off a massive tower of sushi rolls.

"What would you say to them?" Misato had asked her, nursing
her white wine.

"Oh! Hmm . . . no . . . oh! Yes!" Jenny adopted a prophet's posture, shoulders back, hand outstretched to her invisible followers.
"Humanity will live among the stars, my glorious children, but not
in your time or the time after. But fear not! You will be reborn,
reincarnated into their bodies so that you may one day live in a
dreamer's dream. So for now, pull your heads out of your asses and
live your damned lives already."

They both dissolved into laughter, Jenny's so raucous she dropped
a spicy tuna roll into her lap.

"Shit. Still good."

With her newly dyed fuchsia hair and fuchsia lips, Jenny looked
at home among the exotic fish. Misato admired her above her wine-
glass, content just to listen. Just to watch.

"I could see doing it," she then said thoughtfully.

"Doing what?" Jenny asked.

"Joining a cult," Misato replied. The lights in the restaurant dimmed another notch, and Jenny wagged her eyebrows suggestively. *Mood lighting.* "They're a part of deep belief. How are scientists any different?"

"Well, for one, you can actually test your theories and see if they work. Have you ever tried teleporting to a comet? Not so easy." Smirking, Jenny snatched another roll with her silver chopsticks.

"But maybe we could. One day. Teleport to a comet, I mean. It only hurts us if we stop daring to wonder." Misato was getting sleepy, and she wanted to crawl into bed soon with her two cats. "One hundred years ago a stable colony on Io was unthinkable. Now look at us."

"Sure, sure. You dream big," Jenny allowed. "But you dream smart. Colonies are useful, aimless trips on comets considerably less so."

"Oh, I don't know." She fidgeted, restless, and downed the last of her wine. "It might be nice to just sit and look and have nowhere to be and nowhere really to go."

That's how she pictured Rayan, sailing along on a comet of his own, taking a long and lazy tour of the stars. She had loved him, in an abstract way, in the way a teacher can love a pupil. Before the Foxfire, and maybe even after it, she saw so much of herself in him. He had a relentless, open mind and a thirst for understanding that rivaled her own.

There was no incense, but Misato found a quiet corner in the lab, compiling and sorting the notes Rayan had made while studying Foxfire. Research was its own kind of meditation, and she couldn't think of a better way to honor his memory than to look at what he had found. His notes weren't particularly organized, and they became less so as time went on, the Foxfire making a messy scrawl of his handwriting by the end. Rayan had experimented on himself relentlessly, but nothing physical seemed to make for much of a change. She, too, suspected that once the spores were ingested, it was too late. More interesting were the complex charts Rayan had made tracking the mental progression of the Foxfire, taking careful stock of how frequently he felt himself hallucinating or losing control.

The trend was clear, day by day the episodes increased, but he had found other connections.

Worse today: Memory of my mother, her perfume, her wrinkled hands, Foxfire stronger then, electric, live wire at the base of my neck. The hallucination calls itself my mother now, uses her voice. Troubling. Fascinating? It's learning our weaknesses.

And then, the next day, a single circled note after his tally of hallucinations:

This phenomenon is obsessed with increase. Children. Us.

Misato waded further into his meticulous notes, tracking the time he attempted to lock them into separate parts of the ship, a clever effort to see if separation slowed the Foxfire's power over them, removing the nearness that seemed to amplify its control, like a signal that grew stronger the longer they remained in proximity. And Rosalyn's arrival was cataloged, too, an explosion of hasty, scrambled ideas . . .

Someone new is here. Mother is louder and louder, she wants the salvager. Why so desperate? Ship is infected, time on Foxfire's side. Why the urgency? I smell lemons all the time now, hear a distant laugh. My brain is on fire. Something has changed.

Misato finished reading, allowing herself to feel the sharp sting of sadness when the notes trailed off for good, all but illegible. Standing, she gathered up the personal possessions Rayan had laid out on the drafting table, and placed them in a small, cozy storage bin. Tuva's went into a separate bin next to his. She didn't store the complicated biological notes Rayan had made, the ones that looked like another language to her. Those, she kept out prominently on the lab's drafting table. If the *Brigantine* was ever found, she wanted that science, that potential understanding, easily found. Maybe whoever found their wreck could pick up the thread and unravel what Rayan could not.

She closed the lid of Rayan's crate and sat next to it, feeling the heavy mantle of loss settle on her shoulders. Even at her age, even after burying so many friends and family members and lovers, it still felt like a fluid going down the wrong passage, a knot in her throat, an endless hollowness in her belly. Her mother had been a Buddhist, not a very good one, but the rituals had given her comfort when the typhoon hit. Misato only remembered the ravaging aftermath because of the archive footage. She remembered the too-strong floral scent of the incense. When she grieved, she always thought she smelled burnt jasmine. She had never been close to her mother, but still, she grieved her, grieved the love that never seemed to grow between them, a garden planted but never tended.

Misato was no monk and she didn't know the correct order of things or the chants, but she lowered her head and closed her eyes and thought instead of having a conversation.

"I know you have him," she whispered, placing her palms on her knees. "Some part of him must still be with you."

With his mother, you mean.

"Forget it," Misato muttered, opening her eyes. But Foxfire wasn't done with her. When was it ever? The voice, which always seemed to come from every direction at once, filled her head loudly

SALVAGED

enough to hurt. Before it took the guise of her mother, until it realized that wouldn't build any roads inland.

*We miss these talks. We know you are afraid of what they became, of
what you saw . . .*

"Boo-hoo." But she didn't move, knowing that once the thing
inside her became talkative, there was usually no shutting it up. Her
coffee was all the way on the other side of the room, and besides, she
was admittedly curious about where this was going. Usually their
conversations were so confrontational, but this had a different tone.
Rayan's research indicated he was sure Foxfire was evolving, changing its methods constantly to outwit and seduce them. This seemed
like another evolution and not even a subtle one. Perhaps it realized
the aggressive method had backfired, turning Piero and Rayan into
easily identified and therefore readily resisted threats.

Misato vowed not to forget that.

*We are curious. When we have these conversations, what do we look like
to you?*

This was new. Before, Foxfire almost always asked the same repetitive questions: Why wouldn't she give in? Why didn't she want
to join the family? Why was she so foolishly stubborn? And on and
on . . .

Misato closed her eyes again, and at once the vision of the blue
woman came to her.

"A woman dressed in blue. Her skin is blue, too, and her eyes.
She's . . . covered in vines, or maybe those are her veins. I can't tell.
When I still slept I dreamed of her. That's how I picture you," she
murmured. "But that doesn't make any sense."

Oh?

"You don't have form, not . . . human form. You're just spores,
some kind of network bound at a molecular level but also a tele-
pathic level. I don't have to understand the nuances of that to know

255

you aren't a human woman," she said. "So it's either a trick, or there's something here I don't yet understand."

You were always the smartest one.

"Ha. Nice try. Flattery is an old tactic, and even we simple *Homo sapiens* know that."

"What are you doing?"

Misato had been so distracted by the exchange that the intrusion made her gasp. Snapping her eyes open, she reoriented, relaxing again when she realized it was only Edison. He stood at the entrance to the lab, and she must have looked awfully strange, wedged in the corner, facing the wall, a box placed before her as she knelt.

Standing, she brushed at nothing on her pants and turned to face him. "Putting some things to rest," she said. "How's Rosalyn?"

Edison drew in a deep breath and fiddled with his glasses, as he always did when he was anxious. "Shaken. Angry. I left her alone to clean up."

"You should talk to her." Misato bent down and picked up the box with Rayan's things, then returned to the crew lockers and put the crate in his. Then she went back to the drafting table where she had left her coffee, and swigged it. This time it was mixed liberally with vodka. "I think she could use a little kindness."

"We could all use that," Edison said. She held out the cup to him and he took it. He drank without sniffing, then coughed. "Jesus, that's strong."

"I needed a little something after . . ." Misato blinked and shook the cobwebs out of her head. "When you dream, do you see a blue woman? Can you smell lemons?"

Edison nodded, seemingly unfazed by the question. They had all compared notes at the beginning, but then Rayan locked them in seclusion, and that triggered private battles with the demons within.

Misato had heard the others go mostly silent except for the occasional bout of rage as they tried to get Rayan to let them out.

"Yeah, it freaked me out. But she—it—always tries to look like my mother. Why?"

"Just something I've been thinking about," Misato said softly, retrieving her cup from him and sipping it. She let her mouth rest on the lip and glanced up at him, noticing a new, ugly bruise spreading along his jaw under his beard. "Why would it look human? Why would it be a woman?"

Shrugging, he faced the drafting table and passed his hands lightly over Rayan's favorite place to work and the laminated scientific notations Rayan had left behind for them. Some of his observations were even written permanently onto the table. Edison had changed into a fresh uniform, and the tight shirt clung to his muscled shoulders. She wondered if the Foxfire made him continue his exercise or if it was his own impulse, another way to remain more human. "Sympathy, I think, or trust. Better the devil you know, right? Mother figure is less threatening than a form we can't empathize with."

"Yes, yes, that's good," Misato agreed. "But then why is she blue? Why the lemons? My mother smelled like jasmine. That's not familiar. Why take a similar form for us at all? My childhood was not like yours, mm? This thing is intelligent. It learns. By now it should know to appear as something pulled from our fondest memories." She sighed and joined him in his shrugging. "Or I'm full of shit, and this leads nowhere."

"When I'm awake I see my mother, when I try to sleep it's the blue woman. I don't know what that means, Misato, but Rayan was clearly very busy," Edison observed. He picked up a plasticky card. It was reusable and shiny, but the marker on it wasn't faded or smudged. "Nanomechanical oscillations," he read. "Organic anchor theory? What's that?"

"Plants can communicate on the smallest molecular scale with vibrations, the closest thing on Earth to telepathy," Misato explained, sidling up to him and peering at the card in his hands. She pointed to it. "But this? OAT. I've never heard of that. I was a hobbyist biologist compared to Rayan."

Edison seemed to unfocus his laser-blue eyes, but Misato recognized it as a person consulting their AR display. He would be searching his hard database for anything on OAT. Quickly, however, he shook his head and put the card back down, making sure to replace it in its original spot.

"Not much," he said. "Most of the linked studies are on crackpot archives. SpaceAsk, I Want to Believe, all the usual suspects. Still, something to look into. I can do some reading later."

"Please do," Misato replied, offering him another sip from her mug. He took it, but more gingerly this time. "I'd like to think Rayan helped us beat this thing. Or, you know, outrun it long enough to see it destroyed."

"That's the idea." He winced from the strength of the vodka. "You all right? I know you and the kid were close."

She took the cup with both hands and padded quietly to the lockers, then opened hers and fetched a bottle of the good stuff. Not vodka, of course, that wasn't his style. She remembered nights of cards with Edison sipping a few fingers of whiskey, his ring finger tapping rhythmically on the glass. That was his tell. Misato brought him the bottle and leaned against the drafting table.

Vodka was her drink of choice, but she opened the whiskey and took a swig herself before offering it to him.

"Does that answer your question?" she asked.

"I should've done more," Edison said to the bottle, holding it close to his chest. "This thing . . . It eats away at what's good until all that's left is the deep dark shit you tried hard to forget."

Misato put a hand on his shoulder, not knowing if it was appropriate or not, but sensing he needed it. He seemed to sag under her touch, or maybe relax. "Then make something else good; I don't want to know what happens if it gets you. We owe it to Tuva. To Rayan. To whatever little part of Piero wasn't monstrous. We're all that's left of the fight."

"And Rosalyn," Edison said with a sad smile.

"Yes, and her. You and me and her, *that's* something good. Try not to forget that."

34

There had been five little stones in the memorial garden for the crew; now three actually belonged there.

Rosalyn had spent as much time as she could stomach scrubbing out her old suit and blasting the new one in the decontam chamber. At some point, she told herself, she had to leave cold storage. The tedium kept her focused, kept her from listening over and over again to her father's messages, old and new, and it saved her from sinking into her mother's texts and Angela's.

She ate, chewing and swallowing the food without tasting it, then pulled on the fresh and clean-smelling suit they had given her. God, she had to laugh. She could just imagine Edison and Misato carrying her to the room, trying not to breathe in the toxic-to-them diffused and decontaminated air while also making sure she was all the way inside with her new gear.

At first, it seemed like a no-brainer to just sit there and read old messages on her display. But the idleness of it, the quiet, made it easier for the demons to come for her. She couldn't shake the feeling of Piero crawling on top of her, his slavering ghoulish face and silver eyes, the sense that history was repeating itself all over again. Music wasn't doing much either, because she felt paranoid without full control of her senses. And there was a soothing quality to the sound of the thrusters churning away, the *Brigantine* leaving behind the coordinates and the *Salvager 6* and her last chance at escape.

Rosalyn wiped at her eyes before the tears even came back. She was locked in now, really locked in, determined to see this thing through and wipe Foxfire out for good. But it was lonely, waiting there with ugly thoughts lurking in the shadows of her mind. That was probably how it felt to be infested with Foxfire, always on the verge of turning the wrong mental corner, surrounded in your own body and head.

A small icon blinked on her task bar. An unread message. Well, it wasn't exactly a mystery who it was from, but Rosalyn was curious all the same.

Hey. You up?

She rolled her eyes and composed a quick response.

Yes. Don't be vile.

It was a legitimate question, he replied. *You were pretty crashed out before.*

Pardon me for that, we all almost died.

She watched the little ellipses scroll and scroll, disappointed in herself for wanting him to reply quickly. Eventually the icon blinked again.

I have whiskey, he wrote.

I'll be right there.

Josh Girdy could hardly blame her for drinking on the job at this point. Rosalyn double-checked the seals on her new suit, acclimating to the slightly different design. These were made for experimenting in labs and collecting samples, and were therefore lighter and less unwieldy. It was still Merchantia issue, however, and similar enough in style to work in similar ways. She stretched, testing it out. They were all standard sizes, and at a guess this one probably was made for someone petite like Misato. A bit tight. It had come with fresh oxygen filters, but she knew she would be compulsively checking the levels anyway. She hopped into the decontam pod and blasted herself one more time for good measure, then left the room and resealed it as quickly as she could.

A shudder rattled her as she prepared to turn and go down the corridor. The Foxfire was still everywhere, glowing with unnerving, slow pulses. She could still see Piero's hideous blue skull of a face in the shadows, hovering there, a disembodied threat. No. He was gone. He was gone and she wasn't going to let the lingering trauma keep her from a stiff drink.

Fight back.

The floor buzzed underneath her feet, the reassuring vibrations of the thrusters carrying them toward CDAS. Not that their destination was at all a pleasant thought, but she preferred movement to the idle, sitting-duck feeling of drifting through space. This *was* their plan coming to fruition, she reminded herself, even if it didn't look the way they had originally imagined. With her AR synced to Edison's, she could keep tabs on the flight time and ETA. At their current level of fuel dedication and speed, they would reach CDAS in approximately forty-eight hours. Two days. A lot could change in two days. She only hoped Edison and Misato could hold on, that she wouldn't run out of filters, and that the Foxfire wouldn't find new and scarier ways to sway their minds.

She had started filling the time as best she could, trying to make herself useful, finding small comfort in dreaming up a solution to the Foxfire still gripping Misato and Edison. A dream it would remain unless she could get her hands on the kind of lab she had used on Earth. Engineering implantable chips was her forte, and in theory, she didn't see why the same technology couldn't work to combat the spread of Foxfire. Without proper tools, she could only sketch and plan so far, but it was something. Something.

A stupid, errant thought entered her head as she called up the schematic and navigated back to the spare storage room Edison had made into his bunker. The stupid thought was this, that maybe she was part of the solution to that precarious forty-eight hours. She was, after all, the only uninfected member of this ragtag crew. Maybe the untouched nature of her humanity was a weapon of sorts, something to use when the call of the Foxfire grew too irresistible. That was easy, in a way, because she liked Misato, and she liked Edison, too. It had shocked her, how cold it felt to be faced with his death, and how much relief she felt to find that he and Misato were relatively unscathed.

Relatively. There was no telling what was happening on the inside, Rosalyn reminded herself, a fact that she would need to pin on her task bar just in case the whiskey stirred up dangerous thoughts.

When she reached the storage area, she was surprised to find no sign of Edison. There was even less sign of Foxfire. She noted little traces of dirt on the floor, flecks of something grayish, but he had managed to scrape the ceiling and bunk area clean. An extendable sweeper and an automated cleaning drone sat just inside the open doors. The growth of Foxfire along the ceiling crept up to those doors but went no farther. Whether it was symbolic or practical, it made her feel more welcome. Safer.

Rosalyn poked her head inside, peering around. Nobody.

"Hello?" she called. "I'm here for the whiskey party?"

Nothing.

She dared to shuffle inside, finding that the dimmers had been switched to a pleasing level, just warmly lit enough to see, but not blinding or glaring. A work tablet was open on his "desk" and she approached it, hands behind her back, leaning over to find a series of handwritten poems done with a stylus. His handwriting was disarmingly artistic, with big, fine loops and a definite slant to the right. Smirking, she read over a few of the verses, then flicked the screen to the left to see more. It was a bit voyeuristic, but that feeling was swiftly quelled. The poems were childlike. One digital tablet simply read, frighteningly enough, TEETH.

"Sorry, I stepped out."

Rosalyn jumped, then spun and tried, pathetically, not to blush. "I was definitely not prying."

Edison shrugged and strode purposefully toward her, setting down a full bottle of single-malt whiskey and a tumbler. Only one, she noted, a little sourly.

"I'm only embarrassed that it's so bad."

Rosalyn glanced over her shoulder at the tablet. "You're a closet poet?"

"I'm not," he said, tapping the side of his head. "She is. Mostly children's rhymes. Basic stuff."

"Oh. Oh, that's . . . weird, actually."

Edison peeled the foil off the top of the bottle and yanked the cork out with his teeth, spitting it into the corner. The cleaning drone, a small, flat disk with three antennae, came to life and chased down the errant cork, sucking it into its round body before going back to sleep.

"Weird? A grown man sitting alone in his storage unit writing children's ditties is weird, you say?" He poured out a measure of whiskey for himself and then reached into his pocket, pulling out a package of sealed cylinders filled with amber-colored liquid.

"No, well, yes," Rosalyn said, taking the cylinders he handed to her and staring down at them dumbly. "Weird because I recognize some of it. Your unwelcome guests are plagiarizing."

Edison paused at that, his eyebrows climbing slowly upward. "Are you sure? When I do it—when the Foxfire makes me do it—it feels like it's organic, you know, original."

Lilting jazz music filtered through the intercom, something chosen from his AR display. She didn't know the artist, but it was relaxing to have the silence filled, even if this all was beginning to feel ominously like a date.

"It's definitely not original." Rosalyn took the tablet and showed it to him, running her finger under one of the lines. "This I know from my childhood. It's Shel Silverstein. And this? My best friend, Angela, knew some of these ones, bits of it. She would read it to her kids over vid calls at work." Her eyes widened. "This next one? That's Maisy Teng. My mom had a first-edition Maisy Teng signed and under a locked display. She'd read it to me before bed when I was a kid. I never got to touch it." She blinked a few times and put the tablet down. "And if that isn't a metaphor for our relationship, then nothing is. What are these, by the way?"

"I found them in Piero's junk," Edison explained, tossing the tablet aside and taking her by the shoulder, turning her gently to the side.

"Wow, well then I definitely don't want anything to do with them. Probably laced with poison. What are you doing?"

"Relax, they're brand name. It's just an injectable; you can use them in the suit port. These capsules are compatible with our lab wear, in case you get hungry or thirsty in the field. They link into the suit from the packaging, totally clean." Edison held up one of the sealed capsules for her to see. "You cool?"

"Yeah," Rosalyn mumbled. "Yeah, I'm cool, I'm very—ow! *Jesus.* You didn't say it would sting!"

"Sorry. Thought it would be better to just get it over with, you know, rip the bandage off."

"Warn me next time, geez," she wheezed, rubbing at the closed port on the side of her hip. Then she opened her eyes wide, the direct injection of alcohol making her head spin. "That's . . . effective."

"Which means I need to catch up." Edison grabbed his glass and lifted it, then clinked it lightly against her helmet visor. "Cheers."

"That's not funny," she told him. "I don't even get to taste the stuff."

"And that's a shame because it is *oooh*. Very smooth."

"Yeah, yeah." Rosalyn waved him off with a grin, taking the tablet again and pacing away from the table. She couldn't let this go. It was too odd, too specific. "Why would Foxfire know these poems? Are you sure you don't recognize them?"

Edison didn't follow, leaning against the table and swirling his cup. He put one arm across his middle, just under his pectoral muscles, which had the uncomfortable result of showing off his physique. Rosalyn squinted down at the tablet diligently.

"Maybe I heard them when I was a kid and I just don't remember. Foxfire could be digging through my memories, whether they're ones I'm aware of or not. Rayan took a ton of notes on it, creepy stuff, tracking the way it all changed, the way Foxfire tried different things to get to him. Not the most pleasant thought." He shivered and chased off the shake with some whiskey. "Childhood is nostalgic. Powerful."

"Mm-hmm," she agreed. "Which means it's dangerous."

"I know some of this, like the 'Are you sleeping?' song. My ex-wife would sing that one to her kid when he had nightmares."

Rosalyn coughed softly. "You were married?"

"Yeah, you?"

"No . . . no, never. Close, maybe, but it was a disaster. My mother was really pushing for it, I know she always wanted to plan a wedding."

Edison beckoned her over, and when she came near, he took the tablet out of her hands and dropped it on the table. He looked tired, but there was a new liveliness in his eyes and a better color in his cheeks. Probably from the booze. "You and your mom, you didn't get along?"

"That's a nice way to put it," Rosalyn told him, deciding there was no real harm in being honest. They were all on a suicide mission, why hold it in? "We don't talk. Or rather, she talks at me and I avoid it at all costs. Never good enough for her, et cetera. I'm sure you know all about it, with your military mom."

"And dad?"

"We were close," Rosalyn admitted, eyeing another whiskey capsule. She was going to need the whole package if they were doing a deep dive into her family. "Really close."

"Were?"

She snorted and dug into the cylinder packet, ignoring his look. "You noticed that, did you? Yes, we had a falling-out recently. I quit the family business over . . . over some serious disagreements. I screwed up, he screwed up, and we both said things you can't take back, so I left."

"That can't possibly be true," Edison said with a chuckle, tilting back his head. "What work was it? Salvaging? You gotta excuse me for saying so, but you don't strike me as a lifelong salvager. You've got grit, and I guess salvaging takes grit, but you're holding out on me. That's a fancy accent for a deep space janitor."

"I'm not," Rosalyn assured him, injecting another whiskey capsule and sucking in a breath through her teeth. God, it was nice, more than nice, taking the edge off in a way she wanted badly. She just had to be careful she didn't go too far. "I just don't want you to feel sorry for me."

"Because?" he prompted, drawing out the word and then drowning it in a sip of whiskey.

Rosalyn caught his eye and held it, losing her smile. "Because whenever I tell someone the whole story, they look at me differently afterward. They always promise it won't happen and they're always full of shit."

She expected him to press, like they always did. She expected a big speech about how he was trustworthy and different. Instead, Edison nodded and finished his glass, then poured another few fingers.

"My wife left a year ago, just after my mother passed. Cancer that spread to her marrow, they slowed it down but eventually that wasn't enough," he said all in one breath. "She was adopted, hated her family, my dad had split, so I was the one that had to decide to pull the plug when she went into a coma."

"Edison . . ."

"See? Now you're looking at me differently, too." He dredged up a smile for her, then quickly hid it behind his glass. "I'm okay. I think you're okay, too. You don't have to tell me, I just thought maybe if we both look at each other sideways, it would cancel it all out."

Rosalyn walked deliberately away from the capsules and sat on the makeshift bunk pushed against the far wall. "That's an interesting theory. I guess we can test it. It's, uh, a long story but the condensed version is that I had a big, important job at a big, important biotech firm. My dad runs the place, and I made the rather poor decision to date a colleague. He was . . . not a nice man, let's put it that way. Treated me terribly, but was all smiles on the outside. Nobody but my best friend believed me when I told them what happened. He got tired of me one night and just . . . All the times, all the little warnings, they all made sense then, that he could just hold me down and hurt me that way."

Drawing in a huge breath, she let it out hard through her nose.

"Dad didn't fire him until, oh, a few days ago. For my birthday. But late, of course. At least he sent an apology of sorts."

He pushed away from the table with his hip but then leaned back against it, checking his whiskey before looking across the shadowy floor to her. "So you got the hell out of there."

She reached, reflexively, to push hair that wasn't there behind her ear. Her fingertips bumped the shield and smudged it. "Yes, and I told myself I might go back, but even hearing about him getting fired didn't make me feel much. He deserves so much worse."

"Now, when you say 'fired,' do you mean *set* on fire or . . . ?"

At that, she gave a dry laugh. "Unfortunately, no. But I like where your head's at."

Edison opened his mouth to say something else, then quickly ducked his head and clacked his teeth together. "I remember you said something before, something like you knew what it felt like to be controlled by someone else."

"I do know, in a way, what you're experiencing. Some days I even want to claw my own skin off."

He nodded. "When the Foxfire feels like it's going to take control? It kind of feels like, I don't know, like that lump you get in your throat when you know you're going to be sick and can't stop it. Like that, but in your brain. Brain . . . vomit."

Rosalyn tried not to laugh at him, biting down hard on her lip. "Brain vomit. Mm, I think it's safe to say you're not the poet in this arrangement," she teased, pointing between him and the tablet.

"Told ya." He took a few steps toward the bunk, examining his glass as he went. She preferred staying on safer topics, though the odd shift she had anticipated after their mutual sharefest remained absent. Whatever awkwardness she felt was from his being a relative stranger, not from the fact that he now knew one of her deepest secrets.

"Where were you before the *Brigantine*?" she asked. His dossier would give her all of that information, at least his postings, but it felt like a natural question.

Edison stood a few feet in front of her, in line with the door, resting his cup in the crook of one elbow. The music shifted to a more upbeat song, a scattershot trumpet blasting up and down scales while mellower drums tried to keep up.

"I bounced back and forth between Merchantia Solutions campuses. Tokyo Bliss Station for a while, but they didn't have much work for me there, it's a small outfit. Vancouver for a while, then mostly space-based deployments after Candace and I split up." He took a sip of whiskey and tsked softly. "I ran with this crew for quite a while, but we rotated security positions. Piero was a new guy. I've known Rayan for, oh, a while now. He was a good kid. So damned smart."

"I'm so sorry," she murmured. She felt suddenly cold and wrung her gloved hands together, trying to get warm. "Rayan, I could have helped him. I think . . . I think he was still in there somewhere."

Edison took three giant steps and knelt, ducking his head until he could find her steadily avoidant eyes. "No. *No*. You don't get to wear that one around your neck. I'm the captain of this ship, I make decisions about my crew, and I made a decision to flush the storage bay. Trust me, I didn't enjoy doing it, it endangered you and killed two men, but I did it. Leading isn't for everyone. After a while, it isn't for anyone."

She nodded, but his words didn't chase away the cold. "There's something else," she whispered, flustered. Rosalyn had to get away from him. The proximity was too intimate, too like real friendship, or . . . She had to get away. The whiskey capsules called to her so she found refuge there, struggling with the packaging to get another tube out.

"At the end, when he knew he was dying," she said quietly. "His eyes . . . they were brown again. Human."

"That doesn't change anything. It could've been a trick of the light. You were in a panic, so was he . . ."

"I suppose," Rosalyn agreed. "I just—"

Something on the packaging had caught her eye. The capsules were trapped in a vacuum-sealed white packet, which had clearly been peeled away from a duplicate, the perforations noticeable along the top edge. Small gray letters were stamped under the tiny puncture dots, an expiration date, serial number and distributer.

"What is it?" She had been so distracted she didn't hear Edison come up behind her.

"Beta Tech," Rosalyn read, showing him the packet and frowning. "Wouldn't Merchantia provide all the rations for you guys? Why would Piero even have this?"

Her last conversation with Josh Girdy floated back to her through her hazy memories and the whiskey. He had mentioned Beta Tech. And Belrose. And ISS. The room spun a little. That pile of connections she had noticed adding up started to shake under the weight of another coincidence.

Edison took the biodegradable package and inspected it for himself. He didn't seem alarmed, turning it over and then shrugging. "He's new. Maybe it's from an old gig. We know he's been around, with ISS at least, maybe he had other secret jobs, too, other identities."

"Maybe," she echoed, but her skin prickled like it always did when her gut wanted her to follow a hunch. "It doesn't make any sense, though. Beta Tech is earthbound; they don't even run space missions. All of their experiments are done in Canada, they just contract out to get whatever samples they need."

Rosalyn snatched the capsule packet back from him and turned, hurrying out of the storage area and into the corridor, finding her way quickly back to the labs. As expected, Edison followed, grabbing the whiskey bottle on the way.

"You said this was in his locker?" she called over her shoulder.

"Yeah, why? What's wrong?"

"I don't know yet," Rosalyn said grimly, remembering Josh Girdy's smug face. His double finger guns. His favor-for-a-favor proposal. "Maybe it's nothing. Maybe it's everything."

35

So much for their nice, quiet evening.

Rosalyn cut through the ship like a shark in chummed waters, scenting something important. He followed, pouring himself another round for whatever the hell was coming next. *Idiot.* It should have been his first move to sort through Piero's things after his death, but he had been so distracted by Rayan's death, by worrying about Rosalyn, that he had neglected to check. They knew Piero had poisoned Tuva, and they had found his fake identity with ISS. Now that he was gone, there was no stopping them from looking deeper. He was the newest among the crew, and he had fallen to the Foxfire the fastest, though Edison still wondered if that was due to his apparent willingness to kill his crewmates or the fresh head injury. The most injured among them seemed to fare the worst, just one more pitfall to fastidiously avoid. He rubbed at the bruise on his chin and winced, hoping it wasn't enough to empower the Foxfire against him.

I don't need a wound. I need my children. Piero . . . Rayan . . . Our family is breaking apart.

It was easier to ward off the voices with Dick Friday playing over

the intercom; now he felt more vulnerable to the lurking suggestions. Edison tossed back a drink, close behind Rosalyn as she all but
sprinted into the lab, continuing through as she caught sight of the
crew lockers at the back of the room.

"Here we go," she said, rubbing her hands together and crouching. His locker was on the bottom row, right next to Edison's. They
were arranged alphabetically by surname. Once upon a time they had
been locked with codes that were forwarded to their VIT monitors,
but once the code blue hit, the locks disengaged and the doors swung
free. Edison hadn't given it much thought; he had nothing to hide in
his. Without an implant, Tuva had opted for the more traditional
locker at the foot of her bunk, and they had already found the secrets
hidden there.

There was no decoration of any kind inside the locker, just a neat
pile of belongings. Edison had found the capsules right on top next
to a very nice bottle of synthetic dolcetto. Rosalyn removed the
bottle of wine to make room for rummaging, then pulled out an
employee ID pass and stood, the plastic square dangling on the end
of a twisty red lanyard.

"Looks like what all the security guys get," Edison said, huffing
when Rosalyn tossed it at him to hold. She went back to work,
coming back up for air with a personal work tablet.

Rosalyn nestled it in the crook of her arm, turning it on and
making a soft sound of interest when she found it unlocked.

"No code," she whispered to herself. "Strange."

The camera lens at the top brightened, a small red dot next to it
indicating it was recording.

"Paranoid much? That feed probably goes directly to his AR
display," Rosalyn explained. "A few guys in our labs did this. I always thought it was insane, you know, just choose a personal code
and make it a long one."

"Right. Why would you do that?" Edison asked, leaning over to watch her flick through the few icons on the tablet.

"Added security. Nobody can touch this thing without being recorded, so Piero, if he was still with us and his AR chip was functioning, would know if anyone tampered with his stuff. I guarantee you there's a keylogger, too. We all used them at . . . at my work," she said. Edison caught the hesitation, flagging it for later. She had freely mentioned that she worked somewhere important, but now he wondered just *how* important.

Rosalyn stopped, squinted, then faced him squarely and held up the tablet, showing him the usual start-up screen.

"Anything strange about this to you?"

Edison raked his eyes over the three icons. Mail, ScribNotes and Trash.

"It's a little bare-bones," he said. "Kinda sad. *Very* sad."

"We can't access new mail without a signal, but look." She opened his inbox. It was completely empty. "Does your inbox look like that? Mine certainly doesn't."

"A killer with a scrubbed inbox," Edison gave her. "Or he doesn't get much mail. Would *you* send him messages?"

"God, no, he's a creep, but no professional has a completely scoured inbox. It's shady, Edison. Everything about this is shady. Tuva. The badge. The note. He's starting to seem like way more than just hired security." She swiveled the tablet back around, navigating into the trash, which was also empty, and then into ScribNotes, which was filled to the gills with . . .

"Code," she murmured. She scrolled and scrolled, her eyes getting wider as she went, so wide Edison felt a cramp of nervousness in his gut. "We should have Misato look at this. Here."

Her fingertip moved over what looked like a screen name in the otherwise unintelligible, garbled language.

pe_BRITO711007

Rosalyn stared at the little slice of code for a long time, then her shoulders began to tremble. He watched her crumple in on herself, then slowly, carefully turn toward him.

"That's an employee ID code," she said, her voice oddly robotic. "I recognize it. I have one just like it; all Belrose Industries employees are assigned one. Oh my God, Dad, what were you getting us into?"

Rosalyn clutched the tablet to her chest, going suddenly pale behind her visor. He instinctively reached to touch her shoulder, and she leaned into him almost imperceptibly. There was a tremor in her fingers, a dull sheen to her eyes.

"We're connected to this," she went on with a shake of her head. "Belrose Industries. *My family.* What would my dad want with this stuff? What would *anyone* want with this stuff?"

"You didn't say you were part of Belrose Industries. Holy shit. Are you sure that's the ID code?" Edison asked. He observed Rosalyn's back while he sat perched on a stool in the lab and she studied Rayan's notes.

"Yes, I'm sure." She thumped her fist against her visor in frustration. "My father sent a message for my birthday, I didn't listen to it until I was here, but . . . he sounded spooked, spooked that I was working with MSC, that I was salvaging at all. It's dangerous, sure, but it was more than that. He sounded *terrified.*"

Edison felt his mind spinning out. He worried that the confusion would give Foxfire an easy in, a way to use his jumbled thoughts against him while he sorted out what Rosalyn was sort of telling him. "Then your dad is famous. Really, really famous."

"Not really, just famously jumped up his own ass."

"Still. I get what you meant now, about your company being a big deal." She went quiet, and he noticed a pronounced tension in her shoulders. Even through the suit, he could tell she was nervous. He understood why; with the way her father had treated her, handled things, it would make anyone uncomfortable to think about their former life. She had run so far, about as far as a human could go, and all to get away from her father and that job.

"Do you know that feeling you get when you walk right by someone you know? Your eyes just . . . cancel them out. Or they blend into the surroundings. That's how I feel right now looking at this," she said, gesturing to the table. "Like I should know what this all means. Like I should pick out the one thing that will make this all come together and make sense." Sighing, she put both hands on her head and swung listlessly from side to side. "If I could rub my eyes right now I would. Tuva. Piero. My dad. What if this is his fault?"

"Can I make a suggestion?" Edison asked.

Rosalyn peered over one shoulder at him, distraught.

"Let it go. Not forever, right? Just for now. You just survived a major ordeal, and as much as I want to understand how we got into this mess, it isn't . . . it isn't important." Edison stood, wobbled, realizing just how much of the whiskey he had consumed. Steadying himself, he joined her at the table. "That didn't come out right. I'm a little tipsy. Anyway. It's important, but it's not . . . urgent. I can see it in the way you look at us, like we're just . . . another problem that needs a solution. Like if you just turn us the right way in the light, all will be revealed. You weren't here when it hit, Roz. You didn't see how hard we tried to understand it."

Turning toward him, she pulled her lips to one side and raised a brow. "What did you call me?"

"Roz. Sorry. Remember? Tipsy."

"It's fine," she told him, wrinkling her nose. "Better than 'chick-adee.'"

"Clearly I'm missing something."

She stretched her arms over her head, no longer able to resist yawning. Before he had seen her trying to hide it, swallowing her exhaustion with big, rounded cheeks and a gulp. Her hands came down with a slap on the table and she leaned against it, head drooping.

"It's what Misato calls me. I have no idea why."

Edison chuckled, feeling the whiskey swirl heavily through his veins. He had avoided drinking recently, finding that the hangovers were brutal, as if he were experiencing them twice, once as himself and once through the Foxfire. He wondered if he would sleep, if he would dream of the blue lady, or if instead, by some miracle, he would dream of Rosalyn. The last human woman he would ever live to see.

"You're eminently nicknameable." The words came out on their own, rather than staying put in his head where they belonged.

She glanced at him sidelong and rolled her eyes at him yet again. "And you're drunk."

"Guilty. And you're exhausted."

"Guilty." Another yawn, one that turned into a helpless laugh. "This is all . . . so much. But you're right, knowing how Belrose is wrapped up in this mess would make me feel better, but it won't speed up the trip to the station. I guess that means I should try to sleep, if I can. I'm still wiped. God, I wish I could fit a whole mattress in the decontam pod."

Edison watched her tap her fingers one last time on the table before she walked toward the rounded door.

"Wouldn't risk it," he called after her on impulse. "We need to keep you healthy."

"Only half of you thinks that," Rosalyn reminded him, but it wasn't cruel.

"The important half. The half you find devastatingly charming, mm?"

She was through the door, just a vanishing silhouette, a shadow becoming a longer shadow, becoming nothing. "Ha! You wish. Good night, Captain."

Then she was gone, and he stood for too long watching the place where she had been. There were other minds in the cluster with him, but that didn't keep him from feeling intensely alone. In a way, it was more isolating, because he didn't trust any of the thoughts that came spontaneously, prone to finding they weren't his at all. Did it matter? Was this him staring longingly after a woman forever trapped under glass, or was it Piero? Was it Misato? Was it an unknown and unseen person far away, someone receiving his tics and habits, someone walking around with an inexplicable hankering for single-malt whiskeys?

Does it matter?

The strangest thing had happened weeks ago, when they first noticed the effects of the Foxfire. A phantom flavor tickled across his tongue. Chocolate syrup. He didn't have a sweet tooth, but his mouth was suddenly oozing with chocolate and he couldn't explain it. A few hours later he opened the crew refrigerator to find a bottle of chocolate syrup hidden in the back, behind the more practical foods. A little piece of tape was over the label, reading M.I.

It was like he had been right there, squeezing the syrup into his mouth in a moment of late-night weakness. He understood it now, but at the time he had felt insane. *Psychic.* When he found the bottle he made sure nobody was around and then swiped an ice-cold, sluggish drop of syrup onto his finger before tasting it. *Horrid.* Pure sugar. He spat it out, wondering how he had been tricked into enjoying it during that odd moment of transference.

Edison stuffed the urge to take another swig of the whiskey. He couldn't tear his eyes away from the empty doorway. Was this just transference? If he saw those big hazel eyes up close, touched the light roughness of her shaved head, would he regret it? It could be just a trick of the Foxfire, some other heart in some other place skipping a beat, not his. Or it was the whiskey. Or the loneliness, or the certainty that any minute now he would lose the capacity for admiring another human altogether.

Was it someone else's ache masquerading as his own?

Maybe, but he didn't think so. He really didn't think so.

36

The whiskey wore off and with it, her terrible urge to sleep. She tried to make a serviceable nest out of the two environmental suits and one of the cushions from a desk chair in cold storage, but the sticky material and the flat pillow only exacerbated how not cozy it all was. Anytime she shifted, the suits squeaked and stuck to her skin. Briefly, she considered kitting up again to get more of those alcohol injectors, but that felt like too much work.

She stared out at the corridor, daring something to come for her. Her mother used to tell her, when she came screaming into their bedroom, convinced of boogeymen, that the best way to banish a bad dream was to meet it head-on.

Imagine the worst thing that could happen and you'll never be surprised.

"If only you could see me now, Mom," she whispered to the ceiling, then softer, "Jesus, Dad, what did you get yourself into?"

The blue flowering growth outside the shield seemed dimmer, as if in mourning after the loss of Piero and Rayan. Rosalyn had met Misato briefly on her way back from the lab. The engineer was doing her best to patch up JAX, but it wasn't looking good. They needed far more replacement parts than they had available on the ship, and she would spend the rest of the night trying to 3-D extrude replacements, though it wasn't the best solution. His hard drive hadn't fried, which was something, but that only guaranteed that he could be put into a new body and retain the information, images and data he had already processed.

At that, the two women had exchanged a long look. When they had access to a signal again, they needed to get that information back to HQ. Merchantia—hell, GATE and the *government*—needed to know what had happened here so it never transpired again. JAX had recorded so much of the struggle, but Rosalyn couldn't help but be thankful that he hadn't been around to record the deaths among the crew. Nobody needed to see that. Rosalyn herself wished she could scrub it from her mind.

She had left out the part about her family business potentially being in league with ISS, Beta Tech and Merchantia. And Piero. Rosalyn couldn't make heads or tails of it herself; she definitely did not want to dump that mess into Misato's lap until it made marginally more sense.

Damn. She should have just gone through the trouble to suit up and get those whiskey capsules. It was the only way she was going to get rest, she thought, because she was too keyed up and too close to bad memories to turn her brain off. A sour taste filled her mouth, bitter and familiar—it was so like the nights just after Glen attacked her. She had tried every drug and every drink in the universe, even experimental ones, but nothing worked. Her nights were spent tossing and turning, dipping into twilight sleep only to come awake gasping and sputtering seconds later. Sometimes, after dawn, her body finally relented and let her grab a few thin hours of rest, but she never felt really awake, suffering on top of suffering, the booze and drugs giving her jarring hand tremors.

And there was something more, something that bit at the back of her brain, a bug bite that wasn't satisfied no matter how much she scratched. Because, really, she didn't even know where to *begin* scratching. It was a puzzle app glitching out, and with no base image to use as a comparison. The blue woman. Her family's company. Piero. The little fragments of poetry that she *knew* she knew.

Rosalyn threw her arms over her head and inhaled deeply. Edison was right. It was stupid fussing over all of these clues when they were about to get back to where it all started. Even then, she had to prepare herself for the possibility that they might not learn anything at all. They would arrive and dock, and because they couldn't communicate with the station, they would immediately be flagged as suspicious and probably escorted in. Then she would have to find some way to communicate that nobody was to come aboard. How would she even do that? Interpretive dance? After that, she had to convince the customs and quarantine agents that she wasn't harmful, just the other two, but that they really, really with a cherry on top needed them to scan for a few specific serial numbers.

It sounded crazy to her; what would it sound like to them?

And *this* was why she would never get to sleep. Endless questions. Endless plans to be made. Belrose Fucking Industries.

She could not believe her father figured into it. Rosalyn had cut off contact with the man for months, true, but she still thought better of him in the big picture. Maybe he believed a scummy guy in accounting more than his own daughter, but that didn't make him ethically questionable enough to play around with something as scary and volatile as Foxfire. She listened to his most recent message again, knowing it was no use trying to sleep, mining the little snippet of confession for whatever truth she could find.

"There are things we've done here, places we've gone, that were wrong. There's tech we messed about with, samples we found, that we should have turned over to GATE right away. Maybe it's better that you're gone. Not because I don't want you here, because I do, and not because I don't miss you, because I do, but because it might be safer. But then, your mother tells me you're with Merchantia now, so maybe not."

The one time she should have responded to the damned message and this was it. Why did he have to be so infuriatingly vague? He was afraid, that much was clear, and he ought to be, if he was in some kind of shady alliance with Merchantia and ISS. And God help him if he had some connection to the Foxfire samples. Charitably, she wondered if maybe he was being threatened or extorted. Or, another charitable thought, perhaps he simply had no idea what Foxfire really was. Xenobio samples were the most precious resource around for a tech company; maybe the flashing dollar signs had blinded him to what might be at stake.

Imagine the worst thing that could happen and you'll never be surprised.

Okay, Mom, what's the worst imaginable reason?

In theory—*in theory*—if her father knew what the Foxfire was capable of, or what Merchantia researchers suspected it was capable of, then the most valuable aspect of the fungus was what? Its aggressive nature was not really marketable. But telepathy? That . . . that was priceless. As a scientist, she couldn't even pin down the most marketable aspect because it was all marketable. And *dangerous*.

Telepathy. Regeneration. The Foxfire had kept Rayan alive despite a mortal head wound; if that healing property could be extracted and controlled . . . something like that would change medicine forever. What CEO with a hungry board could resist?

Her task bar chimed, alerting her to a new message. Of course Edison wasn't asleep, he never would be. Well, she wasn't exactly busy, so she opened the message and noticed the attachment. It was kind of sweet, even if she couldn't download it. No signal. No network. She copied the title and searched her hard database, finding it easily among popular songs from the last five years. It had made a few "best of" jazz playlists. Rosalyn closed her eyes and put the song on repeat, then she composed one last message before trying to sleep.

Thanks for the suggestion. If this actually works I might have to burn you for witchcraft.

Not five seconds later his icon blinked with a new message.

Can't burn what's already scorching hot. OH.

Rosalyn snorted, shaking her head and draping one arm over her mouth, laughing into her forearm.

You really have to let this go.

This time his reply took longer. *Why? Got big plans?*

She had to laugh, because if she didn't, she would certainly cry. This wasn't fair. None of this was remotely fair. Why did she have to go to the ends of traveled space to find someone that made her want to be in her heart and her mind and her body again? Why hadn't they crossed paths on campus? In another universe, another reality, they bumped into each other in the cantina and she spilled her soda on him, he brushed it off and smiled, then introduced himself. When, after the first date, she tried to disappear, he let her, and then she changed her mind, messaged him, and they went on a real proper date. Forager in Little Paris on Tokyo Bliss Station. Or they stupidly went for ramen and ended up splattered and liquid-bellied. She would tell a best friend, almost certainly Angela, that he was hot, but not too hot, that he was the second-professor-you-got-a-crush-on kind of hot, not the first professor, because that one was who everyone crushed on, the guy who always ended up being a douchebag. The second professor was when you were older and smarter and realized how much you liked elbow patches on a blazer. Angela would say something like, "Oh, honey, you've got it bad," and then they would laugh and laugh over their grapefruit mimosas.

In another reality, the first time she saw his name wasn't on a grave marker.

You know why.

This is for your own good, she thought. Our *own good*.

Ten seconds . . . twenty . . . thirty . . . She had scared him off. Why did that fill her with so much regret?

Then: *A man can dream.*

Rosalyn nodded, hoping he stopped responding after her next message. She didn't like how this felt. Like drowning a kitten. Like killing a good and innocent thing.

So can a woman—time for bed I hope. Good night, Edison.

She woke to a *crack* that split her dreams open like the heavy *thunk* of a cleaver. At first, drowsy and in the dark, she thought something had malfunctioned with the ship's thrusters or that they had run into some kind of floating debris. But then she saw two glowing white slivers, eye height, and the face of the man she had just wished good night.

"Edison?" she whispered, sitting up fast, head spinning, eyes adjusting too slowly. "Edison! *NO!*"

His head slammed into the shield again, then his fist, right over the fissure Piero had left. Scrambling to her feet, Rosalyn tumbled off of the hazmat suits, kicking her legs out to untangle them from the twisted pile they had become. He wasn't going to stop. He wasn't himself. Her only defense was the suit, and then . . .

And then?

The multi-tool had gone into space with Piero. She had nothing. *Nothing.* Another *crack*, and the sound of spidering fractures racing along the barrier, threatening to implode. She had to think, clearly and quickly, and protect herself from what was coming headlong through the shield at any moment. Crying out to him, pleading, she shook out the newer lab suit and climbed into it, jumping to pull it faster up her body and over her shoulders, her fingers useless and shaking as she reached for the toggles and seals. This was it. Unless Misato came rushing to her aid, she would have her helmet ripped off and her lungs exposed to the spores.

She heard Edison collapse against the shield, going limp. He was still upright, one fist resting above his head, his forehead bloodied and digging against the barrier. His eyes were still bright white, but tears tracked down his cheeks, darkening his beard.

"Please," she heard him whisper. Whimper. "Please . . . I just . . . Can I just talk to you? Can we just . . . just . . ."

I and then *we*. He was slipping in and out of the Foxfire's control. That explained the tears. Rosalyn knew it was reckless to ignore him, so she grabbed a pouch of food out of the decontam pod and tore it open, slamming it down, choking but eating anyway. Cold, gelatinous pork. She ate another, and a third, knowing it might be the last time she could eat at all.

"You don't have to hurt yourself like that," Rosalyn said, closing the seals on her visor and swallowing desperately around a mouthful of bland mush.

Crack.

"You don't have to listen to those voices!" she cried, racing to the shield. This was a better hope, she thought, her only hope. Cornered in the tiny room, she would never overpower him. She had seen what a beating Piero could take, and so she sided with compassion, gasping as she felt his head thump against the shield.

"Hey!" Rosalyn tapped on the barrier. Then again. "Hey, look at me, Edison. Really look at me." She watched the fissure closely. The diffusers were on, and if the milky air from her side seeped into the corridor, she would know the room was breached.

Edison's startling white eyes found her, his mouth turned down in a pitiful frown as he smeared his blood across the shield, struggling for air. "I don't want to . . . I don't want to—*ach.*"

His head crashed against the shield again and a sob escaped his lips, a desperate prayer. Rosalyn felt her own tears coming on, a rush of heat behind her eyes so strong it stole her breath away. But she licked her lips, steadied herself, tapping her fingers on the barrier until he locked gazes with her again.

"It's okay, Edison, it's okay. How does the song go? Here, I'll try to hum it," she said, the trembling in her voice giving away just how much she wanted to curl up in the corner and hide from him. Not him, the Foxfire. She could see him fighting it, hear the *I* and not the *we*. God, she had heard him hum that damned song so many times but the beginning eluded her. Softly, softly, she heard his low bass voice begin the horn's line, climbing higher, then holding for half a second. *That was it.*

"Yes, like that," Rosalyn cried. She picked up the song, humming along, her voice higher, not quite in harmony with his but following closely. Blood dripped down the shield between them. Her fingers smoothed over the tight circles of the fissure, a noticeable dent there but nothing sharp. Nothing breaking through.

Crack.

The blow to his temple interrupted the song, but it only made Rosalyn hitch and continue, humming as calmly as she could, trying to keep the thread of the melody while Edison joined in again, just a rumble in his throat, hardly more than a growl.

"You love this song," she reminded him. "Dick Friday, right? You just sent me another one of his. I want to listen to it, Edison, but I want to listen to it with my own ears. Do you understand? Don't come through this door. Don't make me listen to that song with someone else's ears."

She hummed again and she would do it for as long as it took. He looked as if he were falling gently to sleep, lulled away from the Foxfire's call and toward the lullaby of the familiar song. His fingers touched the shield on the other side of the fissure, blood running along his skin, tunneling into the barrier.

"Shhh, shhh," she repeated, and it had the unintended side effect of soothing her, too, banishing the fluttery panic in her chest.

White became pale turquoise, which became light blue, then darker, then the hue she had come to consider "normal." It would have to be enough. It was certainly better. Rosalyn felt one hot, fat tear escape, rolling over her cheek and splashing at the bottom of the visor. Her helmet clinked quietly against the shield as her humming grew less and less, until it was just a wisp on her lips, a heavy breath.

"Are you all right?" she murmured. Their fingers would have met if not for the shield.

Edison looked up, a swipe of blood across his forehead and nose. The tussle with Piero had broken his glasses on one side. He had repaired them, but now they were bent again.

"I should be asking you that."

It was bone-deep relief to hear his true voice again, husky, hoarse, but human.

"What happened?" she asked, watching him wipe at the blood and tears on his face. "You were fine in the lab and then—"

"It's you." He cut her off, not meanly, but with a shuddering sigh. His eyes were wet again. "It's you. The Foxfire is . . . trying to use you against me. It thinks it can, I don't know, dangle you joining the cluster in front of me like some sort of prize. It's disgusting. First my mother, now you . . . Whatever I care about is just turned against me."

Rosalyn flinched, but didn't move her hand, and Edison was still. "Edison . . ."

"You don't have to say anything. You've been pretty clear about what you think of me."

"No, I haven't been," she said. "But I don't think hope is a

289

luxury we can afford right now. I run every scenario over and over again, and it doesn't look good. Maybe in another life. Maybe . . . God, I don't know, maybe if we get to CDAS and they greet us with champagne and a perfect cure for you and Misato."

Edison pulled his lower lip between his teeth and glanced away, his forefinger working against the fissure nervously. "It wasn't the song."

"What?"

"The song. It helped, sure, but it wasn't the song that brought me back," he said.

She wanted him to go on but he didn't. He didn't need to. Rosalyn felt a lump rising in her throat, sharp and unavoidable. "What if I'm not there to help next time?"

"I don't know," Edison admitted. "But I've tried swallowing this down deep, and it doesn't seem to be working out so well. I won't speak for you, and I won't tell you what to do, but me? I'm going to try running toward the light instead of away from it."

Rosalyn tipped her head to the side. "I'm the light in this metaphor?"

"It's not perfect, I admit. I didn't exactly have time to workshop it, okay?"

"Take a step back," she said. "Please."

Edison put both hands up, rolling his eyes, not at her, she knew, but at himself. "I get it. I'll leave you alone. No need to ask twice."

"Just a step." She reached for the door panel. "You are terrible at following directions."

"I'm the captain, I'm usually giving them."

The shield lifted, wisps from the diffuser spreading into the corridor before she crossed into the hall and shut the door behind her. She reminded herself that she was being incredibly stupid, and then reached for his hand, holding it lightly in her gloved palm before he returned the gesture, twining his fingers in hers.

"I guess there's something romantic about tragedy," Rosalyn muttered, glancing up at him.

"Stop it," he said, but he was half grinning.

"Hey, tragic endings can be beautiful. Here." She poked her left forefinger against the shield, approximating above her cheekbone. "One," she said. "Just one."

"Just one," he repeated gently, as if saying more might spook her. He leaned down and down, crossing the distance with what felt to her like reverence. Maybe she imagined it, but Rosalyn let herself.

The kiss fell light as a snowflake on her visor, the only evidence it had ever happened the slightest smudge and the roses in her cheeks.

"The perfect start," Edison whispered, backing away into the darkness, "to a tragic ending."

37

Misato stood in front of the cockpit display, inputting Rosalyn's credentials to keep the thrusters burning. She increased their fueling rate, impatient to reach CDAS. The time they spent as a crew on the station had gone by in a flash. Leaving the confines of the ship was always a treat—better food, new people to talk to and more room to stretch the legs. But Piero had been in such a rush, convincing Edison that it was better to pick up their allotted samples and supplies and keep moving. He was security, he said with his usual bluster, and CDAS wasn't officially a Merchantia property. It was a neutral station, technically in Canadian waters, but parceled out to different research, development and corporate entities. For the right price, anyone could rent space there to work in antigravity labs or to test orbital reactions, and Piero didn't trust it.

"The Wild West," he had said, antsy, fidgeting in the cockpit. "You know what the Wild West is? It's like that. Not a good place, you don't want to spend too much time hanging around here."

That seemed like an exaggeration, but Misato caught the vibe in the station that nobody really cared who they were or why they were there. Everyone kept to themselves, their uniforms branded with whatever corporation they were associated with. She had at

least gotten enough time to grab some half-decent grilled chicken
and a glass of wine.

After they left, she hadn't given the station much thought, but
now the opportunity to return consumed her. It was unnatural, this
preoccupation, manifesting not from her own psyche but an indirect
feeling. Foxfire. Edison had described the sensation to her once,
saying it was like passing by an advertising node and having a
cheeseburger pop up in your AR display. Ten seconds ago you didn't
want that cheeseburger, but now you couldn't help but crave it.

Hamburger, hamburger, hamburger. Relentless.

She sat in one of the swiveling chairs and placed her palms on
her knees, trying to remain at ease, but it was not so simple. The
Foxfire inside her felt . . . effervescent, like tiny bubbles rising
through champagne. That same giddiness echoed in her own breast.
She hadn't felt the invader inside her react that way to anything. It
had experienced a kind of joy or anticipation when Piero and Rayan
fell under its influence completely, but that held a sinister edge. This
was something else, and, inexplicably, it frightened her more.

Misato closed her eyes, falling into herself. It was a technique she
learned with Jenny at a meditation retreat. The suite on Tokyo Bliss
Station had been painted an inviting sky blue, puffy white clouds
drifting through the lobby via their AR integration. Soft, twinkling
sitar music filtered down from the ceiling, and attendants dressed in
crisp white robes glided out to meet them. Everyone who worked
there was so serene, composed, as if nothing could jar them out of a
benignly smiley mood.

"It's a good day," the woman said as she came to her and Jenny.
A helpful cloud popped up above her head, spinning, the name Solaris printed across it. "When you join us here, friends, every day is
a good day."

Solaris gestured to the open hall to her right, past the registration desk. They had reservations, so they were allowed to walk right on through.

"Kuh-reepy," Jenny muttered as they went. "Her name is Solaris, because of course it is."

"Give it a chance," Misato chided.

The guru led about twenty of them through holotropic breathing exercises in a brightly lit rotunda. Most meditation seminars Misato had attended were held in dim rooms filled with enough pillows to make a nap seem like a good idea. But this rotunda was almost blindingly yellow, the lights and walls a cheerful buttercup color. They sat on hard mats after their breath work was done. She heard Jenny snigger as the guru, her long hair braided to her waist, began chanting.

"Are they going to turn the lights down? My eyes hurt."

"It's part of the experience," Misato explained. "You have to fight against it, keep your eyes closed so completely that no light slips in."

Jenny sighed. She hated it.

Misato didn't know what to think. She had never tried to sit in direct sunlight with her eyes closed for that long. After a while, she noticed the red, glowing nature of her closed eyelids, as if her skin had become a lantern, lit from within. The chanting became rhythmic, mesmerizing. She went back a second time without Jenny there to distract her and found it easier to fight the bright light, to venture so deep inside herself that even the floor beneath her and the chanting disappeared.

Meditation never worked for Jenny because she could never quiet her mind. Misato agreed it was extremely difficult to master, but after a while she developed a way to turn off the thoughts and questions that normally plagued her. *What's that bump on my leg? What should I make for dinner?* To turn it all off she pictured a black wall that stretched in every direction, and a glossy black pool at her feet. She walked slowly toward the wall, timing the guru's chants with her steps, clicking off the thoughts in her head like light switches until everything was blank and dark. Then she would sit in that void until ideas offered themselves up.

Misato had found that the same technique worked, unexpectedly, with Foxfire, but instead of leading her to a void, it led her to an empty room where she could face the voice inside her head with greater clarity. And there, they conversed.

She hadn't tried to talk this way with her parasite since the incident with Rayan and Piero. It was too painful to consider, and she didn't trust herself not to simply explode with rage instead of listening and responding with deliberate composure.

But the excited buzzing in her head and body told her it was time to investigate. While everyone else fought the Foxfire, she had hoped to negotiate with it. So far, neither method produced encouraging results, but all things being equal, she would prefer to fight this battle with open ears and compassion. Losing gracefully was a victory of a kind.

This time, when she returned to the blank room, she found it occupied. That was new. A function of losing Rayan and Piero? Or did it have to do with their proximity to CDAS? She cleared her mind. The meditative state would break if she allowed in too many rushed questions.

"I've seen you before," Misato told the figure calmly.

It was the blue woman, though she appeared blurry, as if being viewed through a lens smeared with gel. The woman said nothing, floating an inch or two above the black floor, her arms loosely at her sides. Her skin and hair were cerulean, her body not fully concealed but draped in a light cloth that billowed around her.

"You're from my dreams," she added. "Our dreams. We've all seen you."

No reply.

Misato hazarded a few more steps toward her, but the farther she went, the blurrier the woman's image became. There were no foolish questions in meditation, and so she asked, "Are you God? A vestige of God? Or are you my own creation, a way for my mind to process the abstract? Fungus doesn't look like much to us. Is this form supposed to be more familiar?"

Nothing.

It would be easy to get frustrated and stop, but Misato had been successful in luring the Foxfire into conversation before. Forbearance, she thought, patience would see her through.

Misato tried walking faster toward her, but as soon as she came within touching distance, the blue woman transformed, becoming first a liquid blob and then a body again, but it was Rayan. He looked whole. His eyes were a soft, inviting brown.

"It isn't really you," she said sensibly.

"No," Rayan, or the image of him, agreed. "We are part of the cluster. Our image, our actions, and the knowledge gained before my departure. We're all her children."

She could feel her temper rising. *Departure.* That certainly was a word for it. He wouldn't have wound up floating in outer space, dead, if not for what the Foxfire had done to them all.

"You're excited about something," Misato observed. Even this figment squirmed with expectation, fingers curling and flexing, a playful smile on his lips. "Things . . . are going well for you."

"Yes," he replied simply. "We are closer now. We will all be with her soon."

"I don't think so," Misato said. She found it best to keep her voice level; any hint of aggravation or despair chased the Foxfire away. She couldn't help but wonder if this monotone, calm medium

was somehow conducive to the organism, that human emotion created an unstable or untenable environment. Rayan believed, and she
did, too, that not all of its structure was purely physical—its ability
to send signals telepathically must make it extraordinarily sensitive
to changes in mood.

"We have proved you wrong before."

"You have," she allowed. Rayan stood in one place, visibly trembling with enthusiasm. "But your methods are changing, which
means we must be resisting successfully. You were thoughtful, then
friendly, then aggressive . . . What will you be next?"

Rayan blinked and when his eyes opened he had multiplied,
until a row of copies stretched out on either side, for infinity. His
smile became tranquil, beatific.

"Multitudinous."

Then he was gone. Misato waited, reining in the urge to scream
in frustration. This was nonsense. Foxfire was already everywhere
in the ship, its ability to spread easily observable. *Multitudinous.* Minutes passed but Rayan did not return and neither did the blue
woman. Misato breathed deeply and emerged from the meditation,
sighing as she dropped her head into her hands. What a waste of
time. She should've been studying Rayan's notes instead of playing
hide-and-seek with unseen monsters.

There was a soft tap on the door outside the cockpit, and she
swiveled in the chair to find Rosalyn waiting there, dressed in the
shiny white Merchantia lab suit.

"Is now a good time?" she asked.

Misato nodded, beckoning her forward. The salvager had a tablet in her hands, a standard-issue work pad given to everyone on the
crew. Rosalyn's eyes drifted to the flight display behind her, scanning quickly side to side.

"I thought I heard the thrusters kick up. Was that you?"

"This needs to end before I go nuts," Misato replied. "I'm tired of waiting around on this ship. Anything is better than waiting to be consumed."

"Did you ever try that AR adventure at the Dome? They had a great one with dragons on Mars, and all these characters you could team up with," Rosalyn said, going to the cockpit chair next to her and sitting down.

Misato let out a chirp of laughter. "*Red Mountain Runner*," she said fondly.

"Yes! God, I was absolutely obsessed with *RMR*, I think I played it sixteen times. I had to see all the endings," she replied, shaking her head. "And, uh, see all the romances, too."

"I did the same thing," she said. "Who was your favorite? I liked Kali'rahn."

"She was completely epic, for sure, but I had a soft spot for Dantis."

"Ahhh." Misato fluttered her lashes. "The classic hero. He usually died in my runs."

They both laughed, and Rosalyn leaned back in the chair, gazing up at the ceiling. "I would cut off my left arm to be in the Dome right now, fighting space orcs."

"What made you think of it?" Misato asked. "Besides finding yourself in this hellscape with us . . ."

"Just something you said, you know, about being antsy, about just wanting to get this over with. Whatever *this* is." Rosalyn pulled her head back down and leaned across toward Misato, turning the tablet around. "Before I tried *RMR* for the first time, I asked a friend who had gone through it for spoilers. I wanted to get the good ending the first time; it gave me massive anxiety to think about messing it up."

Misato took the tablet, chuckling. "Shut up, I did the same thing! My girlfriend forgot to retrieve the protective amulet for Janie and had a total party wipe in the foothills. She was a ball of anxiety until she got to go back and do it over again."

"I would be, too," Rosalyn snorted.

"But you're not here to talk *RMR* strategies, I take it."

"Correct." Rosalyn sighed, clearly reluctant to switch topics. Then her brow turned down fiercely with concentration, and she woke up the tablet she had brought, opening a writing app.

"It's recording me," Misato noticed, pointing at the little red camera light shining in her eyes. "Security measure?"

"Yup. It's Piero's. He was up to something serious with you guys. I looked through some of his code and searched his username. It's tied to . . . well, my old company. My family owns Belrose Industries, and he has the same sort of employee ID we all used. I have no idea how this all fits together, but I can't stop thinking it all connects. Anyway, I'm not much of a coder, so I thought maybe you could take a look, see if any of it makes sense to you."

Misato stared unseeing at the screen for a moment. That was a lot to process. Of all the crew in the cluster, Piero had always felt the most remote to her, closed off. Now it was obvious why. He was holding in a secret, maybe many, and trying to keep them from finding out.

"I . . . sure. Tuva's death makes more sense now. He was protecting something big." Misato took the tablet, squinting down at the tiny rows of code. She increased the text size and dug in, going quiet for a long time. It wasn't awkward; Rosalyn let her work without seeming bored or impatient. In fact, she turned to the flight screen and seemed to be inspecting the way Misato had increased thruster usage while maintaining the lowest rate of fuel burn-off.

```
[pe_BRITO711007@ip-72-39-
181-61 ~]$ poe.sh -a -P
Checking ports . . . . . . . . . . . [OK]
Allocating space . . . . . . . . . [OK]
Running . . . . . . . . . . . . . . [OK]
[pe_BRITO711007@ip-72-39-181-61 ~]$
```

She scrolled and scrolled, then pinched her forehead, wishing she had something more interesting to report. "This is pretty basic stuff. It looks like common enough code he just wanted on hand for convenience's sake."

"So it won't hack Merchantia's bank accounts? That's a letdown."

"No, but this is important," Misato said, pointing to his handle. "We can use this when we get to CDAS. If he modified anything in their code, he might have left this behind. The amount of Foxfire samples we took on board seemed odd to me. Too much. He could have modified the manifests on the station to make it look like we only took the correct number of samples."

"And it all does what?" Rosalyn let her keep the tablet, collapsing back into her chair. "He's dead. Foxfire is loose. It doesn't matter if we prove he took extra samples or didn't."

"It does, Rosalyn, it does matter." Misato set the tablet aside and reached for the young woman's knee, putting her hand on it lightly. "Whatever happens to Edison and me—no, listen—whatever happens, you need to show all of this to HQ and then to the Global Alliance."

Rosalyn's head drooped on her shoulders. "Merchantia had you guys take those samples, though. We have no idea who's really to blame. Hell, it could be *my dad.* And anyway, Piero had some Beta Tech junk in his locker. Before I left for this assignment, this HR guy told me about several partnerships that were causing issues.

Merchantia is linked to them, too. I don't want to say vast corporate conspiracy but—"

"Vast corporate conspiracy," Misato breathed. "Sounds like something out of a Dome scenario."

"I know this is going to sound crazy, but I wish the asshole was still alive," Rosalyn said. "I'd like to ask him a few pointed questions."

"Wouldn't we all . . ."

"Thanks for looking at it," the salvager added, wheeling back toward the flight screen and staring at it blankly, one gloved knuckle tucked under her visor. "You can keep looking through the code if you want. Maybe there's something juicy hidden in there."

"Or here," Misato ventured, pointing to her forehead. "He was part of the cluster. There are . . . vestiges of Rayan left in there. I've seen it. Maybe if I go deep, I can find Piero, too."

That drew Rosalyn's attention. "If you think you can handle it. I mean, I'm sorry, that sounded really condescending, but isn't that dangerous? Isn't that playing right into the Foxfire's hands?"

"I've practiced quite a lot," Misato told her with a wink. "This old girl still has a few tricks up her sleeve."

38

The starboard observation deck remained in complete disarray. When the ship ran smoothly, before Foxfire swept through it and the crew, Edison had found the area somewhat peaceful. A band of thick windows wound around the entire middle, and one could sit for hours and hours, just staring at the stars, marveling that they were right there, close enough to touch. The motorized cleaning drone worked alongside him, sweeping broken bins, benches and bits of signage into a pile. Edison worked on the dirty floor, the bottom of the wet mop stained with blackish blood. A web of blue filaments arched over them, a twinkling canopy as bright as the stars through the window.

It wasn't peace, exactly, but he found pleasure in the work. He captained the *Brigantine*, disastrous as it was, but this small act of cleaning and ordering seemed right.

Other things felt right, too, but he wouldn't let his mind touch those things yet. His mind wasn't a safe place.

The canopy above him lit up, brighter, and he closed his eyes. He felt her there, Mother, behind him, before she ever spoke, the ghostly presence prickling the hairs at his nape. Glancing over one shoulder, Edison found his mother, Diana, watching him, though she appeared covered in a fine, shimmering blue dust.

"Is she good for you? Is she good *to* you?"

Edison remembered that conversation well. Candace, his ex-wife, was never up to Diana's standards. She didn't have a job, and preferred staying home with her child. To a woman that had dedicated her entire life to dangerous terrestrial and extraterrestrial missions for the Global Alliance, stay-at-home mom just didn't cut it.

"Yes, ma'am."

Forty years old and he was still calling her *ma'am*. Edison leaned against the handle of the mop, then rubbed the bottom of it hard against the black plasticized floor. They hadn't been on a ship then, but in his temporary office on Tokyo Bliss. He would transfer to Merchantia's campus soon after, and he had just finished his own career with the military. It felt like the right time to marry Candace and help her with her kid. Diana saw it another way.

"That boy is going to need discipline. A lot of it."

"Sure." He shook his head. "That's up to Candace."

"It should be up to you. I know what it's like to raise a boy on your own. How much it takes out of you. That's what your children do. Take and take and take."

Edison blinked, turning fully to face the apparition. This part of the conversation stung, unfamiliar, and the vision of his mother shifted, jangling out of tune. It hadn't gone that way. She had wished him well, told him to message if he had any questions about being a parent, and then she made some joke about it being romantic to get married in the stars.

"Selfish," Mother said. "That's what you are. All of you. But you? This is the worst betrayal. You were my favorite."

The blue woman floated closer, flickering between the face he knew to be his mother's and a stranger's. She reached toward him, fast, her hand lashing out before he could move and closing around his throat. Foxfire was in him, controlled him, wound seamlessly into his nervous system. He felt his throat closing, his chest suddenly tight. His forehead still ached from slamming it so hard against the lab barrier, and now his neck prickled with heat. Suffocating. He was suffocating himself. Edison clawed at his throat, trying to pry her hand away, but there was nothing there.

"I can take this from you," Mother said. "Baby. *Baby.* My baby. She eludes me, but I can take you from her. Children take, Mother can take, too."

He didn't know how to plead with the monster in his own mind, but he tried, breathing deep, forcing himself away from the edge of panic. Foxfire controlled his pain receptors and now he *felt* it.

What did it want? Why would it kill him? The Foxfire needed hosts, needed people to carry it forward. But darkness closed in. The prickling in his throat spread to his eyes. Gurgling, scratching, he tried to paw at his throat again, but there were no hands there to bat away.

You killed me, baby. You killed your own mother.

He had, it was true. He had told the nurses to end it. They had known for months she wasn't coming back, but selfishly he let her hang on, sitting next to her each day, finding he didn't have it in him to lose his mother and his wife at the same time. Candace had stopped coming to see him at the hospital. Too hard on Joey, her son. Edison held his mother's hand while the machine quit living for her, and sang a quiet song, one she had showed him on his record player.

You killed me.

His mother's voice, and an accusation he couldn't deny, even if he knew deep inside it was a mercy. She was gone, and it was his responsibility, his need, to let her go.

Something beyond the blue woman caught his blurring vision. Soon, without oxygen, he would lose his sight altogether, but a figure stepped through the archway into the observation deck. Then she was running, closer, closer, until she slid through the shimmery blue outline of his mother and grabbed him by the shoulders.

"What's happening? Edison. *Edison*. Are you choking?" Rosalyn pounded on his chest, a crude attempt at chest compressions. Then she shook him a little, waving a hand in front of his face, and the turquoise glow she stood within vanished, dispersing around her, a halo that faded away into the twinkling ceiling.

Edison bent double, gasping, slapping at his own cheeks to see if they had feeling.

"I don't," he wheezed, "understand."

"Did Foxfire just try to kill you?" Her eyes were wide behind the visor, and she helped him kneel on the damp floor. "That doesn't make any sense." Rosalyn trailed off, glancing away from him, but then her mouth tumbled open, a squeak escaping. "Unless . . ."

"Unless?"

"Rayan's notes . . . He was convinced Foxfire evolved. It keeps appearing as people you all know, right? Maybe you're changing it as much as it's changing you. You're a connected system, and it could go two ways. That thing, Mother, is becoming more human, and humans are petty."

Edison nodded slowly; it made a terrible sense. The cleaning drone bumped around them, then whirred away toward the edge of the room and the padded benches. "I wanted revenge on it, now it's taking revenge on me."

For my own mother. No, he thought, it didn't know him. It didn't know how long he had waited before saying goodbye. A captain for years by then, and it was the hardest order he had ever given.

"And here I was hoping to give you good news," she muttered.

"I could use some right now." He felt safer with her there, more himself. Just her arrival had chased away the vision, and he hoped her presence would anchor him there, far from any tainted memories.

"Here," Rosalyn said, pulling a folded piece of paper from her pocket and showing him. It was covered in what looked like scribbles and tiny drawings, one of a fairly standard rectangle, another that was labeled as a close-up and a cutaway. Underneath were lists of chemicals and compounds, some crossed out, some with question marks next to them.

"What am I looking at here?" he asked, adjusting his spectacles.

She chuckled and started pointing to random elements. "It's a modified version of the chip tech we used at Belrose. We were using a chemical coating to encourage protein production on a cellular level, which keeps your body from deteriorating. It's meant to help with longer and longer space travel when Ionese ore can't jump us quickly enough," she explained.

"That makes a little more sense," Edison said softly, touching his bruised throat. "I think."

"Rayan tried to break down the fungus at a molecular level," Rosalyn went on. "I'll skip a lot of the technical stuff, but in theory we can find a chemical coating that will bond to those molecules. We've had success with other coated chips attracting unwanted pathogens. When the blood tests come back clean, the chip is removed. It's like . . . it's like if you stick a magnet into a bunch of metal filings and pull it out. Find the right coating, and the Foxfire molecules bond to it, then *boop*." She mimicked pulling a magnet out of her palm. "No more Foxfire."

Edison stared down at the schematic, the corner of his lips twitching. "This is amazing."

"It isn't amazing yet," she said softly. "Not until I find the right coating and the right lab to run tests, but I'm hoping—if *you're* right and CDAS is still functioning—that they'd have the proper equipment to work out a solution. If not, I know we have it back in Montreal. Time isn't on our side, but it's better than giving up."

"Look at you," he said softly, handing her the tablet. "Suddenly Little Miss Optimistic."

He noticed a dark blush creep across her cheeks. "I want to help you. If my family's company had anything to do with releasing Foxfire, then, God, it's the least I could do."

"Not to ruin the moment, but don't you think I'm probably too far gone for this?"

Rosalyn stared at where he was still touching his neck. "I hoped you wouldn't bring that up."

"It's . . . Still. It's still something. It's hope. Thank you."

She grinned across at him and nodded. He wanted to lean over and kiss her, or the shield, but stopped himself, just enjoying her look of momentary satisfaction and shyness. Of course he had known she was smart and resilient, but to see it turned toward a cure to help them felt like an act of compassion. He looked down into her shining eyes and felt his heart clench; she had leaned a little closer and put her hand firmly over his.

"You're welcome."

39

Station approach still made her jumpy and nervous, even after dozens of longer flights and casual interstation hops. From where they all stood, watching the flight screen intently, side by side, JAX's small, square hard drive cradled in Misato's hands, Coeur d'Alene Station appeared normal enough. Six concentric rings around a central powering core, with elevators running along the core exterior, a docking flat at the very bottom. Most modern stations were organized similarly, and Rosalyn felt an anxious itch at the back of her neck.

They were getting closer, closer, and the silence in the cockpit made her ears pound.

"Nothing," Rosalyn whispered. "Christ. They aren't hailing us. Why aren't they hailing us? Customs should have—"

"I know," Edison interrupted sternly. "Look at the docking flat. There's no movement. No shuttles. No ships."

Rosalyn covered her mouth with both hands, landing on her helmet visor. "Can you dock us manually?" she asked. *Do you even want to?*

"This is going to be bumpy," he replied darkly, sitting down at the central cockpit chair. "I suggest you take a seat."

She moved wordlessly to his right and dropped like a stone, fumbling with numb fingers for the safety belts. The feed was mesmerizing in its horror. It looked fake, like a toy floating out there in the thin mist of space, light asteroid debris drifting by, oddly placid given what must have taken place within.

From across Edison, she heard Misato's belts click into place. "They could have evacuated," Misato said. "We don't know anything yet."

But Edison glanced Rosalyn's way and she stared back, jaw set. She had been right; something terrible had happened on CDAS, and all his lofty optimism was crashing down around his ears. He looked stricken, a sick, green cast to his dark skin, as if he might be ill at any moment.

"Can you feel that?" Misato whispered.

Rosalyn stayed quiet, knowing the question wasn't for her. All she felt was the cold dread in her body and the nauseating certainty that she needed to harden herself against what was to come, and fast.

"Yes," Edison said. "She's excited. Mother is . . . happy."

"Do we have any weapons?" Rosalyn asked, determined not to give in to the tempting pit of hopelessness yawning before them. It wasn't too late to turn back, but she knew nobody would allow that, including her. If nothing else, this confirmed that there were answers on the station. Being hailed and asked for corporation clearances would have meant that there was a small, small possibility of the Foxfire remaining innocuously on the docks. She hoped against hope that Misato was right, that the contamination had been detected early and evacuations had started immediately.

But she couldn't help but fixate on the ships motionless on the docking flat. Nobody going in or out. If there had been an evac, those ships would surely be gone.

"As soon as everyone started hearing voices, I incinerated Piero's security kit," Edison said. "I didn't know if we would turn on each other or ourselves. I've heard some dark stories about deep space mutinies."

"I can't blame you," she said. "I've cleaned up some of those deep space mutinies. I think you two should suit up," Rosalyn added. "We don't know what we're going to find in there. It would at least offer a little protection, and the atmosphere could be nonexistent."

"Not a bad idea," Misato agreed. "But you're in my suit."

"How long until we dock?" Rosalyn asked, unbuckling.

"Not long. Like I said, it could get dicey."

"I'll be fast," she said, grabbing the top of her chair and hoisting herself out. She heard Misato shrug out of her safety belts and follow.

"I won't make you wear my old stuff; I have no idea what it smells like in there," Rosalyn muttered.

They were silent after that. It was a tense jog to cold storage. Rosalyn hadn't even considered that this was likely the last time she would see that weird little haven. She wouldn't miss sleeping on the floor or the constant decontam showers, but all the same, sadness pulled at her like an insistent child until she distracted herself with the business of changing out of the suit, decontaminating it and the old one just to be sure, and dressing again. Misato chewed her nails on the other side of the shield, eyeing the crack in it and the blood-stain there.

"Rosalyn."

She worked at the toggles on her helmet and turned to face Misato, then crouched to gather up the other suit and fold it over her arm. "Yeah?"

The *Brigantine* shook as they neared the station, and Rosalyn flailed, reaching for the kitchenette counter to steady herself. Misato braced in a wide stance, managing to stay upright.

"Remember what we talked about."

It wasn't a suggestion, but a command.

Rosalyn avoided her gaze, dropping the barrier shield and handing over the cleaner suit. There was a detectable vomit scent clinging to the inside of her helmet.

"I'm not making any promises until we get on that station," Rosalyn said, marching past her.

But Misato caught her by the wrist, making her spin. "Listen to me. Whatever is happening between you and Edison is none of my business. What happens between you and me, you and the future? That's my business." She held up the rectangular hard drive. JAX's brain. "I'll download whatever relevant data we find on CDAS, but then you'll be taking it. You're the only one of us healthy enough to go back to society. You have to . . . you have to tell our story."

Rosalyn squeezed her eyes shut. "I hate this. I hate this so much."

The engineer reached out and took Rosalyn's hands, holding them tightly. "I know you do, but this can't all be for nothing. There's going to come a moment when you want to stay, and it will feel like the right thing to do. But, Rosalyn? Running can be brave."

It was Misato who had called her a survivor, even after she confessed to running from home and her pain. Could she know what it really meant, to have that choice validated? She didn't ask and it didn't matter. Rosalyn listened and squeezed her hands back, then pulled Misato toward the cockpit.

"We should get back," she said.

"Rosalyn? Chickadee."

"I heard you," Rosalyn told her, flinching away. "I heard you."

After all of Edison's warnings, the landing turned out to be routine. He expertly maneuvered the *Brigantine* to the lowest level of the station, cutting the main thrusters and using the smaller precision boosters to glide them gradually to an open bay. The ship bumped into place, but the usual magnetized clamps didn't engage. Without them, the *Brigantine* would float slowly away, unmoored.

"Shit. I'll have to secure us manually," Edison muttered. Misato had brought his environmental suit to the cockpit, and he struggled into it while nodding toward the flight screen. "Misato, keep us steady while I take a look out there. I should be able to secure the ship from the mobile platform, but if not, I'll have to find the dockmaster's terminal."

"I'm going with you," Rosalyn announced.

Edison shot her a warning look. "It's too soon. We don't know what it looks like out there."

"We're not staying here no matter what," Rosalyn replied, planting herself near the air lock in the gallery. "I won't wander away, I just want to get a look."

"Stop wasting time and let her go, Edison."

"You know, for a while there, I thought I was the captain," he groused, yanking up his suit with an irritated growl. "Fine. Pressurize and prepare for outer doors."

Misato seemed quite at home in the captain's chair and quickly followed his instructions, though it was doubtful she needed them. Rosalyn watched him approach and lightly adjusted one of the loose toggles on his helmet seal.

"Are you nervous?" she asked softly.

"Don't leave my side," he said by way of answer. "I'm serious, Roz."

He knew something. She read it in his face, in the way his jaw ground and ground; his eyes, even transformed by the Foxfire, were distant and distracted. And if he knew something, then that meant it had to do with his malady.

"The samples," Rosalyn whispered as the air lock doors hissed and shrieked. The *Brigantine* rocked. "You can sense them, can't you? They're close."

Edison's eyes flashed at her. He looked on the verge of tears. "It's more than that. A lot more."

They waited together side by side at the doors, then he stepped out first, into the pressurizing antechamber and then through the round open portal to the platform. Rosalyn heard her boot land on the flat like a clap of thunder. She could have heard dust settle if she tried. It was silent, completely abandoned, ships left docked and empty, no sign of any workers or crew. Edison gazed around, twisting to look up at the higher docking bays and toward the central flight control tower with its huge, rectangular bay windows.

He stopped at the end of the short ramp leading from the ship to the docking flat, then turned right, finding the mobile terminal assigned to this bay. On a normal shift, a Servitor or human worker would be there to assign them to a specific customs line, double-check the crew manifest and confirm how long the ship intended to stay. When everything checked out, the crew would be allowed to leave the ship unattended.

But there was nobody. Edison leaned down to inspect the terminal.

"Well, it's functional," she heard him say as she stopped at the end of the ramp.

"But?"

They both jumped and reached for each other as an earsplitting blast came from the intercom. It was an emergency tone from the flight tower, a swath of orange light traveling across the flat in time with the jarring horn.

"Reactor breach detected, evacuation in process, please proceed to emergency pod bays on levels 1-B and 1-C. Do not run. Use caution when engaging elevators and shuttles."

The automated voice sounded far, far too calm, given the circumstances.

"Reactor breach?" Rosalyn repeated when the air around them was again leaden and dead. "That's not a failure, right? It could even just mean some hardware malfunction. Maybe that's why everyone is gone, they evacuated already."

Edison hunched over the mobile terminal and sighed. "I know I teased you for being a reformed pessimist, but the reactor breach is the least of our problems."

"What do you mean? They called for an evac; the station is probably completely empty."

He closed his eyes and shivered, his hand falling slowly over the manual lock lever. "No, you have to listen to me. The station isn't empty. It isn't. I can feel them, Roz, and they're everywhere."

40

Half of a Servitor's body lay slumped on the ground just beyond the mobile terminal. Rosalyn hurried to inspect it, crouching and poking at its lifeless husk.

"Look at this," she whispered. Even her own voice, filtered as it was through her suit, was startling in the dense silence. She could swear it echoed.

Edison joined her after securing the ship, and she could hear movement from inside as Misato cut the boosters and engine, powering down the *Brigantine*. He knelt and pushed over the Servitor, then pointed to the joint where the main chassis had been severed from the lower half of the machine's body.

"It's like it was pulled clean in half," he said, then turned and looked down the walkway leading to the customs platform and the control tower. "Rosalyn, I think you should get back on the ship and stay there. Coming here was a terrible idea."

"What? No! No, we're finally here and I'm not going to just *hide*."

"Something's not right," Edison continued, taking her hand and pulling it close to his chest. He flattened her palm over his heart and waited until she stopped arguing. "There is Foxfire everywhere but it's . . . it's like they're dormant. Sleeping. I can sense them, but

315

MADELEINE ROUX

they're not moving or communicating. Misato and I can go deeper and have a look around, then come back for you. This way, if anything happens, you can at least autopilot back to campus."

"I agree." Misato stood with arms crossed at the end of the ramp.

"Not you, too! This is ridiculous. I survived this long and I can survive this, whatever it is!" Edison opened his mouth to fight her but she clapped her hand over his visor. "I'm the way you keep it together now, Edison. You can use that song, but you know I'm the stronger anchor. I can keep you in yourself, you know I can."

He pulled her hand away, breathing heavily. His shoulders slumped. "She's right, Misato, but first thing's first: We need to find her a weapon. And we should move fast; I don't like the sound of that reactor breach."

"We need to get to the maintenance hub for diagnostics. None of the ordinary terminals would allow access to that kind of information. I'm sure I can . . ."

She trailed off mid-thought, staring straight through Rosalyn. That wasn't good. They watched Misato's eyes flicker once, twice, and then blaze into pure, blistering white.

"Oh, shit," Rosalyn whispered.

Edison put out a hand to silence her. Rather than the usual swift attack on Rosalyn's helmet, Misato didn't seem to notice her at all. Or she *saw* her, but quickly lost interest. Instead, she drifted by them, as if pulled along by an invisible string or an intense magnetic force. She said nothing, immune to their wide-eyed staring as she marched down the walkway toward customs and processing.

"Misato?" Rosalyn stage-whispered. "What's happening to her?"

"She's being called somewhere, summoned," he murmured. She hadn't actually expected a coherent answer from him, but was grate-

316

ful that he hadn't gone white-eyed and spooky. Taking his hand, she pulled him forward, following in Misato's trail.

"I can't explain it," Edison went on. "It's calling me, too, but it's . . . like there's a time delay. Each word bounces around in my head for a while. It doesn't sound anything like the Foxfire I'm used to. It's Mother, but coming in a hundred different voices."

"What did that sound like?" Rosalyn asked, trying to keep Misato in range. She was going faster now, walking with real purpose.

"Mother but flat, no emotions," he said. "Still a woman's voice. She sounds . . . kind. Worried, almost."

"Right, I wouldn't fall for that."

"Stay close," Edison told her, latching onto her arm. "We're going to need each other."

Rosalyn wasn't complaining. The thought of being alone and hunted by Foxfire-infested people in that massive space station while it went into core breach made her stomach burn with anxiety. Clinging to the bigger, stronger Edison at least allowed the illusion of safety, or the illusion of prolonged survivability odds. The vast dark echoed around them, safety lights illuminating the path forward, blinking yellow, then green, then back to yellow. She had no idea where to look or for how long, convinced that danger could be and was lurking in every possible nook. The other ships might not be empty, she thought, glancing at them with hostile suspicion. They could be filled to the brim with white-eyed, crazed passengers just waiting to tackle her and bring her into the cluster.

She froze, certain she saw a shape move among the windows hanging above them, where the Servitors and ground crew organized and cleared incoming and outgoing ships.

"Up there," Rosalyn whispered, pointing with a nod. "I saw something move. My AR isn't picking up a signal, but I don't trust anything anymore."

"I'll watch Misato, you watch our backs."

"And then? We're not exactly armed," she reminded him.

Edison had no answer for her. Rosalyn kept her eyes fixed on the windows, but nothing moved there again, and she promised herself it was just a trick of the eye, or one of the flashing emergency lights reflecting oddly. They reached the customs kiosks, completely abandoned, work tablets still poised and at the ready. A Servitor's foot, cleanly severed, still stood, as if the body had been whisked away mid-interview. A handful of crates to be inspected were stacked next to the foot, unopened. Misato disappeared into the shadows on the other side of the rounded walkway leading through customs and toward the main elevators.

They needed to hurry. Edison nudged her along with greater haste while Rosalyn peered in every direction, a cold, slimy feeling crawling over her neck whenever they passed an open doorway.

"Kenopsia," she whispered, head turned and eyes trained behind them as he hauled her toward the elevators. Misato waited for a car to be called, her body unnaturally stiff and still. The doors were opening, a friendly golden light spilling out onto Misato's head.

"What?"

"It's like that bizarre feeling you get when you're in a place that should be filled with people but isn't."

Not just a weird feeling, a hollow one, an eyes-on-you-from-every-direction-at-once feeling. Which was ironic, considering Rosalyn hadn't spotted another soul on the station except for Misato. But she trusted Edison's instincts, so perhaps it wasn't so strange to feel as if she was going out of her skin with untold numbers of Foxfire agents waiting for them somewhere inside.

The central bank of elevators led to the last security staging area, which was a mandatory stop before getting clearance and being allowed access to whatever segments of the station involved your stated business. The cantinas and retail spaces could be reached by anyone, but many of the corporate offices required an additional step, usually a rotating pass card or code. Rounded banks of stories-tall windows looked down onto them, and as they neared the elevators and Misato disappeared into them, Rosalyn felt her heart sink to her toes.

"You were right," she gasped, gazing, transfixed by the pulsing blue light pouring out from the windows above. "They're every-where."

Rosalyn collapsed with relief as the elevator doors closed with a *hush*. Sheer terror and Edison's arm had been keeping her upright, but now the full weight of what she had seen barreled into her, dropping her to the floor. Vaguely, she heard Edison programming the elevator. Of course he knew which floor. That thing was calling to him, too. If she hadn't been there, close to him, he would be going to it as blindly as Misato.

She tried to make sense of the mayhem. The glittering growth of Foxfire along the *Brigantine*'s walls and ceilings was disturbing, but this was far worse by comparison, like a typhoon next to an after-noon shower. The only word that came close to describing it was *hive*. It was like a hive, blue and webbed and shining. It was much worse than the ship, worse than a smatter of blackish, lichen-like growth with twinkling blossoms. No, it was an overwhelming riot of color. Nothing that she could see moved among it, yet it *breathed*.

Rosalyn hugged herself, feeling the dread in her gut spiral into panic. *Breathe*, she reminded herself, drawing air but only suffocat-ing. The harder she tried to breathe, the less air came in. Wheezing, groaning, she rocked back and forth, squeezing her middle hard until it ached, until she felt like her chest was caving in. How long would her oxygen filters last in an environment all but choked with dangerous spores?

"Talk to me."

His voice cut through the attack, her face hot and covered with sweat. She blinked up at him, pursing her lips, sealing a sob inside her throat.

"You were right," she hissed. "I should have stayed on the ship."

"No, *no*. We knew it could be bad. Remember? You told me to prepare for the worst," Edison told her, holding her and leaning into her in a rocking motion. Somehow it felt better, less painful when he did it with her. "We're in the worst now, and I need you to help me get through it. We can help each other now."

"It's too much. You saw it. It's too much . . ."

He cupped her visor, raising her face to his. His eyes were still that too-bright blue and it frightened her, but at least the color seemed warmer beaming from his face. She expected platitudes or begging, but all she wanted was to stay there on that elevator floor until it could go down again and bring her back to the ship. The floors dinged by, moving fast, bringing them swiftly to that horror she had glimpsed from below.

"Tell me the plan," Edison said, touching his helmet to hers.

Rosalyn blinked. The plan. Her mind spun into a frenzy without her meaning for it to. A plan. She licked her lips, which were cracked and stickily dry. "M-Misato has JAX's hard drive. We need it."

"That's good. What else?"

"Search the manifests," Rosalyn whimpered. "Search Piero's handle, find out where he got the Foxfire in the first place and make sure this was the only point of origin. We should be able to check the numbers we found with his badge, too, see if those launch dates coincide with any pickups."

Oh God. The elevator stopped, the door opening with an eerily cheerful chime. With the evac, the floors should have all been lit for the emergency, flooded with whirring yellow warning lights. But it was all turquoise, glittering like the insides of a sapphire struck by a sunbeam. She couldn't close her eyes, couldn't look away, even while every reasonable fiber in her body begged her to blink.

Edison raised her unsteadily to her feet and she slumped against him, only moving forward because she refused to be dragged.

And the worst part. The worst part . . .

"What's happened to them?" she breathed.

They stood just outside the doors, which closed with another happy chime, a sound from out of time, not this time, not this nightmare. The floors were covered in the same gummy webbing and growth as the walls, lapis bright. Strands of it, ropes of it, hung between railings, over visitor signage, over the lights, blotting out whatever the station floors might have looked like, covering it instead in brilliant blue. It almost hurt her eyes to look.

But the people. Most were in a state of decomposition so advanced it rendered them inhuman. Mounds of rounded fungus protruded from skulls and abdomens, bursting from bellies with reaching, arcing stems. Spores puffed out of the flowering ends, sending streamers of particulate white into the air, a winter-dense snowfall of pollen. Other workers and occupants were less disfigured, simply sitting hunched against the wall. One man looked as if he were napping, head tilted against his shoulder, mouth parted as if to snore.

"Is this what you become?" Rosalyn whispered, clinging fiercely to his side, then realizing the true horror of it and tearing herself away. She had forgotten Misato. The plan. The looming *and then* that she had no answer to.

Edison seemed almost not to hear her. He looked beyond her shoulder, to the curving, tall corridor of the fifth floor, where the blue carnage butted up against a glass office door. No, not butted up against, spilled from. It was quite obviously the epicenter of whatever had happened here, most likely an unwitting customs worker opening a Foxfire sample, not knowing what they were unleashing on the station.

"That way," Edison said. He shrugged helplessly at her. "The call, the voice, it's coming from that direction."

"Wait." Rosalyn tugged hard on his arm, pulling him away from the hideous mounds of overtaken people to the waist-high directory across from the elevators. A low panel, lit from each side, showed a layout of that corporate floor, with directions to each separate company. Blue film covered the map, but Rosalyn wiped it away, leaning down to study the schematic. Her AR chimed, pairing automatically with the kiosk.

"Look at this," she told him, holding fast to his wrist. "ISS. They have an office here. We have Piero's ID; maybe it will get us through the door."

"Misato," he said, shaking his head. "We have to find her. Look at this. *Look at it.* We have to get a signal out. We have to send a warning." He spun and laughed, a little crazed, half tripping on a corpse covered with purplish-blue growth, colonized and consumed.

"And we will get a warning out. But there's more to this, we know that. Piero was trying to cover his tracks, and he was working with my dad's company and ISS *and* Merchantia." She licked her lips nervously, pulling him away from the left-hand side of the corridor and toward the less hideously overrun area leading to ISS. "I've been thinking about this. It's all I've been thinking about. What if they already know? The man I spoke to in HR this week at Merchantia seemed suspicious of this big new partnership. He wanted me to investigate the *Brigantine* for him. What if they all know? What if Foxfire wasn't an accident but . . ."

She stopped herself. It was too evil to consider.

Edison nodded along as she spoke, listening intently, letting her guide him toward the large, black doors, INNOVATIVE SHIPPING SOLUTIONS spanning them both in bold, red print.

"But?" he prompted.

Checking her suit pockets, Rosalyn shoved aside her schematic and message chip, finally finding the copy of Piero's ISS badge.

"But an experiment," she said. A box at about shoulder height flashed with a holographic beam and ID reader. There was no telling if the 3-D printed copy would be enough to get them through without trying, so Rosalyn took a deep breath and placed the badge up to the scanner.

The scanner beeped once, twice, then chimed, and the doors to her left began to open. Something had jammed them, Foxfire growth no doubt, and she rushed forward, bracing herself in the gap.

"Help me with this," she said, and they each took a door, throwing their weight against it until the blockage gave and the doors screamed open, locking in place.

"Welcome, Danny Russo. Please have a productive day!"

The voice that drifted down over reception had once been bouncy with enthusiasm, but the recording had corroded, twisting the message into a broken whine.

A body slumped forward in its chair, leaning against the surface of a half-circle reception desk. It was covered in a thin, blue skin of mushrooms, and Rosalyn couldn't tell if it had been a man or woman. She skirted around the edge of the desk, holding her breath as she eased over the frozen body and carefully moved one of its hands aside. A puff of spores drifted upward, and Rosalyn stifled a scream, watching the fingers all but disintegrate.

"Sorry," she whispered, then booted the computer. It woke up, already logged in, one spot of luck. "I practically grew up at Belrose," she told Edison while he watched the doors for them. "Summer job at reception. Not paid, of course, because hard work is its own reward according to my dad." After a brief pause and a stuffed urge to babble nervously about her internships, Rosalyn found Danny Russo, Piero, in the employee ID log.

"He came through when the *Brigantine* docked here," she said, squinting through the haze of spores lingering in the air. "Just a quickie. Picked up a package for them."

"Working all angles," Edison muttered. "That definitely sounds like Piero."

"And making a mint, too." Whistling, Rosalyn shook her head, glancing up from the monitor. "They paid him a small fortune for this. Package included . . . let's see . . . ah! Perfect. Single-use experimental vaccination. Beta Tech–brand rebreather. Dangerous biocontaminant. Xenobiological samples. There's just an address here, but it's this same station, only a different suite."

Rosalyn looked up again, consulting her AR, checking the floor schematic against the suite address.

"It's on this floor," she said, unfocusing her eyes from her display, training her eye not on Edison but what lay beyond him, through the doors. "One guess where it is."

"Piero knew what he was doing. Bastard. He brought the Foxfire on board knowing it was dangerous." Edison swore again and again, pacing in front of the open doors. "And the dates we found with his badge?"

"He's a bastard, certainly, but there are a lot of bastards here. ISS is a shipping point, a middleman." She backed out of the manifest proving Piero's mission and called up the complex calendar, layered with icons. A small box in the corner, like a map key, allowed her to choose what information the calendar displayed. "Scheduled pickups." She had memorized the sequence of numbers that coincided with the Merchantia launch dates, only a quick scroll through the calendar away. "There." She poked the screen. She felt like she might choke. The dates were too close to be a coincidence. "There. Danny Russo had a stopover with ISS before each of those doomed launches. They weren't accidents, Edison, all of them took deliveries from this place, and all of them went dark. *Shit.*"

Rosalyn pulled back from the computer, bumping the receptionist and watching as it dissolved into a flurry of bluish-white specks, like a dandelion blowing into the wind. She stumbled back toward Edison, pointing frantically at the back of her environmental suit.

"My filters. They're not handling this level of contamination. I've probably got another hour, maybe two."

"That's more than enough to send a warning and leave," Edison told her, taking her by the hand as they ran out of the ISS lobby and back onto the main floor of the corporate level, bringing them face-to-face again with the horror that had taken place. "We find Misato and get that hard drive, we send whatever warning we can, and then we get out. Bringing these assholes to justice will have to wait; you're more important."

Rosalyn wanted to scream, but held it in. Every step they took toward the other office suite degraded her oxygen filters further. She didn't want to bump another body and watch it float away. There was the terror of the ship, and then there was the terror of this place, almost too bizarre, too inhuman to fully take in.

"They might be one and the same," she whispered. "Misato is in there somewhere, and that's where ISS got the Foxfire samples. It's ground zero."

Edison took her arm again, waiting until she walked of her own volition to lead her toward that office door and the octopus-like explosion of thick tendrils that had forced its way through the glass.

The whole seething mass of it and every thickened growth around them pulsed in time, the same way it had on the ship, not steadily, but with a hitch, with the rhythm of a human heartbeat.

"You need to tell me something," Rosalyn whispered, no longer trying to hide the deep tremor overtaking every inch of her. "You need to tell me if these things . . . if they're still alive. Still . . . still human."

She watched his chest expand with a stabilizing breath and knew the answer. "Yes."

"Can you sense them like you did the others?" Rosalyn hadn't looked closely at his face in a moment, but saw now that he was as tremulous and damp as she was. His eyes swept anxiously back and forth, his neck and shoulders stone stiff.

"Yes."

"How is that possible? They're . . . practically muck."

He chose each word carefully, articulating himself with great effort. "I'm doing my best just to hold it together, but they're waking up now that we're here. Imagine five hundred voices all talking at once, right into your ear. Some are your mother. Some are your ex-wife. Your best friend. They all want you to join them. They're all confused. Afraid. *Hungry*."

"*What?*"

It at least shocked her out of the gripping panic. Edison paused, looking down at her blankly, and then he frowned, realizing what he had said. His eyes slid gradually to the right, and Rosalyn heard the sound of flesh unpeeling from flesh, a wet, swampy slide and slip that corresponded to a mossy blue body rising from the ground. There was no face to see, no eyes to look into, just a fur of tiny mushrooms covering a naked body.

"Run. Now."

Edison took his own advice first, sweeping her down the

corridor at a speed she could barely match. The thing that had woken up moved slowly, shaking itself out before pursuing at a crooked lurch. But it wasn't alone. More bodies in every state of transformation and decomposition began rising around them, finding their mark and following. Rosalyn stopped glancing over her shoulder, screaming as a human-shaped mass of stems and twinkling, sucker-shaped fungus pulled itself up out of the sludge in front of them. Edison didn't slow down, and Rosalyn braced with her elbow out in front of her face as they plowed through it, showered in a flurry of heavy blue sparks.

"Not again. Help me push!" They reached the door, sliding up to it and throwing their weight against the panels, the glass creaking from its compromised core, the pulsing tentacles speared through its center adding unbelievable density.

Rosalyn kept her eyes closed. She didn't want to see how close doom crept. Edison roared as he gave another full-bodied shove, and at last the door began to move, inch by inch, allowing a space just big enough for them to tumble through and then back up against.

She spun, watching as a blond, short woman with half a face covered in growth walked right up to the glass, her nose bumping against it. Then she went still, as if the light in her head had dimmed. Nothing pursued them inside this apparent sanctuary, they simply froze in place, silent, pulsing watchers.

"Let's go," Edison said, taking her wrist gently. She glanced toward him, her feet so heavy with pitiless terror they felt fused to the floor. "We're close now. For better or worse, we're close."

41

Like an aquarium, teeming and blue, the office pulsed with growth all around them. Rosalyn picked her way across reception, finding there was almost nothing to explain where they were or what was meant to happen there. All of the employees, it seemed, had fled, then succumbed to Foxfire out on the landing or elsewhere in the station.

"Are you all right?" she asked Edison, watching him closely as they moved deeper through the junglelike tendrils, the living blue sinews as thick around as a tree.

"No, are you?"

"No," Rosalyn said. "If you're going to give in—"

"I won't," Edison promised her, helping her over an overturned desk. "We've come too far for that."

"I don't think that will matter. If this is where it all began, it will only get harder and harder. But I'm here. Just don't listen, okay? Whatever it tells you, whatever it promises you . . ."

Edison nodded, and from the draw of his brow, she could tell he was nervous, or maybe embarrassed. His eyes flitted quickly along the walls, and his hands shook as he and Rosalyn helped each other over tumbles of ruined and scattered furniture. They traveled deeper, through doors lodged open by thick blue growth. The mottled light glittered down on them through an unbroken web of thin turquoise threads, adding to the sense that they were wandering through a fish tank.

Holding her hand, he squeezed it often, too hard, but Rosalyn refused to show him how much it hurt. She imagined each squeeze was an attempt the Foxfire made to sway him, and if he needed to pulp her fingers to stay with her, then so be it.

"I hope that money was worth all of this, Piero," she whispered, gazing around at the utter destruction. "That vaccination tab in the manifest? A rebreather?"

"I know," Edison replied, strained. "I don't want to think about it. Let's keep moving."

Rosalyn could think of nothing else. That someone had willingly taken a payment to unleash Foxfire on unsuspecting crewmates made her heart wither. How could anyone be so selfish? So shortsighted. It didn't give her satisfaction that Piero had succumbed to the Foxfire first and hardest, but it did seem like a sort of dark, cosmic justice.

"Are we getting closer to Misato?"

"Yeah," Edison said. "She's not far."

At the sound of her name, the living blue vines and mushroom clusters surrounding them shivered. Rosalyn went silent, hardly breathing as they stepped carefully through the office suite, stopping when they reached a split corridor. One way led in the same direction, another door, open, waited to their left. Rosalyn watched the Foxfire shudder as she wiped her hand across the wall near the doorway, searching for a label.

"It isn't storage," she said. "It's a rented lab."

The shivering of the walls intensified, a rattling sound chasing around the room. The two of them huddled close as the shaking took form, creating words and then a beat, a song. Glowing with each hum and word, the office lit up around them.

Busy the bee goes, "Buzz, buzz, buzz!" Dizzy the dog goes, "Woof, woof, woof!"

"I know that story," Rosalyn murmured, easing through the doorway and away from the sudden buzzing song. "Angela told it to her kids. I saw it in your bunker."

"Mother recites it all the time," Edison replied, blinking rapidly. "Candace would tell it to Joey . . . or maybe not. I'm . . . it's hard to remember now."

"Stay with me," Rosalyn pleaded, keeping him close. "Keep moving. I don't think we should give it a chance to make a plan."

Busy the bee goes, "Buzz, buzz, buzz!" Ollie the owl goes, "Hoot, hoot, hoot!" and Mother goes: "I love you" . . .

Rosalyn couldn't imagine anything more unnerving than a thousand sizzling voices chanting a child's rhyme at her, but it kept on, louder and louder, chasing them into the rented lab. Two hallways opened up around a shared wall and desk, and Rosalyn chose the right fork, which seemed less choked with singing vines.

As they went, as the song followed them, Edison squeezed her hand harder and harder, until she couldn't help but wince.

"Stay with me," she told him again. "Don't forget the plan. Misato. Hard drive. Warning. Then we run."

He grunted, nodded, sweat pouring down his face. It hurt to look at him, to see him struggling against the voices. If it was that bad on the outside, she dreaded to think what he heard in his own mind.

The narrower hall opened up into a familiar sort of space for Rosalyn, a lab similar to the one she had spent countless hours in at Belrose. Even the layout echoed the labs at her old job, a coincidence that worried her more and more as they navigated between the

evenly spaced rows of desks, piled with equipment for experimenting and recording. The little pipettes looked the same. The trays.
The *mugs*.

Everything could have been picked up from their labs in Montreal and put down there, on a distant station overrun and destroyed.
Rosalyn felt her hand go numb, and then her lips, her oxygen and
Edison a distant thought as she raced up the alley between the desks
and to where Misato knelt as if praying to the woman seated at a
central, lower desk, shimmering and blue, perfectly preserved.

She might have been a statue, still but completely lifelike, a paler
blue light emanating from her chest, beating slowly, a bright glow
of a pulse. The children's rhyme filtered through the blue-tinted lab,
the vaulted ceiling and kneeling Misato giving it all the strange,
cold reverence of a church.

"I . . . I *know* her," Rosalyn whispered. Was she hallucinating?
Had Foxfire taken her? How was it possible that she knew this
woman, the clear, obvious heart of the infestation? The tendrils of
blue that grew to overtake the lab and then the station sprang out
from her fingertips, spiraling down from the desk to spread and
spread.

Edison inched up behind her, then leaned hard against Rosalyn's
shoulder for support.

"She looks just like the woman from my dreams," he said.

"That's because she is the woman from your dreams," Rosalyn
whispered, afraid to take another step toward the epicenter of all this
destruction. But it really was her friend. They shared a birthday, a
passion for work, a love of singing silly songs to her kids over video
chat. Strange flashes of familiarity, almost déjà vu . . . "The poems,
the rhymes, the smell of lemons? Parts of her were in your head.
Angela. She was a mother, a mother who took this job so far away
from her children. God, no wonder she wanted to convince you all

to join some family." A shocked sob escaped her throat. "We would go out together sometimes . . . and get lemon drops. That's why I seemed so familiar to you. You recognized me because *she* did."

Rosalyn felt her knees buckle. More of it slotted into place in her mind. Edison had used a saying she had only ever heard from Angela. Her kids, her family, were everything to Angela, and leaving to oversee the first Belrose lab in space had torn her to pieces.

"We did this," Rosalyn breathed, seeing but unseeing, feeling more of her heart break each time she looked at Angela's soft, blue face. She had a cherubic look, always, curly blond hair and plump cheeks, a permanent, wry smile and pixie chin. "Our company did this."

"No," Edison managed through clenched teeth. "She did this. This lab did it. It's all around us; they had no idea what they were experimenting with, but they sure found out. You couldn't have stopped it, not if you stayed, not if . . . *agh.*"

"Edison!"

He collapsed, both hands clamped over his helmet. His mouth dropped open in a contorted scream, veins bulging from his temples. Misato didn't budge, frozen, still in a prayer position. Rosalyn dropped down next to Edison, trying to force his hands back down, wiping her hands over his visor. But his eyes were shut against her, and his scream drowned out the lilting children's song drifting up from the choking vines.

"I'm here! Edison? Edison? Come back to me! I shouldn't have brought you this close, I shouldn't have . . . Angela! Let him go. *Let him go.*"

His screams abruptly ended, and his hands dropped to his sides. Going still and calm, his face relaxed and then his eyes opened, a blazing, terrible silver.

42

A hush fell over him, and everything was quiet. The hospital smelled like pain and antiseptic, a smell he would always associate with death. He wouldn't step foot in a hospital again unless it was life-threatening; just one whiff of that air and he wanted to run.

"Eddie, baby, you're here!"

"Of course I'm here."

Edison looked down at his mother on the hospital bed. He had brought her a special blanket, one he had shipped from their house on Earth. It was crocheted with little blue and orange flowers, and cheered up the dreary white and gray sheets folded over her legs. Diana, shriveled, small, spoke to him through her oxygen mask.

"You're awake," Edison said, frowning. "But you've been asleep for months . . ."

"It's you," she said, patting the bed by her knees. "You woke me up. Where are Candace and Joey?"

"He doesn't like it here." Sitting next to her, he could feel the scary thinness of her leg through the blanket. He ran his hand over the blue and orange flowers. "It upsets him."

"It upsets you, too."

Edison didn't say anything, swallowing around a lump.

"But you come to see me, it upsets you but you come to see me," she said, smiling as much as she could through the mask. "Because you love your mother, baby. You've always been such a good son."

A nurse came in, sighing, consulting an overstuffed clipboard. Her name tag was blank, and when Edison tried to look at her face, it was nothing but a smudge, a blur. He squinted, but she never came into focus.

"Something isn't right," he whispered.

"Mr. Aries? I think you should leave now," the nurse said, her voice warped, almost a garble. But he knew what she said, and what she wanted.

"I'm staying with my mother."

"That's right, baby. You stay here with your mother." Diana reached for his hand, and he took it, cradling the baby-bird lightness of it carefully in his palm.

"It's time for you to go," the nurse said, never putting down her clipboard. "Now."

Diana sat up, struggling, leaning toward him. She smelled sour and dusty, her hair badly in need of a wash. "Don't let her take me, baby. Don't let her kill your mother."

"What?"

A nurse wouldn't do that . . . It was his decision. Of course it was his decision. But his mother had woken up, hadn't she? The life support could be taken away. They would run some tests, of course, make sure she was in good enough shape to get off the oxygen, but then she would be better.

He stared at the nurse for a long time, trying to make a face out of the fuzzy space where a nose and mouth should be. Soft, strange noises came from her, as if something were stuck in her chest, a hiccup, but louder and more like a voice. He strained to hear it, but nothing became clear, and then he saw her darting forward, toward the bed. Toward the machine.

"No!"

Edison lurched for her, taking the nurse by the shoulders and wrestling her away, down to the ground. She was tall and strong, but he fought her back, pinning her to the floor. The bizarre, muted cries from her chest became louder. His head ached, hard, almost blinding, and he cried out, then fell to the side, feeling her knee slam into his crotch.

The nurse jumped swiftly to her feet, scrambling toward the machine.

"It's not your mother! It's Angela. It's not your mother!"

Edison froze, trying to stand, and hearing, at last, the strangled words caught in the nurse's chest. She was close to the machine now. She was going to unplug his mother. Kill her. But if she was awake and well, why would it matter? Why did she need the machine?

"Don't let her touch me! I don't want to die, baby, I don't want to die. You wouldn't kill your mother . . ."

Diana's face, wet with tears, shimmered under the oxygen mask. He could remember when that face was full and healthy, when her shoulders were more than desiccated knobs. This was a memory, but it was all wrong. *All wrong.* He knew how it went. He remembered the way his hands shook and then became strong as he reached for the machine himself. His mother wasn't there anymore. She had died a long time ago.

"Stop!" he shouted at the nurse, grabbing her by the waist and pushing her to the side. "I have to do it. Me."

"No, I'll help you. We can do this together, all right? Together. It's a mercy, we can't leave Angela like this, we can't let her hurt anyone else. That's not who she was, she was a good friend, a good person, and she wouldn't want to stay like this." The nurse looked different then, familiar. Beautiful. He trusted her big hazel eyes, and he nodded, knowing her again. The knowledge made him feel strong. Rosalyn.

"Help me," Edison whispered. Rosalyn stood out from the rest of the room, richer in color, realer and more vivid than the faded memory around him.

Diana thrashed on the bed, rising up, clawing at him, no longer a frail woman but a skeletal creature of talons and flashing teeth. Blue. She was explosively blue, and her sharp hands lashed out toward him. Rosalyn shifted to block her, trying to hold her hands still while Edison struggled to reach her life support.

"You wouldn't kill your mother!" she screamed and screamed, tearing at Rosalyn's side. "I'm your friend . . . your friend. Everything went to pieces, Rosalyn . . ." So he was no longer the focus of her anger, Rosalyn was. He watched the salvager brace herself and shut her eyes tight, but Mother—Angela—went on shrieking and pawing at her. "Don't take this away from me. My children . . . All of this was mine, my project. I gave up everything for this, don't take it away!" They pierced, her screams, fracturing his headache into a million stabbing pieces, but he went to the machine himself while Rosalyn held Mother at bay.

"Do it, Edison." Rosalyn opened her eyes, finding his.

"I'm your friend!" the creature on the bed wailed. "I'm your *mother!*"

He found the display on her life support. He knew this memory.

"You're not my mother." Edison blinked through the pain in his head, gazing at the pitiable creature writhing on the hospital bed. The little crocheted blanket fell on the floor. All the hate had gone out of him, and all the fear. "I'm sorry."

Light shot in every direction. Edison opened his eyes to find Misato and Rosalyn staring at him, both with mouths open, their hands reaching out toward him.

His head felt better. Clearer. The pain lingered but gradually slipped away. A pile of blue ash scattered across the desk in front of him, and with it came a wave of nausea. The tendrils of iridescent turquoise spreading from the desk, from the woman that had been there but was no more, blackened, shriveling up like charred leaves.

"You fought back," Rosalyn whispered, unblinking. "You helped me fight Foxfire."

"Mother," Edison rumbled. "She was . . . the first one. Angela. Alpha. Mother. The first one infected. I don't know what happens now."

"You and Misato tried to stop me, but then something changed," Rosalyn told him, standing and backing away from the cloud of spores dancing above the desk. "Then you just . . . snapped, and went for her. 'Help me,' you said. Poor Angela . . . She gave up her entire life on Earth for this, and look at it. A nightmare. In her last message to me she said they were going to change medicine, she must have thought the Foxfire's regenerative properties could be isolated, but this . . ."

"The road to hell," Edison murmured, not bothering to finish the idiom.

"There are no intentions good enough to justify this," Rosalyn replied.

"Worry about her later; the others, the ones that were totally consumed, totally her children, they're angry," Misato said, biting her lip. "Very angry. They're untethered now. Nothing is controlling them. Not Mother. Nothing. They were listening to her but now it's all a panic," she said. "Can you hear it?"

Edison did, the distant buzzing that became a roar.

"There's nothing human about them anymore," he said quietly, sadly.

Misato jumped to her feet, squaring herself in front of Rosalyn. "I destroyed JAX's hard drive before you could get here. Mother told me to do it and I . . . I couldn't resist her. You're the record now, Rosalyn. Go. One of the engineers tried to trigger the reactor breach before the Foxfire took him. Mother—Angela—was furious. I can finish it."

Misato turned, staring straight ahead, in profile to Rosalyn from where she stood near Angela's desk. "They are mindless now, monstrous. They'll try to stop you, but Edison can get you to the evac pods."

"You're both coming with me," Rosalyn shot back stubbornly. "This can be over. She's gone now. That has to *mean* something."

But she knew she was outnumbered. Edison was giving Misato's shoulders one last squeeze before continuing on, arriving at Rosalyn's side to take her gently by the forearm. He slid an arm around her waist, saying softly, "The worst thing you could do right now is argue."

"Then I'm doing the worst thing. We can all fit in an evac pod." Rosalyn jumped to see over Edison's shoulder as he hid Misato from her view. "Misato? Come with us. *Come with us.*"

She heard the engineer give a husky laugh. "It can be brave to run, Rosalyn. Don't forget that."

43

It was impossible to find the edges of her relief. At last, all the voices in her head were silent. She couldn't sense Edison, or the seething mass of thoughts and feelings assaulting her from the concentrated hive of the cluster. It was just input from her eyes, her ears, her nose, and the jarring silence of her own mind.

If left to ponder it, she might consider it lonely, but there was no time for reflection. She didn't watch Edison as he dragged Rosalyn away. In the end, the salvager went freely. That was good. Misato would have forced her on the pod if she had to, but she trusted Edison to do the right thing. They had shared half a mind for so long, she could practically guess each word before he spoke it.

That left the reactor. The remaining Foxfire-infested humans were in a frenzy. They were far, far gone, not a shred of human thought remaining in their minds. The jittery, crazed ramblings she had heard from them when she was still connected through Angela left her skin cold. It was hunger. Fungus needed nutrients, after all, and the cluster had spread through the station too quickly, consuming everything, leaving very little for food. They wanted her for food, of course, and Edison and Rosalyn. She would make sure they understood not only true starvation, but destruction.

At first, the hive had contained an exquisite beauty. Lost in the labyrinth of voices and opinions, Misato couldn't see it for what it was—life, in all its messy, scattershot determination, out of control. Life wasn't always some magical, mystical thing to be protected and cherished; sometimes it was simply greedy expanding chaos, a teeming, overwhelming force. The Foxfire had grown wild, shoveling food and people and knowledge into its mouth like a toddler left unsupervised at a buffet. A mother desperate and hungry for more children.

She could still feel the bite of the warmed plastic in her fingers as it broke in two. Unforgivable, she thought, even while controlled by Foxfire. She knew better. That was their research, their thoughts, their experiences, their knowledge, gone in a blink, and if Rosalyn did not survive, then nobody would be warned. Even with Angela gone, Misato felt instinctively that Foxfire would find a way to survive. Life was tenacious that way.

The reactor access was less webbed in gooey blue strands. She reached it through the maintenance elevators, grateful for the breach opening access to all doors and hatches. It was a given that if a breach warning went out, nobody was going to stay to loot the place; they would grab their loved ones and bolt for the pods. Radiation was probably already spreading through the station, and she wondered if that hadn't contributed to the intense mutating nature of the cluster.

Purely academic, useless thoughts, she chided herself. *Focus.* She found the engineer that had tried so valiantly to obliterate Angela and her cluster. She was still as a statue, standing at the manual flow controls out on the platform near the plated core itself. The desperate thing hadn't even bothered to put on a suit, exposing herself to dangerous levels of radiation. Clearly, she had thought it worth the risk, and Misato agreed.

She couldn't help but feel a pang of sadness for this woman. Misato climbed out onto the platform, the great humming, thrumming plated core spinning in hypnotic intervals. It was the kind of sound that, if heard from a distance, would put one to sleep nicely. A rhythmic pulse. A steady, comforting whir. Now it was too loud to be of any comfort, like the blurred blast of a drum vibrating through her chest as it turned. So close, she heard the almost imperceptible problem, the slight out-of-kilter hitch to the turn. The engineer had tried to force the core out of its gravitational trap, but stopped just before the alignment triggered total meltdown.

Misato took her time, measuring her steps, never peeling her eyes away from the flow controls. These would almost never be used, and probably hadn't been touched since the station's construction. But the maintenance hub would never allow her to attempt station-wide sabotage; in fact, the engineer had been forced to use a power hammer to wedge a gap in the safety railing separating the maintenance tower from the far-more-precarious walkway. The platform leading to the shielding and the controls was wide enough but shook from the massive, spinning core, juddering as if a bullet train were passing by. She approached the engineer, her skin hanging in red, irradiated clumps from her face. Her eyes were closed, her mouth slightly open, as if she could not believe she had come so far and failed.

The CDAS security badge hanging around her neck read DE-SHAWNA ADAMS.

"Good work," Misato told her. "I'll finish up here."

The controls were already unlocked, a USB key dangling from the side of the LED screen. The core breach alert blared inside the station again, but so near to the core the sound was muffled, a distant warning, and not for them. This was not where someone went to escape unharmed. She closed her eyes, wishing she could summon her connection to Edison. Had they made it out okay? Regardless, she knew what had to be done, but she would feel a lot better knowing Rosalyn was safely away. And if she wasn't? Well, there would be nothing left of their story to tell. This core was going to kill them all, and the Foxfire with it.

Misato froze, listening to a coughing wheeze from over her shoulder. She turned, Deshawna listing forward, sucking air with trouble through her drooping mouth and the holes torn through her neck by the radiation.

The Foxfire had kept her alive. It was monstrous, not Deshawna, but what the infestation had done to her. Slow radiation deterioration was enough; this was a second, worse punishment. Misato grabbed her, feeling the brittleness in her bones, the wet, sloughing slide of the woman's skin as she touched it. But Misato had the strength of determination behind her, and hauled Deshawna forward, pushing her hand over the flow controls, the LED screen flashing, screaming warnings at them as their fingers moved across the display.

There was a sudden ping as the core shifted, scraping the metal plating that contained it, knocking loose a casing that zipped over their heads, lodging with a metallic clang in the maintenance tower behind them.

It was starting.

Misato had no idea how long it would take for the breach to destroy Coeur d'Alene Station; she only knew that she and Deshawna would go first. She let go of the woman, watching her fall to her knees and then over onto her side. Misato sat with her, feeling the platform rattle and bounce, the key chip falling out of the control screen, plunging down before being whipped into the erratic orbit of the core. Watching it disappear, she felt a pit open up in her stomach, a longing she hadn't expected or wanted. She could have retired. She didn't need this last adventure.

There was never any guarantee of another side, of more adventures. There was only the flood of last-minute regrets and the taste of Jenny's lip gloss, the last memory she wanted. The only memory she needed.

Deshawna looked like she was at rest, curled up, the remains of her hair blowing in the draft of the core. And so Misato lay down next to her on her back, folded her hands over her chest and closed her eyes. She could feel Jenny's hair sliding through her fingers as she settled her head on Misato's chest to sleep. Their cats, Charlie and Wrex, wove between Misato's legs with their warm, slinky bodies, wrapping themselves around knees and ankles until at last contented, huddled safe beneath the covers. It was so, so warm. Her skin itched, and if she touched it, she feared it would fleck away like ash.

"Okay," she murmured to the hot spinning fires above. She was warm and safe, her work was done. "I love you, Jenny. *Bye*."

44

The thick, strange tentacles bursting through the office door sagged, leaving a gap wide enough to see through, wide enough to show the field of rigid, waiting obstacles in their path. It was like they had thrown a matchstick into a beehive, and now all the riled, furious insects wanted to act, wanted to sting.

"There's too many," he heard Rosalyn whisper at his side.

She hadn't spoken since he held her back from following Misato, and her bitter, silent fury had wounded him as much as seeing his friend go. He didn't have time to explain to her that this was how it was always going to happen, that they both knew it, and that surely she had run this scenario in her head enough times to see that they were knee-deep in the cluster's final moments. That she hadn't really counted him and Misato among the cluster's numbers touched him, but made this all-too-predictable betrayal harder. But Misato would fulfill her promise, and now he had to fulfill his. What he knew and Rosalyn didn't was that no matter how many of the dying cluster's sentinels remained, he would get her on that evac pod.

Only her desperation protected her from the truth.

"Just stay close." Edison hadn't been looking out the doors but down at her. Maybe he was the desperate one, frantically sucking up every detail of her face, her posture, her frame, imprinting it deliberately on his memory. He had no idea how long it would take for the core to destroy the station. It wasn't something he had read about or seen before; no station had ever suffered catastrophic core failure. Would it be loud and fast or painful and slow? Would he burn up in a moment or fall gradually to pieces, shredded by prolonged radiation poisoning?

He watched his gloved right hand push at the doors, fighting the stringy bands that had grown up around the glass and clung to it like overgrown jungle vines. The station workers that had fallen to Foxfire were waiting, standing in haphazard places, pulling themselves up from whatever wall or floor had become their last resting place and turning toward them, vigilant. They had failed to protect their mother, and now they were ready for the one who had done it.

"Don't let go of my hand," Edison added.

They pushed out into the hall, both of them raising a forearm in defense. Rosalyn was shaking so hard it was difficult to keep hold of her, but nothing could make him let go. He was the captain, and she had become part of his crew. Every member of a crew had a duty, a mission. Misato was completing hers, and soon Rosalyn would perform her final act as a portion of the *Brigantine*. He had hated that ship when it first came under his command. The assigned Servitor was old and poky; the thruster tech could be newer; the layout seemed cramped and ill conceived; the toilet pipes leaked.

Now he ached to be back on board, curled up in the odd little bunk he had created out of repurposed crates and half of a crew bed. Rosalyn could come with him. They could sleep and sleep and sleep while the *Brigantine* flew them home. She would work on that coated chip tech while he waited in quarantine, biding his time until her genius saw them through.

Edison was shouting, barreling down the hall, shoulder checking softened bodies out of their way, heedless of the scrabbling hands that pulled at him as they went, ignoring the tear that opened up in his suit and the blood that poured freely from his arm.

Slam. They were at MSC, laughing because he had gotten tired of the quarantine food, worse than the cantina food, as if he was being punished for falling sick. Rosalyn smuggled in Twinkies when she visited, the strawberry kind, because she gave a shit and couldn't stand to see him on the bland diet.

Crack. She needed her old equipment back on Earth and had to leave for a while to finish the prototype. The way she talked about it wasn't just endearing but intoxicating. Her eyes lit up when she explained the ins and outs of the process, what recovery would be like for him, and all the associated risks. But she was confident, too, that it *would* work, that if she had time and focus she could perfect a chip with the cure, and he would sleep the sleep of the deeply anesthetized while the lifesaving chip was fused to the AR implant. While she worked, he would dream of this moment, of how close they had both come to failure and annihilation.

But that was a fantasy. The station creaked all around them, the floor beneath their feet tilting suddenly, sending them careening into the corridor wall. The mass of tangled growth cushioned the impact, and Edison let Rosalyn fall against his chest as they and their pursuers struggled to stay upright. A head, torso and one arm pulled itself toward them, flowering blue sprouts as small as clover waving as the remnant of humanity, the evidence of Foxfire's cruelty, made a pathetic attempt to stop them. Edison kicked it hard into the wall out of mercy, putting his boot through the mushy face and grinding before yanking Rosalyn toward the elevators.

She was crying.

Hiccups punctuated every sob as she gasped for air, keeping pace with his run. Edison felt his heart twist to the side as he glanced down and saw how red her face had become, shining wet with tears. The elevators were so close. Did she think they wouldn't make it?

"Tell me something funny," he rasped out, not realizing how out of breath he was, how fast and hard they had been sprinting. His arm hurt so badly that it had gone numb out of pity for his pain receptors. But he *did* feel it. No more voices, plenty more pain. Foxfire was losing its grasp on his mind.

"What?"

Edison slammed his entire hand into the elevator controls, pressing the CALL square way more times than was necessary. Maybe it was necessary. On the periphery of his vision shapes moved, sliding ever closer, bodies and parts of bodies clamoring to stop them, to take her.

"Don't look back. Tell me something funny. Anything."

The elevator doors opened and Edison half tackled her into the safety of the car. He knelt and repeatedly jammed the CLOSE button, then their destination. Docking platform. Evac pods. Salvation.

Rosalyn crawled into his arms, and they sat huddled against the wall, rocking, while the elevator lowered. They dropped with unnatural speed for a second, the elevator shifting from side to side, jarring them as the station tilted further out of alignment. He held Rosalyn tight. Misato had completed her objective, now it was time for him to do the same.

He tipped Rosalyn's head against his shoulder, wishing more than anything that he could've touched her once, just once, out of that suit.

Maybe her mind was on Misato, too, because she whispered between hiccups, "What do you call a sad canister of coffee?"

Edison smirked, realizing his face was wet, too. "I don't know, Rosalyn, what?"

She gasped, squeezing him around the middle so hard he winced. The elevator dropped again, the voice announcing the floors warping from the terrifying speed of it. Then the voice resumed, normally, as if they hadn't just free-fallen twenty feet. He watched the floors count down. Close. They were so close. He didn't mind that she held him that tightly.

"Depresso."

He snort-laughed, or sob-laughed, whatever it was, and tears splattered against the inside of his helmet. That made him laugh, too, and she joined in, glancing up at him, her big hazel eyes blurry behind the tears that just kept spilling out.

"That is the worst joke I've ever heard," Edison said through his chuckles.

"I have more," she warned.

"I can't wait to hear them."

They arrived. He almost dreaded the doors opening. The doors opening meant he had to stand up and take Rosalyn with him. It meant he had to take her to the evac pods, put her in one and watch her hurl into space away from him. Away from him. Selfishly, he considered the alternatives. He could go with her. He could master whatever was left of the Foxfire in his mind. There could be a cure, there had to be a cure, the mother of it all was dead, the first infected human, so didn't that mean something? *Didn't that mean something?*

Somehow he stood. Somehow he herded her into his arms and hug-walked her out of the elevators and down the platform. Somehow he followed the signage. Somehow he kept them upright as the station listed, threatening to catapult them against the gravity field. Somehow he put one foot in front of the other, guiding her to the bank of pods on the far left-hand side of the flat, where two dozen circular hatches in two orderly rows waited, green lights shining brightly on every little door.

Somehow he opened one of those pods and saw the crisp white cushions inside, and somehow he let her go.

45

"It's so spacious," she joked, turning around and sitting down on the lip of the pod hatch. "Just like being back in cold storage."

Edison scrunched his eyes up but didn't laugh. She hadn't noticed how many shiny tracks had fallen down his cheeks, sparkles nesting in his beard. For some reason, he stood down at the bottom of the short ladder leading into the pod. At least her hiccups had stopped.

"What are you doing? Get in," Rosalyn told him, tugging on the slack part of the suit over his chest.

Edison took her hand, touched it to his visor and then returned it to her, folding it gently against her own chest.

"You know I can't do that. You know this is where we part ways."

"No," she said, shaking her head hard. "We didn't agree on that. I didn't agree to that!"

"Rosalyn. *Rosalyn.*"

She slapped at his shoulders but he carefully fended her off, waiting until her fury was spent, waiting until she sank back down and looked in every direction for help. There was no help. There was the sharp bite of the pod's edge under her ass and the tearstained face in front of her, his lips in a grim line, his eyes . . . His eyes.

"Edison . . ."

"I'm not having this fight," he blurted. "It's hard enough watching you go, I refuse to argue about it. For once don't be stubborn. *Please*."

"Shut up," she breathed, reaching out slowly and holding his helmet. The flat under them seemed to roar, then shake, nearly throwing her out of the pod. But Rosalyn ignored it. "Your eyes. They're . . . they're yours. They're brown. They're *beautiful*."

He stared back at her, dumbfounded, searching her face with, for once, eyes that were purely, wonderfully *human*.

"Isn't that a sign?" she whispered, feeling stupid and heartsick and berserk.

Edison put his hands over hers, tipping their visors together. She heard his long, long sigh and shivered. "No, Rosalyn. There are no signs. There are no signs for us, only decisions. It doesn't matter what my eyes look like, I'm a liability. That stuff is still inside me and all over me. You're the only record of this we have when the station goes. The station will be gone. The *Brigantine* will be gone. Foxfire will be gone. Misato and I . . . we'll be gone, too."

"No," she cried. "You can't make me do this alone."

"You've done so much alone, so many incredible things," Edison told her, his voice trembling as steadily as her hands. "This is just one more incredible thing, and I know you can do it."

"But I don't want to, I don't want to go without you. Please. *Please*. Not after all of this, not now. Your eyes, they're human, you have to believe me."

Edison was silent while the station around them screamed, every fail-safe failing, every safety measure inadequate against the plated core being forced off its axis. She didn't care if the whole thing came down around their ears, she wasn't leaving without him.

There were so many times—so many times—when she wasn't

believed and when she didn't believe in herself, but this was not one of them.

"Believe me," she whispered. "Please. Just . . . believe me. Look into my eyes. I can finally look into your eyes, so look into mine. Do it. Do it and listen: Believe me. Believe that there's a chance you can be truly, wholly human again."

Edison turned toward her and climbed up the ladder, trying to keep his balance as the station rocked and he nearly flew off the platform. They didn't have time. The station was collapsing. Rosalyn's filters wouldn't last much longer. She watched and watched, and told herself there would be enough oxygen in her canisters to make it back. Even if he was still infected, even if she had to go down to the least possible intake, they could make it. His chin flexed, and she felt stuck in that place again, the place between screaming and sobbing.

"All right."

She stared, then nodded, then smiled, watching him go up one more ladder rung. And another.

"I believe you," Edison said, taking her by the waist, helping her duck into the pod. She didn't let go of him, wouldn't, and he tumbled in beside her. His fist came down hard on the release mechanism, which closed the hatch, locking it, the hydraulics hissing as the Mylar around the seal drew tight and her stomach dropped, the evac pod jetting out into space, so fast, so cruelly it stole her breath clean away.

"I'll always believe you."

The stars rushed out to greet them. They were away, safe. Together.

EPILOGUE

Rosalyn bounced her knee as she waited outside the GATE conference room, muttering through the speech she had spent all night preparing and practicing. *Aboard the* Brigantine *and* Coeur d'Alene Station, I, *along with Misato Iwasa and Captain Edison Aries, discovered undeniable proof of a conspiracy to test and release unimaginably dangerous xenobiological samples. The unethical—not to mention reckless and disgusting—behavior of those responsible at ISS, Merchantia Solutions and Belrose Industries cannot be emphasized enough . . .*

That part always made her flinch. The mere thought of saying the name of her father's company aloud in court made her flush with embarrassment and rage. But the next part of the speech—tracing Piero's whereabouts and involvement in the conspiracy to transport and test the deadly samples—gave her a surge of confidence.

Sometimes when she slept, she still dreamed of his glittering blue skull, haunting her forever from the dark recesses of her memory.

It would be at least six months before the trial began, and every minute of it felt like torture. This deposition was just the first step. She rubbed her thumb lightly over the lip of her coffee cup and breathed in the dark scent of it, thinking of Misato and her coffee obsession. Whenever she poured herself a cup, she always pictured the old woman's smiling eyes, her cheeky grin, her silver bob swinging as she dumped more caffeine down her throat.

"You can do this," she whispered, knowing she would be facing down more than a judge and a team of lawyers. This time it would be harder. Personal. Waiting for the patent to clear on her chip was miserable, but the angel investments had come quickly once she started telling her story. The original design she had created aboard the *Brigantine* bore little resemblance to the final product, but it had been a start.

"Just tell them what you know," Rosalyn added under her breath. The door in front of her was crisp and white, unmarked. That seemed fitting for a path leading to the dangerous unknown. She slid the sleeve of her shirt down on her right arm, reading the little words over and over again to herself as she waited, terrified but undeterred. If only Edison were there with her, but he would tell his story from quarantine. It wasn't so bad, he kept insisting, at least there was plenty of Jell-O.

With nothing to do, he had sent many, probably too many, jazz playlists for her to listen to while she built her new company from the ground up. It would have been so much easier with him there to hold her hand and wink from behind his spectacles, but Rosalyn would manage. Her hair had begun growing out, and she pushed a strand defiantly behind her ear, standing up straight.

Survivor. That was what Misato kept calling her. Maybe she was right. If she could survive Foxfire's desolation, an exploding space station and the collapse of her family's reputation and business, then she could survive a simple testimony.

"What does it mean?"

Rosalyn started, spilling some of her coffee. To her right, Josh Girdy fidgeted in his signature gray suit. His hair looked extra shiny.

He looked just as nervous as she did to tell the GATE agents what he knew.

"*Ikke gi opp*," she told him, butchering the Norwegian. But she smiled and adjusted her sleeve, the door in front of them hissing open. It was time. "Fight back."

ACKNOWLEDGMENTS

First and foremost, a tremendous amount is owed to Anne Sowards for her insight, patience and guidance on this project. I'm also extremely grateful to the team at Ace for their hard work, patience and creativity. Kate McKean for being the best in the business and a reliable partner. My friends and family for their love and support during this difficult project, especially Marcella Waugh for her scientific insight and Alex Cautley for his tech help. A huge thanks to Henry Eide and Kjersti Kirkeby for their Norwegian expertise.

Photo by Colin O

Madeleine Roux is the *New York Times* bestselling author of the Asylum series, which has sold in eleven countries worldwide, and whose first book was named a Kids' Indie Next List pick. She is also the author of the House of Furies series and has made contributions to Star Wars, World of Warcraft and *Scary Out There*. A graduate of the Beloit College writing program, Madeleine now lives with her beloved dog in Seattle, Washington.

CONNECT ONLINE

madeleine-roux.com

🐦 Authoroux